MW01178436

Liz —

The best to you, and
I hope you enjoy, darlin'!

♡ Rivi

Finding
JUSTICE

RIVI JACKS

ACKNOWLEDGMENTS

A heartfelt thank you to my Street Team, Rivi's Rebels.

Y'all mean so much to me, and you truly are the best!

Laurie Schmidt Lee, Michelle Engler, Jacquie Denison, Jessica Johnson Welch, Leigh Ann Panorelli, Melissa McCarty, Suzette Warren, Lisa Molina, Crystal St. Clair, Linda Delaney, Nancy Young, Rachel Rae Palmer, Lacey Smith, Debra Hiltz, Niki Bass, Gail Goodin Crowell, Tessie Arse Sexton, Katie Rose, Tonya Mae Labasan, and Claire Louise Ingram.

An additional thank you to these ladies for beta reading for me.

I'm sincerely grateful to you for taking the time to help me.

Angela Cetrangola, Jo Hoover, and Diane Buckner.

And I would be remiss if I didn't thank my readers.

Thank you for taking the time to read an unknown author. Thank you for contacting me to say how much you liked Seeking Justice and thank you for your reviews.

I hope you enjoy the conclusion to Liam and Cait's story.

CHAPTER ONE

Three weeks later.

T HE POUNDING WON'T STOP.
I roll over, pulling the pillow over my head. Whoever it is needs to go away and leave me alone.

It's not Paul or Julie — they have a key, and a habit of marching in as they please. I don't mean to complain; I'm not sure I'd have survived the last few weeks without them.

It's been pure hell. Days spent in mental anguish over losing Liam and then the onset of the flu, unable to rest with repeated rushes to the bathroom to vomit. When I do manage to sleep, Liam fills my dreams and I wake crying.

But whoever is pounding on my door is determined. I slip on my robe and tuck loose strands of hair that have escaped my braid behind my ears. Passing my hallway mirror, I grimace at my reflection.

Looking out the peephole, I moan and press my forehead against the door. I only open it, holding on for support, because I can't take the pounding that resonates through my brain.

Valerie raises her eyebrows and then steps through the doorway into my apartment.

"You look like shit, Caitlyn."

I close the door and move cautiously toward my kitchen. Sudden movements make my head spin.

"Would you like something to drink?" I murmur.

"I thought Paul told me he and his wife brought you food every evening. You've lost weight."

It's hard to eat when you feel like you're dying inside. I don't tell her that, though.

I take the bottle of ginger ale out of the refrigerator and pour a glass.

"Would you like something to drink?" I ask again.

"No, thank you."

I sip at the soothing soda under her watchful eye.

"Caitlyn, I think you need to see a doctor."

I set my glass on the counter top.

"I did. I have the flu." My legs are already beginning to shake. "If you don't mind, I need to sit down." I head back to the living room.

As I curl up on one end of the couch, Valerie walks over to my entertainment center where I have pictures of my parents. I pull the afghan throw from the back of the couch and drop it over my lap. I hope she gets to the reason she's here as I'm on the verge of lying down.

"Caitlyn, I'll get right to the point." She replaces my parent's anniversary picture and then turns. "I want you to come back to the magazine."

"You're offering me a job?"

She gives me one of her wry smiles. "Your old job, yes."

I settle down into the couch. "I...I'm not sure if I'm staying in Chicago. I may go home for a while."

She's quiet, and I feel her watching me as I pluck at the yarn on the afghan, avoiding her gaze.

"All this over a man," she says softly.

My eyes flash back to hers. There's a glint of surprise, which is an emotion you don't often see from Valerie Sharp.

"You're in love with him," she states bluntly.

The acute pain that settles around my heart is unbearable.

I slowly sit up and bring my legs down to stand. I'm not talking to her about Liam. I am not thinking about Liam. I can't. Not if I want to keep my sanity.

"I need to lie back down, Valerie." I swallow convulsively against the slight nausea that the dizziness always brings on.

"Perhaps you need to go back to the doctor."

"I'm...better, really. Thanks for coming by Valerie." I move slowly toward the door. "I appreciate your job offer but I really think I'm going home."

This is something I hadn't even considered. I only said it as an excuse. But now, I realize I have to. I can't stay and chance running into Liam.

I wrap my arms around my waist in a protective reaction against the intense yearning to see him.

Just one more time.

Valerie surprises me when she reaches out and lays her hand against the side of my face. It's such a maternal action that I blink at the sudden dampness in my eyes.

"Think about the job offer, Caitlyn. Pining away does not fix a broken heart. Talk to him."

My eyes widen. Increasing my dizziness, I shake my head gently. "He hates me. He thinks I'm a horrible person who lied and slept with him to get information. He thinks I'm the one who tried to break into the files at

Justice House." I wipe at the tear that spills from my eye. "He thinks I betrayed him," I whisper.

"Then it's important that he knows you did not," she says.

I exhale sharply. "I'll never get the chance to talk to him again."

After Valerie leaves, I crawl back into bed, pulling the covers up to my chin. I lie quietly and then my sob echoes around the room.

I'd thought the numbness would help me pull through my devastation. Face turned into the pillow, I let the tears pour from my body in what I pray will be a healing catharsis. I've been so afraid to let go, knowing I might not be able to stop. If nothing else, maybe this purging of emotions will relieve my tension and I'll be able to sleep.

I drag myself out of bed a couple of hours later to shower and then make my way to the kitchen. I promised Julie I would eat some of the soup she brought the day before, but just the thought of food makes my stomach churn. I pour myself another glass of ginger ale and drink it while I sit at my breakfast bar.

All that crying was for nothing. I didn't sleep and now my head feels full of cotton and my eyes are swollen.

I jump at a loud knock on my front door. I look through the peephole shocked to see Holly standing in the hallway. I step back.

She knocks again.

I smooth my loose hair back and straighten my robe, taking a deep breath before opening the door.

"Hi."

"Oh, Cait!" The combination of concern and compassion her voice and face express is almost my undoing.

I swallow against the lump in my throat. "Come in."

"I've been so concerned about you," she says as we sit in my kitchen.

"Thank you. I'm... okay." I can barely get the words out. I want to ask her about Liam.

"I'm not going to lie to you, Cait—you don't look okay."

I self-consciously tuck my hair back. "Would you like something to drink?" I stand and step to the fridge. "I'm going to have a ginger ale, would you like a glass?"

"How much weight have you lost?"

I hold up a glass.

"Yes, thank you," she says to my silent question.

As I sit back down, Holly sips at her drink. "Cait, I'm *really* worried about you. Have you been to the doctor?"

"Yes, right after—" I close my eyes briefly at the thought of that day. "I have the flu," I say weakly.

She snorts. "This is more than the flu. You look as if you've lost weight—a lot of weight. You have dark circles under your eyes and frankly, your color is alarming."

I bite my lip at the sudden urge to cry. I feel so weary; I just want to crawl into a hole.

"I can't sleep," I whisper brokenly. "I can't keep any food down. I'm miserable, going over and over in my mind what I should have done." I take a deep breath. "I can't let myself think of Liam, but every thought goes back to him," I say miserably. "I miss him so much, Holly."

She reaches over to squeeze my hand.

"I promise I never betrayed him—or any of you."

"I know, honey. I never thought you did."

"Thank you." The relief I feel at her words, relieves a little of the pressure around my heart. I worried that Holly thought I used her friendship to get to Liam.

"When you first revealed that you worked for Query magazine, I was upset because I knew how Liam was going to take it. Just so you know, Bryce never thought you betrayed us either. We've put a timeline together of everything that happened." She grins. "Ryan gave us tips on preparing our case for you before we —" She hesitates.

I know she was going to say, *before we gave the evidence to Liam.*

"Cait —" she takes my hand in both of hers " — he just needs time." She frowns, looking down. "Your hand is as cold as ice.

"Okay, go get dressed." She stands. "I'm taking you to see my doctor." She pulls her phone from her purse.

"Holly, I just have the flu and I'm exhausted. It will — pass."

She puts her phone to her ear.

"Well, we'll see about getting you something to help you sleep. Now go — Hello, Dr. Lyle please, Holly Phillips calling." She raises her eyebrows and gives a motion with her hand for me to get up.

I'm not even aware of what dress I pull out of my closet and slip over my head.

On the way, I learn Dr. Michelle Lyle is a friend of Holly's. I listen as she tells me about the good doctor, but honestly, all I want to do is lie down.

"Cait — maybe I shouldn't tell you this but Liam isn't getting through your break-up un-scathed." I look at her, my heart lurches in my chest at the thought of Liam hurting. "He's as grouchy as an old bear with a thorn in its paw." She frowns then and I know she's thinking of something she's not happy about. I don't want to know.

We don't have to wait once we arrive, we're ushered right back to the doctor's office.

Dr. Lyle is an attractive, pleasant woman, about ten years older than Holly. She has a reassuring confidence in her manner and she sits and talks to me as if she has all the time in the world.

When she questions me about what else is going on in my life, other than the flu, Holly speaks up, informing her that I quit my job and boyfriend at the same time. When I look at Holly, she winks.

"If I could just sleep, I know I could get over this," I whisper.

"Well, let's run a couple of tests for my piece of mind," she says smiling.

Those tests are expedited too, I realize as we arrive back at the doctor's office in what has to be the quickest lab work-up I've ever experienced. And with my dad's condition, I've been exposed to a few.

"You okay?" Holly asks as we sit waiting on the good doctor.

"Yes."

Dr. Lyle walks in, glancing through a chart. She looks up and smiles before sitting behind her desk.

"You said you saw a doctor two weeks ago, correct?"

"Yes, almost three weeks." My inner voice is shouting a warning. "Not my regular doctor, it was on a weekend."

"I had the lab tech repeat the test to be certain."

From the corner of my eye, I see Holly sit forward in her chair.

"Cait, you're pregnant."

Holly gasps and slowly turns to me, eyes wide and her mouth open.

The air is sucked right out of my lungs and I struggle to draw a breath. I shake my head.

"No I'm not."

"That's why I had the test re-checked, to be certain. You are pregnant." Dr. Lyle smiles gently at me. "From what you've told me you're about nine weeks, but I'll schedule an ultra-sound to confirm."

I shake my head again. "No," I whisper. *Oh, God.* "I was on my period when I went to the doctor." Holly looks as shocked as I feel.

"It can happen, Cait," the doctor assures me. "It's not that uncommon."

"I can't be pregnant, we used... " I close my eyes; nausea rears its ugly head.

"But?" Dr. Lyle coaxes gently.

"I started birth control; it was one of the mini-pills, but..." I bite my lip.

"You had unprotected sex when you first started the pill." She finishes my sentence for me.

"Yes," I breathe. "It was just one time."

"That's all it takes," she says.

"What now?" Holly asks.

I tune out what the doctor says. Panic renders me unable to process anything past the fact that I am going to have a baby.

Liam's baby.

And he hates me. I grip the arms of the chair, a buzzing sensation beginning in my head.

"Cait, I would like to check you into the hospital for a few days."

"What?" I shake my head slightly.

"Why?" Holly asks, looking at me.

"Morning sickness is considered a normal part of a healthy pregnancy. What is not normal is persistent vomiting and excessive weight loss. The inability to keep fluids down leads to the risk of dehydration."

"So Cait's dehydrated?"

"There is slight dehydration, yes. At this point, I'm more concerned about her electrolyte imbalance, which if not put in check can lead to severe dehydration."

"Is that dangerous?"

"Cait will be fine, Holly. We'll administer a medication through an IV to stop the vomiting and start her on vitamin and nutritional supplements."

The room is quiet and I look up to see the doctor and Holly both looking at me.

"Cait, I know this is a lot to take in," Dr. Lyle smiles kindly at me. "But I don't want you to worry. You and your baby will be fine." She looks back at her paperwork. "I'll have my nurse call and make the arrangements for your admittance—"

"No." I shake my head. "No hospital."

Dr. Lyle's eyebrows lift in surprise.

"Cait," Holly says. "Michelle thinks you need a few days stay—"

"I'm not staying in the hospital," I say firmly.

"Cait—"

"Holly." Dr. Lyle raises her hand and gives a slight shake of her head before looking at me.

"I will *not* check into any hospital. You said I'm only slightly dehydrated, and I can take medicine without having to be in the hospital. I will do whatever you say I need to do." The steam goes out of me and I whisper, "But please, no hospital."

Rivi Jacks

I can't look away from her discerning stare.

After a moment, she pulls open a drawer and takes out a pad.

"I'm going to give you a prescription for something to help with the nausea, and I want you on a bland diet. I'm also going to start you on vitamins and supplements." She looks up. "You are to get these filled—you can do that downstairs in our pharmacy before you leave—and start the doses immediately." Her expression becomes firm. "I want you in here every day for the next three days, if there is no improvement... I *am* checking you into the hospital," she says, her voice adamant.

She notices the tensing of my body. "It would only be for 2 to 3 days, Cait, just long enough to push some fluids into you."

"I'll do what I need to." I nod. "Thank you."

"And I will help her," Holly adds.

I close the door of Holly's car and sit back against the seat. She does the same and neither one of us says a word.

This can't be happening. I place my hand on my stomach. I've never even thought about having children.

"What am I going to do? I'm twenty-four years old and I don't have a job. I was going to go back home but now..."

Holly turns to look at me. "You can't leave, Cait. You have to tell Liam and he won't want you to leave."

I look at her then, unable to control the shock on my face.

"Cait, you have to tell him!"

I shake my head, feeling a little dizzy from the movement.

14

Finding Justice

"I can't," I breathe. The thought of how he'll react terrifies me. I'm too vulnerable and won't be able to stand up to his anger.

He hates me.

I'm suddenly sick with the thought that he might want me to get rid of the baby. My hand moves protectively over my stomach.

"Cait, he has a right to know and... I know Liam; he will do the right thing."

My eyes open wide in alarm. "I don't want him to do the right thing!"

"There is no way he will turn his back on his child. He will help you."

I drop my head down, covering my face with my hands.

"Why did this happen?"

"Maybe... because you and Liam are meant to be together."

My wry laugh sounds hollow. I lean my head back against the seat.

"He's hurt, Cait. And... he decided a long time ago, after his mother died, that he wouldn't let anything hurt him again."

I look over at her.

"He would be so pissed at me for telling you this but..." She nods as if to assure herself that she's doing the right thing. "You are the only woman he's ever let in. He's never had a steady girlfriend. Oh, he's had lots of women and most of them wanted to insert themselves into his life but... he wouldn't have it.

"Before his mom... died, he felt she needed him, and I know he felt he had to stay focused for her." Holly's gaze meets mine. "His dad..." She shakes her head.

Oh, Liam.

"When he lost his mom the way that he did, we thought he'd lose it. His mom was such a good person and they were so close. She didn't cling to him... they were just close and he adored her."

I reach up to brush a tear from my cheek.

"I know, Cait that he'd never abandon his child." She reaches over to rest her hand on mine where it still rests on my stomach. "He will want this baby and if you wait even one day before telling him about his child..." She squeezes my hand. "You have to tell him. Today."

I close my eyes and rest my head back against the seat.

She starts the car and as she pulls out of the parking lot, I know we're headed to Justice House. I have to tell him, I know that. I'll probably need help through this. Emotional support. I won't take money from him, though. I'll figure out a way to make it financially.

A wave of despair washes over me. I'm not sure how that will work out. I have no idea how long I'll be able to work before the baby is born or how long until I can go back to work afterward.

My breath catches. I'm going to have a baby.

I press my hand against my stomach suddenly knowing that I'll have to accept Liam's help if I'm going to provide for my child. At least at first. I can't go home to my parents, they can't afford to support me and a baby. I won't put that kind of pressure on them. I'm not even sure how they'll make ends meet once I'm unable to send them money. They've never let me give them much and it's never been a burden to send them what I do each month but that will have to end. I'll have to let them know about the baby, soon.

I'm at once overwhelmed and panic-stricken. Okay, I need to calm down, stressing over this right now isn't good for the baby and it's making me nauseous.

As Holly slows the car and pulls through the gates of The Justice, I honest to goodness feel a flutter in my abdomen.

At my soft gasp, Holly looks at me.

"It'll be okay, Cait. What? What is it?"

"I think I just felt the baby," I whisper.

Her eyes widen. "Really?"

I nod. "Yeah."

This has to be a good omen.

Holly knocks on Liam's office door. When I hear him call out, I panic and step back but Holly grabs my arm.

"It'll be okay," she reassures me.

I feel light headed as we step into his office.

He's at his desk and glances up briefly at Holly before looking back down. "Holly, I reckon you're here for—"

When it registers that I'm standing right behind her, he quickly looks back up and then stands abruptly.

"Are you fucking crazy?" He glares at Holly.

"Now, Liam just listen—"

"No! Get her the fuck out of here!" his voice booms, echoing around the room.

"I'll go," I say softly.

Holly quickly turns my way. "No, you will not! You stay right where you are."

"Holly, so help me—" Liam hisses through clenched teeth.

I drink him in. He's livid, but he's never looked more handsome. His eyes are just as striking as I've dreamed.

His hair looks its usual sexy disarray and the dark scruff on his face only adds to his good looks. He does look tired though, but the dark circles under his eyes only seem to intensify the blue.

Although I can't take my eyes off him, he hasn't looked at me. I might as well be invisible. I do have the satisfaction of knowing my presence does upset him, but I'm not sure that's a good thing.

"Liam, Cait has something to say to you and —"

"I don't give a fuck! Do you understand me, Holly? Now get her the hell out of here."

It hurts, more than I could ever have imagined. He means so much to me. I bite down on my lip to keep from bursting into tears.

"Just listen to her Liam, it's important." His whole body is rigid with anger. "Please, Liam, give her two minutes. For me. Please."

Liam closes his eyes and for the fraction of a moment, I think I see pain etched on his face, and then it's gone and I know that I must have imagined it.

"Two minutes, starting now," he growls.

Holly turns quickly, takes hold of my hand and squeezes, then heads for the door.

No! I need her to stay. I watch as she walks out closing the door behind her.

"You have ninety seconds."

I look at him and he's finally looking at me but it's as if he's looking right through me. It chills me to the bone.

The buzzing in my ears, that I experienced at the doctor's office is back. I'm suddenly light headed and I'm having trouble breathing.

Oh, please don't let me be sick.

"Caitlyn!"

I jump at his hard, angry tone. At least he's focused on me now. I realize this might be the last time I'll ever be this close to him and I commit every detail of his dear face and his haunting scent to memory.

He frowns slightly. "You have thirty seconds."

I can't get the words out, I'm paralyzed with fear and a sense of total loss.

"You look a little peaked, darlin'. What's the matter, feeling guilt over your subterfuge?"

I shake my head, feeling nauseous. I swallow and draw in a long breath.

"No," I whisper, my eyes meeting his. "I'm pregnant," I say softly.

I see the shock in his eyes and then the shutters come down. His expression becomes impassive as his eyes bore into mine and then he cocks his head.

"Congratulations, darlin'."

CHAPTER TWO

INHALE SHARPLY AND MY BREATHE rushes out in a soft gasp.

Okay. That's it then. He doesn't want us. I'm on my own.

Everything goes fuzzy black and I think I'm going to pass out, but I will myself to keep standing and the moment passes.

I take one more look at his handsome face. God, I love this man, I think I have from the very first. And I'm not sure what hurts more, that I'll never see him again or the fact that he'll never know his child.

I give a small nod. "Thank you," I breathe.

Turning on unsteady legs, I make it to the door and manage to get it open without disgracing myself further.

Stop me.

Stop me.

Stop me, please.

I close the door behind me, suddenly feeling as if I'm at the end of a long tunnel.

Goodbye, Liam.

The tunnel closes in.

Mmm. He smells so good. I turn my face slightly against the pillow.

Liam.

I hear the din of voices but I'm unable to open my eyes. I seek refuge from my pain in the darkness and Liam's incredible scent.

"Why doesn't she wake?"

Liam.

"She's exhausted. From what I've learned from Dr. Lyle and Mrs. Phillips, she hasn't been resting or sleeping well."

I feel him.

Liam.

It's quiet.

I turn my face more fully into the pillow seeking the comfort of Liam's scent. I slowly open my eyes, disoriented by the fact that I'm in his bedroom. *Why am I here?* The room is dark but someone has left the bathroom light on with the door slightly ajar, giving the room just enough light for me to see him. He's asleep in a chair, pulled close enough for him to prop his long legs up on the bed. His face is in shadow but I can make out the deep crease between his eyebrows and I want to smooth it away.

The urgent need to pee overrides any other thought and I move my arm to pull back the cover but it won't work right. When I look, I see my arm strapped to an IV board with an IV line running from the back of my hand up to a bag of solution hanging on a pole. I hope the pole rolls; I need to pee in a bad way.

My free hand moves to my stomach. I know my baby

is okay. I don't know how to explain it, but now that I know I'm pregnant, I can feel her presence. Or his.

"Liam." My throat is parched and his name comes out in a whisper, but he hears me. His eyes open and even in the low light I'm submerged in deep blue.

The crease deepens between his brows as he puts his feet on the floor and sits forward in the chair.

"What happened?"

"You fainted."

I swallow against the dryness. "I need the bathroom."

He stands, but he's uncertain.

"Please," I won't make it if he doesn't help me right now.

He leans down over me. "We'll have to be careful," he says gruffly.

I place the arm taped to the board on his shoulder and my good arm around his neck. He lifts me up into his arms.

It's almost my undoing — being held this close to him again. I turn my face into his chest, inhaling deeply. When he doesn't move, I look up. He has his eyes closed as if he's in pain. I breathe his name so softly I'm not sure he hears but his eyes open and he looks down, his gaze meeting mine.

There's the little flutter again, low in my belly and I want to tell him but I hesitate, uncertain of his reaction.

He moves then, supporting me with one arm and pulling the IV pole with the other, setting me down in the brightly lit bathroom. I gasp when I see my reflection in the mirror over the sinks.

Someone braided my long hair but strands have come loose and it's an untidy mess. I raise my untethered hand to tuck the loose hair behind my ears. I still have dark smudges under my eyes but my eyelids look purple and my complexion is sallow. None of my coloring goes well with my dark brown eyes, adding to the just-stepped-out-of-a-horror-movie look. And for the first time I notice I'm only wearing one of Liam's white T-shirts. It's large on me and I suddenly feel like — little Orphan Annie.

An overpowering need to cry causes tears. I look down in abject misery.

"You're fine," he says a little brusquely.

I don't feel fine. I blink away the tears.

"Do you need further assistance?" He sounds impatient.

"No." I sniff.

He reaches to lift my chin, his eyes meeting mine and he holds my gaze. "I'll be right outside," he says gently, before stepping out, closing the door behind him.

After relieving myself, I remain seated and give in to the tears.

I'm pathetic, I tell myself as I drag the IV pole to the sink, I don't even know why I'm crying. I wash my hands as well as I can with my arm strapped down and splash water on my face. As I look up, reaching for the towel, I see Liam's reflection in the mirror.

"Ready?"

"Yes, but I can walk."

"I don't think so." He scoops up both the IV pole and me, depositing me back on his bed before picking up the house phone.

"Ms. Shaw is ready for a bowl of soup. Thank you." He replaces the phone.

"Could I have some water, please," I whisper.

He crosses the room to the bathroom and comes back with a glass of water, then helps me sit up to drink. My hand trembles in response to his nearness as I hold the glass, and he reaches out to steady it. Just as I finish the cool liquid, there's a soft knock on the door.

Liam steps over to the doorway and a small gray haired woman enters, carrying a tray. She sets the tray on the bedside table.

"How are we feeling, dear?" She doesn't wait for me to answer as she plumps the pillows behind my back.

"Fine," I say softly. I look toward Liam but he's standing at the glass doors, looking out at the night.

She lays a towel across my lap. "Do you need help with eating?" she asks as she reaches for the bowl that's sitting on the tray.

"No, I... can manage, thank you."

"Liam you need to bring in one of those rolling trays, like they have in the hospital," she says, handing me the bowl.

Liam turns.

"This is fine... really," I assure her.

The soup is delicious. Chicken noodle and I'm sure it's homemade. I'm conscious of Liam and the woman watching me as I eat, but I don't care. I finish every drop, amazed that I seem to have my appetite again. I'm so hungry, I think I could eat another bowl, but it's as if a switch flips and my eyes are closing as I take that last bite. Liam reaches for the bowl taking it from my limp fingers. I vaguely hear him as he speaks to the woman.

When I open my eyes next, the room glows with a soft light. Not knowing if it's early morning or early evening adds to my disorientation.

An older man sits in one of the rooms chairs, one leg

crossed up over the knee of the other as he writes on the papers balanced there.

I glance at the door wondering where Liam is.

"Ah... you're awake." He smiles kindly and sets the papers aside as he stands. "I'm Dr. Hines." He takes hold of my hand lying across my stomach. The IV is gone.

"I removed your IV a couple of hours ago. As long as you continue eating and are able to keep food down, you'll do just fine. How do you feel?"

"Good," I whisper, and he lets go of my hand to pour a glass of water from a carafe that's sitting on the bedside table. This time my hand is steady as I hold the glass to drink.

"No nausea when you were awake and up moving around early this morning?"

"No."

"None now?"

"No."

"Good," he says, smiling.

He waits for me to finish my water and then he returns the glass to the table before moving to sit down, picking up his pen to resume his writing.

"You may get up from bed as you feel able, but I want you to take it easy for the next couple of weeks while you regain your strength. I'm prescribing an antihistamine for nausea, it will also help you sleep. Follow the instructions Dr. Lyle gave you with the vitamins, get plenty of rest and this bout of morning sickness will pass." He looks up to smile at me again.

"Thank you."

"You are very welcome, young lady."

I'm still somewhat confused by all this. "Why am I here instead of in the hospital?"

I think he's trying to suppress a smile. "Mr. Justice wouldn't hear of it. And since Annie is retired from nursing — we thought you might do better in familiar surroundings."

Annie? Who is Annie and why would Liam insist on my staying here? I close my eyes; this is all so confusing. I wish someone would explain why I'm *here*.

Where is Liam? I look to check the time but the clock that usually sits on the bedside table is missing.

"What time is it?"

The doctor snaps the top of his pen, pocketing it before looking up. "It's five thirty."

"Evening?" I ask in surprise.

He has a pleasant laugh. "Yes. You slept another twelve hours from the last time you were awake."

No wonder I feel so good. I've been sleeping sporadically for the past 3 weeks.

"What day is it?"

"It's Thursday."

"What?" I gasp softly. It was Tuesday afternoon when I came here to tell Liam about the baby. I've slept over forty-eight hours straight, except for the short time I was awake earlier that morning.

The doctor stands. "Well Miss Shaw, I'll be on my way. I'll stop in to check on you tomorrow."

"Thank you, Dr. Hines."

He smiles and picks up his bag to leave. No sooner does he step out than the woman who brought me soup earlier, comes bustling in with a tray.

"How about a nice bowl of tomato bisque?"

I sit up straighter, scooting back against the headboard.

"That sounds delicious."

She's brought a bed tray this time and places it over

my lap. Besides the soup, there are little crackers shaped like fish, a glass of milk, and a small bowl of pudding.

"Now just eat what you can, dear."

"Thank you."

"You're welcome. Would you like to shower after you eat?"

"Yes please," I say right before I spoon in another mouthful of her delicious soup. Once again, I'm certain the soup is homemade.

"Are you Liam's housekeeper?"

"I am. Did Liam not tell you?" She shakes her head. "That boy," she tsks, which makes me feel like laughing, the thought of her tsking Liam. I haven't laughed since the day I left Justice House.

"My name is Annie and I'll be living in for the next couple of weeks to help you."

I quickly swallow the sip of milk I've just taken. What?

"Would you like me to get things together for your shower?"

I don't have any things here but I assume she's talking about towels and possibly another one of Liam's T-shirts, so I'm more than a little surprised when she comes back out of Liam's closet with one of my gowns and matching robe.

My eyebrows rise and the spoon stalls half way to my mouth. She pauses on her way to the bathroom when she catches my expression.

"I believe, Ms. Holly went to your apartment and packed up some of your clothes, dear."

"Oh," I say softly. Now I'm really confused.

I finish all of the food and Annie sets the tray aside, standing close as I slide out of bed. I feel weak but no longer shaky. She moves along with me to the bathroom. When she's satisfied I'm able to stay upright on my own, she assures me she'll be right outside the door if I need anything.

The shower feels so good. I stay under the spray letting it soothe my sore muscles. When I step out, I find my make-up bag lying on the counter. Thank goodness, Holly packed my toothbrush. I braid my damp hair in a loose side braid and gather up my robe. I feel guilty about taking so long with my shower, knowing Annie probably has better things to do than wait on me.

As I step out of the bathroom, I come to a quick stop when I see Liam. He's standing at the open French doors. He turns, his eyes gliding over me, and my body responds to that look. Why does he have to be so damn good looking? And it's not just the face, it's everything about him. The easy grace with which he moves, his slow, sexy, melt-a-girl's-panties voice, his laugh, that smile of his, and those eyes... oh those eyes.

I'm at once embarrassed. I didn't put my robe on and my nightgown is very revealing. I quickly slip it on, and when I glance back at him, he's still watching me.

"How are you feeling?"

"Very well, thank you." My voice sounds breathy.

"Sit down Caitlyn, we need to talk." He motions toward one of the rooms chairs.

The warm breeze coming through the open doors has me wanting to seek the outside for a bit of fresh air.

"Could we sit out on the balcony or maybe up on the roof?" I love it up there and I know Liam seeks it out for relaxation. There's something about being up high, like in a tree that has a calming effect.

"No. Out here will be fine." He stands back and as I

pass by him, I inhale deeply. I've missed his positively mind numbing scent. The air seems to crackle between us and I bite my lip, looking up into his hooded gaze.

I sit in one of the chairs next to a small table, reveling in the soft breeze that carries the sweet scent of flowers. Liam didn't follow me out and when I look back he's coming through the door with a glass of water, which he sets on the table, pushing it toward me before leaning against the railing of the balcony, his long legs stretched out before him.

"Thank you," I murmur, feeling my body flush just looking at him.

"I have a few things to say, Caitlyn."

I frown slightly at his tone. "Okay."

"First off, you'll be moving in here to stay."

What? What is he talking about?

I sit forward. "Liam—"

"I'd appreciate it if you'd hear me out, please." He raises his eyebrow.

I sit back. His tone makes me uneasy.

"You are under doctor's orders to take it easy for the next few weeks and I want to make sure you take care of yourself so you don't get into this shape again."

My mouth drops open. He makes it sound as if I don't know how to care for myself.

"Don't give me that look. You obviously need someone to look after you and the baby."

Oh!

"You no longer have a job, what savings you do have won't last long with the expense of doctor visits, not to mention the hospital bill you'll accrue with the birth of the child."

I almost choke on my sip of water. *What savings I*

have! "You—looked at my bank account?" *How the hell can he do that?*

"Suffice to say, I know you won't last long on your own."

I look at him in disbelief. "I can find a job, Liam."

"And if you come down ill again?"

"It's—only morning sickness." I feel myself growing tense and I take a deep breath to calm down. He's raising questions for which I have no answers.

"It's my responsibility to take care of you while you are pregnant with my child." There's an underlying anger in his voice that I now realize is what I heard in his tone earlier. "Caitlyn, you *will* move in here."

I look away, no longer able to look into those discerning eyes. I don't want to be a responsibility to him. I don't want to be here because he feels obligated.

What did you think, Cait, that all would be forgiven? I'm here for one reason and one reason only. But regardless of how he feels about me or how I feel about the situation, I will need his help.

"Dr. Hines said I only need to take it easy for a couple of weeks until I get my strength back. By then I'll be close to my second trimester, and Dr. Lyle said morning sickness usually subsides by then." I take a deep breath and look at him. "I agree to stay that long but then I'll be going back—" My voice trails off as Liam's eyes narrow on me. He studies me for a moment before uncrossing his legs. My eyes are drawn to the bulge in his jeans. Is he always aroused? When I raise my eyes to his, he tips his head and smirks. I can't stop my blush.

He pushes away from the railing. "There's no reason to discuss this further." With that said, he walks back into the bedroom.

I huff an exasperated breath. *The arrogant ass!* He can't—

I sit stunned for several minutes, contemplating what to do and then I follow after him. He's left the room and I head out, stopping when I reach the living room. Not finding him, my next stop is the kitchen where I find Annie stirring something in a bowl.

"Do you need something, dear?"

"No, thank you, I'm looking for Liam."

"I believe he went to his study."

"Thank you."

"Would you like to have your dinner in the dining room with Mr. Liam, or in your room?"

I hesitate. "I'm not sure." I'm starting to feel as if I need to lie back down.

"I'll check with you before dinner is ready then."

"Thank you, Annie." I head back toward the other side of the apartment. Liam's study is next to the media room if I remember correctly.

I knock softly on the closed door, scolding myself for being nervous and for the fact I want to scuttle back to the bedroom. But I know I can't let him browbeat me into doing whatever he wants. I need to set some ground rules here.

"Come in, Caitlyn," he says as he swings his door open.

He knew I'd follow him. He's toying with me.

I step in, my gaze sweeping around the room. I opened the door to his study when I was conducting my self-tour a few weeks back. I wanted to come in then, to explore, but I respected that it was his private space.

It's a lovely room with filled bookshelves lining the walls. My fingers positively itch with longing to inspect each one. A large cushy looking leather couch sits before the fireplace and I can envision cold winter days curled up on that couch with a good book.

The dominating feature of the room however, besides Liam, is the large desk where he has a computer. It looks like he's working as there are files lying out on the desktop.

Liam closes the door behind me. "What can I do for you, Caitlyn?"

I glance back at him and then step close to inspect a row of books.

"You can start by calling me, Cait." It hasn't escaped my notice that he's not once called me, darlin', except when he sarcastically congratulated me on being pregnant. I look at him again.

One arrogant eyebrow shoots up. "That's what you're here to discuss with me?"

I hate his cold impersonal tone.

I walk down to the next section of books and see an intriguing title. I reach up on tiptoe, grasping at the book. Liam is suddenly behind me, pulling the book from the shelf, handing it to me. His scent and nearness evoke all manner of wicked reactions in my body. My stomach muscles clench, nipples tighten, and a dull ache forms between my legs.

Holy hell!

My breathing is even affected and I can feel the fine hairs on the nape of my neck and arms stand on end. I close my eyes taking a deep breath, willing my suddenly activated libido to calm down.

I open the book, giving a semblance of interest when the only thing that interests me at this point is Liam taking me into his arms. I snap the book shut and move to the next section, away from his electrifying proximity. It helps — somewhat.

"Why" — my voice sounds breathy — "do you keep an office here when you have one close by downstairs?" I move away.

"The office downstairs is for the business of Justice House, I use my study for my personal business."

"Oh." I look back at him and catch his frown. "This is a beautiful room. You must—"

"What do you want, Caitlyn?" His voice is sharp and impatient.

I turn to face him with trepidation. Why does he have to be so intimidating?

I swallow nervously. "I—think we need to further discuss... my staying here."

"There's nothing to discuss," he snaps.

"Liam we need to come to a mutual understanding." When he doesn't say anything, I take advantage of what I hope is his possible consideration of what I am saying. "I agree with you that I will need—help, but there is no reason for me to move in here with you beyond my recuperating time." The irony doesn't escape me that if I'd been upfront with him from the first, I might possibly already be living here with him.

His expression is impassive as he continues watching me in silence.

"After the baby is born I will need to find a place of my own anyway, so I think it will be best—for all concerned— if we keep our living arrangements as they are."

I'm physically melting under his silent countenance and my need to lie down.

"And how do you plan, financially, to live out on your own?" His voice has an edge to it.

I take a deep, fortifying breath. I realize now that I don't have a choice.

"Well, I think I might go home to my parents" —I watch his face darken in anger— "just until the baby is born." I'm suddenly pissed that with my waning energy, my voice has lost every ounce of confidence.

"Absolutely not," he seethes. "You will not take my child from me." There's a foreboding menace to his tone, and his eyes flash dangerously.

I take a step back, wilting visibly under his anger. "I would never—"

He advances on me, pulling me into his arms. I cry out from the suddenness of this action as his hand flattens across my belly.

"This is my child. Mine." He speaks forcefully. "There was no decision on my part, no hesitancy, when I first learned you were pregnant. No denial." His eyes blaze with intensity. I tremble in his arms but I don't know if it's because I'm afraid—or aroused.

"I will be a full time father to this child and neither you nor hell—will keep me from him. Do you understand?"

I know better than to apprise him of the fact that the baby might be a she.

"I would never keep your child from you," I whisper, looking down where my hand lies against his chest, over his heart with his medallion nestled against my palm.

Liam suddenly swings me up into his arms, and I grip his shoulders as he strides from the room. He carries me back to the bedroom and lays me down on his bed. Without another word or glance, he turns and leaves the room.

I wake at some point during the night and roll over to go back to sleep, which eludes me. The glass and carafe are missing from the nightstand and I decide to make a trip to the kitchen for a glass of water.

The apartment is dark and quiet as I walk down the hall. When I reach the kitchen, I decide I should probably eat something too. I find a plate in the fridge with fresh fruit, cheese, and cold chicken. I sit at the center island and nibble as I think over the scene earlier in the library.

Liam said there was never any hesitancy on his part about wanting or believing the child was his when he learned I was pregnant. He could have fooled me at the time. I do concede though that his reaction was probably from the shock of hearing he was going to be a father. He clearly is determined to be in his child's life. And as much as I am happy that my baby will know his or her father, Liam needs to understand that he can't control how I live for the next seven months.

As I head back to the bedroom I wonder where he is, where he's sleeping, but I'm not about to start opening doors looking for him.

I fall back to sleep almost instantly when my head hits the pillow.

CHAPTER THREE

B RIGHT MORNING SUNLIGHT WAKES ME, and I roll over to check the time, glad that someone thought to return the clock to the bedside table. Going by the time, I know that Liam is probably at the morning meeting right about now, and I've slept another twelve hours.

Sheesh.

I pull the spare pillow over against my chest, but Annie changed the bedding yesterday, so no more heady scent of Liam on the bed linen.

I'm loath to hurry out of bed. Now that I feel human again, I realize that I have nothing to do, nowhere to go. It's not a good feeling, and what's worse—I know I'll never be welcome downstairs again. I can't imagine that Miranda has kept quiet about what happened or the reason why Liam fired me.

I roll onto my back. If I move in here, what will I do, sit around all day? What is Liam thinking? I know he's concerned I'll keep him from his child. He doesn't know me well enough to know I would never do that to him or my baby. I can sense that Liam will be a wonderful father and I know he will always be here for his son or daughter, but how could he possibly want me to move in with him? It's evident that he's still angry with me, still believes I betrayed him. It breaks my heart how he looked at me in the library last night. How will he deal with having to see me for the next seven months? And what happens after the baby is born?

I sit up on the side of the bed, raising my arms above my head stretching. How can I live here craving Liam's touch and loving him as I do? That hasn't changed.

The ringing of my cell pulls me from my unsettling thoughts. I answer after looking at the caller ID.

"Julie, I am so sorry I haven't called—"

She laughs cutting off my apology. "It's okay, Cait. Liam has kept us up on your progress."

What? "He has?"

"Yep, called us the last two evenings. How are you this morning?"

"I feel so much better. I just woke and I'm starving!"

Julie laughs again. I'm still trying to process the fact that Liam called them.

"Liam said you were going to be staying with him." I hear the unasked question in her voice.

"I'm supposed to take it easy for a couple of weeks so—can you come over? We can find something here for lunch." I need to see her, talk to her.

"Sure, but I don't get lunch until one today."

"Perfect. I'll have something ready."

"See you then."

"Wait!" I don't have a clue how to reach Liam's apartment other than through his office. "Call when you're on your way."

"No problem. Bye."

I look around the bedroom. Surely there's another entrance to his apartment, if for no other reason than a fire escape.

I might as well take my shower and then I can go in search of Liam.

Someone has hung my clothes up in Liam's closet. Annie I suppose, but I don't think she would have without Liam's okay.

And why am I in his bedroom to begin with? He has other bedrooms, why not put me in one of them?

I get what I need and head for the shower.

I leave my damp hair hanging loose to dry while I finish dressing. The jeans Holly packed for me to wear are loose. I have lost weight. Too much weight. It's a good thing I have my appetite back and that I'm now able to keep food down.

I wonder, not for the first time, how much of my loss of appetite and my inability to sleep for the past 3 weeks was directly connected to my break up with Liam. And what happens when he tells me to leave again? My hand goes to my stomach at the thought.

There's a soft knock on the bathroom door.

"Yes?"

"Ms. Shaw, Mr. Liam would like to see you in his study."

I open the door slightly. "I'll be right there as soon as I finish dressing. Do you mind letting him know?"

"Of course not, dear."

"And Annie, please call me, Cait."

She smiles and nods her agreement, turning to leave as I shut the door.

I pull my pale pink, form fitting T-shirt over my head and smooth it down over my stomach. I wonder how long before I begin to show? I need to google about that and other questions I have. I probably should also check into what a baby needs and get started on that.

My hair is almost dry as I wind it up into a loose bun at the back of my head.

I hope Liam won't keep me long, I'm so hungry I'll probably eat twice as much as I need. I pad, barefoot down the hall to his study.

As I get close, I hear voices coming from within. Liam has company. I knock softly on the partially open door.

"Come in, Caitlyn."

The door's promptly pulled open and I'm surprised to see Ryan.

"Ryan! Hi."

"Cait, how are you feeling?"

"Very well, thank you." My pulse quickens. I can feel Liam's intense gaze on me.

"Holly informed me congratulations are in order." He smiles gently at me.

"Thank you," I murmur, glancing toward Liam.

Holy hell.

He's dressed in slacks and a white dress shirt, sleeves rolled to expose his strong forearms. His tie is loose at the neck and he stands casually giving the impression he's relaxed but I can feel his tension.

"Caitlyn, come in and sit down, please."

Why do I feel so apprehensive and why is Ryan here?

As I approach his desk, Liam motions to the chair I am to sit in. Ryan takes the chair next to mine as Liam sits behind his desk.

What's going on? He doesn't leave me wondering for long.

"Caitlyn — I've made a decision." He looks at me, his

face void of any expression. I search his eyes, hoping to see something that will help me discern his mood.

"I've given the situation serious thought and I have come to the conclusion that the best we can do for our child—is to marry."

My eyes widen and my mouth drops open. "You're... kidding." I honestly think that he is, that he's making a joke for Ryan's sake.

Liam leans back in his chair. The weight of his narrowed gaze rests on me like a sensual veil. With an elbow propped up on the arm of his chair, he strokes his bottom lip with one long finger.

The skin on the back of my neck tingles. He's not making a joke.

"You're serious," I say softly. He cocks his head to one side. I look at Ryan but he avoids making eye contact.

"Liam," —My voice sounds desperate— "we don't have to marry to raise our child together. That—is a crazy idea." I shake my head. "I'm not getting married."

He pushes his chair back and stands. His eyes have chilled to blue shards of ice as he moves around the desk. Reaching down he grips my arm, pulling me to my feet.

"Ryan, please excuse us for a moment."

I glance at Ryan and it looks as if he's fighting a smile. I can't possibly see what he finds so amusing. Maybe it's the fact that Liam has taken leave of his senses.

Liam practically drags me from the room and as soon as we step out to the hallway, he pushes me against the wall, bracing one arm above my head.

It takes every ounce of strength not to cross that whisper of space between us and press my body to his. His mind numbing scent surrounds me, intoxicating my senses, rendering me helpless. The heat from his body and that—electrical charge that infuses the air every time we are close, reminds me that he is the one, the only one who knows how to bring my body to life.

My breathing is rapid and shallow as he looks down into my eyes.

"Please, Liam," I plead softly as the air pulsates between us.

"Please what?" he whispers.

I pull my gaze from his, looking down focusing on the shape of the medallion resting beneath his shirt, against his chest. I shake my head.

"Caitlyn," he begins softly. "You *are* going to marry me."

My gaze flashes back to his. "Why?" I ask sharply, but I know it's because of the baby.

His brow lifts. I've surprised him I think. "Why?" he repeats. "Because I say so."

I huff my breath out in irritation at his arrogance or maybe it's my disappointment, I'm not sure which. I take a step to move out from under his arm. He immediately pulls me back, this time pressing his body to mine.

I gasp at the contact as he brings his face close.

"Why, darlin'?" he asks from between clenched teeth. "Because I feel the need to secure my position in my child's life. Because I don't trust you to not run. *Because* of so many more reasons that I should have my fucking head examined for even considering the idea of marrying someone like you, someone I can't trust!"

I stare at him wide-eyed, willing myself not to cry.

"Cait—" He closes his eyes briefly. "I'm sorry, I didn't mean—" He lifts his hand to my face and then he steps back, running his fingers through his hair.

I feel a sudden urge to console him, which irritates

me. His words hurt, but I know he's hurting too. I take a deep breath. He believes I betrayed him and he's scared. Afraid that he might lose a child he already desperately wants to love.

He steps close again, his voice soft and persuasive. "Caitlyn, this is what is best for our child — a marriage of convenience, yes — but a chance to provide a home with two parents for an innocent child who deserves to have stability and security in his life."

"Single parents do that all the time," I reason.

"Not an option here," he snaps.

I look away from his intense gaze, my hand unconsciously going to my stomach. I want the best for my child but — if I do this, how will I protect my heart? I mentally shake myself and take a deep breath. How can I possibly consider marrying Liam? I love him but he doesn't love me. Is a marriage in name only, where one of the two people involved doesn't trust the other, conducive of a happy environment? How can all this add up to a good home life for a child?

"We don't have to marry to do the best for our child." I place my hand on his chest when I see him visibly tense. "I will stay here — for as long as you want me to."

He steps back and my hand drops to my side.

"Not good enough." His eyes regard me closely and I become nervous under that calculating stare.

"You leave me with no choice, Caitlyn."

"What? What do you mean?" I ask nervously, uncertain of what he's going to say.

"I will have Ryan file the documents that I have already signed to petition the court for full custody of my child."

I shake my head, unable to speak.

He looks down at me with his hooded gaze, completely implacable in his decision.

I feel fear, the likes of which I've never experienced. And then, anger. "You bastard!" My hands ball into fists.

His mouth lifts at one corner. "Yes. I can be if warranted."

My breathing has escalated but no longer from his nearness. I'm so mad I want to spit in his face.

"What's it going to be, Caitlyn?"

I glare at him, our eyes locked in silent combat. The fear returns with the knowledge that with his connections, his money and my lack of both, he possibly could succeed in taking my child from me.

He cocks his head in a slightly mocking manner and steps away, reaching toward the door of the study.

"Yes," I hiss. Anger wells in my chest to the point that I think I'll choke with the emotion.

He looks back and raises that damnable eyebrow. My first task as his wife is going to be shaving that eyebrow while he sleeps.

"Are you sure? I wouldn't want to force you to do something you didn't want to do darlin'."

"You bas—"

He's instantly in front of me pushing me back against the wall, roughly pulling my arms above my head to bring them together in one of his large hands as the other grips my chin. His mouth comes down on mine in a punishing kiss, his tongue forcing my lips to part as he seeks entry, stroking my tongue with fierce determination.

Desire blasts through my body like dry timber going up in flame. I moan into his mouth as my body seeks to get closer to his. He growls, deep in his chest, which further incites my lust.

When he lifts his head, we're both breathing heavily. I raise my eyes expecting to see humor or satisfaction, but what I see is his bewildered gaze and his brow furrowed in confusion. I jerk my chin from his grasp.

"Let me go," I demand.

He holds me a moment longer, then releasing me, he steps back.

We enter the study to find Ryan talking on his phone. "I'll meet you downstairs for lunch in about an hour, baby."

My legs are shaking as I sit back down while Liam paces behind his desk. Ryan's conversation reminds me of Julie and I close my eyes. I don't want to talk to him, I just want out of this room, something to eat, and a place to lie down and come to terms with this new situation.

"May I use your phone, please?" I look up to find him watching me.

He frowns. "Can't it wait?"

"No."

Ryan hands me his and when I look at him he gives me a smile.

"Thank you, Ryan."

Julie answers on the second ring, curiosity in her voice at the unfamiliar phone number.

"Hey, I'm sorry but I need to cancel our lunch date... No, I'm fine." I glance up to see Liam listening to my conversation. "I'll call you later, okay?" I listen as she informs me she and Paul won't be home until late. Would I like to do breakfast with them the next day?

"I would love to," I tell her, conscious of Liam glowering at me.

I hand Ryan's phone back to him. "Thank you."

"If you are quite finished, Caitlyn, I'm needed downstairs." Liam glares at me.

I sit back, placing my hands in my lap, not saying a word.

He slides a batch of papers across the desk to me. "You need to read and sign this prenuptial agreement."

I reach for the papers as he picks up the house phone. First a NDA and now a prenup.

"Annie could you come to my study for a moment? And bring Ms. Shaw a water with you, please?"

"Do you have a pen?" I ask.

"You'll need to wait for Annie. She'll need to witness your signature. It'll give you time to read the prenup, Caitlyn." His voice is somewhat condescending.

I stare at the contract, but I don't read it. I don't want anything of his. Except his child.

There's a knock on the door and Ryan rises to open it, admitting Annie. She's not only brought me a glass of ice water, but a muffin too. I smile gratefully as she hands it to me.

"Thank you." I promptly pull off a piece and pop it into my mouth, wiping my fingers on a napkin she hands me.

Ryan motions for Annie to sit in his seat, explaining she is to witness my signature on a document.

"Can I sign now?" I look up to catch Liam's scowl.

He leans forward. "Didn't you eat breakfast?"

"No, I didn't get the chance," I say in a mocking sweet voice.

His eyes narrow dangerously.

"Here, Cait." Ryan hands me a pen. "Let's get this finished," he says in Liam's direction.

I promptly flip to the last page to sign.

"Cait — you need to read the prenup first. I can explain any of the legal terms you are unfamiliar with," Ryan offers.

I glance up and catch Liam glaring at Ryan.

"That's okay." I sign and hand the pen back to Ryan. I give the documents a little shove to slide across the desk and Liam catches the papers just as they fly off. He gives me a raised brow as I stand.

"Is that all you need from me?"

"Cait." I look at Ryan. "Let me go over the contract with you — "

I interrupt him. "It's okay, Ryan." I turn back, making eye contact with Liam. "I don't want anything from you. When I leave here, it will be with the clothes on my back — *and* my child." I don't wait to see how Liam responds as I quickly turn and walk out.

When I wake, it's early evening. Annie fixed me a light lunch earlier after I returned from the meeting in the study, but I'm already hungry again.

"You're going to make me fat, aren't you?" I say, looking down, rubbing my flat belly.

"Caitlyn" —Liam walks into the room— "Dr. Hines should be here shortly."

I look down, suddenly shy knowing he surely heard me. I avoid looking at him as I flip off the throw, sliding over to sit on the edge of the bed. It's only then that I look up, my breath catching. He's staring at me with those incredible eyes. His white dress shirt is unbuttoned; hanging open to give me a glimpse of his toned chest and hard abs, and I swallow deeply as I look down at his bare feet. No matter how angry I am with him, I know that I will never be immune to his sexual magnetism.

"Did you hear me?"

I look back up to meet his gaze. I give him a dismissive look as I stand and turn toward the bathroom. Before I can take two steps, he's gripping my arm, pulling me to a stop as he steps close.

"I asked you a question, Caitlyn." His voice is dangerously low and I don't dare look up. I am utterly shocked at the level of intensity in which my body responds to his touch.

Dark, insidious desire courses through my veins, pooling in my belly, leaving me a quivering mess. It's so unfair that he affects me like this. Even if I don't elicit the same feelings in him, can't he feel how I am affected?

"Answer me." His tone is gentler.

"I heard you."

We stand for several moments and then he releases his hold on my arm. I immediately move away from him, and he doesn't stop me this time as I continue to the bathroom, closing and locking the door behind me.

I stand with my hands resting on the vanity as I look in the mirror. I make a decision. I refuse to be anxious, nervous, or continuously angry during my pregnancy. I don't want those types of feelings or unhappy vibes. If what I ingest has a direct effect on my baby, than it only stands to reason, my emotional well-being is just as important.

Somehow, someway, Liam and I are going to have to work through this. He doesn't trust me? Well, I lost trust in him too when he threatened to take my child from me. If I'm willing to look beyond that, he can certainly try too.

I reach into one of the drawers for the hairbrush,

pulling it through my hair. I need to call my parents and let them know I'm getting married. I'm not sure how they'll react to that news. I've not even mentioned Liam to my mom, so they'll be asking a lot of hard questions. I can handle it, make them understand, but telling them they are going to be grandparents is a whole different story.

There's a light knock and the doorknob rattles.

"Caitlyn — open the door."

I finish wrapping the hair tie around the end of my loose braid before I open the door. Liam is standing directly in front of the doorway, so close that I can't pass.

"Excuse me." He makes no move to step aside.

"Why the fuck are you locking the door?" I look up into his burning eyes.

"I didn't do it consciously, it's a habit." And it is.

"Don't lock a door against me again," he says, his drawl holding an angry edge.

"I have a right to my privacy, Liam."

I think he's about to say something, but he turns and walks across the room. "Dr. Hines is here, I'll send him in."

To my annoyance, Liam stays in the bedroom while Dr. Hines takes my blood pressure and listens to my heart and lungs. Then I realize I shouldn't be annoyed. I have no reason to be. Liam said he was going to be involved in his child's life. The baby and I are very lucky actually. I'm really only annoyed at his high handedness.

In between the doctor's ministrations, I steal occasional glances at Liam. He's wearing shoes again and even with his shirt buttoned to cover his sexy abs, he's more handsome than any man has a right to be. He's leaning against the chest that sits against the wall across from the foot of the bed. Long legs stretched out in front of him.

It's Friday night and I know he'll be leaving soon for the nights activities. He usually spends Friday nights going back and forth between the second floor and the nightclub. Sometimes, I know he's down in the basement or dungeon as everyone refers to it. The thought of him leaving makes me feel lonely but I push those feelings right back down.

Just at that moment, Liam looks up. Smokey blue eyes lock with mine, and the heat I see there is unmistakable.

I pull my attention back to the doctor as he starts the verbal part of the exam. Liam listens closely as the doctor questions me about nausea and dizzy spells.

"And you say your appetite is back?" the doctor asks as he fills out his paperwork.

I giggle softly as my hand goes to my stomach. "Oh, yes."

The doctor looks up smiling and when I glance up at Liam, a corner of his mouth lifts. His eyes meet mine and I quickly look away.

"Well Ms. Shaw, I'll be back in a couple of days that is unless" —he turns to look at Liam— "you'll allow me to send my assistant now?"

Liam gives a slight nod.

I frown, wondering what that's about.

"Very good." The doctor sounds a little annoyed. "Continue getting plenty of rest and fluids," he says as he stands. "Don't forget to call Dr. Lyle's office for your appointment with her."

"I won't," I say softly. "Thank you, Dr. Hines."

"I'll walk you out, Greg. I have a couple of things I need to discuss with you."

What?

If they are going to discuss me, I have a right to hear what they have to say. I sit for a moment after they're gone and then I'm hurrying down the hallway to the elevator. Liam and Dr. Hines have already left the apartment and I consider following, but the thought of running into someone downstairs stops me. So I stand in the apartment's beautiful entryway and wait.

It's not long before the elevator is on its way back up. I lean against the wall directly across from the doors. The same wall Liam had me pressed up against a few weeks before. I close my eyes willing the erotic memories of that night to fade.

When I open my eyes, Liam is standing in the open doors of the elevator, watching me intently. My breath catches as my stomach muscles clench.

Stop this Cait!

I close my eyes again, praying that the craving I have for this man ends. I need to remember that he threatened to take my child away from me.

With my eyes still closed, I know when he steps close. That connection we share when we're near each other causes the hair on my arms to rise. My nipples tighten into hard buds, and a dull ache centers right between my legs.

Oh!

I bite my lip when I feel Liam lean in close. I hear him inhale deeply, and I'm finally able to draw a good breath, along with his delicious scent. I feel the air move as he steps back, and I open my eyes to find him still watching me, his brow furrowed.

"Liam." I breathe his name.

"Dinner will be ready shortly."

What?

I want to tell him I couldn't care less about dinner, but he turns and walks back into the apartment.

I follow slowly, a little shaken. This is not going to work. I want him. I want him desperately. Nothing has changed about that for me. Even with his threat to take my baby from me, just being close to him fills my body with blatant need. How am I going to survive living with him? Being married to him?

I come up short as soon as I walk through the bedroom doorway. Liam's just stepping out of the closet. He's changed into jeans, he's bare chested and just all kinds of sexy man. My gaze slides down to his bare feet, and I follow him with greedy eyes as he pads over to the balcony doors, pulling on a black shirt that he leaves hanging open.

Oh, hell.

"I thought we could eat out on the balcony but it looks as if a storm is rolling in." He turns to look at me.

I realize I probably have this goofy, drooling expression on my face and I promptly compose myself, turning away.

"It's Friday night—aren't you needed downstairs?" My voice sounds breathy.

I hear movement and then I feel the heat of his body at my back. I squeeze my eyes shut.

Shit. Shit. Shit! I am not going to lean back against him.

"I thought we should spend the evening together—since tomorrow is our wedding day."

I whirl around to face him. "What?" I shake my head. "What are you talking about?"

He's still standing close. Too close. His eyes have darkened to a stormy blue.

"We're flying to Lansing, in the morning, where we will be married." He's watching me closely as if he's on guard in case I run.

I glance around the room, looking for an escape.

"We can't get married tomorrow, it... it's Saturday and we don't have a marriage license and—" I feel panic set in. I know without him saying, he's already taken care of all that is required for us to marry.

"Well, darlin', I flew to Michigan yesterday and took care of everything." He steps over by the bed and picks up the phone.

I feel nauseous. Married. Tomorrow!

"Liam—"

He holds up a finger. "Annie, has the delivery arrived?" he glances at me. "Yes, but we'll eat in the dining room." He turns to look out the windows again. "Yes, I do think that sounds perfect. Thank you." He hangs up the phone and turns to level his gaze on me.

"Liam... I have... breakfast plans in the morning. I can't—"

"I spoke with Paul and Julie already and I do believe they're going with us." He crosses his arms over his chest.

"What?" I sit in the nearest chair before I fall down.

"I spoke with them earlier and they agreed to join us for the ceremony." His eyes move over me. "We'll pick them up on the way to the airport."

"I don't have anything to wear." I almost laugh at how that sounds. I'm grasping at straws.

Liam's lips twitch. "I took the liberty of buying a dress for you to wear."

I gape at him and then I try to force the overwhelming panic down. "You have it all figured out, don't you?"

He lifts an eyebrow. "Well now, I'm sorry that the thought of marrying me distresses you, darlin'," he says dryly.

I bite my lip as my gaze grows misty. I shake my head and look down at my hands as my fingers twist together. "I—" I look back up at him "—I'm scared," I confess, my voice sounding ragged.

He frowns and then he's crouching in front of me, taking my hands in his.

I sniff.

"Don't cry," he orders softly.

I give a choked laugh. I look back down at his hands holding mine. His thumbs slide back and forth over my knuckles as he watches me and I do my best to control my emotions.

"I'll tell you a little secret," he says at last, his slow drawl soft and growly at the same time. "I'm scared too." I look up in surprise. He smiles and leans a little closer. "I've never been married before either."

I smile a little at his teasing, looking back down to escape his discerning gaze.

"This is scary for both of us, sugar. It's all very— sudden, but we're doing it for the right reason."

Are we? He's still angry with me. What happens twenty years down the road when our child is grown and we're alone, on our own? But—if we don't marry, who's to say what we'll be doing all those years from now anyway. There's no guarantee for happiness either way. I frown. This is one of the hardest things I've ever had to do.

"Caitlyn—" he gives my hands a little shake "—can you do something for me?"

I search his beautiful eyes. There's not much I wouldn't do for him. "Yes."

He looks down at our hands and then back up, this time searching my eyes.

"Trust me, darlin'." My breath catches. "Trust me to take care of you and our child. Trust me with your future."

He's so serious, so sincere, his eyes boring into mine that I'm nearly overcome with the need to throw myself into his arms.

"Say yes, Caitlyn," he urges softly.

I know without a doubt that he will always protect and provide for his child and me. I will never have to worry about anything.

Except — for him breaking my heart.

I close my eyes and breathe in his unique scent, my lips parting when his finger brushes, with the lightest wisp of a touch, down my cheek to my jaw. I bite my bottom lip and his finger gently plucks at it to pull it free from between my teeth. He strokes my lip softly and it's deeply erotic, stirring a need in the pit of my stomach.

"Say you'll marry me," he breathes against my lips. I nod slowly. "Say it, darlin'."

"Yes, I'll marry you," I whisper.

His hand moves to grasp a handful of hair at the nape of my neck, holding my head in place as his tongue replaces his finger to lick across my bottom lip. My tongue comes out to lick the same path. When he sucks on my lip, that need he awoke suddenly flares into a roaring fire. My hands grip his shirt, trying to pull him close. When he doesn't budge, I try to scoot forward on the chair seat but his grip on my hair holds me in place. I open my eyes. The satisfaction I see in his eyes is unmistakable. He leans in, taking my mouth in a deep kiss, his tongue stroking, inflaming my need for him. My hands move to his bare chest, lightly grazing his skin with my nails and he growls softly.

Pulling his mouth from mine, he grins wickedly, and I think my heart stutters.

"We best stop this right now or we won't make it for the special meal I've ordered," he says as he leans in to kiss my forehead.

I blink. He just seduced me into saying yes. I don't care about eating and I don't want to stop, we can always reheat the food. I don't say anything, though. I'm still unsure of anything between us right now.

I decide at that moment, since he's asking me to trust him, I'll do the same. "Liam, since we're talking about trust..." I begin hesitantly.

He leans back and it's like a curtain coming down, not only over his eyes, but over his whole face. "Don't go there, Caitlyn."

"I think we need to talk about what happened —"

"No, we do not." He drops my hands and stands. "You best change for dinner. I want you to wear the red silk dress you wore the first night I saw you out with your friends."

I frown. *Holly packed that dress and brought it here?*

Liam mistakes my frown for confusion. "The night I assumed Paul and Julie were your lovers."

"I know what dress you're talking about!" I snap in irritation at his resolve not to listen to me. He considers me guilty of all manner of ugliness since the day he discovered that I'd worked for Query Magazine and hired on here at the Justice in order to investigate him.

His unwillingness to listen to me, to even consider my side of the story is beginning to piss me off.

"You told me one time that sometimes things are not as they appear." When he frowns, I can't help myself. "You know the day I walked in on you groping Miranda's ass."

It's not what I say, but the condescending manner in which I say it. His eyes flash with anger and then he's leaning down bringing his face close to mine.

"I do believe, darlin' that you need to go change for dinner before you piss me off." His eyes bore into mine before he straightens and steps back.

I'm more than happy to escape his sudden anger. Upon reaching the closet doorway, I glance back to find him watching me intently. I hesitate as his seductive eyes meet mine, holding me captive in their depths.

He finally breaks that grip on me, striding from the room.

CHAPTER FOUR

M Y WEDDING DAY IS LIKE a dream, as if I experience it all in a hazy, dreamlike state.

The day begins with a flurry of activity, for everyone but me. Liam won't let me do a thing, telling me when I complain, that I need to keep my strength up and let him handle everything.

Annie fixes a delicious breakfast, but after the dinner we had the night before, I'm still full and not very hungry. Liam arranged for a well-known chef to come in and prepare his signature dish for us. It was possibly the best meal I'd ever eaten.

We ended up dining in the living room at a small table placed before the open French doors. The table was set beautifully with fine linen, china, and crystal. It was simply lovely with the soft glow of candlelight, and as we dined, we watched the play of lightning across the darkening sky. The turbulent atmosphere of the approaching storm only added to my already heightened senses affected by Liam's nearness. It didn't help that he watched me with a dark, brooding sensuality that kept me aroused throughout the evening. Nothing more was said in reference to our discussion before dinner, but the buildup of tension was still there between us.

Now I sit and pick at my breakfast, as the apartment becomes a hive of activity. Even Annie is put to task and quickly disappears. Mike comes up, with another security guard, to carry a couple of suitcases and garment bags down to the waiting car. He doesn't speak; he just nods in my direction.

All too quickly we're headed to the airport, stopping to pick up Paul and Julie on the way.

At Chicago's Executive Airport, Mike drives us right out onto the tarmac so we can board a sleek Lear Jet. Our flight is a short one to Lansing, Michigan and as we exit the plane, a white limo is waiting for us.

After I enter the limo, to sit opposite Paul and Julie, Paul leans forward.

"Are you okay?" His forehead creased in the way it gets when he's worrying something over in his head.

I smile. "I am." But I don't sound okay, even to myself. Julie reaches over and squeezes my hand as Liam slides in beside me.

We ride in silence. I want to ask where we're going but I'm too nervous and to say I'm shocked when we arrive at our destination is an understatement. As we pull up to the curb, I glance up at Liam to find him watching me. His mouth slowly lifts into a smile.

The church is a beautiful, old Romanesque and when the driver opens my door, I'm surprised to see Holly and Ryan waiting for us.

"They came along with me yesterday when I applied for the marriage license and stayed behind to take care of some of the arrangements," Liam says.

That's not my last surprise. Holly leads Julie and me to a dressing room off the chapel so I can change. When

Holly unzips the garment bag and pulls out the dress that Liam bought, she's almost giddy.

The dress is exquisite. Liam chose well. White lace over shimmery silk, with a plunging neckline that ends well below the valley of my breasts. The back and cap sleeves are sheer lace in an intricate design with the skirt of the dress draping beautifully as it falls to the floor. It is sexy and very tastefully feminine. I love it. It also fits as if made for me.

Julie is ecstatic over the dress as she carefully takes it off the padded hanger. "I know this designer," she says with a raised brow.

"Hush," Holly says, taking it from her.

"This is from Holly and me." Julie hands me a flat white box with a large silver bow. It contains lingerie of the finest silk. Delicate, almost sheer in a beautiful shade of ice blue.

"You'll only be able to wear the panties and garters with your gown, but we wanted you to have the complete set," Holly says.

"Something blue," I say softly. "It's so beautiful. Thank you, both." I blink against the tears.

"And" —Julie holds out her hand— "something borrowed."

I take the small jewelry box, looking up in surprise when I see the necklace inside. "Your grandma's necklace."

She beams at me before taking the diamond, hanging on a fragile looking chain out of the box. "As you know, she wore it on her wedding day and then my mama, me and now you."

"Julie—" I'm at a loss for words. I know what this necklace means to her and for her to allow me the privilege of wearing it, brings tears again.

"Now stop. No tears on your wedding day," Holly admonishes gently.

I laugh and sniff as Julie hugs me.

They help me with my makeup and hair, working over me as if I were a doll without a thought in my head, which is fairly accurate at this point. The whole experience and preparation is surreal.

There are two distinct moments though that I will retain in my memory for as long as I live. When we enter the chapel and I walk down that aisle toward the spot where Liam stands, he turns toward me and my breath catches.

He chose a dark blue suit for the day that highlights his eyes, turning them to a dark, cobalt blue. He's tall, broad shouldered and strong.

My body tingles with awareness as those eyes move over me in a slow leisurely caress, coming back to hold my gaze. I don't mistake the hunger I see there.

My heart feels as if I'm running a marathon by the time I reach him. He takes my hand and gently pulls me close to take my mouth in a soft kiss. My senses drink in his scent, his taste, and I feel our bodies connect with that nearly tangible flow of energy that is so uniquely ours.

When he raises his lips from mine, his eyes seem to reflect what I'm feeling, what he surely must see in mine.

"Do you feel that?" he whispers in awe.

My held breath escapes softly from between my lips. "Yes," I breathe, our eyes locked in the wonder of the moment.

He reaches out to stroke his finger down the side of my face, his forehead furrowed slightly as if he's puzzled at what is transpiring between us.

"You are the most beautiful, exotic creature that I have ever had the good fortune to lay eyes on, darlin'."

I feel my cheeks heat.

"So pretty, sugar," he whispers, his mouth lifting in a slow smile as his finger brushes across my cheekbone.

The minister clears his throat, asking if we are ready to begin. I hear someone, Ryan I think, laugh softly.

I know that I repeat my vows correctly because neither the minister nor Liam corrects me. When Liam takes my left hand and slips a band of fiery diamonds on my ring finger, all I can do is stare at the dazzling brilliance. It is as equally unexpected, when he hands me a gold band and I repeat after the minister before slipping the wedding ring on Liam's finger.

I vaguely hear, "You may kiss your bride," before Liam is pulling me into his arms bringing his face close. I close my eyes, lost in the moment, feeling his warm breath against my lips as he softly says, "Mine." The word is barely a whisper, but I know I don't imagine it. My eyes fly open, meeting dark and seductive blue before his lips take possession.

Strong arms hold me tightly as he kisses me with hungry fervor. His kiss leaves me totally unsettled when he releases me.

My legs are shaking as Julie and then Holly hug me before Paul wraps me in a bear hug.

"Be happy," he whispers in my ear and when he lets me go, I catch Liam's narrowed gaze.

"Congratulations, Mrs. Justice." Ryan gives me a quick peck on the cheek.

I blink and look at him as if he's sprouted two heads. He laughs out loud. I'm still in shock at just the *thought* of being married and now — I am.

"Let's go." Liam sounds disgruntled as he holds out his hand. I go to him, wondering where it is he wants to go.

Amid the good byes and remembering to get my things from the dressing room, we're pulling away in the limo before I realize that we're leaving everyone else behind standing on the curb. I turn to look out the back window.

"Paul and Julie will be traveling back to Chicago with Holly and Ryan," Liam says softly from the seat across from me.

I turn back around to find him watching me with an unreadable expression. We didn't take time to change and he's still in his fine, dark blue suit. His pristine, white shirt sets off his dark hair, brows and lashes to perfection. He is simply — gorgeous.

His stare is unnerving and I look down, smoothing the skirt of my dress across my lap.

"Thank you, for the beautiful dress."

After a moment he says, "You're welcome. I wasn't sure if you'd think I was being presumptuous in choosing your wedding dress."

My eyes meet his. "I would never criticize the gift of this lovely dress, Liam." My fingers stroke the material. "I don't think I could have chosen as well." I give a sharp laugh, my nerves beginning to tell. "It's more than most brides expect for a shotgun wedding."

Liam's eyebrow lifts and I look back down, my thumb rubbing against the band of my new ring.

When he doesn't say anything else, I look back up. His head is resting against the back of the seat and he watches me from under hooded lids. My body responds with a will of its own, to my embarrassment. My nipples tighten and I know that he notices, as nothing seems to escape him. I press my legs firmly together as my body tightens under his silent perusal. I inhale deeply, willing myself to relax. The sexual need he is able to bring forth with just a look has not diminished with the absence of intimacy. If anything, the urge for him to assuage the ache he instills is stronger.

I crave his touch, long for the sexual control he so expertly wields over my body. Is this overpowering carnal need I have for him a weakness in me or because it's been weeks since we've had sex. Or maybe it's just a side effect of pregnancy. I turn my head to look out the window. I'm sure he's had sex since we broke up. I fidget in the seat as I try to control the surge of jealousy that courses through my body.

Liam remains quiet, no doubt he's wondering what he's going to do with a wife. Probably cursing the night he let his lust override his common sense and didn't use a condom. Then again, maybe he's just pissed by the fact he's had to marry the woman who carries his child because he feels the need to solidify his place in that child's life. He'd said as much to me the day he dragged me out of his study into the hallway to threaten me.

Now what? He's whisking me back to Chicago and I don't have a clue about... anything. I worry my bottom lip between my teeth as I feel my anxiety rise. It doesn't help that he won't stop staring at me. After several minutes, I've finally reached my breaking point.

"What, Liam?" I turn to glare at him.

One dark brow lifts arrogantly.

"What? You keep staring at me and I know you want to say something, so just— say it!"

He raises his head, levelling those killer eyes on me.

I swallow uncomfortably, unease settling in the pit of my stomach.

"You know, I do like that you are feeling better. And a part of me enjoys that sassy attitude of yours." His voice holds the slow seductive drawl that causes my stomach muscles to clench in reaction. I nervously lift my hand to brush a loose tendril of hair behind my ear. His eyes follow my movement, his gaze feeling like a sensual touch and when it slides down my neck to my chest, following the plunging V-neckline, I almost moan. My nipples harden painfully and my breasts rise and fall noticeably with my arousal.

I bite my lip.

"Actually, darlin'" — his voice is raspy now — "I enjoy it very much, relish it even. I find it refreshing." There's a ghost of a smile in his expression.

He sits forward, his forearms rest with deceptive ease on his thighs, his hands hanging between his spread legs.

"But I feel I should warn you, sugar, you best watch how far that sassiness goes." His expression hardens perceptibly and my mouth goes dry. "You being pregnant won't change the fact that I'll still turn you over my knee," he threatens.

He leans back his arms going up to rest along the back of the seat. He props one leg up over the knee of the other.

"Hmmm." The sexy sound comes from deep within his chest. My mouth opens slightly, and I blink slowly. "The thought of you, your belly swollen with my child, lying across my knees as I spank that sweet ass of yours..." His eyes narrow seductively and he tips his head slightly, humming again.

Muscles deep within, clench in a painfully delicious way.

Oh!

I bite my lip, closing my eyes.

Liam suddenly grips my arms and hauls me across the seat to his lap. I cry out softly and he lays a finger against my lips.

"Shhh."

His hands take hold of my wrists, pulling them to the small of my back to hold in one large hand. My chest pushes forward and he brings one of his long fingers up to slowly stroke down the length of my throat, between my breasts to where the neckline ends. I moan softly closing my eyes again.

"I do believe what you need, darlin', is a good, hard fucking." His voice is husky and when I open my eyes, I see he's not as cool and unaffected as he seems. Sitting on his lap, I feel his hard erection pressing against my bottom. I know he's toying with me but his words wash over me like a tidal wave, eliciting a need that shakes me to my core. I mentally shake myself. I can't let him reduce me to a trembling mess like this.

I look out the window when I realize the limo has come to a stop beside the plane. I pull a hand free from his hold, bringing it up to lie against the side of his face.

"Don't say things like that to me." I pull my other hand free and slide off his lap to return to the opposite side of the limo. When the driver opens the door, I look back just before I exit. "It's my wedding day."

We're on the plane, in the air and Liam is watching me again with an unfathomable expression. My body feels flushed as I recall what he said about what I need. I wish I'd asked him if he were offering his services, but my sudden streak of courage left me right after I exited the limo and Liam gripped my arm possessively, guiding me up the steps, into the plane.

I look around the luxurious cabin of the jet, my attention returning to Liam when he stands to remove his jacket. My belly flip-flops and it has nothing to do with air turbulence. Why is a man dressed in a suit so hot? You would think it would be just the opposite, too many clothes. But I know from girlfriends who have had the same reaction, it's like the equivalent of us wearing lingerie for them. So. Damn. Sexy.

When Liam steps close, towering over me, he begins to roll his sleeves up. I feel a frisson of unease slowly work its way up my spine. He said he'd spank me. Would he?

"Are you hungry?"

I look up from watching him roll his sleeves, and notice the flight attendant coming toward us carrying a tray.

I nod. "Yes, I'm starved," I admit. I see a ghost of a smile on his lips.

The attendant beams as she sets the tray down and places covered plates in front of us before lifting the lids with a flourish. She turns that beam on Liam and if possible, I believe it brightens.

"What can I get you to drink, Mr. Justice?" she asks her voice low and throaty.

Seriously? We're sitting here in our wedding apparel and she's coming onto my new husband.

"What would you like, darlin'?"

"Apple juice?"

His mouth lifts at the corner. "My *wife* will have an

apple juice and I'll have a glass of white wine, please."
The attendants smile dims a little at the subtle reprimand.

I dig right in and I don't think a steak could taste
any better than the club sandwich that I proceed to put
away. I flush, embarrassed when I look up to see Liam
watching me.

He wipes his hands on his napkin and picks up his
plate, offering me the remaining half of his sandwich.

Looking down I whisper, "No, thank you."

He sets his plate down. "Don't be embarrassed,
Caitlyn. As they say, you're feeding two." When I look
back up, he gives me a wink. "We'll have a proper meal
when we land."

I pause as I reach for my glass of juice. I glance out
the window.

"We're not going ho—back to Chicago?"

Liam picks up his glass and I watch as he takes a long
sip of his wine. My eyes slide down his throat, watching
the play of muscles in his neck as he swallows.

Is there one thing not sexy about this man?

I raise my eyes to meet Liam's pensive stare. He sets
his glass down.

"We're flying to St. Louis."

"What?" I gasp.

"We're going to visit your parents. I do believe it's
time they met me in person, don't you?"

"What?" I repeat. *We're going to my parents?* "Liam—
I... I haven't said one word to my mother about you—"
His eyes narrow ominously. "I need to talk to her first.
They're going to be—surprised that I'm married, that I
didn't tell them. They are going to want to meet you, of
course but—"

Shit!

I feel like pacing the length of the plane. Maybe running laps up and down the aisle. When I meet his gaze again the blatant anger throws me. I frown as I recall what he's said.

"What do you mean, that it's time they met you in *person?*" I search his expression.

He leans back in his seat, his anger still evident as he stares right back at me, arrogance written all over his masculine features.

"You called them," I say with certainty, leaning back in my seat. I shake my head, resigned to the fact that my parents must be confused by the situation. As am I. "What did you say?" My voice sounds anxious.

"Well now, you seem a tad upset at the prospect of introducing me to your parents, darlin'." His voice holds anger and something else.

"No." I shake my head and look down. "That's... not it." I turn the diamond band on my ring finger with the opposite hand, not noticing what I'm doing.

"Why don't you tell me what it is then?"

I sigh. "I've barely spoken to my mom in the last three weeks. My parents know I've been ill, but now I'm going to show up out of the clear blue and introduce them to a man they've never heard a word about. A man who is their new son-in-law."

Liam picks up his wine glass, the polished wedding ring on his finger gleams, and downs the contents before setting the glass down.

The flight attendant immediately steps through the curtain with fresh drinks. I turn to look out my window. This will be so odd taking Liam home to meet my parents. Not that they won't accept him, they will for the simple fact that they think I've chosen him. And I have no doubt that Liam will charm them. I just don't want this to hurt their feelings, beside the fact it might make them worry. My dad especially will be quick to see through any subterfuge.

"Mrs. Justice?"

"Caitlyn."

I look back to see them both looking at me. I feel my face warm when I realize that the attendant just referred to me by my new name and I didn't respond.

"Would you like anything more?" she asks, politely, her professionalism back in check.

"No, thank you."

She removes our plates and leaves us again. Liam sips at his drink, regarding me thoughtfully.

"Caitlyn—I took the liberty of introducing myself to your parents when I called, advising them of the situation."

My eyes widen. "You what?" My hand moves to my throat.

"I told them" —his voice has an edge to it— "how we dated briefly, broke up, and how I seized the opportunity when you came back into my life, and you agreed to marry me."

I gape at him, uncertain of what to say.

"I then asked your father for your hand in marriage."

I'm stunned at that last bit of information.

"You seem a might surprised, darlin'." His voice is slightly mocking.

I don't know what to say to him. "Did you tell them about—" I stare at him.

"About the baby?" His eyebrow lifts, his expression somewhat derisive. "No, darlin', I thought we'd share the happy news together." His words are heavy with sarcasm.

I blink before looking back down, my fingers moving over the soft lace of my dress. How are we going to do this? I'm suddenly tired, not sure of what we think we are doing here. Regardless of what Liam said about us marrying for the right reason — the fact still stands that he continues to be angry with me. He'd shut the door on our relationship, ending things between us, and if it weren't for the baby — I wouldn't be sitting here, married to him.

Can we really make a happy life for our child? And what of *us?* What type of life are we supposed to build together? My doubts of earlier raise their ugly head. What happens if after a few years Liam decides he can't do it — can't face it with me any longer? I'm not sure how I'll be able to survive the devastation of losing him again.

"I... I'm not ashamed of you, if that's what you're thinking. It's just—" I keep my gaze cast down, not wanting him to see my uncertainty. "I'm confused by all this, Liam." I take a deep breath. "My parents, especially my dad, are going to notice the — the tension between us. And when they hear about the baby—" I bite my lip. "I don't want to disappoint them," I whisper.

"Cait," Liam says softly, leaning forward in his seat. "Fuck!" He abruptly stands, scoops me up into his arms and sits back down with me in his lap.

I wrap my arms around his shoulders, burying my face against his neck and breathe in his amazing scent. It comforts me, and I relax against him, his arms tightening.

"We will make this work, baby," he murmurs near my ear. I nod, my face still pressed to his neck.

If I could only remain like this, in his arms...

"Caitlyn."

I hear him but I can't move. I'm too comfortable. His hand rubs my back and I shift slightly.

"Time to wake up, darlin'. We're fixin' to land."

I give one of those croaky whines. His answering chuckle is low, seductive. I turn into his body more fully. He's so warm. I moan slightly as I raise my head to meet his hooded gaze. His eyes are that hazy shade of blue that is so seductive, sensual even and I no longer see mockery in their depths. No. What I see in his eyes, can only be described as intense heat. The response in my body is instantaneous.

This pent up sexual need I constantly seem to be experiencing is building and becoming more difficult to control as it vibrates throughout my body.

His mouth lifts into a wicked smile. "You need me to fuck you, don't you darlin'?"

I blush at his words, desire pooling low in my belly, an intense ache settling between my legs.

"Answer me," he demands, his voice taking on that edge that calls to my libido.

"Yes," I breathe, looking up to see his eyes darken.

He gives me a lazy grin as the flight attendant walks down the aisle toward us.

"I'm sorry to interrupt, but we will be landing shortly and you will need to fasten your seat belts."

Liam stands and I clutch at his shoulders when he acts as if he's going to toss me over to my seat. He laughs softly as he gently plops me down.

Bastard!

Leaning over me, he brushes my hands away to buckle me in himself.

"Never fear, sugar. I won't be as gentle with you in bed." His face is level with mine and he stares boldly into my eyes, his ablaze with fire.

My breath catches at his seductive promise and then he leans in, taking my mouth in a hard, swift kiss.

Liam suggests we change clothes in the plane's bathroom and I have to ask him to help me with my dress. His breath is hot against my bare back as his fingers deftly release each pearl button down the back of the gown. When he runs his finger along my spine, I can't stop my shiver.

"There you go." His voice sounds hoarse.

"Thank you," I whisper. When I turn, he's already stepped out, closing the door softly behind him.

A hired car is waiting for us as we disembark. It seems Liam was very thorough in his arrangements for our trip.

As we enter the SUV I ask, "How long are we staying?"

He glances at me before looking back down at his phone. "Just until tomorrow."

Liam charms my parents, as I knew he would. And they are genuinely happy for me. I see it on their faces and hear it in their voices. I catch a look pass between them, and I can read the whole gamut of emotions in that one exchange between them. They had been worried.

My father is unable to go out for dinner, and it is so unexpected to find that Liam arranged in advance for a local restaurant to bring dinner to us. They bring it all, everything needed to set a beautiful table. Liam even helps my mom assist my dad into his wheelchair so Dad can sit and eat with us.

We have a delightful time together, lingering over the incredible meal, and while we enjoy our after dinner coffee, my dad and Liam discuss the current baseball season. I watch the animation on my father's face as he shares his passion for the game.

When I look at my mom, she smiles, shaking her head, and then leans close. "I want to show you my new project, Caitie."

"Okay." I glance at Liam as we stand and he quickly stands, giving me a slow smile.

My mom moves behind my dad's wheelchair, squeezing his shoulder. "We'll be right back; I want to show Caitie the quilt I'm working on." My dad reaches up to pat her hand.

Liam leans close. "Caitie?" he whispers and then grins when I subtly elbow him in the side.

At the doorway, I look back meeting Liam's gaze, and then quickly follow my mom.

Holy hell. How am I going to live with that man and refrain from jumping him?

Mom has always kept her sewing machine set up in her and Dad's bedroom. It keeps her close to him and sewing is her thing. She made most of my clothes while I was growing up and she's really good at it. I always had a new outfit for any occasion.

She proudly spreads the squares of fabric she's piecing together out on the card table that sits beside her sewing machine.

"I love these colors, Mom," I say, knowing although she's happy to show me her start of the quilt, that's not why we're here.

"I'm making it for you, sweetie."

Turning my gaze from the pieces of fabric to my

mother, I say, "It's going to be beautiful. You know I'll love it."

"If I'd known, I would have started with a Wedding Ring pattern."

"Mom, I'm so sorry I didn't tell you about Liam. Everything has happened so fast and—"

"Caitie, I didn't bring you in here to scold you." I can't help but smile. I don't think she's ever scolded me about anything. "You know I married your father on our third date."

"Yes. Love at first sight."

She turns to face me fully. "Was it that way for you?"

Her question catches me a little off guard. "Yes," I say softly. "From the moment I saw him he's—turned my world upside down."

She smiles and lays her hand against the side of my face. "Good. Your father and I trust your judgement. You know we only want you to be happy."

"I know, Mom."

"He is a handsome devil. I can understand how he'd turn a girl's world awry."

"Mom!" I laugh.

"Let's get back out there," she says, turning toward the door. "Your father is having a wonderful time. This dinner was very thoughtful and generous of your new husband," she says over her shoulder.

"Yes, it was," I say thoughtfully.

When I nervously tell my parents about the baby, my mom cries with joy. I almost start crying myself when I see my dad swipe at a tear.

After dinner we move back to my parent's room while

the restaurant staff cleans up. I can tell that the time out of bed has exhausted my father. Liam notices too and it's not long before he suggests we take our leave.

My mom wants us to spend the night with them and part of me wants to too, it's been so long since I've visited. But the only other bedroom is my old room upstairs and the bed is only a twin, so we decline the offer. The thought of lying in that small bed with Liam causes my pulse rate to quicken. When she starts to protest, my dad reaches for her hand and she lets the subject go. Liam promises her we'll be over early after breakfast and will spend the day with them, which appeases her and she lets us leave for the night.

I doze in the car on the way to the hotel, my head resting on Liam's shoulder. It's been a long day and all I want is a shower and bed.

The suite is spacious and beautifully furnished, yet that's all that registers with me as I head straight for the bedroom. I unpack the nightgown that someone packed for me. Liam? Obviously new, I hold the short, white chemise up to inspect. It's soft and practically sheer with a plunging neckline. My skin feels hot at the thought of Liam seeing me in it. I'm crossing to the bathroom when he walks in.

I pause. "Do you want to shower first?" I ask.

He looks up and his eyes slide over my body, which tightens on cue.

"No, you go ahead — I'll join you in a moment." He promptly pulls his phone from his pocket as my mouth drops open. *He wants to shower with me?* I grit my teeth against the sudden overwhelming need that gnaws at the pit of my stomach, and quickly turn, continuing to the bathroom.

I strip, no longer tired. My hair is still up in its wedding day hair-do and I yank the pins out, working my fingers through the long tresses, before I step into the shower, letting the water sluice down my body. I feel overheated and anxious waiting for Liam to join me. We've never showered together. When I stayed over, before we broke up, he was always gone; already busy in the mornings by the time I awoke.

I imagine his hands moving over my body, touching me where I most need them. I tip my head back letting the water wet my hair as the sharp spray hits my back and shoulders. I turn and gasp softly when the needles of water hit my sensitive nipples, imagining Liam's teeth as they bite and tug the turgid peaks.

I start guiltily at my erotic thoughts when the shower door finally opens. Liam steps in, gloriously naked except for his pendant. I swallow against the sudden dryness in my throat. I would never have thought that I would forget exactly how gorgeous he is with no clothes, but clearly, my memory sucks.

His shaft is long and thick, standing erect almost half way up his flat belly.

Fuck.

I gawk, unable to look away, my eyes taking in his toned pelvic muscles that form that sexy V.

Fuck.

He reaches around me for the shampoo and his medallion swings off his chest and hangs close to my face. It's the first time I can see that there is engraving on the back. As I reach up to take hold of it, Liam grabs my wrist. I look up and his eyes bore into mine. He shakes his head.

Why?

"Turn around."

When I make no effort to move, he repeats firmly, "I said, turn around."

I quickly do and hear the lid pop open on the shampoo, and then his hands are tangling in my hair, massaging the shampoo against my scalp with the tips of his fingers. I moan as he works the shampoo in.

"Step back."

Tugging gently on my hair, he pulls my head back so the water rinses the shampoo clear. He reaches around me for the bottle of body wash.

"I want you to put your hands behind your back and keep them there," he says near my ear and I shiver.

I do as told, interlocking my fingers together.

"Very good, darlin'."

I feel the quiver start low in my belly, and I bite my lip in a bid to control my rising desire.

When his soapy hands encircle my neck, I step back against his front and then I almost moan when I feel his impressive erection nudging against my clasped hands and lower back. I close my eyes in pure bliss as his hands slide down my throat, across my shoulders. He works the soap down my arms, and then back up to slide down over my breasts.

I arch my back, thrusting my breasts forward more firmly into his hands. I love when he touches me like this, strong, demanding. As he squeezes and massages, I feel my tender breasts swell in his hands. I moan, unashamed of my desire for this man.

He works me into a frenzy as he holds the weight of each breast in his large hands, his strong fingers working to the tips, plucking at my nipples. I moan softly and when he squeezes both nipples tightly between his fingers, I buck back against him, this time crying out.

"You are exquisite, darlin'," he murmurs against my ear.

His hands move with soapy slickness down over my stomach, rubbing soap gently, almost reverently over the skin of my belly.

I bite my lip as his fingers continue their path down, working the soap into the curls between my legs. One hand moves behind me to my bottom, rubbing the soap over and between my cheeks. I mewl softly and squirm, my anticipation building.

"Hold still," he orders.

I don't think I can.

He shifts until he's at my hip, continuing his sweet torture. Cupping me firmly between my legs, he parts the folds of my sex as his fingers move over me.

"Liam..." I whimper as my body begins to tremble.

"Turn around," he says gruffly.

When I turn to face him, placing my hands on his chest, he uses the hand on my bottom to anchor me solidly against his front, his erection rock hard against my stomach. I slowly raise my eyes to his. They glitter from beneath half-closed lids, sending a thrill through me. He is so damn sexy, and he owns me with just a look.

He at once drops his hands from me, reaching for the body wash as he steps back.

"You can wash my back now, darlin'." He hands the bottle to me.

What? I need— I close my eyes, knowing it won't do any good to beg. He says when. Okay. I take a deep breath and take the bottle from him. I feel as if my insides are quaking.

I smooth soap across his shoulders with shaking hands, working it down his back.

Holy shit. His body is amazing. So muscular and strong. My hands move down to his firm backside, and I bite my lip as desire grips my insides, twisting with a vengeance as I rest my head against his back.

"You're not washing," he murmurs as he reaches for the shampoo.

I take another fortifying breath and go down to my knees. I work the soap down his muscular thighs and by the time I reach the top of his feet, my teeth are permanently imbedded in my bottom lip.

Liam turns to face me and my eyes move slowly up his body. I unconsciously lick my bottom lip and when I reach out to touch him, he reaches down and grasps my arms, pulling me to my feet.

His jaw is taut as if he's gritting his teeth. He quickly pulls me under the water, and I rest my forehead against his chest, hoping the water that rains down on us, will rinse away the raging desire that smolders in my belly. Turning the water off, he reaches out to grab a towel, which he shakes out before wrapping it around me.

"Liam—" I breathe.

"You're clean." He opens the shower door, and with his hand at my back, pushes me gently toward it. "Go to bed."

What? "But—"

He reaches for a towel and begins drying his leg. "I said go to bed." The look he gives me brooks no further argument.

I dry off quickly and slip into my nightgown. It's practically transparent, my nipples displayed provocatively. I blow dry my hair until it's just damp, watching Liam from the corner of my eye as he steps out of the shower. The towel wrapped around him, sits low on his hips and his erection juts out, titillating my senses. Just knowing how long and hard — how thick he is — I mentally shake myself and try to hurry.

His mood has turned almost surly and I hasten with my bedtime ritual so I can leave the bathroom and his overpowering presence.

I climb into bed and when he walks into the bedroom a few minutes later, the slow burn in the pit of my stomach roars to life.

He's wearing boxer briefs that prominently display the size of his erection. My eyes follow him as he walks out of the room.

What's he doing?

When he walks back in, he has a glass of ice water. I watch as he walks toward the bed, still fully erect. I do believe that the man has a perpetual hard on.

"Like what you see, darlin'?" he asks as he sets the glass on the nightstand.

I look up to catch his cocky grin. I lift my chin. "Yes," I say boldly, my face heating.

His eyes instantly burn.

"Come here."

I hesitate for just a moment and then I'm sliding across the bed to stand in front of him. Under his gaze, I feel my nipples tighten painfully. The sudden throb in my clit has me fidgeting. He reaches out a finger and touches the tip of my nipple. It's as if an electrical current enters through my breast and heads straight between my legs.

I gasp and at the same time lift my hand to my breast.

Liam hisses from between his teeth and then he's yanking me into his arms, his mouth coming down on mine, kissing me almost violently. I moan into his mouth as dark desire explodes in my body. He has my arms pinned down and I can't reach up to touch him as I'd like. I work an arm free running my hand over his chest, sliding up to his shoulder. His skin is hot and his muscles ripple in response under my touch.

I melt. My legs feel like jelly as his tongue explores my mouth. I make a distressed sound when he jerks his lips from mine and cry out in alarm when he painfully grips my arms and shakes me.

"What the fuck are you doing to me?" he asks angrily.

Doing to him? What is he doing to me?

I shake my head and cry out again as he sweeps me up into his arms. He takes the two steps to set me down beside the bed and before I realize his intent, he's gripping the front of my gown, ripping the silky material right down the middle and lets it falls to the floor around my feet.

I gasp, surprised and unbelievably aroused, as I stand naked before him.

Holy Shit!

Nervous excitement courses through my body. This is — freaking hot!

I look up, and his eyes are ablaze with fire, his jaw gritted tightly, but as I watch, the shutters come down.

"Go to bed," he orders harshly.

"What?"

He turns and crosses the room.

"Liam — "

He pulls the door closed with a resounding thud behind him.

I stand there stunned for a moment before embarrassment assails me.

He doesn't want me.

I crawl to the center of the bed, pulling the sheet up over me. As I lie there staring at the ceiling, I decide that being rejected on my wedding night has to be the most humiliating thing I've ever experienced. If he only wants a marriage in name only — why did he join me in the shower? Why the kissing and sex talk?

I roll to my side. He's angry. Still holding onto his belief that I deceived him. Angry I'm pregnant. Angry he's married to me. The list is endless. And daunting.

I draw my knees up, my arms crossing protectively over my stomach as I huddle beneath the sheet. The air conditioning has nothing to do with the chill that settles over me.

I swallow down the tears, determined not to let him totally break my heart.

CHAPTER FIVE

I ROLL OVER AS I STRETCH; clutching the sheet and blanket to my breasts. I look down at the blanket covering me. Liam must have come in during the night and placed the blanket over me. The thought of him watching me sleep —

I look up as the door opens and he walks into the room. I'm unable to stop the blush that I feel heat my cheeks and the need to avoid him supersedes all other thought.

"Good, you're awake. We need to shower; breakfast will be here shortly."

He's been exercising somewhere. His sleeveless, gray T-shirt is sweat drenched and his hair is damp. Wow. I look over at the alarm clock. I don't think my body would be up for any type of exercise this early in the morning.

He rucks the bottom of his shirt up, exposing his delicious abs as he wipes his face.

Shit! My stomach muscles tighten as a place deep inside of me stirs with desire. I can't believe he can do this to me after last night. I look away, determined to ignore my bodies yearning.

"Let's go, Caitlyn."

Is he serious?

"I'll wait to take mine after you—" My voice tapers off. He's already shaking his head.

"No. We shower together. Let's go."

I shake my head. "I'm not showering with you," I whisper, appalled at the thought after his rejection of the night before.

He reaches for the sheet and I wrap it firmly as I scoot away from him across the bed.

His eyebrow lifts arrogantly as he stands looking down at me.

"There's not an inch of your body that I haven't seen, nor tasted for that matter." He motions toward the bathroom. "Now."

The man is crazy if he thinks I'm going to allow a repeat of the night before.

"I *am not* showering with you," I say firmly, keeping my face turned down. When he doesn't say anything, I surreptitiously look up from under my lashes. He's staring at me, his forehead creased.

He walks to the bathroom and at the door he looks back at me. "The longer you dally, the shorter your time with your parents."

That's just fine. I'll skip my shower if I have to.

We eat breakfast at a table out in the main room of the suite. It sits before a large window that offers a panoramic view of the city, the famous Arch in the distance. I'm wearing one of the fluffy white robes provided by the hotel with my wet hair wrapped in a towel, turban style. Liam's dressed in nice jeans and a white linen shirt with the sleeves rolled up. I would never have imagined, before Liam, just how sexy a man's forearms could be. And no matter how upset I am at him, I'm not immune to his appeal.

"We'll spend the day with your parents and then fly back home late afternoon." He pushes a glass of juice closer to me.

"Okay," I mutter around the bite of granola I've just taken. I frown slightly. Home. I want to ask him what that means.

"What is it?" he asks as he refills his coffee cup.

I shake my head and spoon another bite.

"Look at me, Caitlyn," he says firmly.

I swallow the cereal and slowly look up.

"Are you feeling okay?"

"Yes." I look back down at my cereal, stirring the contents before spooning another bite.

When he doesn't say anything, I look up to catch him studying me, his expression impassive. I squirm under that penetrating gaze.

"Caitlyn, if you have concerns about anything regarding your pregnancy you *will* tell me. I don't want you ignoring any problems, thinking they'll go away."

I inhale sharply. "I'm not stupid, Liam."

"I won't have you jeopardizing your health or that of the child."

My eyes open wide. I don't know why his words surprise me. He's already made it clear that he thinks I don't know how to take care of myself while pregnant. I set down my spoon and turn my attention to the view. I'm also well aware of the cold, hard fact that it's the child he wants in his life.

He sets his coffee cup down. "I mean it, Caitlyn."

I continue staring out the window. I hear his heavy sigh and then the ringing of his cell phone.

"Justice."

I lay my napkin on the table.

"What!"

At his tone, I turn to look at him. He stands abruptly and I watch as he runs his hand through his hair.

Oh, no.

"When?" He glances at me. "What the fuck!"

I sit forward in my chair.

"My computer?" His eyes land on me again and narrow as he regards me. "We'll swing by Caitlyn's parents and then we'll be on our way."

He ends the call, his eyes still on me.

I feel unease trickle down my spine.

"What's going on?" I ask.

Very gently and precisely, he lays his phone on the table and then looks back at me.

"You tell me."

I frown "I don't understand. What's wrong?"

He continues to study me before finally saying, "Someone broke into my office last night."

"What? Why?"

His gaze is assessing as he continues his regard, his eyes boring into me.

I frown again in thought. "You don't keep member's files in your office, do you?"

Why would they target one room at a time? If it was info on a particular member, why didn't they just hit Lara's office again? Unless, they knew what they needed would not be found in the membership files. What type of information does he keep on his computer?

"Liam, before I... after the first break in before I — left, it occurred to me that whoever broke into Lara's office wasn't working alone, they had someone on the inside helping them. I'm sure you and Mike have come to the same conclusion."

He remains silent.

Why is he acting like this, not saying anything, just staring at me as if he's trying to work his way into my brain.

Oh!

My eyes widen and my breath ruses out in a small exhalation. "You think that I had something to do with the break-in?" I shake my head. "Liam, I've been with you. I had nothing to do with this, *or* the first break-in."

His eyes shift away, finally.

"You don't believe me." My words, uttered in disbelief bring his eyes back to mine.

"I don't know what to believe, Caitlyn." He throws his napkin down on the table. "All I know is that you've lied to me already."

"I didn't lie to you!"

He's suddenly looming over me and it's all I can do not to shrink back into the chair.

"You. Lied. To. Me." He glares down at me, one hand on the table and the other on the arm of my chair, effectively pinning me in.

I glare right back. "I *did not* lie to you."

He straightens to his full height. "Call it anything you want but you weren't honest with me," he says harshly. After a moment, he grabs his phone and as he crosses the room, he says in a hard voice, "Get dressed!"

"Are we talking about honesty here?" I ask softly but he hears me, stopping to look back. I take a deep breath and try to tell myself not to do this now, but his continual mistrust has pushed me to this point. "How honest were you with me yesterday and then last night?"

He narrows his eyes on me. "What are you talking about?"

"You made promises yesterday, vowing to love, honor, and cherish." I stand slowly, keeping my eyes on his and I see something fleeting cross his face. "Is that what you did last night?"

We stand there staring at each other until I drop my gaze and walk past him to the bedroom.

We sit in strained silence on the ride to my parents. But to Liam's credit he acts perfectly at ease with them as he explains our need to hurry home. I'm the one who acts in a manner that worries my mother. While Liam discusses our flight home with my dad, Mom gets me aside.

"Are you sure you're okay, Caitie?" Her discerning gaze searches my face.

"I'm just tired, Mom. The last two days have been so busy. I'll be fine once we're... back home." What I say must pacify her because she visibly relaxes.

With promises to come back soon, we say goodbye.

"Bye Daddy. I love you."

My dad holds me in a weak hug, his arms nearly useless. "I love you too, baby. Call us tomorrow and let us know how things are," he says.

"Bye, Mama." I have to steel myself against the sudden need to cry in my mother's arms.

As I let her go, she places her hand against my cheek. "You take care, and I'm going to hold your new husband" — she glances fondly at Liam — "to the promise that he's bringing you back soon. We'll go shopping for the baby."

My eyes are teary as the limo pulls away to whisk us

to the airport. I feel the weight of Liam's gaze the whole way.

It is a relief when we arrive back in Chicago and head for Justice House. I'm glad that no one will be around since it's Sunday, the only day that the club is closed. I'm nervous about seeing any of the members or the people I previously worked with. I know I will eventually have to face them but I'm not up to it yet.

There are several cars parked in the circular drive as the cab pulls up into the driveway and I glance at them anxiously. I think one of them belongs to Bryce.

A security guard comes out of the guardhouse to help unload our suitcases. He and Liam talk quietly for a couple of minutes while I wait. We use the elevator just inside an alcove off the main hallway. I've never used it before and I'm surprised when the doors open just outside the apartment. The area we're in is actually the rotunda part of the main entry hall downstairs. The first day I arrived for my interview, I looked up to the stained glass ceiling, two floors above me. Railing encircles the open area and I can look down into the entryway below or up to the exquisite, multi-colored ceiling above.

"Oh, Liam it's beautiful!"

He comes to stand beside me, his hand resting on my lower back. We haven't said a word to each other since this morning. Our flight was quiet and I tried to rest, which proved impossible with the sense of Liam's eyes on me and the replay of our morning's conversation.

"This is the reason I bought this place."

I smile up at him. It's a relief that he doesn't sound mad any longer.

"I apologize for not showing it to you sooner." He steps away to a door situated beside the elevator doors, opening it to reveal a stairwell. "Fire escape."

I nod. Good to know.

He moves to the door I assume leads inside the apartment to scan the same card he uses for the elevator. It lets us into the long hallway just down from his study.

Before I can enter, Liam scoops me up into his arms, and I let out a small "eek" of surprise. He laughs and his gaze locks with mine.

"Welcome home, Mrs. Justice."

My breath catches as I look into his eyes. "Thank you."

He promptly carries me across the threshold, and continues down the hallway. I'm taken aback to hear voices as we near the living area. I'd already forgotten about the others being here. I squirm a little but Liam makes no move to set me down. I see Bryce as he steps into the hallway, smiling broadly.

"Here they are now," he says as he heads toward us. Liam at last, sets me on my feet.

"Glad to see you have enough sense to carry your bride into her new home," Bryce jokes as he shakes Liam's hand, pounding him on the back.

"I have been known to get a few things right," Liam shoots right back, giving me a wink.

My lips part at his suggestive wink.

Bryce rubs his hands together. "Now to welcome the bride."

Liam reaches for his arm but Bryce is already stepping toward me, and before I realize his intent, he's pulling me into an embrace. Just before he bends me back over his arm, I hear Holly calling to Liam. Bryce proceeds to give me more than a friendly kiss. When he raises his lips above mine, he whispers, "Let's stay like this a moment." I have a second of confusion before he's being jerked away. I grip his arm at the suddenness, feeling as if I'm about to fall.

"What the fuck!" Liam hisses, reaching for me.

Bryce laughs out loud.

Liam glares down at me as he pulls me to his side. "Are you okay?"

"I'm fine."

Liam scowls at Bryce. "Fucker!"

I almost laugh then, but catch myself. They're like a couple of adolescent boys.

"Cait!" Holly's suddenly beside me, giving me a quick hug. "We're here to welcome you home." She laughs as Ryan walks up behind her.

"Hi, Ryan."

"Cait." He smiles and puts his hands on Holly's shoulders. "Babe, let's move out of the hallway so they can get through the door to sit down."

"Is Mike here?" Liam asks as we all move to the living room.

"He's on his way," Bryce says, handing Liam a beer.

Liam sits on one end of the couch and pats the cushion beside him. I gratefully sink down, feeling drained of energy.

"Bryce since you're playing bartender, would you mind fetching a glass of juice for, Cait?"

"No problem."

I shift to rise. "I can get it."

"Stay put," Liam orders and I sit back.

"Did you enjoy your visit with your parents, Cait?" Holly asks.

"I did, it was good to see them."

"Did you behave yourself, Liam?" Holly asks with a laugh.

"You know me Holly." Liam laughs and looks down to give me another wink.

Oh, my.

"Here you go, Cait."

I tear my eyes from Liam's and take the glass of juice Bryce hands me.

"Thank you, Bryce."

Bryce proceeds to plop down beside me, grinning over at Liam. I look up and catch Liam shaking his head.

"Your friends, Paul and Julie are a great couple, Cait," Holly says. "We had so much fun with them."

"They are good people." I glance up at Liam. He's looking down at me.

He leans his head toward me. "Drink your juice."

"How are you feeling, Cait?" Bryce asks.

I finish my sip and lick my lips. "Very well, thank you."

He grins. "I guess it's too early to feel the baby moving?"

"Not for our little Justice it isn't," Holly says.

"Really?" Bryce sounds surprised.

"When was this?" Liam asks, frowning down at me. His voice sounds irritated.

"Just a couple of times—" His eyebrow lifts.

"You've felt the baby kick?" Bryce asks.

"No." I glance at him. "Just a faint flutter."

"Mike's here," Holly announces.

Bryce stands and goes to greet him.

"When?" Liam asks again.

I frown at him. Why does he sound cranky? "The day

I came here to tell you about the baby," I whisper. "As we drove through the gates."

"And the second time?" He leans in closer, placing his arm up along the back of the couch behind me, effectively enveloping me in his heady scent. His gaze holds mine and there is something so intimate in the moment, I truly forget about the others.

"That first morning that I was here, when you picked me up—to carry me to the bathroom."

I see something flicker in his eyes. His hand comes down beside my ear and he caresses the lobe as my eyes drop to his mouth.

"Stop looking at me like that," he growls.

My eyes flash back to his. They are smoldering in their intensity.

Holy hell. He's so damn confusing.

"Hey, Mike," Holly greets the big guy.

Liam's eyes drop to my mouth and then he looks up at Mike. "Did you bring what I asked for?"

Mike nods.

Liam pulls his arm from behind me and stands. "Holly, will you keep Cait company please, while we have our meeting?"

Her eyes shift quickly to mine. "Of course."

Liam leans down and grips my chin, tipping my face up to his. "We will discuss you keeping things from me concerning our child later." His voice is low, so I know the others don't hear him and it probably looks like an intimate moment between us. Before I have a chance to respond, he's crossing the room to speak with Mike in a tone so low I can't hear what he's saying.

"Cait?"

I tear my gaze from the two men to look at Holly.

"Are you hungry?"

I grin. "What do you have in mind?"

What Holly has in mind is a trip downstairs to the restaurant's kitchen where she rummages around in the large walk-in cooler. Within minutes, we're enjoying cold, roasted duck, thick slices of a delicious Russian cheese, which makes me giggle when Holly attempts to pronounce the name, and strawberries.

"Chocolate covered strawberries?" I ask as we sit at the kitchen counter on stools Holly rustled up.

She hesitates with a strawberry half way to her mouth. "You've never had a chocolate covered strawberry?"

I moan around the mouthful of heavenly goodness as I shake my head.

"What planet have you been living on?"

"Clearly the wrong one," I say. I lick my lips and reach for another. "These are good for you, right?" They have to be. They are my new favorite food.

"Oh, yes." She grins. "And they have no calories." I blink at her and then we both bust out laughing. Grinning she stands. "Be right back."

She disappears into the cooler and is soon back with a jug of apple juice, pulling a couple of glasses down from a shelf.

"You certainly know your way around this kitchen."

She smiles as she hands me a glass. "I help myself— frequently." She raises her glass to toast and I do the same. "To you and Liam and our little Justice."

I clink my glass against hers.

"You okay?"

I nod. "I am."

She eyes me speculatively as I nibble on a piece of

cheese. "So how was the honeymoon, besides being short?"

I think back over the last twenty-four hours. "Well, considering the fact that Liam wasn't acknowledging my existence a week ago, and that he considers me a big, fat liar who is possibly conspiring to destroy him — I think it went fairly well." I nod my head, agreeing with my own assessment.

Holly laughs out loud. "To Liam." She lifts her glass in another toast and we both sip our juice.

"You had nothing to do with the break-ins," she says as she sets her glass down. "He knows that... he's just frustrated."

I'm not so sure about that — about him believing that I had nothing to do with what has been happening — he made that plain this morning. "Holly, there has to be someone on the inside," I say softly.

"Yeah, they know that. At first, they thought that it was someone working alone, tapping into the security systems computer to disable the alarm. But after they had a meeting with the security company, Mike is now convinced that it is someone who is either a member or an employee helping them."

Or me. I'm sure Mike favors that possibility.

"The first break-in happened on a Sunday night, when the club was shut down, so it had to be someone who knows the security system and how to disarm it. The intruder last night" — she shrugs — "there were only a few of us here late and Mike set the alarm himself. He and I were the last to leave a little before 3 a.m. The gates were locked behind us by the guard left on duty." At my frown she adds, "The guard has worked for Liam and Mike for years."

Maybe it's from working as a reporter for the last couple of years, I don't know, but every instinct in me wants to investigate this further, even pull Paul in on it. But I know I can't, because I'm still a suspect. The fact that I was with Liam should prove to him that I had nothing to do with any of this.

Holly leans close. "The really odd thing is—"

"Holly," —I interrupt— "I think it would be best if you didn't tell me anything else."

Her eyebrows lift in surprise. "Cait—" She shakes her head and I know what she's going to say.

"Please, I think it's for the best... the less I know."

She gives me a sympathetic smile. "Okay. Change of subject."

"Thank you."

"I want all of us to go out together, dinner and dancing. A party since you didn't have a reception. We can invite your friends, Paul and Julie. I really like them and Ryan does too."

I smile, not committing. I have no idea if Liam would want to do something like that with me. We've never been on a date. We made a baby but we've never actually dated. I must be getting tired because everything is starting to make me feel weepy.

"We girls should go out to lunch. You need to become better acquainted with Emily. She's wonderful." Holly looks thoughtful for a moment. "Actually you two are a lot alike."

All at once, I feel a tingling at the nape of my neck. I turn on the stool knowing Liam is behind us.

He's leaning against the doorway between the kitchen and the dining area.

How long has he been standing there?

Bright eyes pierce me with their intensity, causing my breath to catch. The tingle at my neck converts into a full-blown shiver down my spine.

Holy hell.

I'm a hot mess in a matter of seconds as carnal need floods my senses.

His eyes move over me in a possessive manner as he pushes away from the doorframe. He moves with sensual purpose, his gaze holding mine.

I can't take my eyes from his, I'm held captive in his sexual thrall.

"Holly," he says softly.

She turns, surprised to see him.

How the hell she couldn't feel the electrical charge in the air is beyond me. Light bulbs should be blowing with the surge of energy sparking back and forth between us.

I inhale deeply as I look up at him. My hand moves quickly to my belly as I feel the faint flutter.

Liam's eyes drop to my hand and then come back to meet my eyes. I watch as his pupils dilate.

"Ryan wants you upstairs, Holly," he says firmly.

From my side vision, I see her look at him and then back to me.

"Okeydokey," she says. I pull my gaze from Liam's to look at her and she gives me a wink as she stands. My eyes slash right back to Liam's as Holly pulls the kitchen door closed behind her.

Liam doesn't hesitate, pulling me up from the stool into his arms. His mouth comes down on mine with an impassioned kiss. His tongue plunging deep into the recesses of my mouth and then back to stroke my tongue.

My hands have a mind of their own as they tangle in his dark, sexy hair. Although I press my body tightly to his, I'm unable to get as close as I need. My hands are actually shaking as they stroke the soft scruff on the side of his face. He moans deep in his chest, the sound reverberating against my tongue, further inflaming my libido.

I grasp the front of his shirt, my knees ready to buckle as he sucks and bites at my lips.

Gathering my hair, he wraps the length around his hand. When he pulls his mouth from mine, I mewl softly and try to regain his lips but he spins me around so that my back is to his front as he pushes his hard erection against me. Pulling my hair, my head tilts back and my neck arches. He licks and sucks his way up the side of my neck.

"Liam," I whimper, my voice barely above a whisper. "Please." My irritation over the night before forgotten as the need I feel for him settles into a dull throb between my legs.

"No," he murmurs against my neck. "I am not going to fuck you in here."

I whimper. *If he'd only stop doing – that, we could go upstairs and –*

He tugs my head back farther and his free hand lands flat, splayed across my stomach. "Did the baby move?" His voice is deep and husky at my ear. For some reason his words are so erotic, or maybe it's just the timbre of his voice.

I moan, my hands reaching behind me to grasp the sides of his thighs.

"Hmmm?" His tongue follows the curve of my ear.

"A... A flutter!" I gasp.

He bites the lobe and then steps back, releasing my hair to grip my hand.

"Let's go."

"Where are we going?" I ask as he pulls me along behind him.

"Upstairs."

I sigh inwardly. I don't want to go back upstairs where everyone else is.

We enter the elevator in his office and before the doors close completely, he turns me to face the back wall and then he's pushing against me. His body flattens against mine, trapping me in place. One warm hand encircles my throat as he buries the other in my hair. I moan relishing the sensation of his hands on me like this.

His mouth finds my ear and takes the lobe between his teeth, biting gently as his hand slides to the back of my neck and I feel the zipper of my dress slide down.

I reach behind me squeezing his erection through his jeans. *Oh! I need him.*

He pushes my dress down, off my arms and I shiver when the cool air from the open elevator doors flows over my body.

"Hands against the wall," he growls. He still has a fistful of hair in his grip, holding me in place. His free hand moves down, caressing my lace covered breast, sliding over my stomach to grip my hip.

"I like this," he murmurs against my ear as his fingers slide seductively under the wide lace strap of my thong, following the line of it around the curve of my bottom between my cheeks. His foot abruptly pushes against mine, causing me to take a step apart, allowing him to slide his hand more fully between my legs. He pulls my head back and to the side, his mouth coming down on my shoulder.

My whole body shivers at the sensation of his hot

mouth on my bare shoulder. I can't believe how badly I
need him. A part of me knows I always will.

I groan loudly, when he bites the sensitive spot where
my neck and shoulder meet. He pushes more fully into
me as he sucks.

"Fuck!" He licks the throbbing spot. "You taste good."

He releases me and places his hands over mine against
the wall. His breathing is a little fast but he's in complete
control as I lean my forehead against the elevator wall,
pulling in a ragged breath.

After several moments, he turns me around. Gripping
my chin, he tilts my face up, his eyes impaling me with
their intensity. He frowns slightly.

Uncertainty grips me. "What?" I whisper.

His eyes move down to my lips and then his hand
falls away as he steps back.

"You look tired, you need to lie down and rest."

"What?" No, I don't.

He turns and heads out of the elevator as I scramble
to get back into my dress.

"Don't bother dressing, there's no one here but us,"
he calls back.

I grit my teeth. One of these days I'm going to strip
him of his clothes, but leave mine on and then we'll see
how he likes that. I snort softly. Who am I kidding? I
give a little sigh as I follow him down the hall.

He stops at the bedroom door and turns, his eyes
sweeping over me. And then he flashes one of his full-
blown, panty-dropping, give-a-girl-a-good-time smiles.

I stumble to a stop and he reaches out to steady me.

"Humor me, darlin'."

Oh, for Pete's sake! "I don't want a nap," I whine.

He snorts softly. I know I sound like a petulant

child. What he doesn't know is that I'm about ready to stomp my foot and maybe beat his chest in frustration. He drives me crazy when he does this to me. I have a disquieting thought. Maybe he really doesn't want me. I've heard stories about men who don't find pregnant women attractive.

He stares down at me, his gaze all too knowing. "Are you going to do as I ask?" His mouth twitches suspiciously.

My eyes narrow. I'm glad he's finding this so amusing. "Maybe."

Without warning, he hauls me into his arms, his mouth taking mine firmly.

I hesitate for a fraction of a second, caught off guard as I usually am with him, and then I press my body against his. I try to pull my arms free from between us but I'm trapped by the circle of his.

He lifts his head his eyes shining incandescent. As I watch, his mouth lifts slightly at one corner. "Careful, sugar," he says in a warning tone. "I might should let you know that I punish bad behavior, and you're already on the short list."

I bite my lip at the sexy implication in his voice. "Is there anything sexual involved in that punishment?"

I see something in his eyes. "I can definitely give you a little taste of the sweetness that comes with the pain."

Holy shit!

Is he teasing?

"Why am I on the short list?" My voice is barely above a whisper.

He cocks his head, his eyes narrow slightly and I suddenly wish I hadn't asked.

"Well now, darlin', I do believe we need to discuss

the problem of you keeping things from me." He raises his eyebrow. "Again."

He's talking about me not telling him about feeling the baby. "Liam, I—" I look down and then back up to meet his unfathomable expression. "I wasn't trying to keep it from you. This is all new to me too and at first—I wasn't sure what you wanted to hear."

The mood has definitely changed. He drops his arms and steps back from me.

"I need to work for a bit and you need to do as the doctor ordered and rest." His jaw is set in a hard line. "I'll wake you in a couple of hours and we'll go out for dinner."

CHAPTER SIX

I'M STARVING AS WE DRIVE to the restaurant a few hours later and my hunger is for more than food. What's wrong with me? I feel like an oversexed teenager. This surely has to be a side effect of the pregnancy. Of course, since I met Liam, I have behaved like I'm oversexed. He seems perfectly relaxed, whistling a familiar tune while he drives. Why does it please him so much to keep me in this state? Maybe if he weren't so damn sexy... but right now — everything about him annoys me. From the subtle scent of his aftershave to the sexual energy that pulsates between us.

"Do you need to whistle?"

He glances at me, his eyebrow lifting in that sexy way of his. When he laughs it does funny things to my stomach, and I grit my teeth.

"Would you prefer the radio?" he asks as I gaze out the side window.

"I'd prefer an orgasm," I mutter.

"What's that darlin'?"

"I'd prefer silence please."

His chuckle is full of self-satisfaction.

He whips the car into the next lane before pulling to the curb. He didn't say where we were eating but it doesn't matter, I'm beyond hungry. Liam exits the car and I watch as he moves around the front of the vehicle to open my door. He's wearing a beautiful gray suit that fits him perfectly. Just looking at him causes my pulse to race. He holds out his hand and I place mine cautiously in his.

After I step out onto the sidewalk, he pulls me into his embrace his mouth coming down on mine, his kiss heating my body. I feel a little unsteady when he releases me.

"Ready?"

I give a little laugh. "Yes, more than ready."

He doesn't pretend not to know what I mean. He takes my arm and leads me around the car, his hand sliding down to take my hand as we step forward to cross the street.

"Do you want me to fuck you in one of the bathroom stalls?"

I look up, catching his smirk and I choke back a laugh. "No!"

"Well then, darlin', I reckon you'll just have to wait until we get back home."

My heart rate accelerates. "Can we just go for fast food?"

He laughs. "Oh no my little impatient one. This is one of my favorite restaurants and we are going to enjoy a good meal."

I sigh with exaggeration and look up. I stumble and Liam pulls me in tight against his side, his arm going around my waist.

Holy fuck!

My step falters but Liam pulls me along. I feel the need to run but his grip on my waist lets me know he is not about to let that happen. When Valerie created a cover for me, my last place of employment was here — The Carriage House.

As we reach the door, I look up to meet Liam's unfathomable expression. I swallow nervously as we enter.

"Good evening Mr. Justice," the Maître d' greets us. "Your table is ready, if you will follow me, please."

He leads us to a secluded alcove. The restaurant is full of patrons but our little space is quiet and private.

My pulse has kicked into overdrive as we're seated. I can't bring myself to look around and I don't want to look at Liam. I'm waiting for him to stand, pointing his finger at me, announcing to all of the customers that I am a big, fat liar.

"You look beautiful, darlin'."

My eyes lift in surprise. His are gleaming at me appreciatively. My dress is a strapless silk done in a soft peach and the soft lace shawl draped over my shoulders is a darker shade of the peach interwoven with a soft, silver gray thread. We didn't color coordinate our clothes ahead of time, but we match, with Liam in his fine gray suit.

"Thank you," I answer softly. I can't just ignore the ramification of our being here. I feel the need to explain — or apologize. I'm not sure which. "Liam—"

"Not now," he says as an older man approaches our table.

"Mr. Justice, Andrew said you were joining us for dinner."

"Good evening, Victor." The man gives me a courteous nod. "Victor, this is my wife, Caitlyn Justice. Caitlyn, Victor is the sommelier here at The Carriage House."

To Victor's credit, he recovers from his surprise very quickly. "It is very nice to meet you Mrs. Justice."

"Thank you, it's nice to meet you." My voice sounds nervous. I want to crawl under the table. What must Liam think of me? I wonder how long he's known.

"Do you have a specific wine in mind this evening, Mr. Justice or might I suggest something after you've chosen your meal?"

"No wine for us this evening, Victor. I will have my usual, though." Liam's eyes are on me as he speaks.

Victor inclines his head. "Very good sir."

After Victor leaves us, Liam continues his perusal, which adds to my nervousness.

"What are you hungry for, Caitlyn?" I pick up my menu; I think I've lost my appetite. When I don't say anything Liam asks, "Shall I order for you?"

"Please."

After the waiter takes our order, I reach for my glass of water.

"Would you prefer something else to drink?"

"A glass of wine."

His eyebrow lifts. "I don't think so, and you'd better not let me catch you drinking alcohol."

My eyes widen in astonishment. "Liam, I'm kidding. I can't drink, I'm pregnant."

After Liam's drink is delivered, he continues to watch me, his expression inscrutable.

I look away pulling my shawl back up on my shoulder. I pull it up close to my neck, making sure it covers the bruise from his bite.

"Are you cold?"

I meet his eyes. "No." I shift uncomfortably. "Liam... why did you bring me here?" I ask softly.

His eyebrow lifts. "Well now" — his voice is like slow, sweet molasses— "I do believe I brought you here for a nice meal, darlin', and here it is now."

The waiter places our food on the table and quietly leaves us.

"Caitlyn, I did not bring you here to make you uncomfortable." He picks up his fork and knife, cutting into his steak.

I pick up my utensils and stab at mine. If he didn't bring me here to make me uncomfortable — he's failing miserably. I have wanted to talk to him about what happened but he's not interested in hearing my side of the story. I'm guilty in his eyes, he's made that much clear. Bringing me here, says so much. Nevertheless, I want him to understand that I did try to tell him about my working for Query Magazine. More than that, I desperately need him to believe me.

He sighs. "You need to eat."

"I am."

"Cait..."

I lay my knife and fork down and put my hands in my lap. "I am so sorry, Liam. I truly didn't want to keep things from you. I—"

"Enough!" he says harshly. He leans back and lifts his hand to run his fingers through his hair. "Cait—I brought you here to clear the air between us."

I frown. "What?"

"I know you didn't work here. I've known from the day you interviewed."

My mouth drops open. "Then... why did you hire me?"

"I didn't. Holly did."

I swallow uncomfortably and look away. "You knew I was lying."

"I didn't want to hold it against you. I decided that perhaps you needed the job." He picks up his knife and fork and slices off a bite of steak. "And there was the fact that I wanted to fuck you the moment I laid eyes on you."

I huff a soft laugh. Even in the face of being embarrassed to find out he knew I'd lied, I'm not unaffected by his words.

"Look at me, Caitlyn."

I meet his bold gaze.

"Let's leave it... it's finished."

My eyes search his. "I need you to believe that I meant to tell you, that I —"

"I do."

My brow wrinkles. *Since when?*

"I've had time to — rethink the situation. I think your actions at the time showed your remorse of the deception."

"I wasn't trying to deceive you, I promise."

"Right now I'm more concerned about you not being clear on the fact that I plan to be involved in every aspect of our child's life. That also includes your pregnancy."

Are we back to this? "At the time... I just wasn't able to talk to you about the flutters."

He stares at me long enough that I squirm in discomfort.

"Okay. I understand."

What? It's my turn to study him. "Do you mean that? About believing me and letting go of all that happened." My heart is beating fast. If he could do that and let us start over —

"I do. Let me make this clear though." His narrowed

gaze burns right into me. "Do not *ever*, deceive or keep from me something you know I should hear. From you. Are we clear on this?" His veiled threat in that smooth voice of his sends a slight shiver over me.

"Yes," I breathe.

Holy shit, he can be intimidating.

I take a deep breath. "I only kept the information about my working for the magazine from you because I felt I should tell Valerie first, before I blew her story apart."

The waiter appears in the doorway to our alcove. Liam shakes his head and the waiter discretely retreats.

He turns that intense gaze back on me. "I understand that your loyalties were to your previous employer, but your loyalty is to me now."

A sudden longing to be in his arms is almost over-whelming. "Yes".

His eyes soften. "Good. Now eat your steak, darlin'."

I'm almost giddy as we leave the restaurant after our meal. I had felt the burden of our unspoken words hanging over me like a black cloud. The relief I feel now that I have said what I mostly needed to say and the fact that he believes me is liberating. For the first time I honestly feel that we haven't made a mistake in marrying, that we do have a chance.

I can't keep my hands off Liam when we reach our parked car. I pull him to me and standing on tiptoe, I kiss him with growing passion.

"Whoa, darlin'." He tips his head back, gripping my arms as my lips work their way up his neck.

"Please, Liam... I need you," I plead as I nibble at his

chin. The unyielding passion I felt earlier in the evening is back full force.

His arm snakes around my waist and he lifts me off my feet, his mouth finding mine. My hands delve into his hair, pulling and tugging at the silky locks. Liam continues to hold me up against his body as he ravishes my mouth, his free hand molding around my breast, squeezing and pinching my nipple.

Desire unleashes with a vengeance and my body is trembling as he breaks the kiss and sets me on my feet.

"At this moment, there's nothing more that I want than to bend you over the hood of this car and pound the fuck out of you, but I am *not* fucking you out here on the street." He reaches to open the car door as my body tightens at his words. When I look up, he returns my look with a smoldering intensity. "In you go sugar, I need to get you home."

"Where you'll pound me on the hood of your car?"

He snorts as he grips the nape of my neck. "I was thinking more along the line of a bed, darlin'."

I bite my lip as he leans in to buckle my seat belt. When he's finished, he turns his face to mine, his eyes burning. He gives me a quick kiss and then he's shutting me in.

Our clothes are coming off as we exit the elevator into the apartment. When I don't move fast enough for him, he dips down to gently scoop me up over his shoulder.

"Liam!" I gasp and laugh as I hang upside down over his back.

"Is this okay, it doesn't hurt your stomach?" he asks, concern etched in his voice.

I wiggle a little but everything seems fine. "No, it's okay." I laugh again.

"Good." He smacks my bottom, hard. Really hard. I squeal and he swats me again. "Quiet!"

"Why? Annie's not here." I'm breathless with excitement.

"Well, sugar that is a good thing since I'm going to make you scream my name."

I moan as a jolt of desire hits me right at the apex of my thighs.

When he flips me down onto the bed, I lay there panting, watching him. His hair is in sexy disarray from my hands and his bare chest and the deep V that peeks out from his briefs just beg for my tongue. But before I can move, he comes down on top of me, pinning me to the mattress with his body. He leans his upper half on his forearms, his hands cradling my head.

His eyes are fervent as they look into mine, before moving over my face as a frown forms between his brows.

"What's wrong?" I breathe.

His eyes meet mine again, his thumbs stroking the sides of my face. "We need to talk about last night, darlin'."

Oh. "Okay," I say softly.

"I didn't mean to hurt you, Cait." His hand brushes the hair back from my forehead.

"You were punishing me," I whisper.

He closes his eyes, inhaling deeply.

"Why?"

"I'm sorry, baby."

He brings his face close and kisses my forehead. I close my eyes, breathing in deeply, breathing in his mind numbing scent. My breath suddenly catches when he kisses first one eyelid, and then the other. Next he kisses the tip of my nose.

"Liam," I breathe just before his mouth takes mine in a soft kiss.

I moan, my arms moving up around his neck and then he's rolling over onto his back, taking me with him so that I'm lying on top of him. His hands delve into my hair as it falls down around him.

His kiss becomes more insistent and when he rolls us over again, I groan with the pleasure of his body covering mine. His kiss borders between rough and tender as his tongue plunges in and out of my mouth in a rhythm as old as time. When his hand covers my breast, pinching and squeezing the nipple, I arch up against him, my hands clutching at his shoulders. I raise my legs up around his hips seating him more firmly against me.

He finally releases my mouth, his eyes aligning with mine. I breathe in deeply but he barely gives me time to catch my breath as his lips slide down my neck to my breasts, kissing and sucking the exposed skin above my bra. I arch my back slightly, my hands moving up into his hair. When he bites my nipple, through the lace of my bra, my head falls back as a low moan escapes my throat. His skillful hands move over me, intensifying the ache between my legs.

"Liam!" Oh, I need him inside of me.

He lifts his head and I try to pull him back down, wanting my mouth on his, but he resists.

"Look at me," he demands, his eyes boring into mine when I do. He smiles gently. "I'm — sorry for last night, darlin'. That was no way to treat you on your wedding night." His voice is low and forceful, his gaze fervent as it holds mine. "I seem to lose all reason when I'm with you" — he frowns slightly — "but that's no excuse. I made promises to you yesterday, important vows. I knew you were feeling vulnerable and I took advantage of—" He closes his eyes again, a deep frown forming between his brows.

I reach up with my fingertips to smooth the frown line and he opens his eyes.

"You're forgiven," I whisper.

"No." One side of his mouth lifts slightly. "I plan on making it up to you, darlin'." His voice has taken on a sensual tone that makes me arch up beneath him.

"And how do you plan to do that?" I ask teasingly.

"Well now," —his hand slides behind my back and expertly unhooks my bra— "I plan to do what I should've done last night." His eyes gleam as he holds my gaze.

I draw in a sharp breath as my nipples pucker and tighten in the cool air.

"Oh, yeah—think you can redeem yourself that easily?" My voice comes out breathy sounding.

He grins and my heart seems to stutter.

"Oh, yeah." He nods and then his expression becomes serious again as he cups the side of my face, his thumb stroking my cheek as his eyes move over my face.

"My grandparents were a great love story," he finally says, his voice slow. "They were wed sixty-two years and my grandmother had a needlepoint that was framed and it hung on the wall above their bed. It hung there for as long as I can remember." His eyes are intense as they gaze into mine. "It wasn't until you came into my life that I fully appreciated what it meant."

I can't take my eyes from his. "What did it say?" I breathe.

He reaches to brush my hair back off my forehead.

"With my body, I thee worship." His voice is low and

husky, his eyes burning as they hold my suddenly tear bright gaze.

"Liam." My voice is choked with emotion.

His mouth comes down to claim mine in a kiss that is drugging to my senses as my arms go around his broad shoulders, clasping him to me.

When he lifts his mouth from mine, I make a sound of protest but his lips are already moving down my body, nipping and sucking. When he reaches my breasts, he forcefully suckles each nipple until I'm moaning and writhing beneath him. My fingers tangle in his hair and pull as his ministrations send sharp jolts to the sizzling nerve endings of my clit.

"Ahh! Please, Liam."

His mouth continues sliding down over my skin to my flat belly, his tongue circling my navel before dipping inside. My moans and gasps are loud in the quiet room as his mouth travels even lower.

He looks up at me as he pulls my panties down my legs, almost reverently placing kisses on my thighs. He then lifts my legs up to bend at the knees, pushing them apart to expose me further. The kiss he delivers between my thighs causes me to cry out and he brings his fingers to slide along my slickened folds as I buck against him. He thrusts a finger into me as his mouth covers my clit, sucking gently at first, slow, pulsating pulls on my throbbing nub. A sound that is somewhere between a growl and a moan breaks free of my lips as my hands fist in the sheets beneath me when he sucks harder. My teeth come down on my lip in a bid to silence my cries.

He raises his head again and my panting is loud around the room as I struggle to catch my breath. He watches me closely, his eyes locked on mine. When he inserts a second finger, thrusting his fingers in and out of me, my back arches and I feel the tightening of my body signaling my impending orgasm.

"Liam—" I gasp his name as my head drops back.

When he lowers his head back between my thighs and flattens his tongue between my folds, licking my length, I climax loudly as the waves of my orgasm rip through me with pounding, unrelenting force.

He gathers me into his arms as the aftershocks ripple through my body.

"You are so fucking beautiful, darlin'." His fingers stroke along my spine, soothing me.

In the next instant, he rolls me onto my back and kisses me endlessly as his hands move over me, stroking my sensitized flesh, arousing me with increased ardor.

"I want to fuck you, Caitlyn. Hard," he murmurs against my lips. I mewl softly, wanting that too. "But not yet." He takes possession of my mouth again.

What? I pull my mouth from his. "Liam, I need you," I plead.

"I know, darlin'."

His captures my mouth again as he shifts until his hard erection rubs against my entrance. I moan into his mouth and when he pushes slowly into me, I jerk my head to the side, crying out his name.

He feels so good. I draw my legs up as he buries himself in frustrating slowness.

"Fuck, you feel good," he gasps against my neck. "So fucking tight." He kisses my lips softly, sucking my bottom lip as his hand lowers to rub his fingers over my clit.

"Liam!" My heels push against the mattress as I raise my pelvis closer. "Please. I need more." When my hands clutch at his shoulders, he quickly seizes my wrists, raising my arms above my head.

"Look at me," he orders, his voice raw with restraint. I look up into eyes that sear me with their intensity. "I know you need more." He gathers both wrists into one hand and brings his free hand down to cup my face, his thumb stroking my lower lip. "I want to give you more, darlin'," he says softly.

My breath is indrawn sharply and he pushes his thumb between my lips, into my mouth. My lips close around his thumb and I suck forcefully, greedily.

He moans and then he moves, easing out of me before thrusting back in with agonizing slowness. I whimper as he repeats the move over and over.

His eyes continue to hold mine as the muscles in his arms and shoulders strain and bunch with the tight reign he holds over his body. And mine as I'm lost in the exquisite sensation of his steady, deep strokes.

It's not long though before I'm thrashing beneath him as he leisurely fucks me into sweet oblivion. Just when I think I can't take it any longer, his thrusts suddenly go deeper, harder and then he's pounding into me. My head tips back and my eyes close at the sensation of my orgasm gathering momentum. I have a moment to realize that this one is going to be rough, really rough. And then it crashes into me with a ferocity that slams me against the mattress. I'm conscious of both our cries before I'm sucked into the vortex.

I stir and snuggle closer to Liam's warmth. He's lying on his back and I move more into his side. My leg sliding up and down his until I notice that his medallion, which lies to the side of his chest close to my face, is positioned so I can see the engraving on the back. I raise my head to get a better view.

Remember,
my love is always with you.

"You've made me late." Liam's voice is deep and rough sounding.

I start guiltily.

He rolls over and sits on the side of the bed and I grasp the sheet to pull it up over my breasts. He looks back at me.

"Are you all right?" I nod. "I like verbal answers, darlin'," he says softly.

"Yes."

He frowns and reaches to slide a finger down the side of my face to my lips. "I'd like to stay, but its Monday morning."

"I know." I want him to stay. After what we shared last night, I'm not ready to let him go, and I want to know who gave him the pendant and what she means to him.

He never takes it off.

"Go back to sleep. It's early and you were up late." He flashes me a wicked grin.

My eyes follow him as he stands and a delicious tightening begins in the pit of my stomach. Muscles ripple across his back as he walks across the room to the closet. I bite my lip recalling the pleasures he gave me that kept me up half the night.

I lie back and I must have dozed because the next thing I know, Liam's leaning over me, taking my mouth in a soft kiss. He smiles when I open my eyes. My arms reach up to encircle his neck. Mmmm... he smells good, fresh from the shower.

"I have to go. I'm late for the morning meeting." He gives me another quick kiss and then he pulls away to stand tall. "I have a lunch meeting and I probably won't be back until late afternoon. If you need me, you can reach me on my cell."

"Okay. Have a good day." On impulse, I blow him a kiss.

He gives me his stop-your-heart smile and then he's gone.

I roll over hugging his pillow to me, breathing in his delectable scent. A smile slowly moves over my face as I remember his sharing about his grandparents.

With my body, I thee worship.

It wasn't until you came into my life that I fully appreciated what it meant.

I smile broadly, as I slide out of bed.

The next couple of days follow the same routine. Liam keeps me up late with his sexual escapades and then leaves early the next morning. He's busy during the day and I don't see him until dinnertime. I'm surprised, but pleased that he's home during the evening hours because when I was working in the restaurant, he seemed busy with club business, the whole day.

I don't have a clue what to do with myself during the day. With no job, I feel adrift with no purpose. I'm soon bored, feeling somewhat trapped in the apartment as I'm still not comfortable running into any of my ex co-workers.

On Wednesday, Liam has an appointment away from

Justice House. I don't know anything about it until he wakes me to say goodbye.

"Mmmm, you smell good, baby," he says as he buries his face against my neck, inhaling deeply.

I do my own deep inhale of his erotic scent and then raise my arms above my head, stretching my well-used muscles. I arch my back, hoping to entice him back to bed. It worked the morning before.

I feel his smile against my neck. "Enough of that, darlin'," he says as he stands.

I open my eyes and inhale sharply. Liam in a suit is a fine sight. When he doesn't say anything more, moving about the room to gather up the items he emptied from his pockets the night before, I ask, "Is it dress up day at work?"

He moves to the bed and leans down to give me a quick kiss. "No. I have an appointment." With that he heads for the door. "If you need anything, call Bryce or Mike." He looks back at me. "I won't be back until late." He's out the door before I have a chance to respond.

For some reason I'm extra restless by late afternoon, so I'm especially pleased when Holly stops in before she heads home for the day. I decline her offer to lunch in the restaurant the next day. I know I'm being a coward but too much has happened in a relatively short time and I'm just not up to answering questions. I imagine part of my reluctance is due to feeling insecure of the situation I'm in. I appreciate when Holly doesn't press the issue.

Annie serves me dinner that evening in the dining room and within a matter of minutes I pick up my plate and join her in the kitchen. All she knows is that Liam told her he wouldn't be home for dinner. I wonder what he would do if I left with only a cryptic goodbye. I bite my lip as a shiver runs down my spine. I know what he would do.

Watching TV doesn't hold much interest for me as my thoughts drift to Liam. I've felt so positive after our talk at the restaurant and with our lovemaking of the last couple of nights. But now all I can think about is that damn engraved message on his medallion. I should ask Holly if she knows who gave it to him. Or maybe, I should act like a mature adult and ask Liam myself. Would he tell me? I recall our wedding night when I reached out to take hold of his pendant, but he stopped me. That's why I believe it's from a previous lover. Does he still see her? Is he having dinner with her tonight?

Gah! I toss the pillow lying beside me on the couch across the room as I stand.

I am not doing this.

I give up on the TV and head for the bedroom where I take a quick shower and crawl into bed.

I wake when Liam slides in next to me, reaching to pull me close, burying his face in my hair.

"You smell so fucking good." His hands move over my body, creating a spontaneous reaction as I sigh softly and press against him. He rolls me onto my back, his mouth coming down to take possession of mine as his hand slides down over my belly.

"Spread your legs for me, sugar," he demands when he ends the kiss. He pulls the hem of my short gown up exposing me to his touch.

His words, his voice, I'm panting as I do as bid.

The heal of his hand rests on my pubic bone as his fingertips move lightly over me, tickling and arousing me at the same time. When I start to reach for him, he captures my wrists and secures them in one hand above my head. He slings his leg over mine to hold me in place.

I moan softly at the erotic feeling of being at his mercy. I almost snort at the thought. He never shows me mercy.

His hand returns and his fingers now slip between my folds, opening me wide, sliding over me. "So sweet, darlin'." He leans his head in close and bites one of my nipples through my gown.

"Ahhh..." My cry is sharp.

When he plunges two fingers into me, I moan with pleasure, my back bowing slightly.

He pushes into me hard and then thrusts his fingers quickly in and out, only to slow and thrust at one angle and then another, from side to side.

"Arghh!" My back arches sharply.

Fuck! I'm going to come.

The feeling of being held down, unable to stop him as he thrusts his fingers into me arouses me in a way I don't understand. My head tosses back and forth on the pillow as my body tightens and my insides begin to quiver.

He pulls his fingers from me and moves between my legs, his hands sliding under my bottom to lift me for his use as he impales me in one powerful thrust. I cry out hoarsely and my whole body bows off the bed. Two more deep thrusts and I splinter into a million shards of light. He thrusts deep one more time and calls out my name as he empties himself into me.

Holy shit, that was fast!

I'm panting as I lie beneath his weight, trying to regain a normal heart rhythm. Liam is breathing heavily too, the sound of our ragged breath mingling in the room.

He leans up on his elbows and takes my face between

his hands, gazing down at me. Brushing his lips over mine, he rolls to his side, pulling me close.

"I've been hard all day, knowing you were here waiting for me to come home and fuck you," He breathes against my neck.

I shiver where his breath touches my skin. I'm only able to respond with a faint sigh before sleep takes me.

Liam wakes me the next morning before he leaves for his morning workout and the employee meeting afterward. I roll over and go back to sleep until the alarm wakes me two hours later.

I'm excited as I rise and head for the bathroom. I have my visit with Dr. Lyle this morning. I feel so much better than I did the last time I saw her, and I have several questions to ask.

I decide to take the elevator that will let me out near the back door of the mansion. I hope I don't run into anyone, but I'll just have to deal with it if I do. I can't hide forever and besides, staying holed up in the apartment is about to drive me bonkers.

I hurry out of the elevator and down the hallway, almost making it to the door when I hear Liam call to me.

He's dressed in slacks and a white dress shirt. He has his suit jacket slung over his arm, and as I watch, he reaches up to adjust his tie and collar. *When did he change?*

"Why didn't you wait for me upstairs?"

I shake my head as I watch him walk toward me. Bold eyes pierce me with a level look before roaming over my body. I inhale deeply as I take in those eyes and the dark scruff on his face. He slips into his jacket and then runs his fingers through his already disarrayed hair.

The man is sexy as hell.

"Are you... coming with me?" My voice holds the surprise I'm feeling.

"I do believe that's the idea, darlin'," he says in his deep, sexy drawl.

As we step out the door, I'm relieved we haven't run into anyone. I sigh. This is so silly; I don't usually hide from difficult situations. I usually take the bull by the horn and confront whatever scares me. I glance toward the gates. My cab's not here yet, and I know I called early enough that it should be.

I come to a stop as Liam continues toward the garage. He only takes a few steps when he stops to look back at me.

"You cancelled my cab."

"You didn't need a cab."

"I didn't know that."

He studies me for a moment. "Well, darlin'—now you do," he says softly.

I grit my teeth.

"Let's go, Caitlyn." He holds out his hand and as I reach his side, he takes my arm to lead me to the garage.

As we enter, I glance up at him. "It would have been nice if you had let me know that you were planning to go to the doctor with me." He stops beside the Range Rover looking down at me, his expression unreadable.

I take a deep breath. "I don't like how you decide things for me—"

Liam steps right up to me, toe to toe. It's all I can do not to take a step back. Instead, I slowly look up, meeting his mocking gaze.

He's amused?

"Tell me darlin', are you pissed because I canceled

your cab?" I might see a hint of amusement in his eyes, but his voice holds a warning note.

"I'm not pissed, I just think you could have told me you were planning to go with me to my doctor visit." When he doesn't say anything, I look away.

He reaches out, his hand going to the side of my neck.

"Look at me, Caitlyn."

I bring my eyes back to his and he moves his thumb to caress my jawline. It's still startling to me how the simplest touch from him affects me.

"In the future, I'll be more courteous to apprise you of my plans. But make no mistake, darlin' — I plan to be involved in every aspect of your life."

What? I frown. *What does he mean by that?*

His hand drops and he reaches to open the door of the SUV, his gaze holding mine. I slide in and he shuts the door as I buckle up. I think over what he said. He said he planned to be involved in every aspect of my life, but I'm fairly certain he means he plans to control my life.

I won't let that happen.

I look over at him. "Where was your meeting yesterday?"

He glances at me before returning his attention to the road.

"I mean, was it out of town, since I couldn't reach you?"

He looks at me again. "Why do you think you couldn't reach me?"

"You said if I needed anything to call Mike or Bryce."

He changes lanes before glancing at me. "And they would have known where you could reach me."

I frown and this seems to amuse him.

"Why the sudden interest in my meetings, Cait?"

I shrug. "I just want to be involved in every aspect of your life."

He laughs out loud, reaching over to pick up my hand, bringing it to his mouth. "I'll remember that, darlin'."

I'm surprised at the list of questions Liam has for Dr. Lyle. He doesn't produce an actual list, but it's obvious he's thought ahead about what he wants to know. Dr. Lyle takes it all in stride as if she's used to dealing out crash courses in Pregnancy 101. In all fairness, he does bring up every one of my concerns and some I hadn't thought of. He also requests information on birthing classes.

The one thing he doesn't ask about and I don't either is my increased sexual appetite.

CHAPTER SEVEN

I T'S FRIDAY NIGHT AND WE have dinner plans with Holly and Ryan.

Not knowing how much longer, I'll be able to wear something short and tight, I decide to wear something — short and tight. One of my favorite dresses is a black strapless, form fitting, stretchy knit with the wide ruffle skirt ending at the top of my thighs, just covering enough to be decent. The ruffle and strappy heels make my legs look long and although I haven't been out on a paddle board in a while, my legs still look well-toned. I have noticed a new leanness to my body that I particularly like and I know it's because of Liam and all of the sex that we have. Dr. Lyle explained that I might not start showing for a while yet. She said it was not out of the norm in first pregnancies for a slim woman.

To please Liam, I leave my hair hanging in soft curls down my back, and I'm just touching up my lip gloss when he walks into the bedroom. Our eyes meet in the mirror and then I watch his eyes move down my body and the subsequent lifting of his eyebrow. I turn completely around for his benefit.

His eyes narrow. "You — do not wear that dress anywhere without me."

I grin and spin around again. He's responding just the way I wanted him to. "Well, I'm not sure I'll be able to wear this much longer with *or* without you."

He shakes his head as his sexy lips form the word *no*.

I smile shyly. "So you like it?"

His eyes darken and take on a wicked gleam. "Come here, please."

"Oh, no!" I back up. "When you look at me like that, my clothes have a tendency to come off." I laugh softly.

"I said — come here."

His expression and the tone of his voice make my mouth go dry. I step forward slowly coming to a stop before him. He reaches out suddenly, gripping my arm to pull me up against his body.

Oh!

His hand goes to the back of my head as he leans down to suck my bottom lip.

My eyes close and I moan softly all thought of him mussing my makeup, my hair, gone as his hands find their way into my long curls. My hands rest on his chest and they slide down to his stomach as I lean into him. I moan as he deepens the kiss, and when he lifts his head, my senses are reeling.

"Caitlyn."

I open my eyes slowly, looking up into his hazy blue.

"If you don't want this to end up in bed, you need to move your hand, darlin'."

I frown and then gasp, jerking my hand from his crotch where I've gripped his erection through his jeans. He laughs and I turn red, feeling the heat roll off me.

His phone rings and he chuckles under his breath. "Saved by the bell."

I step away to reapply lip-gloss with a shaking hand as he answers his phone.

"Yes."

I glance at him in the mirror. We decided to go casual for dinner so he's wearing jeans that sit low on his hips and a black, button down shirt left untucked with his sleeves rolled to his elbows. Again, without conferring, we've managed to dress complementing each other. This is only the second time I've seen him wear black and he looks unbelievably sexy.

"That won't be a problem," he says into the phone. He glances up, meeting my eyes. "I'm sure."

He pockets his phone. "Ready?"

"I am."

I'm nervous about the fact that Liam needs to retrieve something from his office downstairs. I'd rather take the back elevator that lets us out near the rear exit than have to walk through the mansion. I'm relieved when the hall is quiet. Strange for a Friday night.

"Is there something going on tonight?"

"Such as?" he asks as he scrolls through his phone messages.

"It's quiet."

He turns his gaze to me, studying me for a moment and then he smiles, a devastating smile. The toe of my shoe catches on the carpet, and I stumble. Liam reaches out, pulling me close.

"You clearly don't need to be wearing heels like that," he says, frowning now.

"It's not the shoes, it's your smile."

A puzzled expression replaces his frown. "You don't want me smiling?"

"I love your smile... just not when I'm trying to walk or – do anything."

His lips lift at the corners. "Well now, are you trying to tell me that the problem you have, walking in *fuck me* shoes is my fault?"

"I don't have a problem!"

"I do believe I remember you falling off a ladder in the storage room." He looks down, his eyes wickedly amused "You do remember that incident... don't you, darlin'? As I recall it was the first time I had my tongue down your throat and my fingers buried in your sweet –"

"I remember!" I pull my arm out of his hold.

Oh! He's just trying to embarrass me now and it's working as I feel my face heat with my blush.

He laughs quietly, pleased with himself and – Damn, I wish he didn't affect me as he does.

I look away, lifting my chin haughtily. "That had nothing to do with my ability to walk! You startled me and –"

Liam grips my arm and pulls me with him out of the hallway. The next thing I know my back is against a wall and Liam has his tongue down my throat and his hand up the skirt of my dress. His fingers slide in under the narrow fabric that covers me, spreading me open, thrusting two fingers inside me. I groan into his mouth and clutch his shoulders.

Holy Shit!

Desire hits me like a dam bursting, roaring through my veins.

He pulls his mouth from mine and thrusts his fingers at a leisurely pace in and out of my wet channel. "So fucking tight."

"Liam!" I cry his name as I feel a quickening in my

lower region. His wicked fingers continue their sweet assault as he looks down, watching me.

"Look at me, sugar."

When I look up, his free hand encircles my throat. He takes a step back, holding me against the wall as he continues to pump his fingers.

"You are so fucking beautiful." His eyes are almost fervent in their intensity. "And you belong to me." He thrusts his fingers deeper and I inhale sharply, my hands clutching at the arm he has raised to my neck. Everything in my body tightens, quivers with my impending orgasm.

And he stops, pulling his fingers from me.

"No!" I cry, shaking my head as much as I can with his hold on my neck. "Please, Liam," I mewl.

He pops his fingers into his mouth and I close my eyes against the erotic sight. Leaning into me, he sucks my bottom lip.

I almost feel faint with the influx of emotions coursing through my body.

"Please don't leave me like this," I beg as I look up at him.

"I like you like this, sugar. You do too."

His hand slides down over my breast to pinch the nipple that prominently juts out. My dress, a lightweight knit, is no match for hard, distended nipples.

"I don't like this." I pout. My insides feel tightly wound and the need for release is strong. *How can he think I like this?*

He chuckles softly. "Well now, I reckon that choice is mine to make, sweetheart. Sorry."

I give him a glare as he steps away to open the door. It's then that I become fully aware that we're in *the* storage room. I hurry past him and his smug grin, thankful that unlike last time, I still have my panties.

As Liam pulls the Range Rover out of the garage, I'm leery when he turns the wheel and steers the SUV under the Porte cochere. I look over at him as he shuts off the engine.

"We're picking up Holly and Ryan. Holly has something she needs me to haul to her place."

He opens the door, sliding out. "Let's go."

I glance about. There's really no activity, no cars pulling in, but nonetheless... "I'll just wait here."

I watch as he shuts his door and walks around the front of the SUV to open mine.

"I don't think so. Let's go." He holds his hand out to me.

Damn it.

"I'll just wait here, there's no reas —"

He grips my arm firmly, reaches over to release my seat belt and pulls me out of the car.

"Please, Liam." My voice sounds a little panicked. "Let me just wait for you out here."

He continues to lead me toward the club, his arm encircling my waist as the security guard opens the door wide, surprising me with his greeting.

"Good evening Mr. and Mrs. Justice."

"Good evening, Matt," Liam says as my steps falter.

Holy crap, what's going on? This can't be good. I'm certain now that Liam and Holly have set me up.

Liam leans down to speak near my ear. "Pick up your feet, darlin' before I throw you over my shoulder and carry you in."

I look up at him. The look he gives me lets me know he's perfectly serious. I bite my lip as we reach the inner door to the nightclub.

Why is he doing this?

The moment we walk in through the door, there is a cacophony of voices directed at us. I pull back but Liam's hold around my waist tightens.

"Cait!" Holly calls out.

Holly and Tansy both rush forward. The next several minutes consist of people greeting us as Liam leads me farther into the club. Evidently, this is a wedding party for us, organized by Holly and Tansy. Most of the people I worked with at the Justice are present, and so many club members I can't keep track of who all is present. Even Paul and Julie are here.

I'm overwhelmed by the genuinely, warm greetings I receive from the people who make a point of coming up to say hello and wish us well. Liam keeps me anchored to his side with his arm around my waist as we slowly progress across the room.

Tansy walks along beside me, explaining how Holly and Liam decided to close the club for the party when they realized how many people wanted to attend the celebration.

I look up at Liam. So he did know about this ahead of time. He looks down at me with a smirk.

We come to a halt as Liam greets a couple I don't know, introducing and explaining that Charles and Deline Niel are long standing members who live in France. They are a middle-aged couple, both very distinguished looking. Definitely not anyone I would ever have thought of as being associated with a sex club.

They both congratulate us in their beautiful accents.

"I'll be over at the table, Cait," Tansy whispers. "See you in a few."

"Okay." I watch her slip away and then turn my attention back to the Niels.

"I had business to attend to in New York. When I heard you had recently married"—he directs a smile my way—"Deline and I wanted to meet the woman who finally managed to capture Liam Justice's heart."

I'm at once embarrassed at his assumption of mine and Liam's marriage.

"We had long given up on Liam ever settling down," Deline Niel says.

I glance up at Liam to find him watching me and I'm surprised at the possessive gleam in his eyes. He breaks the connection when Charles Niel says something to him in French.

I feel Liam's body stiffen slightly.

"I'm afraid so, Charles," he says in a clipped voice. I look up again and notice his jaw clenched.

The Frenchman laughs and then he's shaking Liam's hand and slapping him on the shoulder as he continues to laugh. What he says next, again in French, amuses both he and his wife, but I can tell it irritates Liam.

"We are about to sit, would you care to join us," Liam asks. I notice there is very little warmth in that invitation.

"No, no. We want to say hello to a few friends before we leave."

"You won't be staying then?" Liam asks.

"No. We really must return home. We will be back next month, though. I will be in touch with you about—" Charles Niel stops whatever he was about to say and gives me a quick glance and then shrugs. "Well—"

"Good." Liam takes hold of my hand. "Have a safe trip."

Before the Niels can respond, Liam is leading me away.

"What was that all about?" I ask breathlessly as I keep up with his quick strides. His face is set in taut lines.

He glances down. "Not anything for you to worry about, darlin'." His tone plainly says, no more questions.

I do my best imitation of him lifting his brow. "Uh-huh — right."

He frowns at me.

As we near a large table sitting close to the dance floor, I see the others and Liam slows his pace, pulling me to his side.

"Hey! We've been waiting for you two." Bryce grins as he stands, giving me a hug, and laughing when Liam pushes him aside, calling him a "fucker."

I'm pleasantly surprised to see Emily and she stands, giving me a hug too. She really is quite sweet.

"Yeah, we've been waiting so we can order." Bryce grins again. I can tell he's in an extra ornery mood.

"I can see that." Liam laughs as Bryce lifts a beer. There are bottles and glasses scattered around the table.

"Did you have any idea, Cait?" Bryce asks as Liam pulls out a chair for me.

"No, not a clue," I tell him as I sit down across from him and Emily.

He grins and then dips his head to say something to Emily.

Liam pulls his chair right up next to mine, lays his arm over the back, his hand gripping my shoulder and pulls me close. I look up and he gives me a wink.

Oh! Just a simple thing like a wink and my nipples pucker in reaction. His fingers lightly stroke my shoulder and I squirm in my chair.

A waitress stops by for our order and while Liam is talking to her, Paul and Julie join us.

"How long did you two know about this?" I ask as Julie sits beside me.

"A couple of days." She beams her beautiful smile.

I stick my tongue out at Paul, and he reaches with the arm that's over Julie's shoulder to lightly pinch my arm.

I remember my manners and ask Emily if she's met Paul and Julie.

"Yes, when they first arrived."

"There is a buffet set up. Would you like me to fix you a plate?" Liam asks.

"I'm not hun—" He lifts that arrogant eyebrow of his. "Yes, please." I watch as he walks across the room.

"Where's Liam going?" Bryce asks.

"To the buffet." I see Bryce frown as he looks in the direction Liam left.

Our waitress delivers our drinks but Liam's several more minutes before he returns. It gives me time to watch Emily and Bryce together. He's very attentive and can't seem to keep his hands off her. She gazes at him with adoration on her face. Do I look like that when I look at Liam? I'm thinking that I must since everyone seemed to realize I was in love with him almost before I even admitted it to myself.

"Long line?" Bryce asks.

I look up as Liam gives Bryce a look and then says, "Long enough." He looks at me and sets a loaded plate on the table before me.

I look at it and then up at him. "I can't eat all that!"

"Well, I should hope not." He sits. "Relax. I'll eat some too."

"Are you sure you wouldn't rather have a juice?" he

asks as I pick up my water with lime. His breath is warm as it caresses my ear. The music isn't as loud as normal, so I'm able to hear Bryce from across the table.

"I would have ordered you a Shirley Temple," he says and promptly winks at me. "I think you two should dance. This is your wedding reception."

"Let's all dance," Holly says as she and Ryan join us. "Come on, let's get this party started!"

Liam's arm is still resting on the back of my chair and his fingers tug my ear lobe.

"Would you like to dance, Caitlyn?"

I bite my lip at the low timbre of his voice.

He reaches for my hand and lifts it to his lips. Oh, his mouth on me is so— I feel the flush move over my body as the spark he ignited in the storage room earlier ignites into a full-blown flame. Our eyes lock and I'm lost in the impossibly blue depths of his. I can't read the emotion I see there but they suddenly burn hot.

"Darlin', I've told you before not to look at me like that in public," he murmurs as he stands, pulling me up with him. "We need to work on your self-control."

I huff a soft breath. If another man said something like that to me, I'd probably go off on him. Why is it that when Liam talks to me that way—I just want him to follow through. This game of seduction he plays has me at a loss. I don't know how to resist him; he does it so well.

I suddenly realize that in our *moment*, everyone else has left the table. I also notice that we've garnered the attention of others as I catch their knowing smiles. I'm surprised though when I notice Leon's cousin Tony, a few tables over, watching us with a dark sullen expression. He turns his head when I smile.

Liam leads me to the dance floor drawing me into his arms. One hand settles at the base of my spine while the other continues to clasp my hand. I can feel the warmth of his skin where my hand rests on his shoulder. His delectable scent permeates my senses as I center my gaze on his throat knowing if I look up he'll see the desire in my eyes.

He whirls me around the dance floor to the sultry beat of the music, which only intensifies my need.

"Relax, Caitlyn."

My eyes fly to his. "Stop doing to me what you did in the storage room and then leave me hanging and I might!" I hiss.

Liam's amusement is obvious and then he's laughing outright. He releases my hand bringing his up to slide around to the nape of my neck. His other hand presses low on my back, securing me tightly to his front. His erection presses into my belly, and I almost moan from the feelings he elicits with his possessive hold on me.

He brings his head down, his mouth close to my ear. "I remember the last time we danced. I can recall perfectly how those lush lips of yours felt around my cock as you sucked me off, sugar."

I inhale sharply.

"This might be an early night for the newlyweds," he adds, raising his head. The smug look on his face brings my attention to the fact that my breathing is rapid and shallow.

I'm suddenly annoyed, realizing he's doing this to me on purpose. Keeping me on the edge just as he does when he brings me to the brink of orgasm and then denies me my release.

"Okay, Buddy. Time to share your beautiful wife,"

Bryce announces as he pulls me from Liam's arms, twirling me away before Liam has a chance to react.

I quickly look back to see Liam standing, watching with narrowed eyes.

I am somewhat relieved and it really does serve Liam right. He's driving me crazy. A little space from him right now is greatly needed.

Bryce laughs to himself. I can only assume it's because he feels like he's put one over on Liam.

"You're incorrigible," I tell him.

"What?" he asks innocently. "Liam just has to face the fact that he has to share his bride." When Bryce tries to pull me close, I step on his foot. "Damn, Cait!"

"What?" I ask in mock innocence.

"Maybe I did Liam a good turn."

"It's good to see Emily here," I say changing the subject. Bryce just smiles.

I dance for the next hour, passed from one partner to the next. I'm more than ready for Liam to come claim me for another dance when Paul cuts in.

"Are you enjoying yourself?" he asks.

"I am, it was a wonderful idea and so thoughtful of Holly and Tansy."

"So, all that worry about the response you might receive from everyone was unwarranted." He smirks.

"Yes. You were right, Paul." I say with a teasing tone as I brush a feather off his shoulder.

"I always am," he responds as he swings me around.

I'm pleasantly surprised when Marc Thomas cuts in on Paul. I've not seen him since the altercation, here in the night club, weeks earlier. He is so nice and I'm glad to see him back at the club after Liam suspended his membership. We try to talk but the music is now loud enough that it's almost impossible to hear each other without shouting. Ryan cuts in and as we dance closer to our table, I look for Liam. Earlier I saw him watching me but he's not there now. I look for him as Ryan dances me across the room, delivering me to Holly and Julie, who stand waiting on the edge of the dance floor.

"Let's go to the ladies room where we can talk," Holly shouts.

I turn back to Ryan and I think he hears me when I ask him to let Liam know where I am.

As soon as the door closes behind us it's like a sigh of relief.

"This is a wonderful wedding party!" Julie announces.

"It is," I agree. "Thank you, Holly."

"Are you having fun?" she asks, looking anxious.

"I'm having a great time," I assure her.

"I'm so glad. I was afraid you'd be mad."

"No! I was just... apprehensive about how I would be received by everyone here."

Holly frowns. "Why would you be worried about that?"

Julie meets my gaze and raises her brows. I'd already shared my concerns with her. I step to the sink to wash my hands and wet a paper towel.

"I figured they all knew why I'd left and—" I shrug my shoulders.

Holly stops in the process of repositioning a hair comb in her short curls. "Oh, honey, I wish I'd known. I guess I should have with the way you dodged my lunch invites."

"I'm sorry."

She turns to face me. "Liam forbade any of us to utter one word of what happened. Of course, none of us would have said anything." She turns back to finish her hair. "And Liam had a chat with Miranda."

What?

The bathroom door opens and Emily steps in.

"I wondered where you all got off to," she says.

"We tried to find you. Where were you?" Holly asks.

Emily's cheeks turn bright pink. "Bryce had something to show me in his office."

Holly snorts and Julie and I laugh.

"I like the way their 'showing us something' always leads to something sexual," Julie says.

Emily's cheeks turn a deeper shade of pink and she laughs.

"I was just telling Cait about how Liam threatened Miranda when she left," Holly says. Emily's mouth makes an O.

My eyes widen. "What?"

"I was there for the joyful occasion," Holly says gleefully. "He told her he'd fire her with no recommendation if what happened with you became public knowledge, so she'd better pray no one else gossiped about it."

"He did?"

"He did. You should have seen her face!"

"Bryce said Liam made the comment that it was a small town, when it came to someone else's business, and he didn't want the story to get out and cause unnecessary trouble for you."

Trouble for me? I clearly need to have more chats with these girls so I can glean more information about the time Liam and I were apart.

As if reading my thoughts, Holly says, "Let's all go out for lunch tomorrow."

"That sounds fun," Julie says. "I can go any time after noon."

"I would love that," I add.

"Count me in," Emily says.

"Okay. I'll text everyone in the morning where to meet."

"We better get back out there, Paul's liable to come looking for me and he won't have a problem with walking in here." Julie looks at me and we both giggle.

Heading out the door, I pull a feather from the back of Julie's hair.

I laugh. "What have you and Paul been up to?" I ask her.

She turns around, her brow raised in question, and I hold up the feather. Her eyes grow wide and then she snatches the feather from my fingers.

I laugh again.

"Shhh," she hisses. And then she grins and gives me a wink.

As we near the table, I see that Liam is still not there.

"You all go on, I'm going to find Liam," I say, able to speak normally as the music has stopped.

I veer off toward the bar. I'm stopped along the way by people I worked with and a couple of club members. I try to keep the conversations as short as possible. When I finally reach the bar, I ask the bartender if he's seen Liam. He nods toward the far end of the bar. I look but don't see him. My eyes continue past the bar top and discover an alcove in the far corner of the club I'd never noticed before. I walk that way. When I get close, I see that this is where the buffet must have been set up. There are empty tables and a few of those large buffet servers sitting on a cart. My pace slows and I come to a halt when I see Liam and Miranda.

"Have you told her?" I hear Miranda ask.

"Excuse me?"

Liam's back is to me but there's no doubt of the controlled anger in his voice. I know I should make my presence known or walk away, but Miranda's next words anchor me to the spot.

"Have you told her about Mel?"

Liam's voice is positively frigid when he answers. "Well now, that is none of your business."

I hold my breath lest I'm discovered eavesdropping.

"Miranda," — Liam continues in a deceptively quiet voice — "I'm getting downright tired of you putting your nose where it doesn't belong."

"Liam —"

"Enough!" he snarls. I almost cringe at the anger I hear in his voice. "Now, let me make this clear for you. I keep you on here because you are good at your job. But you're a tad mistaken if you think you are not replaceable." Miranda's face turns pale. "Do you understand me?"

I turn to leave, not caring to hear her answer. But then I stop and stand there indecisive, because I know Miranda saw me. Liam has put her in her place, maybe I need to stay to let her know I'm not going anywhere.

I spin around and walk into the hard body of Liam Justice.

"Going somewhere?" he snaps.

I look up into his blazing eyes.

"No," I answer softly, hoping he's not mad at me too.

"Good. Let's go." He grips my arm and I give a quick look back to see Miranda glaring at us.

He leads me across the room and once again, members

who have yet to congratulate us choose this moment to do so. Liam is very cordial but I can feel the tension in his body.

What were he and Miranda talking about that involved Melanie? I know that she was the hostess before me, the one who left without notice, and I was hired to replace her. Before I left Justice House, Miranda had hinted some things about Melanie, nothing definite just that I needed to ask Liam why Melanie left so suddenly. And on top of all that, when Liam left to fetch me a plate of food from the buffet—he'd headed in the opposite direction from where I now know the buffet was located. I want to ask him about it all, but now's not the time.

Once we reach the table Liam says, "Cait's tired, we're calling it a night."

I quickly cover my surprise at his words.

"Oh, but the night is young!"

"Cait's tired, Holly," Liam says firmly.

I give her, Julie, and Emily a hug and a quick wave to Bryce and Ryan. Paul stands and gives me a hug as Liam watches.

"Come by soon and we'll go to lunch, okay?"

I glance at Liam surreptitiously from the corner of my eye. "I will, Paul."

The music stops playing and Bryce's voice comes over the sound system announcing that the newlyweds are leaving the party. For once he doesn't tag on a suggestive comment.

Liam holds up his arm in a salute type goodbye as we cross the room toward the door that leads back into the mansion.

I'm totally caught off guard as people begin to clap.

"What about the car," I ask as the club door closes behind us.

"Mike parked it back in the garage."

He grips my arm firmly and with long strides, he leads me across the darkened dining room. When we reach the elevator in the hallway, the doors open immediately when Liam slides his card. When the doors close, I look up.

"Are you mad at me?"

He glances down. "Should I be?"

"No," I say firmly as the doors open.

He puts his hand out to stop me from exiting. "Would you like to go back to the party and dance some more, darlin'? There might be a man or two you missed dancing with."

What?

"No," I say a little irritated. "I want to be alone with you." Maybe I should ask him why *he* wasn't around to dance with me. But I'm pretty sure that wouldn't be wise right now either.

He moves quickly, pulling me close, his hands gripping my upper arms to lift me up on tiptoe. His warm mouth has a hint of bourbon as his tongue strokes mine. I moan in response, all thoughts of the night gone as I lean into him. Before I know it, he has me backed up against the elevator wall. I pull against his hold until he releases my arms only to take hold of my wrists, pulling them down and around to the small of my back, grasping them in one large hand. His free hand comes up to encircle my throat.

Oh! I angle my lower body to his. He has the power to make me want him in a heartbeat, and that's one of the things I have always loved about being with him.

I moan into his mouth as he deepens the kiss. My nipples, pressed against him tighten painfully. He growls low in his chest, and then he releases my throat to grip the bodice of my dress yanking it down, baring me from the waist up.

I gasp, unconsciously arching my back, effectively thrusting my breasts forward. His hands mold around the full mounds as he bends, forcefully sucking a hardened nipple into his hot mouth.

It's as if an electrical current travels straight to my clit and I cry out, my head falling back as Liam sucks and nips at first one nipple and then the other. By the time he finishes, they feel raw and engorged and I'm a quivering mess. He maneuvers my dress down over my hips, and it falls to the floor. I'm left standing in my heels and thong.

He releases my hands. "I want you to leave your hands behind you back, darlin'." When I don't say anything he raises an eyebrow.

"Okay," I snap.

His mouth lifts slightly and when he takes a step back, I feel flushed as his eyes move over me.

"Very pretty, darlin'." He reaches out and his fingers close in a tight pinch around a sensitive nipple. I bite against my bottom lip as he rolls and pulls the swollen nub. I close my eyes, my head falls back and his mouth is at once on my arched throat. He sucks and licks his way up over my chin until his mouth hovers over mine, absorbing my soft little pants.

He brings his mouth down hard and controlling on mine, and when he releases my nipple, I moan into his mouth as he rubs his thumb back and forth over the throbbing peak. His kiss robs me of all coherent thought and when his hand slides between my legs, I'm unaware of anything but his touch and his mind-numbing scent.

He lifts his lips from mine, and I open my eyes to find his mesmerizing in their intensity. As he sinks to one knee, my breath catches in my throat. He slowly peels my thong down and then runs his hands down my legs, from the tops of my thighs to my ankles.

"Spread your legs, sugar." His voice is that slow, lazy drawl that makes my insides melt.

My heart rate kicks into overdrive when he presses his nose into my pubic hair, and I groan at the exquisite clenching of muscles. I dig my nails into my palms, desperate to run my fingers through his hair.

"Fuck, you smell good," he growls. He grips one leg and raises it up over his shoulder.

I gasp and almost unclasp my hands to steady myself.

"Relax, I won't let you fall, baby."

He strokes the inner thigh of the leg over his shoulder, and leans in, his mouth latching onto my clit to suck hard. I think I'll go mad with the almost unbearable assault on that tiny epicenter. I'm not even aware that my hands have come around, my fingers tangling in his hair as I arch my hips to give him better access while at the same time, I yank at his hair, desperately trying to pull his mouth from me. I feel crazed with the acute pleasure, crying out as my legs begin to shake and I feel myself losing control. He abruptly releases me, sliding my leg off his shoulder and quickly stands.

I'm trembling as he turns me around to face the wall. "Hands on the wall."

Holy hell! I can barely stand.

He runs a finger down my spine. "So beautiful, darlin'," he murmurs. His hand slides around my waist to splay possessively across my belly as he presses into my back, flattening me against the wall. "And you fucking belong to me," he growls.

"Yes!" I cry, startled by his vehemence.

With his free hand, he gathers my hair and then winds it around his hand. Pulling my head back he asks, "Tell me, Caitlyn, did you enjoy dancing with those other men?" His deep voice reverberates near my ear.

I'm not sure how to answer. "No. I would rather have danced with you," I say breathlessly.

I hold my breath, waiting countless seconds, and then he says, "Would you now, darlin'?"

He turns me around, grips my waist and lifts me in one quick move as his eyes blaze, enslaving mine with their intensity. My legs go around his waist as he presses me back against the wall, holding me there as one hand slides under my thigh to my bottom. His other hand goes to the fly of his jeans, freeing himself and then he lifts me to position the head of his erection at my entrance, holding me there.

"Please, Liam!" I beg, my fingers digging into his shoulders. I need him in me. Right now.

He lets me down, impaling me slowly but not fully seating himself. He's driving me freaking crazy.

"Do you think another man can make you feel like this?" he asks hoarsely.

My eyes widen in surprise. How can he think I'd be interested in any one else? I search his eyes, totally confused. Surely, he's not serious. I look at his beautiful mouth wanting it back on mine. "Never, Liam." My hand cups the side of his face. "I love you," I breathe, leaning in to take his mouth as he buries himself to the hilt.

CHAPTER EIGHT

THE APARTMENT IS QUIET THE next morning as I walk back to Liam's study. He's at his morning workout and I won't see him again until I get back from my lunch with the girls.

Annie's gone for the weekend, thank goodness. I bite my lip recalling our little tryst in the elevator.

As I enter the study, I feel a little like I'm trespassing. I forgot to ask if he minded my using his computer. I could use my phone, but I prefer using a PC when I search a shopping expedition. I definitely need to retrieve my laptop from my apartment. I frown. I need to make a trip there and start packing up my belongings. Hopefully Liam has storage space somewhere.

I sit in the chair behind his desk, moving his mouse to wake the processor. I've decided to leave early and do a little shopping for the baby, but first I want to check and see if any of the local stores have sales going on. I don't have much money left so I need to shop prudently.

My search inadvertently leads me to baby furniture and I am so caught up in my musings of redecorating one of the guest bedrooms into a nursery that I don't hear the door open.

"What are you doing in here, Caitlyn?"

I jump, startled and quickly close the web page I'm looking at. I stand as Liam and Mike step into the room.

"I asked you a question." His brow is furrowed and his eyes narrowed. "Why are you in here?"

"I... needed to look up some things, I don't have my computer."

I glance at Mike, and I can practically see the wheels turning in his head. I'm sure he thinks I'm up to no good.

I walk across the room and stop in front of Liam. "I wasn't doing anything wrong."

He tilts his head to the side. "I didn't say you were, darlin'," he says softly, holding my gaze and then he nods at Mike.

I watch as Mike heads for Liam's desk.

Liam takes that moment to step up close. I look up and meet his eyes.

"What were you doing on my computer, Cait?"

"I told you, I was—" My eyes narrow on him. "You think I was looking at your personal info, don't you?" I work hard to keep the hurt out of my voice.

He continues looking at me, and for the first time since I've known him, he seems taken aback. He glances toward where Mike is checking his computer to see what state secrets I've stolen. Looking back at me, he raises his hand to fun his fingers through his hair.

I shake my head slowly in disbelief. Exhaling loudly, I turn on my heel to head for the door.

"Hey." He grabs my arm, pulling me to a stop. "I'm not accusing you of anything, Caitlyn."

I purposely look across the room at Mike and then back to meet Liam's eyes.

"I didn't go through your things. I only used your computer to search for—" I take a deep breath. I have to get out of this room. I'm crushed that Liam is suspicious of me and mortified that Mike is witness to it. I pull my arm from his grasp and hurry out the door.

Luckily I'm ready to leave, all I need is to grab my bag and phone. I don't want to use the back elevator since I'll have to walk close to Liam's study where he and Mike continue to search for the evil I've done, but I can't use the one that goes to his office downstairs. There's no telling what I'd be accused of if I were caught in there alone.

I move quickly back down the hall on high alert, slipping, as quietly as possible, out the apartment door into the rotunda. I draw a sigh of relief when the elevator doors close.

I already called for a cab at a specified time and I have to wait a few minutes before it arrives. I wait anxiously, knowing Liam won't be far behind once Mike finds out what I was doing. If Liam catches up with me right now, there's no telling what I might do. I'm so mad at him. Just as my cab pulls away with me inside, Liam calls. I silence the ringer. I definitely don't want to talk to him. I need to think about what happened and how he was so quick to jump to the wrong conclusion. He said he wasn't accusing me of anything but he was quick to have Mike check out what I was doing on his computer.

I rub my belly. "Your father can be—" I don't finish the statement as my phone rings again. I don't answer.

I have a couple of hours before I meet up with Julie and the others for lunch, but I'm no longer in the shopping mood, so I decide to have the cabbie drop me off near a bookstore that I know has a small café.

I grab a couple of periodicals and order an herbal tea with one of their pastries. The bookstore is quiet and it's not hard to find a table near a window. I glance through one of the magazines but I really don't see the pictures.

Liam still believes I would betray him. It's as simple as that.

I know he said that he didn't believe I intentionally tried to deceive him before, and he told me we needed to let it go. Evidently, that's not what he meant. The father of my child thinks the worst of me. How do we go on from here?

My cell vibrates and this time it's Julie calling.

"Hey."

"Hey, doll. You okay? Your husband called here looking for you."

I sigh. Of course he did. "I'm fine. I just decided to do a little shopping before we meet up for lunch."

"O-kay," she says. There's a note of doubt in her voice. "Would you like some company?"

"Thanks but I know you are tying up loose ends on that big project of yours."

"Yeah, I am, but I meant for Paul to come and keep you company."

We both laugh. Paul would rather have a toenail removed than go shopping.

"Uh... thanks, but no thanks." I rub at a spot on the table. "I'm fine, Julie, really. I'll see you at lunch."

"Okay. See you soon."

I'm on my second cup of tea when my phone vibrates again.

I know I should talk to him but— he hurt my feelings. And now he's let me know where I stand with him.

I sigh. Now I feel like crying. Damn hormones.

I check the time and decide I might as well head for the restaurant. As I step out of the bookstore, I have an uncanny feeling of being watched. I scan the sidewalk both ways but don't notice anyone paying special attention to me. Just my imagination.

The restaurant Holly chose is charming. It has skylights that are open and lots of windows with an abundance of greenery everywhere. Despite the tumultuous start to my morning, I'm in good spirits as are the others.

"Okay," Holly says as soon as the waiter takes our order. "What's going on with Liam?"

I quickly swallow my sip of iced herbal tea. "He called you too?"

"Yes, he did. Ryan and I were having our usual Saturday morning marathon and the dumb ass wouldn't stop calling!"

Emily snorts a giggle.

"Marathon?" I gasp, trying not to laugh. "I'm sorry."

She winks at me. "It's not your fault."

"He called Julie too," I announce.

"Actually, I didn't speak to him. Paul took the call."

Oh, no! "Did Paul get mad?" I hope Liam wasn't rude to him.

"Not at all. He thought it was funny. He said Liam seemed anxious to find you." Julie grins.

Our waiter delivers our food and Holly waits until he leaves before saying, "Yeah, he was pretty insistent about finding you. Insisted I tell him where we were having lunch."

"Really?" I look across the room.

"Don't worry, if he knows what's good for him he won't show up. I threatened him."

I laugh, but I still think he might show up and I'm not sure how I feel about that.

"What did he do this time?" Holly asks.

I finish chewing my bite of chicken before answering. "He jumped to a—not very flattering conclusion about me."

They all three look at me, waiting for me to say more.

"I wanted to shop for baby clothes this morning. My laptop is still at my apartment, so I used the one in his study. I meant to ask him, I just forgot. He and Mike walked in on me and—" I take a sip of my iced tea "—he thought I was committing—espionage."

"What?" Holly lays down her fork. "I hope you told him where to get off!"

"Not yet."

"By now I bet he feels bad. I'm sure Michael discovered what you were doing," Emily says.

Michael?

"Yeah, I knew it wouldn't take him long. That's all I looked at besides baby furniture."

"Uh... Cait—" Holly begins, but the waiter stops by to check on us, interrupting her.

After he leaves I ask, "What were you saying, Holly?"

She waves her hand and stuffs another bite of salad into her mouth.

"Do you know what theme you're going with for the nursery?" Emily asks.

"No. I haven't thought about that. I guess it will need to be decorated for either a boy or a girl."

"How far along do you have to be before they can tell the gender of the baby?" Julie asks.

"I think the doctor said around twenty-two weeks."

"Sometimes as early as thirteen weeks, but it's more accurate at twenty-two," Emily says.

"Well, I still have a little while." I smile at her. I don't think it's my imagination that she suddenly seems sad.

"Do you have a preference?" she asks.

Do I? "No. I just want her to be healthy."

"Her?" Holly asks.

I laugh softly when I realize what I said. "I think it's a girl."

Holly gives a shout of laughter that has some of the other diners looking at us. Emily's face breaks into a wide grin.

"Oh! That would be priceless. Liam with a daughter." Holly continues to laugh and I chuckle, amused too at the thought of Liam dealing with a little girl.

I suddenly get a lump in my throat at the thought of a little girl with dark hair and bright blue eyes. Most men want a son, but isn't it the little girl who always steals their hearts?

"Oh, I'm sorry." Holly dabs at her eyes as she tries to compose herself.

"Well, well, well." A deep voice interrupts us. "You ladies are having too much fun. What's the joke?"

I look up and almost choke when I see Myles Lea standing beside Julie's chair. I haven't seen him since our catastrophe of a date several months earlier when he kicked me out of the cab.

"Cait Shaw! What a pleasant surprise." He moves closer and I want to scoot father away.

"You'll have to excuse us, Myles," Julie says. "We're having girl time. Sorry."

"And it's Cait *Justice*," Holly says, giving him a withering look.

"Yes. I did hear about that." He leans down close and I lean away. The man makes my skin crawl.

"Did you tell him about us?" Myles asks in what he thinks is a seductive voice.

I turn more fully to face him. "Us? Sorry, Myles. I evidently don't have the same dreams you have."

Julie snorts and Holly laughs.

"That's very amusing, Cait. If you want to keep what we had a secret from your—husband, I'm okay with that." He reaches out to run a finger down my arm and I slap his hand away.

What an ass!

"Myles, go away before I tell the waiter you are bothering us," Julie says acidly.

Holly obviously doesn't have the same compunction about warning him as she has already flagged the Maitre D' over.

Myles steps back and lifts his hands. "Okay, ladies. Sorry, but I can't join you. I have a young lady waiting for me." He looks across the restaurant. I don't look but Julie does.

"It was good to see you, Cait. We need to have lunch and catch up." He reaches out to touch me again and I jerk away. He laughs softly and then turns to swagger off.

"Who the fuck was that?" Holly asks, watching him walk away.

"A jack-ass I work with," Julie answers. "Are you okay?" she asks me.

"That guy is psycho," I say looking at her and shaking my head. I look over at Holly and Emily. "Please, don't think I had anything going on with a creep like that!"

Our little get-together breaks up soon after, and Holly insists on dropping us all off. She lets me out at the back door of Justice House.

It's still early in the afternoon but I'm exhausted and I need to lie down. When I step up to the elevator, I almost laugh. I have no keycard that works the elevators or stairwell doors.

I stand for a moment. I have two choices. I can either go to security or ask Mike to let me on the elevator, but then he'll have to ride up with me to let me into the apartment, or I can go see if Liam is in his office down here in the mansion.

I suddenly feel weary, indecisive of what to do. If I were smart, I'd probably do best to get the hell out of here and go to my own apartment.

The doors to the elevator open and I look up into Liam's angry face, his eyes like cold, hard glass.

"Hi," I say softly.

He doesn't say anything. Stepping to the side, he motions for me to enter the elevator.

I hesitate for a moment before stepping in beside him. He touches the key pad and the doors close. His delicious scent permeates the air and I close my eyes breathing in deeply. We're both silent as we're whisked up two floors. I don't have the energy to deal with his anger, and besides I'm the one who deserves to be angry. When the doors open, I step out and wait for him to open the door, letting us into the apartment.

"I'm going to lie down for a while," I say. When he doesn't respond I turn and head down the hall. Hearing him follow sets my nerves on edge.

Okay, so he's mad because I didn't answer his calls. I'm not going to apologize, though. I've done nothing wrong.

He follows me into the bedroom and I can't help but feel nervous. I enter the closet, kick off my shoes, and deposit my purse. I take a deep breath and walk back out to the bedroom.

Liam is standing in the same spot I left him in and I boldly meet his eyes.

"Who was the fucker in the restaurant?" There is a measure of controlled anger in his voice.

I frown, his question catching me by surprise. "What?"

He steps close, his handsome face darkening in anger. "Who was the fucker in the restaurant who put his hands on you, Caitlyn?" His anger isn't as controlled now.

Holy shit!

"He works with Julie—" Wait. How does he know about Myles? I know that the others didn't say anything to him. My eyes narrow. "You have someone following me?"

"Answer the question, Caitlyn," he snarls stepping even closer, towering over me.

My anger at the fact he's having me watched overrides his intimidation. My voice is angry now as I answer. "His name is Myles Lea. Like I said, he works with Julie." I storm over to the bed and pull the duvet aside. Liam follows right behind me. "She fixed us up on a blind date. He acted like a jerk—not unlike someone else I know— and I never went out with him again."

"He seemed a might friendly, darlin'."

I turn to glare at him. "I know you don't believe me, but today was the first time I'd seen or spoken to him since our date."

Liam frowns. "Why do you think I don't believe you?"

I snort softly and cross my arms hugging my elbows. I am not going to cry. Damn hormones.

"Cait—" He gives a thorough sigh and runs his

fingers through his hair. When he reaches out to take my arm, I resist.

His smile is rueful as his hand lifts to tuck my hair behind my ear. "I feel as if telling you that I'm sorry, for this morning is simply inadequate," he murmurs.

"You said you believed me," I whisper. When he doesn't say anything, I look down, twisting my fingers in resignation. "I've been so hopeful, ever since you told me you believed I never meant to betray you. But now—" I look back up. "How are we going to make this marriage work?" He frowns. "In a few months' time, we'll have a child whose father thinks its mother is a lying, conniving—" Tears sting my eyes. Add to the equation that I'm falling more and more in love with him every day and it's like a disaster waiting to happen.

"Hey." He uses his finger to lift my chin, his eyes hardening perceptively. "I do not think you are a liar or conniving." He sighs and closes his eyes, a frown forming between his brows. "Cait—" His eyes are intense as they look into mine. "Don't let what happened this morning fill you with qualms about our marriage."

"How can it not, Liam?"

His hand comes up and he brushes the back of his fingers down the side of my face. "Trust is a hard thing for me, darlin'."

Now we're getting somewhere. "Because of what happened to your mother?" I watch as his eyes darken and the shutters come down. "Don't do that! I know you don't want to talk about it but—"

"No, I do not," he says firmly.

I don't point out that he did once. The night before he found out I had worked for Query magazine, he finally let me in, telling me about the murder of his mother, asking me to move in with him.

He sighs deeply, looking at me from under hooded lids. When I look back down, he reaches out, his fingers touching my belly.

"Has the baby moved today?"

"No," I answer in a slightly irritated fashion. "It's just a flutter when it happens, Liam."

Dr. Lyle was very tactful about saying it was highly unlikely that I felt the baby move so soon. But I know what I felt and there is no doubt in my mind that it was the baby moving.

"I think you need a nap, darlin'," he answers in response to my disgruntled tone.

"I think you need to let me in if you want to have a life with me," I say, my eyes snapping back to his.

His head tips to the side, and he studies me with an unreadable expression.

"Well now, darlin', that can go both ways," he drawls. I frown. "I reckon we both need to change our attitudes." I frown even more and he moves his face closer to mine. "Answer your fucking phone when I call you," he growls.

I look back down, my face growing warm. He has a point.

"I... just didn't want to talk to you," I say softly.

He doesn't say anything for a minute and then, "I guess I wouldn't want to talk to me either after how I made you feel this morning," he murmurs, suddenly stepping closer. His hand goes to the side of my neck as he leans down to kiss my forehead.

"You need to rest. I need to make this morning up to you, so I've made plans for this evening."

"You have?" I fail to keep the breathiness out of my voice. His plans usually lead to a night of incredible sex.

His eyes hold a measure of humor as they look into mine. "Not those kind of plans. I'm beginning to get the idea that you're insatiable, darlin'."

I feel the blush move over my skin.

Liam laughs softly and strokes a finger over my cheek. "So pretty, sugar." His eyes gleam. "Rest, baby so you'll be ready for tonight."

His smug smile turns into a full laugh, and I glare at his back as he exits the room.

"Please give me a hint," I whisper.

I am sitting in the back seat of the SUV with Liam. Mike is driving us, which adds to the mystery of where we're going. I can't help but feel uncomfortable around him after what happened that morning in Liam's study. Plus I know he doesn't like me. But regardless, I am excited and exasperated at the same time. Liam hasn't given me a single clue of where he's taking me. Dinner must be involved though since he would only let me have a light snack when I woke earlier.

He gives me a quick look and one of those devastating smiles of his.

My breath catches. He's dressed casually in a pair of tan Chinos and a button up white shirt left untucked with the sleeves rolled up his muscular forearms. His dark looks, intensified by the white shirt, stir my libido into action from just looking at him. As usual, breathing his incredible, sexy scent does nothing to curtail my desire for him either. I sigh inwardly. I'm a mess where he's concerned.

He told me to dress casual so I chose a short, polka dot sundress with a halter-top that leaves my back bare to the bottom of my spine. I slipped on a short sleeve cardigan sweater for his benefit since his eyebrows rose when he saw how much of my legs were revealed in the dress. I can't wait for his reaction when I take my sweater off.

"Please," I beg. I simply can't sit still.

He laughs and with the next turn Mike takes, I suspect we're headed for DuSable Harbor.

"Are we going on your boat?" I ask almost bouncing in my seat.

"You're terrible with surprises." He grins, reaching over to tug my earlobe.

"I am," I quickly admit. "But I love them. It must be your boat." Does he have a boat? He doesn't correct me, so —

"No. It's just a little surprise, darlin'. Be patient."

I'm puzzled as Mike takes Lower Randolph street to the lake. When he pulls over to let us out, I look up at Liam but he's already climbing out and reaching for my hand.

"I'll text you," he says in Mike's direction.

"Okay," Mike answers. "Have a good time."

Liam leads me along the walkway to a series of black dock gates. After passing several, he punches a code in on one of the gates and we pass through. I'm beside myself with excitement but I pay attention to my surroundings and check out the boats. There is some serious money here. As we near the end of the dock, I notice a gorgeous yacht.

I want to ask more questions but since Liam is being so secretive, I'll just wait.

He pulls me to a stop when we reach the yacht.

"Ready to board, darlin'?"

I glance up at him and smile, and then back at the boat. She's a beauty with her sleek lines.

A man, in a white uniform suddenly steps forward to greet us. "Good evening, Mr. and Mrs. Justice. Welcome aboard."

"Thank you, Matthew," Liam says as we step on deck. "Caitlyn, Matthew is the steward here on the Heartbeat."

"Hi, nice to meet you, Matthew."

I turn to look around as Liam and the steward talk. There are two levels of deck with the top deck providing cover over the first level. A table, beautifully set for dinner sits near the port side of the boat. This level is a nice open area with a stairway that leads to the second level. I can just imagine how cool and relaxing it would be to sit here on a hot summer day and enjoy the lake. Maybe fish. Do people fish off yachts? I glance at Liam. Does Liam fish?

The sliding glass doors that lead into the interior of the boat opens, and another steward, also dressed in white, sidles through carrying a tray. Walking across the deck to the port side, he sets the tray on the stand near the table.

"I'll show Mrs. Justice the salon while we prepare to get under way, Matthew."

The steward nods his head and Liam takes my hand, leading me toward the darkly tinted glass doors that let us into the main salon. The salon, elegantly decorated, has rich hardwood flooring covered with a deep, plush rug in the center of the room. Comfortable looking leather couches and chairs invite one to sit. It's like walking into someone's living room. And I'd bet my last paycheck that the art on the walls are not reproductions. Lamps and low lighting set the room off to perfection.

"Is this yours?" I look up at Liam to see him watching me.

"No, darlin', it belongs to a friend."

"Some friend," I say softly.

Liam reclaims my elbow. "Come, I'll show you where the bathroom is."

He leads me down a hallway, before reaching around me to open the first door we come to. The bathroom, just as richly decorated as the salon, is all polished wood and luxurious marble, with gleaming fixtures and sparkling glass.

"Don't be long, darlin'."

After taking care of my needs, I hear Liam talking to someone as I leave the bathroom and walk back toward the salon.

"Caitlyn." Liam holds his hand out and I hurry to his side. The steward precedes us out the sliding doors and we exit out to the open-air deck.

"What are we doing here, Liam," I ask softly as we cross to the table.

He inclines his head toward me. "I do believe that we are going to sit and enjoy a nice meal as we cruise around the city of Chicago." He smiles down at me and I can't help but grin. He pulls out a chair at the table for me and I sit. It's set with fine linen, china, and crystal.

Liam leans down. "Surprised, darlin'?"

I look up. "Yes! Liam, this is a wonderful surprise." He lifts my chin with one long finger and brushes his lips over mine. "Thank you," I whisper.

He smiles and then sits in the chair close beside me.

Within seconds, the yacht begins to glide slowly through the water.

DuSable Harbor is located in the heart of downtown Chicago, surrounded by a towering skyline. It gives a spectacular view of the city from Lake Michigan and I feel in awe as the yacht moves out past the other boat slips, the Yacht Club, and the sailboats moored beyond.

When I look back at Liam he's watching me with that enigmatic smile of his.

"What?"

He shakes his head slightly and then glances past my shoulder.

"Hungry, darlin'?"

I teasingly raise my eyebrow in mock Liam fashion. "Yes! I wanted to eat when I first woke but a certain man I know coerced me into following him and skipping dinner."

His eyebrows arch in mock surprise before he leans close. "Well now, darlin', I do believe that you were as eager as ever to my suggestion." His voice and words are seductive in his subtle hint, and my face warms at his reminder that I am indeed always eager and ready for him. He laughs softly.

I bite my lip and close my eyes as his warm breath bathes my neck. I chose to wind my long hair up into a casual knot on top of my head, not thinking about the delicious consequence of exposing my neck to Liam.

"I like this." He strokes the back of his finger down my neck. "Maybe we'll let you—be dessert, sugar." His beguiling voice causes a slight tightening in my lower extremities.

My breath escapes in a soft rush and then Liam sits

back, addressing Matthew who is standing at a discreet distance, balancing a food tray.

He serves us quickly and as he pours wine into Liam's glass, I eye with appreciation the salad of baby spinach, bacon, red onion, sautéed mushrooms, and bacon ranch dressing.

I tuck into the salad after Matthew excuses himself. He certainly is efficient in his duties. Again I wonder at the person who is the type of friend to lend Liam his yacht.

"Do you borrow your friend's yacht frequently?" I ask as I reach for my glass of ice water. Is this something he does to impress dates? I almost smile as I sit my glass back down, picking up my salad fork. The thought of Liam needing anything other than his charms to impress women is funny. I decide quickly that I hope he doesn't answer, I really don't want to speculate on the possibility that he's brought any number of women on board the — What name did he use for the yacht?

"What did you say this boat was named?" I hope this will change the subject.

"The Heartbeat."

"Like the nightclub you took me to the night I met up with Paul and —" I suck in my breath. *Oh, no!* "Not that friend," I say, dismay apparent in my voice.

Liam's brow lifts and I think I see the hint of a smile in his eyes. "Yes. That friend."

"Oh." The only way I was able to deal with the embarrassment of being caught in a compromising situation with Liam was the fact that I would never have to cross paths again with Liam's — friend.

Of course, Liam finds it funny.

"Don't worry, darlin', Jimbo is not in the country at this time so you can relax."

I squirm as Matthew approaches once more with our entrees. I turn my attention to the view. It's a beautiful evening and I can't think of a better way to spend it.

Our entrees consist of Filet of beef in a type of wine demi-glaze that Liam teases me about not eating since I'm pregnant, and a Prosciutto topped chicken breast stuffed with mozzarella, basil, and tomato in a shallot white wine sauce. There are also seasoned, roasted vegetables and heirloom potatoes. I'm stuffed when we finish. I couldn't decide which entrée I liked the best so I sampled back and forth between the two.

Matthew is attentive to our needs, but very discreet.

"Does your friend employ Matthew or is he someone you brought in for the meal," I ask with interest as I lay my napkin on the table, completely sated.

"He's regular staff."

"Oh." Wow. The lifestyles of the rich.

Liam lays his napkin on the table and leans back in his chair. "Jimbo uses the yacht frequently. He basically lives on her in the summer." He looks up at Matthew who has come forward. "I reckon that's fairly accurate, don't you think Matthew?"

Matthew grins. "Yes, sir. Would you like dessert and coffee served here or on the upper deck?"

"I believe we'll take it on the upper deck, thank you, Matthew."

"Thank you, Matthew, everything was delicious," I tell him. He smiles his appreciation and steps away.

Liam stands and pulls back my chair.

"Liam, I don't think I can eat another bite," I whisper.

He smiles and takes my arm. "I ordered something special for you."

I look up quickly. He ordered something special for me?

The view from the upper deck is even better than below. It's twilight and the city is a spectacular sight. There is comfortable seating and soft music playing in the background.

"I can understand why your friend would live on this boat. It would be heaven to enjoy this view every evening."

Liam pulls me into his arms and brings his lips close to mine. "Dance with me, darlin'."

When I shrug off my sweater, Liam is quick to take it and lay it along the back of a chair. His eyes move over me in a leisurely fashion.

"Hmmm—"

The sound from deep in his chest causes a tightening in mine. When he walks slowly around me I nervously look back at him.

"What?"

He runs his finger down the spine of my bare back. "I like this, darlin'."

He suddenly pulls me back against his front, his arms wrapping around me, and then he takes my hand, swinging me out, only to quickly pull me back against him. I giggle at the move and he smiles.

"Yes. This has definite possibilities," he says just before he whirls me out once more, twirling me around and around the deck until I'm out of breath and laughing. Liam grins down at me as he slows our steps until we are swaying in time to the music, dancing beneath the stars as his fingers slowly move up and down my back.

"You're a beautiful dancer, darlin'," he murmurs near my ear.

"I love to dance." I look up. "You're not so bad yourself."

He immediately dips me back, and I laugh with delight. My arms go around his neck as soon as he pulls me back close.

"My parents used to dance."

When I look up in surprise, I see the frown between his brows. "They did?"

He nods slowly. "When I was a kid. They used to dance in the living room after I went to bed at night, but I'd hear the music and sneak down to watch them from the stairway. My mom told me years later that they always knew I was there." He smiles.

"They danced, only when you were young?"

His eyes meet mine. "Before my dad started his hard drinking."

Oh. "That must have been hard for you," I say softly.

He doesn't say anything more and I decide he's not going to when he says, "It was hard on my mom."

The song ends, and he leads me to the seating area at the stern of the boat. While we danced, someone, probably Matthew, lit candles and placed a coffee service on a long, low table in the group seating area. Instead of sitting in one of the chairs, Liam pulls me over to the couch. He hands me a cup and I lift my brow.

"It's herbal tea, darlin'. I've noticed you haven't been drinking coffee."

He has? "Thank you," I say as I take the cup. There's a covered dish on the table and when Liam removes the cover, my mouth drops open. Chocolate covered strawberries. He reaches for one bringing it to my lips. His eyes are alight with wicked humor.

"Bite, darlin'," he drawls.

I blush at his suggestive tone. My hand goes up under his as I bite into the delicious concoction. My eyes close and I hum appreciatively. I glance up at him and his eyes burn with blue fire. His mouth slowly lifts at the corner and then he sucker punches me with that full-blown smile of his.

I lick my lips and his gaze drops to my mouth. "Aren't you having any?"

His gaze is still on my mouth as he says, "Yes. I reckon I will, sugar." His mouth comes down and his tongue traces my full bottom lip before he gently sucks on it. He tastes and licks as I melt against him. Raising his head, his thumb comes up to swipe at his bottom lip. "You taste mighty fine, darlin'."

Knowing I want more, I reach for another strawberry. Yes... this has possibilities too. I rise to straddle his lap facing him and when he raises his hands, I shake my head.

"No. No hands."

The corner of his mouth lifts slightly, he's clearly amused, but he places his hands on the couch. He leans his head back against the back cushion, his eyes hooded as he watches me, a bemused expression on his face.

Holding his gaze, I bring the strawberry to my mouth, and I moan softly as I bite into the rich blend of chocolate and berry. I close my eyes as I savor the flavor.

"Do you want another taste?" I whisper when I open my eyes.

"Yes," he says hoarsely, his eyes hot, fervent in their intensity.

I lean in, careful not to touch anything but his lips, using my tongue to tease his lips apart, delivering a passionate kiss that elicits a low rumble in his chest as he brings his hands up to my waist, pulling my body to his.

My arms go around his neck and before I realize it, I'm lying on my back with Liam stretched out alongside me. His mouth devours mine with determined intent and when he lets me come up for air, I'm breathless. Pulling one of my legs up so it bends at the knee, his hand easily finds its way up under my skirt and between my legs.

"Liam," I whimper, pushing gently at his shoulders, but my head tips back and my mouth goes slack as he pushes my panty aside and inserts two fingers into me.

"Shhh... No one will disturb us, darlin'."

He pulls his fingers from me and then pushes them back in deeper, curling them against that sweet spot that totally annihilates any resistance I might have.

"Please," I moan as he increases his thrusts, twisting his fingers in and out of me. My bent leg splays wide as I lift my hips meeting the thrusts of his fingers in wild abandon.

When he stops all movement, holding his fingers still, I'm panting. I want him. Right now, no longer concerned with who might discover us. This is what he does to me.

He's unbuttoned my halter top and I don't notice until he lowers the front part of my dress exposing my breasts.

"No!" I gasp, reaching to cover myself as the cool night air hits my nipples. He quickly grips my hands, raising them above my head to hold in one large hand. His other grips my chin.

"Stop." His voice is forceful as his bold gaze holds

mine. "If I want to strip you naked, I fucking will. No one is going to see you."

My breasts rise and fall provocatively with my rapid breathing, drawing his gaze down. My nipples elongate farther under his lascivious gaze.

"Liam," I breathe as he dips his head, sucking forcefully on a sensitive nipple. My back bows and I moan softly as he sucks and nips first one and then the other. My hands pull against his hold and when he releases them, I bury my fingers in his hair.

"Look at me." I open my eyes, my gaze meeting his as I lie beneath him panting. "I'm going to make you come." I bite my lip. "I don't want you to make a sound. Do you understand me?"

What? I frown and he raises his eyebrow in warning before lowering his head, sharply drawing a nipple into his mouth, his teeth biting down around it. I almost cry out, and a tiny whimper does escape. His eyes open and he looks up at me as he continues to suck forcefully. The sensation this creates travels straight between my legs. My back bows again and he starts moving his fingers fast and hard against that spot deep inside that turns me into a mindless mess.

I writhe beneath him as my body moves and bucks against his hand. I pull at his hair and push against his shoulders but it doesn't calm the tempest that is raging through me. I feel the tightening, the incredible sensation that makes my toes curl and my legs stiffen, causing my inner muscles to grip his fingers, which only adds to the acute sensation that I know is leading to a mind-blowing orgasm.

"That's right, sugar, fuck my fingers." His wicked words are guttural in their intensity. I can't control my body as I wantonly raise my pelvis meeting each thrust of his hand.

My body suddenly arches up beneath him and I throw my head back in wild abandon as I climax. My scream is silent as I shatter beneath him.

I sit on Liam's lap as we watch the fireworks from Navy Pier. I love firework displays and I've been on Navy pier before to enjoy one of Chicago's greatest summer attractions, but seeing it for the first time out on the lake is truly an awesome sight.

"Are you enjoying yourself, darlin'?"

I angle my head to the side looking up at him and he kisses the top of my head as his hand comes up to cradle the side of my face. His other hand rests on my belly. This has become a habit of his. "It's been a wonderful night, Liam. Thank you."

He leans his head closer. "Remind me to feed you chocolate strawberries more often."

I blush and he seems to know, even in the dark, because he laughs softly.

"How was that for you?" His deep voice holds a measure of amusement. I know what he's referring to.

"Good."

He laughs out right. "Just good?"

Why does he love embarrassing me? "It was intense."

"Ahhh... the thrill of discovery. Yes, that does heighten ones sexual gratification."

He's done this with other women.

Possibly right here on this boat. That's an unwelcome thought.

Our romantic night ends with the yacht making its

way back to DuSable Harbor. Mike is waiting for us and as we climb into the SUV, it's like a switch is flipped and I'm exhausted. It was the best of nights I decide as I rest my head on Liam's shoulder. His arm snakes in behind my back and pulls me as close as our seatbelts allow.

CHAPTER NINE

I PUSH AGAINST THE DOOR OF Query Magazine, entering the lobby. I'm meeting up with Paul for lunch, still floating on the magic cloud Liam weaved around me over the weekend. A small smile plays on my lips as I cross the lobby.

"Excuse me! Ms. Shaw!"

I turn toward the receptionist. "Yes?"

"I'll need to announce you."

I frown. I know Paul informed her that it was okay for me to go on back to his office when I stopped in the last time. But she's new and maybe she forgot.

"That's fine," I say moving closer to the reception area.

"Who are you here to see?"

My eyebrow lifts. I'm mastering that look from Liam. She gives me an *are you stupid* look. What the hell?

"Hey, Cait!" One of the mail boys shouts across the lobby. I turn and give him a quick wave.

"Is *that* who you are here to see?" She smirks.

My mouth drops open and I quickly close it. Why is she so hostile toward me? She was like this the last time I was here.

"No. I'm here to see Paul."

She smiles one of those secretive smiles as if she finds what I just said amusing. She's starting to piss me off. I contemplate just going on back to Paul's office but she'd probably call security on me.

"Ms. —" I pointedly look at her name plaque sitting on her desk "— Rogers, you can call Mr. Sims if you'd like. I'm sure he won't mind your interruption of whatever it is that he might be doing. Especially since the last time I was here, I heard him specifically tell you that it was okay for me to go back to his office unannounced. But I have no problem with waiting here while you announce me; he is expecting me, after all." Wow. Am I being a bitch? I said it nicely.

She narrows her eyes, tosses her head and picks up the phone, punching in what I hope is Paul's extension, while she glares at me.

Nope. I don't think I'm being a bitch.

She replaces the phone and moves to pick up some folders. Seriously? How rude. Does she treat everyone this way?

I sigh and start to walk away but turn back. "Oh, and it's *Mrs.* Justice."

I'm still shaking my head as I knock and then open Paul's door when he calls to come in.

"Hey, Cait." He stands and closes a file, slipping it into a desk drawer. "You're just in time. I'm about to starve."

I laugh. He's always hungry.

"I was afraid that the receptionist was going to throw me out of the building. What's her problem?"

He frowns as he moves from around his desk. "She's a pain in the ass."

I laugh. "Well I'm glad to know it's not just me."

"Ready?" he asks as someone knocks on his door.

"Paul," Valerie says walking in before he has a chance to say anything. Her glasses are perched on the end of her nose and she's rifling through the papers she carries. She looks up. "Caitlyn!"

"Hi, Valerie. It's good to see you."

She motions toward the chairs in front of Paul's desk. "I'm glad you're here. I was going to give you a call, we need to talk, have a seat."

"Oh?" I give Paul a quick glance and hear his sigh as he perches on the edge of his desk, his arms crossing over his chest in a resigned manner.

Valerie sits and looks up expectantly.

"Well, we were just going to lunch—"

"Sit. What I have to say won't take long."

I glance at Paul again and he gives a slight shake of his head.

"Caitlyn, I want you to come back to work."

"Valerie—"

"You and Paul will work together as before, but you won't be going out on assignments. A desk job if you like, but I want you back here."

I would be lying if I said I had no interest in her offer. I'm bored silly sitting around the apartment all day. Shopping gets old fast and all of my friends work during the week.

"I'm taking your silence as a positive consideration of my offer."

"No." I sigh. "Valerie, I'm not sure. I'll need time to think it over."

She stands. "Fine, let me know tomorrow."

"Valerie, I—"

She turns toward Paul. "What did you find out?"

Paul leans back to reach over his desk, picking up a piece of paper. "A phone number is all I was able to come up with." He hands Valerie the paper as he stands.

Valerie gives me a look over the top of her glasses. "*You* would not only have acquired the home address but the work address and the addresses of friends and family by now." She opens the door calling over her shoulder, "I need you back here, Caitlyn."

I look over at Paul, trying not to laugh as he shakes his head again.

"Are you certain you want to get back into work? You know how Valerie is. Don't let her push you to do something you're not sure of."

I pick up my ice water and take a sip. "Honestly? I miss it Paul. I'm bored."

"Not enough going on with shopping and planning for the baby?"

I push my salad around on my plate. "Not really. I'm sure I'll be very busy after the baby comes but right now... I think I really want to do this." I'd been turning the idea over in my head ever since we left Paul's office. A paycheck would enable me to send money to my parents and maybe start putting a little back. My hand goes to my belly.

He looks up to catch the waiter's eye. "What do you think Liam will say about it?"

"I'm not sure." But I am. He won't like it and on second thought, I realize it's probably not a good idea, not since working for the magazine was the reason he fired me from Justice House in the first place. But I still feel the need to work somewhere.

We pay our check and Paul puts me into a cab for home.

"Call and let me know later. I like knowing things before Valerie does," he says.

I laugh. "Okay. Tell Julie hello for me. We need to get together soon."

"Sounds good. Call."

I lean back against the seat. I hope Liam will be okay with this. He's never said one way or the other about my working or not. But then we've never talked about it.

I have the taxi drop me off at a little shop that specializes in baby furniture. Julie met the owner when he was conferring with her company over advertising. She'd mentioned her friend was expecting and he told her to have me stop in and he'd give me a discount.

I take my time looking around the shop. I know that even with a discount, I will never be able to afford this quality of furniture, and I am instantly in love with half the items in the store.

"I'm just checking I don't want you to think I've forgotten about you." The sales associate is a friendly older woman who introduced herself when I first came in. I like that she's let me look around and not pressured me. "I know you are just looking right now, but if you have any questions or would like information on the manufacturer, please don't hesitate to ask." She gives me a friendly smile.

"Thank you, I will."

It's late afternoon when I arrive back at Justice House. It's usually a quiet time in the Mansion, just before the dinner crowd starts arriving. I know Liam will be in his office and I head that way to talk to him. I know working for Valerie is out of the question but I've decided that I am going back to work and I have a secret hope of coming back to work here at Justice House.

I haven't seen Holly in a couple of days and I'm a little disappointed when her office is dark.

I knock softly and enter when Liam calls out. He's sitting at his desk, files scattered across the top. He looks up from his computer as I walk in.

He smiles as he stands and my heart rate accelerates as he walks toward me. Without a word, he pulls me into his arms, his mouth lowering to mine.

Mmmm... he smells so good and tastes even better. His tongue strokes mine in a suggestive way that has me melting against him. Sliding his lips along my jawline to my ear, he tugs on the lobe with his teeth.

"You are a most welcome distraction, sugar." His hand grips my bottom. "If I didn't have to get this inventory entered into the computer, I'd fuck you over my desk."

My body immediately says yes to his suggestion. He laughs and tips my chin up.

"Did you have a pleasant lunch with Paul?" He and Paul seem to have gotten over their animosity with each other, which pleases me.

"I did, thank you."

Liam leads me across the room to the bar area. "Would you like some juice?" he asks as he opens the mini fridge.

"Water please."

He hands me a bottled water, then pulls out a carton of juice, and fills a glass. "Would you like a glass for your water?"

"No, thank you." I do prefer a glass but I don't need

Rivi Jacks

to linger since he's busy. I realize I'm being a bit of a coward too, relieved that I can delay my talk of going back to work.

"What is it Cait? I can tell you're nervous darlin'."

"I'm not nervous."

He gives a soft snort and comes out from behind the bar, stepping close. "Sugar, your breathing has picked up, you keep moistening your lips and you're eyeing the elevator like you're planning your escape route." He reaches out and brushes the back of his finger down the side of my face, down my neck and over my collarbone, softly brushing the tops of my breasts.

My breathing stops altogether.

"Let's have it, Cait."

"It's nothing... it can wait until you're finished here," I say softly.

"I won't be finished until late. You'll be asleep."

"I can wait up." I look up as he steps even closer. My breasts brush against his chest and right on cue, my nipples harden almost painfully. He does this on purpose, knowing exactly what he does to me.

"I don't think so," he says softly as he runs his finger along the swell of my breast, underneath the lapel of my blouse, down into my bra. The tip of his finger just grazes the tip of my nipple and a tingling sensation jolts right to my clit. I gasp, squeezing my legs together. Would he take me over his desk if I begged?

"I don't want you waiting up and overdoing it, you need your rest." He pulls his finger from my blouse and lifts my chin, giving me a quick rough kiss. "I have every intention of waking you when I come to bed, darlin'."

I bite my lip with my body's response at his words.

He turns and moves back to his desk. "I'm going to

ask you one more time, Caitlyn, what it is that you came to talk to me about."

Holy shit! This man keeps my equilibrium in a tailspin. He seduces me one moment then intimidates me the next.

He perches on the edge of his desk; arms crossed, watching me.

Damn. Now I'm really nervous.

"While I was at the magazine today, Valerie offered me my job back—"

"Absolutely not."

What? "You can at least hear me out," I snap.

His eyes narrow and he cocks his head slightly, but he doesn't say anything more.

"Liam, I really want to go back to work. I need something to do. It will only be until the baby comes."

"You have something to do. You have a baby to prepare for. I suggest you forget about working at the magazine for the woman who wants to smear my personal life all over the news." He straightens and moves around his desk to sit.

"Well, I'm sorry you don't understand my need to stay busy and be productive." My temper has flared at his obstinate attitude and I don't try to explain that I have no intention of going back to the magazine. "And Valerie no longer has any interest in doing an expose on you." I take a deep breath, telling myself to calm down. "My going back to work will not take away from my preparing for our baby." I need to work, and there is the fact I still feel the need to prepare for the possibility that I might end up out on my own. "I am going back to work, and you will just have to accept it, Liam." I start to turn away, deciding that I'm going to go look for Holly.

He moves faster than I can blink and I'm suddenly against the wall my wrists pinned above my head.

I can't control my gasp or my subsequent whimper as he presses against me. His demeanor has changed so quickly that fear and passion intermingle as desire unfurls in the pit of my stomach. I'm not really afraid of him but I am unnerved.

He buries his nose in my hair and breaths in deeply.

"You best do as I suggest, darlin' before you get yourself in a heap of trouble." He releases my wrists and steps back, looking down at me.

I gape at him.

"It wouldn't be wise to defy me on this, Caitlyn."

It wouldn't be wise to defy him on anything. Of that I'm sure.

"Liam—"

There's a soft knock on his door and I glance that way, looking back to find him still glaring at me and I glare right back.

"Come in," he says harshly.

I quickly step away to compose myself as Bryce enters.

"Liam, there's something that needs your attention upstairs. Hi, Cait."

I turn back. "Hi, Bryce."

"I'll be right with you, Bryce," Liam tells him his intense gaze still on me.

"This subject is closed, Caitlyn. Do I make myself clear?"

The arrogant— "Crystal," I snap. He'll discover soon enough that this subject is not closed. But I'm not going to fight in front of Bryce.

With one last lift of his arrogant eyebrow, he heads for the door with me right behind him.

"Where do you think you're going?"

I nearly run into his back as he stops abruptly after clearing the door. I take a step back as he scowls down at me.

"I'm going to look for Holly." I don't even try to keep the annoyance out of my voice.

He narrows his eyes and I lift my chin. From the corner of my eye, I catch Bryce's amused grin.

"Holly's out back talking to the gardener," Bryce says. Liam turns his glare on him, and Bryce raises his hands in a gesture that says he'll stay out of it, but he still has that shit-eating grin on his face.

Liam continues down the hall and Bryce quickly falls in beside him as he looks back at me grinning. I follow at a safe distance and when we near the back stairs to the second floor, I slow. I get a funny feeling in the pit of my stomach when I think about Liam going upstairs. I've never been up there in the evening so I'm not exactly sure what goes on but I know it's a party atmosphere on busy nights. I know Miranda is up there and a couple of other girls on the payroll that fill the same capacity that Miranda does in the club. And of course, there are always the female club members. I'd be blind not to notice the glances and smiles Liam gets on any given day when we walk through the mansion. And I can't even bring myself to think of the *dungeon* as everyone refers to it.

Is he ever tempted? It's a disheartening thought and I come to a halt in the middle of the hall. I suddenly wish I'd gone to the apartment as he suggested.

I look up and at that moment, Liam looks back, meeting my gaze. A frown passes over his face and then I make my feet move, hurrying on to the elevator.

It's much later when I hear Liam in the apartment. I'm in the bedroom with the door open and I can hear him talking to Annie. I came in here after I ate the dinner that Annie prepared, keeping me company as she chattered about her weekend.

Holly called when Bryce told her I was looking for her. We caught up on what we did over the weekend and I told her about wanting to go back to work. She knew Liam didn't like the idea without me telling her how he'd responded, and she brought up the subject of me working here in the mansion again. She also told me that there were special guests visiting and the upstairs was busy for a Monday night. I could have done without that information.

When Liam doesn't come directly back to the bedroom I know he's eating his dinner that Annie put aside for him. I toss the Parenting magazine I've been trying to read and head toward the kitchen.

I'm wearing a long sleeve nightshirt that ends at the top of my thighs but it's presentable if Annie is still up. I pause in the doorway and drink in the beautiful man sitting at the kitchen island.

He suddenly looks up with those mesmerizing eyes and I'm at once under his spell, my breath hitching in reaction.

"Hi," I say softly.

One corner of his mouth lifts and he crooks his finger for me to join him as he stands, moving to the refrigerator.

I cross the kitchen, at once self-conscious. He's probably been around scantily clad women all evening, and here I am in a buttoned up nightshirt.

"I thought you'd be asleep. Annie said you went back to the bedroom right after you had dinner."

I sit on one of the high back stools as he comes back with a bottle of wine. "I've been reading."

Oh. I look longingly as he pours a glass. I would love a glass of wine.

I fidget when he gives me a long look.

"You look tired." He sits. "I told you I don't want you over doing it. You're supposed to be taking it easy."

I sigh softly. "I'm not tired, Liam. I've lain around all evening."

"Have you, darlin'?" His eyes run over me and I sit up a little straighter. "Well now, I'm right sorry I wasn't here to join you." His words, uttered in his slow, sexy drawl cause all the muscles south of my navel to clench tightly.

Holy hell!

He takes a drink of wine and then pushes his plate back, coming to his feet. I look up as he reaches for me. His hands go around the sides of my waist and he lifts me up off the stool and sets me on the edge of the counter in one swift move.

I laugh a little breathlessly and then my breath catches as he puts his hands on my knees pushing them apart, moving in between them. I bite my lip in reaction. He pulls me closer to the edge so my body juts up against his. My arms move to his shoulders as his gaze holds mine and he grins wickedly as he smooths his hands over my bare thighs and down the calves of my legs.

He smells so good.

"Tell me, sugar; are you naked under this shirt?" His hands run back up my thighs, under the hem of my shirt, stopping just shy of finding out on his own that I am indeed naked under the shirt.

"Yes," I whisper.

"Hmmm…" He leans in then, his lips brushing lightly over mine. My lips part with a soft sigh. When he brings his hand up to encircle my throat, I moan softly.

He raises his head and there's no mistaking the heat, the desire in his eyes. He reaches to unbutton my shirt.

"Liam—" I glance at the closed door that leads down the hall to Annie's room.

"Relax, darlin' she won't be coming out here."

I'm not so sure about that, but he suddenly pushes my shirt apart, exposing one breast as he leans down drawing deeply on the pouty nipple.

"Ahhh—" My back arches allowing him better access as he pushes my shirt farther off my shoulder. My breath draws in with a hiss when he bites down on my nipple.

He raises his head drawing me even closer and takes hold of my wrists, pulling them down to the counter.

"Lean back on your hands," he says roughly, his hands already moving to finish unbuttoning my shirt.

Holy shit! My breathing is unsteady as my body grows tense with equal measure of desire and panic that Annie is going to walk in on us.

He pulls my shirt apart and it slides off my shoulders, down my arms to fall onto the counter.

"Fuck!" he growls. My body tightens as his eyes move over me. "You are so fucking beautiful."

Oh! My teeth imbed in my bottom lip as I try to control the rising passion that is threatening to ignite. I fight my embarrassment as I think about how I must look. My arms are behind me, propping me up and prominently displaying my breasts, my legs spread wide.

"Lie back, darlin'." He raises my legs to help tip me back.

"Liam! Please, no!" I gasp, leaning forward to grab

his hands. I'm terrified of what he plans to do with Annie just down the hall. He grips my wrists again.

"I said—lie back." His voice has that hard edge that causes me to stop and look up. His eyes burn into mine. Why does he do this to me?

"Oh, fuck!" I hiss angrily as I jerk my hands from his and lie back on the counter, raising my arms to cross over my face. My entire body tightens, knowing what he's about to do.

"Hurry up!"

I lie there pissed as hell at him, but I wait with bated breath, my desire spiking before he's even touched me. What is he waiting for?

"Hurry up?"

I peek up at him from between my arms. His brow raised and his expression is one of surprise.

Oh, shit.

His mouth twitches and as I watch his eyes suddenly sparkle and then unexpectedly, he laughs outright.

I give him a long blink. When he laughs like that with his head thrown back, he is simply the sexiest man. It causes all of my sexual neurons to ignite at once, rendering me a hot mess in ten seconds flat.

"What's wrong?" I'm confused.

He's still laughing as he takes hold of my hands and pulls me up against his body.

He's so confusing. "What's so funny?"

He leans back so he can look me in the face. His smile so beautiful, I just gape at him.

"No woman has *ever* told me to 'hurry up,' darlin'." He grins.

I snort softly. "I just bet they haven't," I grumble as I

push back and pull my shirt up around me. I don't need to be reminded of other women.

"Hey," he says softly.

I don't look at him as I button up my nightshirt.

"Darlin'." He places his hand over mine stilling my fingers, with the other he lifts my chin, his voice still filled with laughter. "Cait, look at me."

I'm slightly mollified that when I do; his expression has sobered.

His thumb brushes across my bottom lip as his eyes search mine. "Cait—" He looks away for a moment as if deciding what he wants to say, before bringing his gaze back to mine. "I take my marriage vows to you very seriously," he says slowly. "I'm not interested in anyone else. I don't *want* anyone else." His voice is low and rough. He leans in and gives me a quick soft kiss, his hand going around the nape of my neck. "I only want you, darlin'."

I stop breathing, his words sending a thrill through me.

His mouth comes down on mine swift and hard, his hands delving into my hair, holding me steady as he devours my mouth. I reach out, gripping his shirt in my hands, scooting closer to him. When he tears his mouth away, we're both breathing hard. He leans his forehead against mine.

"I think we need to take this to the bedroom." His voice is husky.

"I agree," I whisper.

His hands encircle my waist and he lifts me off the counter, bringing me close to his body as he holds my gaze. He lowers me slowly so that I slide down his length.

When my feet touch the floor, he gives me a lascivious smile.

"I have an idea, darlin'. You go on and I'll be right there."

"Okay." I take two steps when I feel the tug on my nightshirt.

"I'll take this." He steps close and then he's raising the hem of my shirt up. "Arms up."

"But—" I glance nervously at the door I'm expecting Annie to come out of at any moment. I raise my arms slowly and Liam pulls the shirt up and over my head.

He throws the nightshirt over his shoulder. "Go," he says firmly, his voice, stern.

Oh! Why do I even bother to dress when he's around?

I give an exasperated sigh as I turn and then exhale sharply when his arm snakes around my waist wrenching me close again, my back up against his front. His other hand comes up to my throat, his mouth at my ear.

"Darlin' you need to do what I tell you without the attitude. Do you understand?"

"Yes," I breathe.

"Go," he growls releasing me. As I step away, he gives me a hard smack on my bare bottom.

I jump and squeak hurrying across the kitchen, looking back when I reach the door. The ass is grinning! I flip my hair over my shoulder as dramatically as I can and walk out.

I feel like skipping down the hallway. The words he uttered in the kitchen, about only wanting me, fill me with an unprecedented joy.

Half way to the bedroom, I stop. He has an idea? My body tightens in response to that thought and I grin as I hurry on.

I'm sitting cross-legged on the bed with the sheet pulled up around my breasts when Liam walks into the bedroom. He gives me a cursory glance and then proceeds to the en suite with the ice bucket he's carrying.

What's he doing with that? I pull my knees up to my chest, hugging my legs with my arms. I almost feel giddy with excitement, wondering what he has in mind. He has such fun ideas.

As he walks back into the room, he doesn't look my way as he continues to the closet. He's unbuttoned his shirt and I get tantalizing glimpses of his chest and hard stomach.

When he emerges, he's changed into sweats. No shirt, no shoes, just sweats, and I know there is nothing under them because his erection juts out.

Holy hell! I'm rendered speechless as he saunters toward me. His dark hair in alluring disarray, his eyes smoky with desire. I lick my lips, breathless with anticipation. His mouth lifts at one corner and I slow blink, my lips parting in response. I lean back as he leans over me, his hands coming down on the mattress beside me, his face within an inch of mine.

"Ready, darlin'?"

My eyes widen. *Ready for what?* I nod. "Yes," I croak.

He flashes a feral grin that unfurls a small quiver in my belly.

Gripping my upper arms, he lifts me to my knees as he stands. The sheet falls to the mattress as he pulls me close, his mouth coming down hungrily on mine. I grip his waist as he fists handfuls of my long hair, our tongues tangling in that age-old dance of lovers. I inch forward trying to get closer, smoothing my hands up over his stomach, loving the feel of his muscles clenching beneath my fingers. His skin is so warm and he smells divine. I moan. I want him desperately and when he breaks the kiss, I mewl softly in protest.

Liam lays his finger across my lips.

"Shhh. Lie down, darlin'." He reaches down to open a drawer of the nightstand by the bed. When he stands, he has soft cords in his hands. He holds them up and I feel nervous tension in the pit of my stomach.

"I'm going to tie you to the bed, Caitlyn." He's only tied me up once and that was a pleasant experience on our honeymoon, but still...

"Why?" My voice sounds shaky.

He raises his eyebrow. "Why? So I can fuck you senseless, sugar."

My breath rushes out in a soft huff.

I can't control my breathing as I lie on the bed. It's fast and a little harsh. I squeeze my legs together. I'm so turned on and he keeps touching me in sensual ways as he binds first one wrist and then the other to the bars of the bed frame. When he finishes he tweaks my nipples.

"Ahhh!" I writhe on the bed.

"You are so fucking sexy," he murmurs, his eyes moving leisurely over me. I bite my lip trying to control my reaction to his perusal of my body.

"Hmmm—" His hand goes to his chin and his eyes squint.

Oh, no. What?

He smiles wickedly and moves to the nightstand again to retrieve more of the ties. "I think I'm going to tie your legs too, darlin'."

Oh, shit! I really want to tell him I don't want that, but I know it won't do any good.

He binds both and I'm spread eagle on the bed. I test

my bindings. He's left a little leeway so that I can bend my legs slightly.

He moves quickly and comes onto the bed between my legs. Leaning down he buries his nose in the curls at the junction of my thighs, breathing in deeply. Oh! My core muscles clench painfully.

"Fuck!" He looks up the planes of my body, his eyes intense with blue fire. "Your arousal smells like sweet perfume, darlin'." He reaches up to pinch my nipples in a hold that feels like a vise. I whimper and my back arches.

"I love the way you respond to me, darlin'," — his voice is low and seductive— "you've never been able to hide that from me." He licks my length before sliding his tongue to stroke my clit.

I buck up and cry out as he sucks hard on my clit. My arms and legs jerk against my bindings as my head thrashes back and forth on the pillow. *Oh!* My back arches up sharply. When he pushes two fingers deep into my channel, I feel the beginnings of an orgasm, gathering energy deep within my body, slowly radiating out.

He hums and the vibration causes a sweet pain in my clit, resonating throughout my body. Thrusting his fingers hard and fast, he suddenly curls them and the action detonates my orgasm as I cry out a semblance of his name. My climax wracks my body, as Liam brings his mouth up over my belly, nipping and sucking his way to my breasts, biting and sucking my nipples.

Before the tremors in my body subside, he's off the bed and then he's holding a blindfold before me.

I vaguely wonder why he's going to blindfold me but my senses are still in his sensual thrall.

Eyes that smolder with intensity hold mine as he

leans over me, taking my mouth in a soft kiss. "You are incredible, sugar," he murmurs against my lips and then he brings the blindfold up over my eyes.

I whimper, feeling vulnerable. "Liam!"

"Shhh, you're okay, baby." His hand rubs gently over my stomach. I swallow deeply and suck in a deep breathe, my chin quivering as I exhale.

The bed tilts and then levels as Liam stands, and I listen as he moves around the room.

I hear him come close and then he's on the bed again, between my legs, his hand sliding under my bottom lifting me. He slides something under me; it feels different from the sheets. I frown. Is it a towel? His hand massages my belly and then slides down to rest on my pubic bone.

"Arghhh!" He rubs something that is impossibly cold from my opening to my clit straight up to my belly button. It's freaking ice cold and I suspect it's an ice cube, but when he brings it back to my opening, inserting it in a short, sharp jab before quickly pulling it from me, I know it's huge whatever it is. I suspect it would hurt if it weren't wet, easing its insertion.

"Fuck!" he growls and repeats the action, this time inserting it a little deeper, giving me two quick short jabs into my channel.

"Liam!" I cry as he runs it over my tissues. The sensation is like wet heat as he moves it over, in and around. He never leaves it in one spot for more than a second or two. My back arches and I writhe as much as I'm able, bound as I am. When his hot tongue delves deep inside of me, I whine, and buck against his face.

Holy fuck!

He rubs the melting ice over my clit as his tongue works me over. I pull against my bindings, and when his hot mouth latches onto my cold clit, my body arches, tearing a low plaintive moan from my throat. Inserting the thick piece of ice at my opening, he quickly inserts it deep into my channel and just as quickly withdraws it. My cry is hoarse as my body jerks, and my arms and legs pull against the restraints. He does this several times while he sucks forcefully on my clit elongating the engorged nub, while his hot fingers replace the ice.

My pants and ragged breath echo off the room's walls.

"I wish you could see how you look, sugar."

I mewl softly and turn my head to the side. I feel him tug at the blindfold, and then I'm blinking rapidly against the bright light as Liam grins down at me. I groan loudly when he touches the ice to my nipple and raise my head, looking down.

Holy shit! The ice he's using on me looks like a frozen penis. I glance up quickly, meeting his amused eyes as he continues to move it around and over my nipple until it feels numb. When his hot mouth latches onto the distended peak, my upper body rears up as far as my bindings allow.

"Mmmm," he hums. The vibration to my breast makes me groan. He raises his head, his eyes gleaming. "We can't neglect this one." He promptly pinches the other nipple.

"Ahh!" I jerk against my bindings.

He leaves me panting as the bed shifts, and I feel him grip my ankle freeing it before he shifts and does the same with the other. Then he's pushing my legs apart and up so that they bend at the knees, opening me wide. He uses the ice again, inserting and then quickly withdrawing from my swollen channel, alternating between shallow and deep thrusts, over and over.

"Look at me," he orders as he comes between my legs.

I open my eyes to see his, hot and burning with his desire. He leans down and kisses me deeply, his tongue tangling with mine. His mouth releases mine and he nibbles along my jawline.

"You are mine. You belong completely to me." His hot breath whispers against my ear, sending shivers over my skin. He rears back and then thrusts his thick, hard length into me, and it's like he's inserting a hot brand.

Liam hisses through his teeth as my back arches. I can't catch my breath as he raises my hips, lifting my lower half off the bed. He drapes my legs over his arms as he grips my hips and batters me with punishing thrusts.

I think I pass out from the intensity of my orgasm because when I become aware of my surroundings again, Liam has untied me and he's lying naked in bed holding me in his arms. The fingers of one hand run through my hair, smoothing it off my forehead. It's so relaxing. The other cradles my breast, his thumb rubbing against my nipple.

"Was that fast enough for you, sugar?" His voice rumbles in his chest beneath my ear.

I snort softly and he laughs.

He shifts looking down at me. "Go back to sleep, baby."

Oddly enough, I feel rested and not sleepy at all, kind of rejuvenated.

"I love you, Liam," I whisper, my voice sounding hoarse and scratchy. And for the first time, it hurts a little that he doesn't say the words to me.

He reaches for my hand and brings it to his chest, placing it over his heart. I blink, holding my breath as I lie perfectly still, wondering if I'm misconstruing the implication of this action. When he rises above me, he still holds my hand over his heart as his eyes gaze deeply into mine, warm and glowing. He raises my hand to his mouth, pressing his lips to each finger, before placing my hand back over his heart, his eyes never wavering from mine.

I breathe again, my heart racing as he lowers his head, capturing my mouth in a passionate kiss.

CHAPTER TEN

'M HUMMING AS I ENTER the kitchen the next morning. Liam's already left, waking me earlier to let me know he'd be gone for most of the day. I won't see him until we meet up for dinner later.

Annie's digging in the refrigerator as I walk in.

"Good morning, Annie," I sing out.

She looks around the refrigerator door at me. "Oh! Good morning, Cait. I'm making out my grocery list, is there anything special you'd like?" She closes the door and poises her pen over pad as she looks expectantly at me.

"Right now wouldn't be a good time to ask me, I'm starving."

She laughs, laying her pad down. "What would you like this morning, dear?"

"I'm in the mood for cereal. Craving it actually."

As I sit, eating my way through a large bowl of Raisin Bran, Annie continues making out her grocery list as she looks through the pantry. I'm sitting at the island counter and I feel my face warm thinking about the previous night.

"Um... Annie, I hope we didn't disturb you last night," I say cautiously.

She peeks around the door and then laughs. "No, not at all." She smiles broadly, noticing my red face. "Playing newlywed games in the apartment last night were we?"

I sputter around my mouthful of cereal.

Newlywed games? I smile. I guess that's exactly what we were doing. I hope we play newlywed games for years to come.

"No, didn't hear a thing, dear and even if I had, Mr. Liam warned me, right after you came to stay, about coming out here at night."

I almost drop my spoon and choke on my cereal.

He what?

Thank goodness, Annie is back in the pantry and doesn't see my face. *The ass!* I can't believe he said that to her. I can't believe he enjoys when I'm as nervous and tense as I was last night, worrying about Annie catching me naked on the kitchen counter.

I pick up my bowl and pour the remains down the garbage disposal, rinsing my spoon and bowl as I shake my head in disbelief.

"Annie, do you have a key for the door that leads to the roof? I noticed it's locked."

"No." She closes the pantry door. "Mr. Liam has the key."

"Okay, thanks. I'll be out on the balcony if you need me."

I change into a one of my bikinis and head outside to sit, putting my legs up on one of the lounge chairs, relishing the warmth of the sun. I wish I could go up on the roof; I love it up there but out here on the balcony is a close second. It's quiet, but occasionally a noise from below catches my attention and I can't help but look.

The back of Justice House is a busy place with all the comings and goings of club members.

After rubbing down with sunscreen I lean back and close my eyes. I need to call Valerie and let her know I definitely won't be going back to work at Query Magazine. I should let Liam know too, that I never intended to go back to the magazine. I know that his argument will be he doesn't want me to work at all, but he needs to understand that I *am* going to work somewhere. I feel the need to save money and there's my parents to think about—

I feel an inner glow when I recall Liam's words last night. That he's committed to his marriage vows. But just as quickly I remember when we spent the night on the roof and he asked me to move in with him. That night he told me that I'd wrapped myself around his heart. The next day he shut me out of his life forever. He only let me back because of the baby, and I know that if there were no baby there would be no—us.

I sit up and take a drink of the ice water I brought out with me.

But there is an us, regardless of the circumstances, and I want to please Liam. I want to be a good wife and mother. I want our child to have a loving home life, just as I had growing up. Not like the battleground that Liam endured. I just know that I can't let him ride roughshod over me. I snort. He does that enough already.

The ringing of my phone is a welcome distraction. The sun is so bright I can't read the caller's name on the screen.

"Hello?"

"Is this... Cait Justice?" a man with a gravelly voice asks, his words hesitant.

"Yes."

When he says nothing further I ask, "May I help you?" I frown. I don't recognize his voice.

"I hope you can. My name is Walter Justice."

Holy hell! I'm too shocked to say anything else.

"My son has told you about me," he states.

"Some," I say softly.

There's a moment of silence and then he clears his throat. "That's why I'm calling you."

"What... I mean... Why are you calling me?"

"I need your help."

I rub my forehead. "I don't understand."

"I need to talk to my son. There is a lot I have to apologize for. I need to make things right with him." He sounds desperate. "I know he doesn't want me in his life and I understand, but there are some things I need to say to him before it's too late."

"Mr. Justice—"

"Please! There is no one else; no one else will help me." His plea ends on a plaintive note.

Something in his voice touches a place in my heart. A place that belongs to Liam. If there were any way I could help Liam heal—because regardless of the fact that he says little about his father, I know he carries years of hurt.

"I don't know what I can do," I say softly.

"Talk to him, please. Help him to understand that we need to talk."

"It's... not that easy, Mr. Justice. Liam is—"

"I know, but there has to be a way. I have to explain to him. Please."

I squeeze my eyes shut, not certain what I should do.

"Let me think about it. I'm not sure if there is anything I can do but... I'll think on it."

"Thank you. I can't tell you what this means to me." There's no mistaking the relief in his voice.

"I can't promise you anything," I quickly add.

"I... I understand. I'll... be in touch... in a few days."

Am I doing the right thing? "Okay, but like I said I can't promise you that I can do anything. Liam—" I don't want to tell him that Liam won't talk about him.

"Maybe you shouldn't say anything about me calling, at least not until we figure this out. Please," he implores.

"O-kay," I say slowly.

I hear his breath rush out. "I'll be in touch. Thank you!"

The line goes dead and I sit there holding the phone, trying to come to terms with the fact I just spoke to Liam's father. I have heard nothing good about the man and I just, sort of, agreed to help him talk to his son.

I would do anything for Liam. That includes facing his wrath if it means he can make peace with his past. But I'm not sure how to go about bringing up the subject of Walter Justice to him. He's so angry at his father, so hurt with what he had to deal with over his mother's death. I'm not sure what I can do, but I want to try.

I tie the belt of the short robe I've pulled on over my suit as I step out of the bedroom on my way to the kitchen. I immediately hear someone knocking on the door that leads out to the rotunda and the elevator that leads to the back of the mansion.

There's no window in the door so I can't see who it is. I glance back down the hall, wondering if I should get Annie and then laugh to myself, knowing it's someone

Mike has let into the elevator or possibly Holly or Bryce. I open the door and I'm surprised to see Emily.

"Hi. I hope I haven't come at a bad time."

"No, of course not. Come in, please." I step back, pulling the door wide.

She comes in like a fresh breeze. She's so pretty and... Emily just has a pleasantness about her. She has one of those personalities that makes you feel as if you're good friends even when you barely know each other.

"Michael let me in the elevator."

I smile. "Would you like something to drink?" I motion over my shoulder toward the kitchen. "I've been sitting on the balcony and was just on my way for an iced tea when I heard you knock." She follows as I take off walking toward the kitchen.

"I would love some."

After pouring two glasses of tea, I ask her, "Would you like to sit on the balcony? It's not that hot and it's beautiful out there."

She laughs. "Yes! I need some sun on these legs." She raises the hem of the very short sundress she's wearing. "I wore this specifically to get a rise out of Bryce only to discover he's at a meeting with Liam."

I lead her back through the house.

"I love this apartment," she says on the way. "It's so beautiful."

I give a loving look around as we pass the living room. "Different than downstairs. More modern but just as elegant."

"I've always thought so too," she agrees as I take her through the French doors that open out to the balcony from the hallway.

As we sit, she looks over. "I really hope it's okay that I just dropped in unannounced."

"Absolutely. I'm really glad you did."

She smiles. "I've wanted to come see you ever since we went to lunch. I... I feel I need to explain."

I sip my tea and set the glass down on the table between our chairs.

"Explain?" I'm puzzled, what does she need to explain?

"Yes. I know you had to notice that I was a little... moody talking about your baby."

Ahhh. Yes I had noticed. I just didn't connect it to the baby. So, Emily is ready to start a family. Maybe that's what Holly was referring to—the problem between Emily and Bryce. I've seen Bryce with any number of women since I first came to the Justice and I wonder if the problem is, he's not ready to settle down.

"You see... I had a miscarriage about four months ago."

"Oh, Emily!" I turn to the side putting my feet down, and lean toward her. "I am so sorry, I didn't know."

"I know you didn't. No one but our families ever knew I was pregnant and they all know what a hard time Bryce and I had dealing with it." She gives a strained little laugh. "They're all careful not to bring it up."

I know that Liam, Holly, and Mike are part of that family.

"I've come to terms with it but Bryce is having a difficult time." Her voice trails off and she gets that sad look again. "He really wanted our baby."

This is too sad. Why didn't Liam tell me?

"I am so sorry. I feel bad about how I kept talking about the baby —"

"Oh, please don't! I love hearing about your baby. Both Bryce and I are happy for the both of you. We can't wait for Liam to become a father." She grins, a mischievous glint in her eye. "I didn't say anything about the conversation we all had at lunch, but—Bryce hopes it's a girl too."

I laugh. He would.

"I wasn't sure about telling you because I think all expectant mothers have the worry of something going wrong early in their pregnancies."

I nod, agreeing. I can't bear the thought of losing my child, I already love her so much. My hand goes protectively to my belly. Liam would be devastated too.

Emily notices and reaches over to pat my hand. I should be comforting her.

"I think Bryce has a harder time with the loss. You know the whole, *gotta be a man*, thing. We women grieve openly and they—" She hesitates and reaches over to pick up her tea. "It caught us by surprise—much like you and Liam. We were engaged at the time."

"You were?"

"Yes." She laughs, the sound soft and musical. "I guess we were careless, maybe on purpose." She smiles. "We were both ready to start a family." She pauses, her gaze growing misty. "Bryce wanted to marry as soon as we found out. He wanted to elope but I said, no." She looks down at her hands, her fingers interlocked tightly in her lap. "Our wedding was a month away and my mom would have had a heart attack if we'd done that."

"You had a big wedding planned?"

"Oh, yes. One of those society weddings all planned out for us." She smiles wistfully. "It's ironic that if I'd done as he wanted, we would be married now."

I reach over and take her hand. She smiles but her eyes hold a world of pain.

"Bryce kind of went off the deep end," she continues softly. "He stayed with me the whole time I was in the hospital and then he dropped the bomb shell that he thought we should wait to marry."

I'm suddenly pissed at Bryce.

"I was so mad at him. It wasn't until my parents whisked me away to Barbados, and I had time to think that I realized just how much Bryce was hurting."

Yeah, but to push her away —

"I think that when he was faced with a loss that devastated him and he couldn't do a damn thing about it — he just shut it out. I was just a reminder of it all." She sighs. "Men are funny like that."

Yeah. I frown. Like Liam shut me out.

"It's how some of them cope." She smiles broadly and swings her legs around to stand. "We need to go downstairs, grab Holly and have some lunch."

"Sounds good. I'm hungry."

Our lunch is enjoyable and the number of people who stop by our table to say, "Hi" surprises me. Leon actually sits with us, telling me he has been on the verge of coming upstairs to see me. He keeps us laughing with his amusing anecdotes. His cousin Tony is working and I give him a little wave but he turns his back, acting busy at the bar.

I also get to meet the new hostess.

Deanna is a beautiful statuesque blonde. She looks familiar and immediately annoys me when Holly introduces us. She is truly unfriendly.

"That was rude," Emily says as we walk out of the dining room.

Holly looks uncomfortable. "Yeah—I knew that was a mistake," she mumbles under her breath.

I sip my tea. "Mmmm," I hum softly.

"Good?"

I look up. Liam is sitting across from me, his seductive eyes watching me closely as his finger rubs across his bottom lip. We've finished our dinner and I'm enjoying a cup of a de-caf tea he ordered for me while he finishes his bourbon.

I bring the cup back to my lips, breathing in the delicate fragrance. "What did you say the name of this tea was?" I sip again, looking back across the table at him. He continues running his finger back and forth across his mouth.

"Darjeeling," he murmurs.

I've been trying to get my nerve up all through the meal and here we are about to leave and I've not brought up the subject of his father. I shift in my seat under his watchful gaze. Tonight there's something more in the way he watches me. The way he keeps stroking his lip is so distracting... my eyes drop, once again to his mouth.

"It's very good."

"Yes. I know it is," he says softly.

My gaze boldly moves back up to his even though I feel my face warm at our innuendos.

He smiles, and his gaze diverts.

"Are you sure you wouldn't like dessert, darlin'?"

"I'm sure." I watch as he nods and the server steps forward to lay the check wallet on the table.

Okay. It's time.

"Liam... can I ask you something?"

He sticks a couple of bills in with the meal ticket. "What is it, darlin'?"

"When was the last time you spoke to your dad?" His hand stills in the process of reaching for his drink as his gaze slashes to mine.

"Excuse me?"

I bite my lip. I know he heard me. "I was just wondering how long it's been since you talked with your father."

He sips at his bourbon and then sets the glass down, holding me in his gaze.

"Twelve years."

Since his mother died. "So he's never tried to contact you?" If Walter Justice hasn't tried to talk to his son in all these years, maybe he doesn't deserve to now. But I'm doing this for Liam, not for Walter Justice.

The skin around his eyes tightens. "Well, now, darlin', I didn't say that."

I frown. So his dad has tried to connect with him? "Oh." I run my finger around the rim of my teacup. "You didn't want to talk to him?"

Liam's eyes narrow in irritation. "No, Caitlyn, I did not. Nor will I ever make contact with Walter Justice."

Holy hell! I take a deep breath under his glare. I knew this wouldn't be easy but... why won't he talk to me about his father. We've spoken more than once about my relationship with my parents.

"Did he remain down south?"

His quiet regard is unnerving because I can feel the suppressed anger radiate out—touching me. "I don't want to talk about this." The finality in his statement is clear.

Drop it for now Cait. I break eye contact.

When he stands, my eyes flash to him. He steps around the table, leans down placing a hand on the table and the other on my chair back, caging me in. My heart flutters. I look up into eyes as dark as midnight, my breath catching. I feel the need to pinch him, just to satisfy myself that he's real. Or kiss him. I look at his perfect lips, biting my own.

The hand he has resting on the table reaches up taking the cup from my fingers, setting it down before returning to rest on the table. He leans down until our eyes align.

"I want to lay you on this table and fuck you really hard," he growls. "And with this line of questioning, I'm not so sure it would be entirely for pleasure." I inhale with difficulty as my stomach does a free-fall. "Ready, darlin'?" I nod slightly, the thought crossing my mine, ready? Ready for him to lay me on the table and fuck me really hard? I swallow deeply.

He straightens, towering over me, his eyes holding mine as I sit looking up at him. When he reaches out, I lay my hand in his, his large hand engulfing mine. He pulls me gently to my feet.

The hairs stand on the back of my neck as he follows me across the restaurant. Once outside, he takes my arm leading me across the parking lot. We're quiet as he walks me around to the passenger side of the SUV and before opening the door for me, he pushes me against it, his hips holding me in place as his hands delve into my hair. He pulls out the pins I used to create my updo, and I gasp at the suddenness of his move as my hair comes tumbling down. Liam fists handfuls as his mouth comes crashing down on mine. His tongue sweeping the inside of my mouth setting off a sizzling response in my body.

I push against him, my hands working their way inside his suit jacket to pull his shirt up and out of his slacks, striving to make contact with his hot skin. His erection presses hard and insistent into my soft belly.

He tears his mouth from mine and my breathing is ragged. I do have the satisfaction that Liam's not breathing any easier.

"Let's go," he growls. He opens my door and I'm more than happy to sit since my legs are shaking. He leans in to buckle my seatbelt then turns his head to look me fully in the face. I'm unsure of his expression in the dim lighting, but I know he's irritated with me. Without a word, he shuts me in, and I watch as he strides around the front of the SUV.

There are cabs and limos already pulling through the porte-cochere as Liam drives through the gates of Justice House.

"It's busy for a Tuesday night," I say as we walk out of the garage. He doesn't comment and when I look up I see him watching the entrance of InJustice. Evidently the *special guests* Holly spoke of are still here and there's a party going on in honor of the occasion.

"Do you need to work tonight?" I ask softly, not sure I want him around all of those beautiful women when he's mad at me.

His gaze swings to mine. "Oh, I plan on working tonight, darlin'. I'm going to work you over until you won't be able to walk tomorrow."

My breath rushes out and when I stumble against him, his arm snakes around my waist. He holds the back door open for me, his expression impassive as if he didn't just totally set my body on fire with merely his words.

He scans his card to open the elevator doors. I still

don't have a passkey, but at the moment, I couldn't care less. The doors open and Liam doesn't wait for them to close. He's on me as soon as I step onto the elevator and turn.

He pulls me into his arms, his mouth coming down on mine. His hands run up and down my body, one hand pulling the top of my dress off my shoulder as the other slides beneath the hem of my skirt. His hand grips me between the legs and I gasp in his mouth.

He jerks his mouth from mine. "Your panties are soaked, darlin'." I feel my skin heat at his words. "Mmmm," he hums.

My hands, flat against his chest curl into the fabric of his shirt.

"Liam," I moan softly.

He walks me backward to the back wall, pressing in tightly against my body. His hands slide into my hair as he gives me a rough kiss, his tongue forcing its way in to quickly stroke against mine. He abruptly releases me and steps back, leaving me struggling for breath as I lean against the wall of the elevator.

"Take your dress off."

I hesitate looking out of the open elevator doors into the rotunda. When Liam grips my chin, I look up into his narrowed gaze.

"If you don't want me to rip it off your lovely body, you better be quick."

Holy hell.

I won't lie about how much he excites me when he's like this. I gather my long hair with shaking fingers and pull it over my shoulder, turning my back to him. A shiver runs down my spine as he lowers the zipper, his fingers sliding over my skin.

"You have a thing for getting me naked in this elevator."

He pushes my dress off my shoulders and it slides to the floor. His hot hands sliding back over my shoulders to the base of my neck. My eyes close as I relish the sensation of his hands on me.

"I reckon I have a thing for getting you naked anywhere, darlin'," he drawls. "It's one of my top priorities."

He grips my hair hanging over my shoulder as his mouth comes down on the opposite shoulder.

I moan softly.

"I've wanted to tear your clothes off you from the moment I saw you walking across the restaurant, coming to me."

His fingers unhook my bra, pushing it off my shoulders. His hand cups my breasts, squeezing firmly as I lean back against his chest.

"I want you to slowly push your panties off your hips" — his voice is deep and erotic — "all the way down your legs. Leave your heels on."

I hurry to do as bid.

"Slowly," he growls.

I push them down bending over the farther I go, down to my ankles.

"Stay right there." He runs his hand over my backside. I moan softly as his hand moves between my legs, and then back up over my bottom. "Stand up."

He steps up against my back and I breathe his incredible scent, deep into my lungs. His arm encircles my waist, his hand flattening against my belly.

"How do you feel?"

"Okay," I whisper.

"Good. Come with me, please."

Does he realize that I'd follow him anywhere?

I step out of the elevator right behind Liam after he scoops up my underwear.

"Did you tell Annie not to come out of her room at night?" I ask as he unlocks and opens the door, letting me precede him into the apartment.

"Yes, ma'am."

I sigh in feigned annoyance. Liam stops unexpectedly, reaching out to pull me close. His hands grip my bottom and he grinds his erection suggestively against my softness. I moan softly, clutching at his shoulders as he lowers his head, rubbing his nose against mine.

"You want an audience, darlin'?"

"What? No!" I choke.

He releases me and clutches my hand pulling me behind him down the hall. When we pass the hall that leads to the bedrooms I wonder with uncertainty exactly where he's taking me. I don't care if Annie's been warned or not about coming out into the apartment, I still feel vulnerable without clothes and I have misgivings about the odd excitement that settles in the pit of my stomach. What is he doing to me?

When he pulls me into the dining room, I frown with confusion. Liam turns to look at the table and then back at me with that sexy raised eyebrow of his. I look at the table and my eyes widen, slashing back quickly to his.

"Lean over the table, darlin'."

My breath escapes in a sharp sound.

He shrugs out of his jacket, letting it fall to the floor and then takes hold of my shoulders to physically turn me, pushing me closer to the table. He molds his body to mine as he pushes against me, bending us both over the table until my chest and belly rests on the cold wood surface with his front against my back.

"I couldn't fuck you like I wanted at the restaurant, but I will here, darlin'."

I lick my lips, suddenly having a hard time catching my breath. I hear him unbuckle his belt and then unzip his slacks.

I say a silent prayer that Annie doesn't come in here.

Liam stands behind me and gathers my hair to hold in one hand as the other runs over my bottom.

"I like your ass with a little color, sugar. I do believe I need to give you a proper spanking."

I squirm and his hold on my hair tightens almost painfully as he presses against my legs and bottom, pushing me hard against the table as panic sets in. He wouldn't, would he?

"Hold still," he demands.

"Please don't, Liam," I beg.

"Relax. Not tonight, sugar. Tonight I'm going to fuck you hard. You need to let me know if it becomes too hard. Understand?"

Just how hard is he going to fuck me?

I'm suddenly awash in sensation as my belly clenches in sexual need.

When he hits my bottom with a blistering smack, I cry out.

"Yes! Yes, I understand!"

Shit!

His foot slides in between my legs, pushing them apart. "Spread your legs and put your arms above your head, stretched across the table. Leave them there."

My breath is indrawn sharply when without warning he sinks two fingers into me.

"Fuck!" He pulls on my hair, pulling my head back. My hands ball into tight fists.

I don't register that his phone is ringing until Liam stills. I hold my breath. He usually just ignores it so I'm dismayed when he pulls his fingers from me and after a moment he answers.

"This better be good," he growls.

When he lets go of my hair and takes a step back, I stand slowly.

"Fuck," he hisses from between clenched teeth. His hand comes up to swipe his fingers through his hair.

I reach down and pick up his suit jacket, slipping it over my nakedness. When I look up, Liam raises his brow.

"No. I'll come down and take care of it."

He pockets his phone while holding my gaze. "I have to go downstairs and take care of something." He walks across the room to where I've retreated. "Are you okay?" His eyes search mine as if looking for his answer.

"Yes."

He sighs deeply. "I shouldn't be long but — don't wait up for me."

What? It's barely ten o'clock.

He pulls me into his arms, his hand sliding up my back, under my hair to cradle the back of my head. His mouth comes down in a soft kiss that ends far too quickly for me.

"I'll need this," he says as he releases me, pushing his jacket off my shoulders. I start to grip the lapels to stop him but decide, since he's possibly going to be around other naked women...

I step back and as he watches with a slight smile on his mouth, I turn my back to him.

"Cait—"

His words cut off as I let his jacket slide slowly off my shoulders. I hold onto the front lapels and let his jacket slide all the way down to my hips. Holding the jacket with one hand, I pull my hair over my shoulder so he has a clear view. I do a little shimmy that I know is provocative and look back over my shoulder. He's not smiling anymore. His eyes are intense as he watches me. I slowly turn, letting his jacket slide toward the floor, catching it at the last second. I swing it up over my shoulder and walk slowly, hip movement exaggerated, toward him. I push down the intense longing to cover myself with the thought of other women flaunting their assets at him, and toss my head so my hair slides behind me, giving him an unobstructed view.

Liam's eyes burn bright, the blue intensified and when I step close enough he reaches out to take his jacket, calmly laying it across the back of one of the dining room chairs. His calm façade is shattered though when his hand flashes out to yank me into his arms. He tangles his hand in my hair, pulling my head back as his mouth comes down on mine in an almost savage kiss.

His forcefulness ignites a fierce desire in me to make sure he thinks of me the whole time he's gone. I grip his erection with one hand as the other clings to his shirt while he ravages my mouth. We're both breathing hard when he breaks the kiss, pressing his forehead to mine.

"I want you waiting in bed—just as you are when I return. Do you understand?"

"Yes," I murmur, dazed from his kiss.

He grips my upper arms and steps back from me, his jaw clenched. "Damn it, Caitlyn."

"What?" I ask innocently.

"You know what." He shakes his head. "I have to go." He shrugs his jacket on. "I'll be back as soon as I can."

"I'll be waiting." I smile flirtatiously and he narrows his gaze.

"You fucking better be."

CHAPTER ELEVEN

I WAKE THE NEXT MORNING WITH the sound of Liam moving around the bedroom. I stretch, wincing at the slight soreness between my legs. I smile and smother a yawn. It didn't take Liam long to sort out the club business that took him from me the evening before and like the good little wife I am, I was waiting for him in bed. Naked.

He comes out of the closet tying his tie and looks up to see me watching him. His sensual mouth lifts at the corners.

"You need to sleep in darlin'."

I smile and stretch for his benefit. "I'm not sleepy. I'm hungry."

He laughs as he opens the dresser drawer and takes out his pocket paraphernalia.

"I have a business meeting this morning and I think you should do some shopping." He glances at me as he slides his watch on. "For you and the baby. But not for furniture, we'll shop for that together."

He walks over to the bed and leans down, his arm sliding under my back to lift me up to meet his lips. My arms immediately go around his neck, my hand sliding into his hair. His tongue strokes mine and I match his moves with equal fervor. His free hand covers my breast, his thumb stroking my nipple.

"Mmmm," I hum.

He breaks the kiss and I mewl in protest when he lets me go and stands.

"I have to go, darlin'. I can't be late."

My lips make a pout. "Are you sure I can't convince you to be a little late?"

"Like last night? And don't think I didn't know what you were doing," he says as he moves to pick up his suit jacket.

"It worked." I smile and bite my lip.

His eyes narrow. "Shopping. I mean it. I don't want you to wait until the last minute. You're going to need new clothes before long."

"Are you saying I'm getting fat?" I ask in mock indignation.

"I hope so."

"Yeah, right."

He smiles. "Okay, I'm out of here. Have a good day." He pulls his phone out of his pocket to check and I slide out of bed, bouncing across the room to him. He looks up and I think I catch him by surprise when I launch myself into his arms to give my husband a proper goodbye kiss.

I break the kiss and take a step back. "Have a nice day, dear."

He gives me the smile that makes me stupid, his thumb coming up to swipe across his bottom lip before his tongue comes out to lick and then he sucks his lip in.

Oh, damn. Now I really want him.

He laughs before striding from the room.

I'm coming out of the en suite after my shower when my phone rings. It's Liam. I grin. He's only been gone about 30 minutes.

"Did you forget something?"

His chuckle is low and sexy. "No. I thought I'd call and ask my wife out to lunch, since you're going to be out shopping anyway. I should be finished with my meeting and able to meet you around one. Unless that's too late for you."

"That will be perfect." I grin.

After he tells me where to meet him, we hang up. I can't stop grinning.

Annie's going to be gone the next few days, visiting her sister, so I rummage through the fridge not knowing what I want. I decide on a bowl of cereal and while I'm putting that away, Holly calls.

"How about a night out?"

"What do you have in mind?"

"I need a girls night out and thought maybe you, me, Emily and Julie could do a little bar hopping. Go for the dancing. Tansy might be able to make it too."

I laugh. "Ryan going out of town?"

"Yes, damn it!" She laughs then.

"It sounds fun. Count me in."

"Okay, I'll get back to you. It won't be until next week."

"Can't wait."

"What are you doing for lunch?"

"I have a lunch date with Liam."

"I thought he had a meeting?"

"I'm meeting him afterward."

"Well, have fun."

"Thanks."

Rivi Jacks

I don't leave the apartment until it's close to one. I don't have far to go and as I exit the cab, Liam stands and heads toward me. I notice other women turning to look at him.

"Is this okay, out here," he asks as he pulls back a chair for me and I sit.

"Yes, it's a perfect day to eat out."

Our waiter is instantly at our table to take our order.

"Where are your packages?" Liam asks as the waiter leaves.

"Um... I've mostly been window shopping." Liam's brow goes up. "I'll go back and buy what I've decided on... later. How was your meeting?"

He gives me a pensive look before answering. "It was satisfactory."

"You have a lot of meetings that take you away from Justice House."

"Too many," he says looking up as the waiter delivers our drinks.

I sit back enjoying the warm breeze that ruffles the umbrella overhead.

"I remember the first morning meeting I attended at the Justice. You were going to a business meeting that day too, and Barry asked if it had anything to do with toys," I say softly so no one can overhear me. Liam smiles. "I was wondering why you'd be going to a toy meeting." He laughs. "I just about choked when I realized what you were talking about."

He leans back in his chair, grinning.

Our waiter interrupts us again to deliver our club sandwiches and we eat in silence.

"You know —" His voice startles me and I look up.

"You're going to have to shop for maternity clothes eventually, Cait."

"I know that," I say softly, wiping my fingers on my napkin.

"Trust me, darlin', if you think I won't find you attractive when your belly is swollen with my child, you are very mistaken."

He thinks I'm worried about the fact that my body is going to change? I fight the smile that threatens. "How do you know?"

He gives me a long blink before a smile pulls at his lips. "Maybe because I fantasize about fucking you when you're large with my child."

I feel my face warm as I glance around to see if anyone has overheard him since the tables are quite close. Liam makes the matter worse by laughing out loud.

I shake my head at a complete loss of what to do with him.

"Sorry, darlin'. It's your fault. You should have thought of the consequences before you let yourself get in this predicament."

I sputter in my drink. I lower my glass and raise my eyebrow. I'm getting so good at perfecting his favorite facial expression.

"Are you seriously suggesting I became pregnant on purpose?"

He cocks his head, his mouth lifting at the corners in a slow, sexy, smile. "Well now, sweetheart, I reckon we both remember when I bred you."

My mouth drops open and he laughs.

I lift my chin. "As I recall it was your fault entirely. Your" — I feel my face grow so warm I need a fan — "lack of control and over exuberance."

He grunts. "As I remember, I explained that I was caught up in the moment." He shrugs. "And I did the right thing."

His words are a blatant reminder that our marriage is a sham.

I swallow against the sudden lump in my throat.

"Cait, I didn't mean it like that." He rakes his hand through his hair. "I—"

The ringing of his phone interrupts him. He glances down.

"Fuck," he mutters under his breath. "I have to take this." His gaze holds mine for a moment before he answers.

I know he didn't say what he did to be mean but I have a panicky feeling that is how he sees our marriage. That he did the right thing by marrying me. How many times did he say it, when he was trying to convince me that our marrying was the *right thing?*

The tone of Liam's voice draws my attention to his phone conversation. "I understand this may be your final offer but you need to understand I have no intention of coming down on the price." He pauses, regarding me steadily as he talks.

I slip on my sunglasses and reach for my bag, making a motion that I am going to go.

"Hey." He reaches out a hand and I step back.

"Excuse me a moment, Phillip."

"Thank you for the lovely lunch" I say as I back away.

"Cait, damn it. Stop." He stands.

"I need to go and... finish up and you need to take care of your business." I don't wait to hear what he says as I turn and hurry to the curb, and as luck would have it, a cab pulls right up. I give a quick look back and Liam is glaring at me, his face set in angry lines.

"Come with me," Julie begs.

"Julie, I'm not sure—"

"Pleeese. Paul won't be back in time and I have to put in an appearance because of work. We won't stay late, I promise."

I am tempted. One of her clients is having a cocktail party to celebrate signing with her company. It might do me good to get out and meet new people.

"What are you wearing?" she asks.

"Nothing suitable for a cocktail party."

"It's not formal. A dress?"

"Yeah, a sundress."

"Perfect! That's what I'll wear, we can accessorize. Being a mixer, it will be fine."

I laugh at her exuberance. "Okay. But you know I can't stay out late."

"Yes! Thank you!"

Liam doesn't answer his phone when I call to let him know what I'm doing. I leave a message telling him I'm with Julie.

The Hyatt in downtown Chicago is one of the city's finest hotels and I'm impressed as we enter the banquet room where the party is being held. I see several familiar faces since I've been to a couple of Julie's office party's.

I come to a standstill with an unwelcome thought. "Julie, is Myles Lea going to be here?" I cannot believe I didn't think of him earlier.

"No, thank goodness. He's on vacation and out of the country."

I visibly relax.

There's plenty of servers but Julie suggests we go to the bar so I can get something to drink other than the champagne being passed around.

Drinks in hand we mingle and head in the direction Julie needs to go to greet the host.

"You might as well meet Mr. Marler," she says.

I guess. A few months back it would have mattered, but since I am not longer working with the magazine, making connections is not really that important.

As we near the corner of the room where the host stands with some of Julie's co-workers Julie says, "Let's do this and then we can hit the buffet and leave."

I laugh and as we step closer, the smile slides right off my face.

Oh, no! This can't be.

I hesitate, ready to turn and flee but it's too late. I see the tall, slim man glance at us, his gaze going automatically to Julie only to flash right back to me, his mouth lifting in an amused smile.

"Mrs. Justice. How nice to see you. Liam didn't say anything about being here tonight."

I groan inwardly and I know my face heightens with color. I just want the floor to open up and swallow him whole. I see Julie looking at me from the corner of my eye.

He raises his brow in question while I stand there like a mute.

"He... he's not here." I stumble over my words.

"Oh?" He grins and then leans a little closer. "I assume he doesn't know you are?" he asks under his breath.

I swallow.

Oh shit.

"Well, I am very glad you're here. Welcome and I am sorry I have not had the opportunity to congratulate you. On two counts, I am told. "

He knows about the baby?

"Thank you," I whisper. I need to leave. This is so embarrassing. I hoped to never see this man again.

"I hope that you enjoyed your evening on the Heartbeat?"

"Very much. Thank you."

He smiles again and then he turns to Julie who's standing quietly beside me taking in our little encounter.

"Julie, it's good to see you."

"Thank you, Mr. Marler."

"I hope you ladies will excuse me, but one of my out of town guests has just arrived and I should greet him."

"Of course," Julie answers for both of us.

"Please enjoy yourselves." He bows his head slightly and then he's walking away from us. Julie turns to watch him but I just stand unmoving, shell shock I think.

She whirls back around and in unison she asks, "What was that?"

While I ask, "Why didn't you tell me?"

I close my eyes and place a hand on my forehead.

"He knows you?"

"Julie!" I hiss. "Why didn't you tell me *Mr. Marler* was the owner of the nightclub?"

She frowns, shakes her head in confusion and then her eyes suddenly widen and her mouth opens in a perfect O. "*The* nightclub?"

"Yes!" I hiss again.

"He's the guy who caught you and Liam naked in his office?" she whispers.

"Shhhhh!" I caution as a server walks by and I set my glass on his tray. "Liam wasn't naked." I whisper back.

Julie slaps her hand over her mouth, her eyes sparkling.

"Yeah, funny," I say wryly. "I need to get out of here." I'm suddenly very tired and I know Liam is going to be mad when he hears about me being here without him.

As I exit the elevator into the rotunda, I have every intention of going straight to bed. I feel positively drained. I should have come straight home instead of stopping with Julie for something to eat.

"Where the hell have you been?" Liam demands as he comes out of the living room into the hallway. Anger rolls off him as he stands glaring at me, his hands on his hips.

I stop in front of him. "Didn't you get my message? I called and told you I was with Julie."

"You didn't say one word about going to a party."

My eyebrows rise in surprise.

"You didn't think I'd find out, did you?" he sneers.

"What? No, I was going to tell you—"

"Don't play fucking games with me, Caitlyn." His eyes flash with anger. "That was hours ago."

I don't know what to say in the face of his anger.

"Where are your packages?" My breath catches in my throat. "You left me in an all fired hurry to finish up your shopping, so where are your shopping bags?"

"I—"

Shit.

I forgot about the bags, and I didn't plan for this confrontation, so I go on the defensive. "Stop trying to intimidate me."

Before I have a chance to walk past him, which is my intention, he takes a step forward and looms over me.

"I haven't begun to intimidate you, sweetheart." His voice is raspy and dangerously quiet.

What the hell is going on here. "Why are you so angry?"

His eyes narrow in warning. "I'm fucking angry because you're lying to me again."

Oh, no. This is not good. "Liam, I—"

"You what?" he snaps.

"I am not lying to you, and I'm tired of you accusing me of lying. I'm not going to discuss this further with you until you calm down."

"You are about to piss me off, darlin' and you really don't want to do that. Trust me."

I'm very certain of that.

He continues glaring down at me and then he says, "Come with me." He immediately turns on his heel and heads down the hall with angry strides.

There's no question of me keeping up as I follow him to his study. He leaves the door open and I stop on the threshold.

He turns and looks at me. "What are you doing?" he asks with a frown.

"Deciding if I'm going to listen to your accusations or not."

His eyes narrow dangerously.

I probably shouldn't poke the angry bear. And why is he so angry? I slowly cross the room.

Liam steps behind his desk opening a drawer to pull out a paper, laying it on the desktop.

"Come closer, Caitlyn. I want you to explain this to me."

I frown and move toward his desk. I pick up the paper, my eyes scanning the information on it.

Holy shit!

"How did you get this?" I whisper.

"I'm asking the questions here, not you. Now answer me."

"You have no right!"

He leans across the desk. "I have every right, you are my wife."

"I don't go through your personal things!" I'm pissed and humiliated that he has the ability to look at my bank account. How can he do that? "This is none of your concern, even if I am your wife. I know nothing about *your* business, what *you* do, or where *you* go."

We both glare at each other.

"Is that all you have to say?" he asks in a tightly controlled voice.

"No! I don't even have a key for the damn elevator!"

I think I catch him off guard. He stands to his full height, his piercing eyes looking at me intently.

"I'm your wife when it suits you." My voice is a little calmer now that I've had my say.

He cocks his head to the side. "Is that what you think, Caitlyn?" His voice is tight with anger.

My anger suddenly leaves me as I'm overcome with weariness. My arms go protectively around my waist and I look down.

There's a measure of silence between us before Liam

speaks, his voice somewhat cooler, but I can still hear the anger.

"I would like for you to explain what you did with the money in your account. There was a little over six thousand dollars in there just before we married and now there's less than five hundred." He walks around to lean against the front of his desk within arm's reach of me. "Now I know you haven't been buying anything on your shopping trips, so what have you done with the money, Caitlyn?"

I know I just need to tell him, but—it's my problem.

"Are you planning to leave me?" My head jerks up, my eyes opening wide in surprise. "Because if that is your plan, I might should warn you, darlin', that I have no intention of *ever* letting you go," he says in a hard voice.

"Liam, no—I—" Is that what he really thinks? That I'm planning to take his child from him? How can he think that when he knows that I'm in love with him. His words come back to me; trust is hard for him.

I take a deep breath. "I gave the money to my parents," I say softly, looking down once more. "When I worked, I sent them a little money each month. They never wanted me to and it wasn't much, but—they needed it to make ends meet. I sent them what I had in my account because I don't know when I'll be able to send them more." I take another deep breath. "I've been trying to figure out how to continue helping them, that's why I've decided to go back to work."

I can't tell him I also feel the need to put a little money back in case he decides— I shake myself mentally. I can't bear the thought of Liam no longer wanting me.

I look up. "I'm sorry I didn't tell you but it was my problem."

I'm standing between his outstretched legs, and he reaches to take hold of my arm, pulling me close. More than anything, I want to wrap my arms around him and just let him hold me, but I resist. I'm still angry that he invaded my privacy, but I'm too exhausted and don't have the energy to discuss it any further. Not right now.

When he lifts me into his arms, I push against his shoulders.

"No! Put me down, Liam."

He doesn't say a word as he carries me back to the bedroom and bending over the bed, he lays me down. He reaches for the coverlet and pulls it over me.

"Sleep, baby." He kisses my forehead before standing to his full height.

"Don't go," I plead, suddenly desperate to keep him near me.

He leans back down. "Shhh." He smooths the hair back from my forehead. "You need to rest and I have work to do." His voice holds a note I'm too tired to decipher.

He stands watching me, but I can't keep my eyes open any longer.

"Cait, when you finish with your breakfast, can you come back to my study?"

I look up at Liam standing in the kitchen doorway. He's dressed in old jeans and a faded black T-shirt that fits tight accentuating his biceps and perfect chest. I bite my lip thinking about what his sexy body can do to mine.

It was late when he came to bed last night and I woke

when he gathered me into his arms, his mouth finding mine in the dark. He was merciless with that mouth, reducing me to begging. He knows just how to play my body, bringing me to the tip of the precipice, holding me there until I am half crazed. He is completely adept at controlling my responses and ultimate orgasm as if he is indeed the master of my body.

"Cait, did you hear me?" His grin is cocky.

The arrogant ass probably thinks I'm daydreaming about him.

"Yes," I snap.

His grin widens and he turns, heading back to his study, whistling a catchy little tune.

I shake my head and carry my bowl over to load in the dishwasher.

Liam's left the door to his study open and when I stop in the doorway, he looks up from his computer. "Come in, darlin'."

He leans back in his chair and watches as I cross the room to one of the chairs placed near his desk. Bold eyes follow me as I sit. I have to remember that I'm still irritated at him.

"What did you want, Liam?" I'm proud my voice sounds unaffected by his nearness.

He gives me a wicked grin. "I want you to know I have made arrangements for your parents to receive monthly deposits to subsidize your father's disability payments."

My mouth drops open. "What?"

He stands and walks around to the front of his desk, leaning against it in his usual stance, long legs stretched out in front of him.

"Cait, you should have discussed this problem with me. I won't have you worrying over things you can't control. It's not good for you and it certainly isn't good for our child."

"Liam—I can't let you do this."

His eyebrows rise. "And why is that, darlin'?"

"Because—they're my parents, my responsibility. I can't ask you to—"

"You didn't ask me and that is the problem." His voice has an edge of anger to it now.

"But the expense—"

"Cait, trust me, I can afford it."

"That's not the point!"

"What is the point, darlin'?" He definitely sounds mad now. "They became my family when we married and I take care of my own. Now it's done and I don't want to hear any more argument about it," he says firmly, and I can tell by the tightening of his jawline that it's best to drop it. For now.

"I have something for you." He picks up a yellow manila envelope from his desk and hands it to me.

I frown slightly as I take it from him. "What's this?" When he doesn't say anything, I look up to find him watching me. I look inside and pull out a passkey.

"Mike said to tell you not to lose it."

I snort softly and reach back in the envelope to pull out a black credit card. I look up in surprise. Liam's gaze is intense, watching me. I look back at the card and rub my finger over my name embossed in plastic. How did he acquire a card so quickly? I tip the envelope to pour out the set of keys, and look up, confused.

"Keys to the Range Rover."

Holy hell!

"Liam—" I look up again. "Why are you doing this?" I whisper.

He reaches for me then, and I exhale sharply when he pulls me up flush against his body, his fingers gripping my chin, forcing me to look at him.

"You are my wife and you carry my child. I need no other reason." He leans down, his lips brushing softly over mine. "It would seem, darlin', that I am forever apologizing to you for one offense or another."

"Liam—"

"I am sorry, Cait." His eyes hold me in their thrall. "I apologize for my inexcusable neglect. Mike and I are the only ones with access to the apartment, not even Holly or Bryce have keys. I'm so used to the way we've always done things around here—" He frowns. "You should have said something."

I can't breathe as my eyes move over his face. As mad as I was at him, he's more than redeemed himself. His generosity toward my parents...

"You looking at me like that, darlin' is going to get you fucked."

I huff a little laugh and then bite my lip. I drop my gaze and then look up at him from under my lashes. "Why don't I get the keys to your Porsche?"

His eyebrows lift in surprise. Then he's laughing. "Too much car for you, sweetheart." I stick out my bottom lip as I smooth my hand over his finely muscled chest.

His cell phone rings and he pulls it from his pocket looking at the caller ID.

"I need to run downstairs for a bit."

"Okay, I'll go talk to Holly while you take care of business." I start to step away and the hand he has down the back of my shorts slides lower before he grips me harder. I squeak as his fingers dig in.

"We have one more thing to discuss, darlin'."

I look up into hooded eyes. I'll be damn if the man doesn't keep my head spinning with his constant change in temperament.

"There is the matter of you going to Jimbo's party last night."

Oh shit.

"I didn't know it was his party, Liam. Paul's out of town and Julie needed to attend because of work. She needed me to go with her."

"The next time you don't call to let me know *where* you are and that you are going to be late, you won't be able to sit down for a week. I give you my word on that, darlin'. And I think it a good idea for you to pass on any of Jimbo's parties. They're not your — style." His eyes hold mine. "Now if you're ready, we'll go downstairs together."

I decide to look for Holly in her office first. On my way, I run into Mike.

"Hi," I say softly, ready to walk on past, but he surprises me when he stops.

"Did Liam give you the passkey to the elevator?"

"Yes. I won't lose it," I hurry to add.

I think I see a small smile before he says, "Good." I watch as he walks away.

Holly is not in her office so I continue to the restaurant. I could text her but I want to see Tansy.

It's a busy spot at this time of day, preparing for the lunch crowd. Saturdays are normally hectic and Tansy and the new hostess are going over the reservations and

I don't want to disturb them. I decide to ask Leon if he's seen Holly.

"Ms. Cait, it's good to see you. What can I get for you?"

"Hi, Leon." I glance around the bar. There are several club members having drinks. "I'm looking for Holly. Do you have any idea where she might be?"

"She came through earlier and said she would be out at the greenhouse."

"Okay, thanks." Looking around again, I ask, "Are you planning on a busy night?"

"It looks that way if the reservation list is any sign. Can I get you something to drink? A juice or water?"

I hesitate before declining. I don't miss his little smile. As I head for the exit, I wonder if he knows about the baby. If he does, do others? Liam hasn't said anything about the staff or members knowing.

The green house is located in the far corner of the grounds past the garage near the spot where the original greenhouse to the estate once stood. Liam had it built when he first bought the mansion at Holly's suggestion and it's a reproduction of the original one, just on a smaller scale. It's gorgeous, looking as if it's right out of the Victorian age. The gardener's wife takes care of the plants and the Justice is filled with fresh flowers every day.

I don't find Holly or the gardener's wife, but when I turn to leave, Miranda is standing at the door with a malicious gleam in her eye.

"Miranda."

"*Mrs. Justice.*" She says in such a way as to be insulting.

I sigh, ignoring her attitude. "I'm looking for Holly."

"She's not here."

"Miranda, I don't know why we got off on the wrong foot—" Which is kind of a lie. We both want Liam.

"How did you do it?"

I shift, knowing I should just leave. "Do what?"

"How did you manage to trick Liam into marrying you?"

Seriously? When I don't answer she adds, "I know you've tricked him in some way. He was done with you. He told me so when he was fucking me after you left." She smiles with ill-concealed malice.

I feel as if a vise tightens around my heart. I actually feel ill at the thought of Liam and her together. My shock and subsequent pain does not escape her as she smiles smugly.

I need to get away from her. When I move to step around her, she decides to crush my heart a little further.

"You know, Caitlyn, if I were you, I wouldn't be so smug in that marriage of yours. I think you need to ask Liam why Melanie left. There was a lot of speculation about that, but—it's a huge secret that no one talks about now, but I know for a fact that Liam was the reason she left and there is something—" She shrugs and brushes her hair behind her shoulder.

She's one of those people who are so beautiful, the angels must have been present at her birth, but her soul is black as hell, and in that moment, I hate her.

I push her aside as I brush past, yanking open the door, and hurry outside to draw in huge gulps of air, desperate to clear the stench of her perfume from my memory. As the door swings shut I hear her satisfied laugh.

Liam slept with that bitch. A part of me knows she is not lying, but the other part holds onto the hope she is.

I cross the grounds, headed back to the mansion. I take the back elevator, not wanting to see anyone; I need some time alone before I see Liam. As I enter the bedroom, he steps out of the closet and stops in the process of checking his phone.

Oh.

"Cait." His eyes roam over me and I curse my traitorous body as it tightens in response to this man who has owned my body and heart from that very first day.

"Are you okay," he asks.

"No," I say softly.

"What's wrong?" His eyes watch me intently.

Oh, I shouldn't be asking him these questions, at least not until I have time to think over what Miranda said.

"Why did Melanie leave?"

There's no outward sign that my question disturbs him. "Why are you asking me about Mel?" He walks to the armoire.

I take a deep breath. "Did you have an affair with her?" I ask softly.

His hand stills as he reaches for something inside a drawer. His head slowly turns so he is looking more fully at me. I don't mistake the sudden anger I see in his eyes. He turns back to the armoire.

"I'm going to put this line of questioning down to the fact that you must be tired."

"I'm not tired, Liam. I'm just asking about the hostess who used to work here. Everyone hints around that she left so suddenly."

"Everyone, darlin'?" He turns to give me a raised eyebrow.

"Did she leave suddenly when your affair ended?"

He turns around, his eyes blazing. "If she did, it's no concern of yours. It was before you."

I look down. He's right, it was before me, but I still wonder at the big secret Miranda hinted about that concerned Melanie. And Liam.

I tuck my hair behind my ear. "Did... you sleep with Miranda when... I left?"

"What the fuck are you doing?" He's in an angry stance now, his legs spaced apart, body rigid. I can feel the essence of his anger fill the room, but I'm not going to let his anger intimidate me.

"I need to know." I gulp a deep breath. "Did you sleep with Miranda after she did everything in her power — and succeeded — in breaking us up?"

When he doesn't say anything, just glares at me, I have my answer. Miranda didn't lie. He takes a step toward me and I take a step back. He stops, his eyes narrowing.

"I don't know what's come over you" — his voice is angry — "but whatever happened with Miranda doesn't matter. You and I were broke up. Now enough!"

I look down at my linked fingers. He's made his point — but to think he'd have anything to do with that bitch — hurts. And if he thinks he can browbeat me into giving up on getting answers, then he is sadly mistaken and it just proves how little he knows of me. Plus, there is something I've wondered about that also needs to be answered. I've kept it pushed down, afraid of the answer. A little voice inside my head says, maybe I should leave unturned stones alone.

I clear my throat. "The day I went up to the second floor — the day I disturbed Miranda in what you called a 'scene,' — you told me that the person who interrupted a scene like that, was usually punished." I look up and take in the tightening of the skin around his eyes. "After you found out the truth — was Miranda punished for her deception?"

He doesn't say anything for several moments, and I know what the answer is. My gut tightens.

"Yes," he finally answers.

I clench my hands into fists. "Who carried out that punishment?"

I see a muscle in his jaw clench as I meet his intense gaze, my resolve unwavering.

"I did."

My chest tightens and I bite my lip, my hand going to my stomach as it churns.

"Cait, it was a punishment. Believe me, she did not enjoy it."

I swallow down the nausea.

"Did you?" I whisper. I hold my breath as my heart beats against my rib cage.

I have my answer — it's there in his eyes.

My hand goes to my mouth. I'm going to be sick.

"Cait!"

I push past him in my rush to the bathroom. I make it to the toilet just in time. Warm, strong hands pull my hair back as I heave the contents of my stomach.

I rest my hands against the toilet tank, my head hanging down. Liam reaches into one of the drawers for a hair tie, pulling my hair into a ponytail. He then wets a washcloth and hands it to me.

I can't seem to stop my shivering or the tightness in my chest that almost chokes me.

"Do I need to call the doctor?" His voice is anxious.

"No. This has nothing to do with the baby." I reach for a fresh washcloth, wet it and wash my face. "I need to lie down," I mutter, not able to make eye contact with him. I brush past him on my way, and under his watchful eye, I crawl onto the bed and curl up on my side, turned away from him.

I feel him watching me and the crazy thing is—I want him to lie down beside me, take me into his arms and just hold me.

It's quiet for several moments and I know he's left the room, so I'm surprised when the bed tilts and I feel Liam against my back before he gathers me into his arms.

Tears threaten as I fight the urge to turn in his arms.

We lie together like this with him just holding me close, his chin resting on the top of my head.

I'm not sure what will happen now, because I can't see Miranda again. The thought of Liam and her— She has her claws in him whether he realizes it or not. She shares a part of his life I have no place in. Right from the start of our relationship, everything he's done and said has led me to believe, this is enough—I am enough.

"I'm sorry, darlin'."

His soft words are almost my undoing. What is he apologizing for?

"Cait—" he sighs deeply "—I've had years of not explaining myself to anyone. I apologize for my short temper."

"Do you have feelings for her?"

"Fuck, no!"

"She's in love with you."

I feel his body stiffen. "Cait, I'm married to you. It doesn't matter if Miranda thinks she's in love with me."

If she thinks?

"Why do you listen to her?" he snaps.

"Because I know why you married me." My voice is barely above a whisper.

He suddenly turns me onto my back as he leans above me, frowning down at me.

"Why I married you? Well, darlin', why don't you tell me why you think I married you?" His voice holds a note of anger as his eyes burn into mine.

I take a deep breath. This needs saying. "You married me because I'm pregnant with your child. If there were no baby" —I close my eyes against the onslaught of his blazing gaze— "there would be no us." My words end on a whisper. I've known all along why our marriage came about but it hurts so much more saying the words out loud to him.

After several moments of silence, I open my eyes. He's watching me with an unfathomable expression.

He reaches out to stroke his thumb across my bottom lip, and my lips part involuntarily.

"If you think, for one moment" —his voice is low and husky— "that I would marry you for any other reason than that I wanted to—you are sadly mistaken." He holds my gaze and then he's off the bad and walking out of the room without a backward glance.

The delicious aroma of food wakes me and my stomach as it growls. Annie has been taking the weekends off leaving us to eat out or prepare our own meals and thank goodness, Liam is a good cook.

I enter the kitchen just as he turns to set placemats on the island counter top.

"Supper's ready," he says looking up.

I step to the fridge to pour a glass of juice, eyeing the

wine bottle that's chilling. I don't think I've ever needed a glass of wine more.

When I turn, Liam is watching me.

"I need to ask you something."

Even several feet away from him I can see his expression become guarded.

"Okay."

"What is your involvement in the club?"

His eyebrow lifts. "I own it."

"I know you own the Justice but what is your — what is your part in what goes on, on the second floor and in the — dungeon?"

He leans casually against the counter, his eyes narrowing.

"Why do you want to discuss what happens on the second floor? You've never shown an interest in it before."

I cross my arms over my chest. "You tell me very little about any of your business and I respect that I have no part in it." He suddenly frowns. "But I think since I'm your wife, I should know what your part is in all of it. You —" I take a deep breath " — said you were the one to carry out Miranda's punishment —"

"Cait —"

"What does that mean, Liam?" I hold his gaze, not backing down.

"So *now* you want to know my involvement in the BDSM community, darlin'?" He raises his eyebrow and I can't stop the flush that moves over me. He pushes away from the counter and steps around it as he slowly walks toward me.

I know how he uses my weakness for him, and I'm not going to have any part of his attempt to silence my questions or distract me with his touch. Because I know that's what he'll do as soon as he reaches me. I step back with each step forward he takes. He suddenly stops. I think I see a glint of humor in his eyes as he pulls out one of the kitchen chairs and sits at the table.

"Sit down, Caitlyn."

I do as bid but it's across the table from him.

He narrows his eyes, assessing my attitude, I think. I raise my chin, letting him know that I'm not backing down. And then he surprises me for the second time that day.

"I own this club—that is my involvement. I saw a chance at a lucrative business opportunity and the rest is history."

I frown. "But... you mean you don't..." *Shit!* I'm not comfortable with asking him these questions. I'm not comfortable with this whole scene. It was truly naïve of me to think I could just ignore this side of his business and that would make it less real.

"No. I have never lived the lifestyle. Have I participated—experimented? Yes." My eyes widen at his confession. "But my sole capacity is owner and manager of Justice House."

I take a deep breath. "But you're so... I mean, the way you are..."

His mouth lifts at one corner. "Controlling? Dominating?"

I give a sharp laugh and look down, shaking my head before looking back. "Yeah, you could say that."

He smiles then, giving me one of those full-blown smiles that knocks the breath out of me. I gape at him and then shake my head to right my senses.

"So, what happened with Miranda?"

"I am not talking to you about Miranda. You wouldn't understand."

"Why won't you talk about her? You said you didn't have feelings for her."

He frowns. "What? I meant her punishment. I'm not talking to you about that."

Oh. "Why?"

"Fuck, Cait!" He runs his hand through his hair. "Why would you want to know that shit?" He glares at me.

"Because you enjoyed it," I say softly.

He closes his eyes, and I look away.

He suddenly exhales loudly and my eyes flash back to meet his.

"Caitlyn... I did not" —his eyes steadily hold my gaze— "have sex with Miranda. Not since before you came to The Justice and certainly not while you were gone."

"What?" I whisper, my eyes searching his.

He slowly shakes his head.

"She lied?"

Liam leans back, resting against the chair, his head down. "Yes. She lied."

"Why would she—" *Because she's a bitch.*

She did her best from the start to make trouble for us. But some of the things she said to me were truer than I want to admit. I take a deep breath. "She said you were finished with me and as mad as you were—"

"I was not fucking finished with you!" He raises his head to glare at me. "I wanted to be— the thought of your betrayal—gutted me."

I shake my head. Sometimes it feels as if this will always be between us.

He sighs deeply. "But I couldn't. I couldn't get you out of my head." He runs his hand through his hair as he leans forward. "You were everywhere. Everywhere here in the apartment. In every room downstairs — in my bed."

I think I've stopped breathing with his revelation.

"For the first time — I didn't want to be here at Justice House. I spent as much time away as possible." His voice trails off and I recall Holly telling me that he wasn't going through the break-up unscathed.

"I thought I was going to go crazy," he says softly.

He looks over at me. "The roof? The reason I have the door locked? I destroyed it up there."

"What?"

"Not one of my finer moments."

"Liam." My voice is thick with emotion. I never imagined that while I was suffering with the prospect of never seeing him again — he was feeling the same anguish.

It's heartwrenching. All that hurt and now having to learn to trust each other again.

"I was just starting to get back into my routine when you came into my office that day."

I clearly recall the pain of his rejection. "You were so angry," I whisper.

He snorts softly. "I was ready to go postal on Holly's ass."

"I was afraid — you wouldn't let me tell you about the baby," I say softly.

He stands abruptly and walks around the table to look down at me. "You were really frightened and I played on that."

I wrap my arms around my middle, not comfortable with his admission.

He rubs his hand over his mouth and then bends down to grip my arms, pulling me up into his. His mouth comes down warm and firm covering mine as my hands flatten on his chest, my fingertips on his medallion. Releasing my mouth he presses his lips to my forehead. "I'm sorry I treated you like I did that day. The minute you went out that door—I was coming after you."

I lean back. "You were?"

He nods. "I caught you as you fainted." He runs his fingers through the length of my hair, brushing it back over my shoulder. His voice is low as his fervent gaze comes back to mine. "I wouldn't let anyone touch you until the paramedics came. You scared the hell out of me, darlin'."

My arms go around his neck and he wraps me in his embrace as we stand together. I can almost feel the trust and strength growing between us.

"Would you believe me if I said that I enjoyed punishing Miranda because of all she'd done to cause trouble for you?"

I lean back my eyes searching his and in that moment, I no longer care. I'm just letting Miranda cause strife in my life. Again. I nod my head. "I do. I believe you."

That frown line I find so endearing forms between his brows as his gaze moves over my face. He tucks my hair behind my ear and then pulls me close. Just before his mouth takes mine, he whispers against my lips, "Thank you."

CHAPTER TWELVE

I LEAVE THE APARTMENT BEFORE NOON the next day. It's Sunday and Julie and I have plans to take in a movie. When I tell Liam I'm leaving, he reminds me he won't be home until late. He and the guys made plans earlier in the week to attend some auto show.

I settle back into the cab and before I have a chance to call Holly, she calls me.

"Hey, I was just about to call you. Do you want to go to a movie with Julie and me?"

"Cait, I really need to talk to you."

"O-kay. Is everything all right?"

"Can you come by here first? Ryan just left."

"I'm on my way."

Holly and Ryan live in a beautiful condo in an old renovated mansion that has quite the history. In the 60s and 70s, it was the infamous residence of a notorious playboy who turned the stately home into a continuous party pad.

Holly answers the door before I can ring the bell.

"Thanks for coming by, I didn't want to talk to you about this at the Justice."

"No problem." *What the hell is going on?*

"Come on back. Would you like some herbal tea? Hot or cold?"

We sit at a table situated in the kitchen's breakfast nook.

"Holly you're starting to make me worry," I say as she hands me a glass of iced tea. "What's going on?"

"Liam fired Miranda."

My mouth drops open. "He what?"

"Yesterday, late afternoon." She sits down and props her elbows on the table leaning in. "I'm in my office with one of the club members and he just stops in the doorway and says, 'Come with me.' I don't think he even noticed I had someone in there with me."

"We headed straight for Lara's office and I ask him what's going on. He tells me to call Mike and have him come to Lara's office, STAT. If Mike's not available — get someone else from security to come. Then he says to call Bryce too.

"I tell him he's scaring me. You should have seen him. He was pissed." She reaches up to tuck wayward curls behind her ear. "He doesn't say anything other than he wants me to call Miranda and have her get her ass down to Lara's office.

"When I hesitate, wondering what the hell is going on, he yells, 'Fucking call her now!'"

I shift in my chair. When did this happen? He must have gone downstairs after I fell asleep.

"Mike and Bryce arrive and Liam doesn't say much more. He just paces the office. I tell him I don't know what is going on with Miranda but he needs to calm the hell down before he deals with her.

"When she arrives, he looks at her, and Cait, I swear he looked as if he wanted to choke her. And I think she knew why she was there. She was as nervous as old Nelly."

Yeah, it couldn't have been much of a surprise. She had to know I would ask Liam about everything she said to me.

"But she was definitely shocked when he told her she was fired. She started crying."

I can't help but feel a little guilty. But I won't lie, I'm glad she's gone.

"Liam told Lara to figure up Miranda's pay and cut her a check." Holly laughs. "Through it all Lara is just as calm as you please. She asks if there is any severance. Liam told her two months. Now, up to this point Miranda is crying and pawing at Liam —"

I sit up straight. She put her hands on Liam?

"When he said two months, the bitch came out. She threw a major fit, accusing Liam of leading her on. That really pissed him off. He just has this way about him when he gets really mad, you know?"

Oh, yes. I do.

"Anyway, Liam told Mike to escort Miranda off the premises. Then he looks at Miranda with that way he has and tells her she is not to come back to The Justice and if she knows what's good for her, she'd do her best to stay away from his other businesses."

He owns other businesses?

"It all happened within fifteen minutes. Mike drug Miranda away and Liam left." She gives me a smile. "I suppose he went back to you."

Miranda is gone.

Why didn't he tell me?

"I'm sorry, I hope this hasn't upset you," Holly says.

"No, it doesn't. I needed to know, thanks," I say absently as my thoughts buzz over what she's said.

"Well—" Her voice sounds apprehensive. "I feel bad, Cait." I look up to catch her worried expression. "When you and Liam were broke up, Miranda was hanging on him like a choke vine and I suspected..."

Oh.

"Please don't hate me. It was so hard not to tell you but—"

"Holly." I reach for her hand. "You don't need to explain. I understand that it put you in a hard place."

"Yes!" Her voice holds relief. "It ate at me not to tell you but I knew it would cause you unnecessary pain."

"No, it's fine." It is now that I know Liam didn't sleep with Miranda.

"He was a mess, Cait. He loves you so much."

I bite my lip.

"Oh, Cait!" She laughs. "He is as much in love with you as you are with him."

I hope so.

"We'd better get a move on if we're going to pick up Julie and make it to the movie on time," I say as I stand.

If anyone would ask me what the movie was about, I'd have to say I don't have a clue. I sit through the entire movie, blindly staring at the screen, laughing when Holly and Julie laugh. My thoughts are wrapped up in my husband as I replay our whole, very brief relationship.

Liam's possessiveness, his asking me to move in with him, telling me I'd managed to wrap myself around his heart. His cold, hard anger over my working for the magazine and his subsequent decision to cut me out of his life. My heart lurches at that memory.

Our marriage was the most puzzling to me. His insistence that we marry. I was so angry at him, the way he threatened me to get his way. And yet, he could have married me in a civil ceremony but instead he arranged to have the service in a beautiful old church, putting aforethought into the arrangements, making our rushed wedding—a special, memorable day.

I recall the enchanted evening he planned for me, watching the fireworks from Navy Pier out on the lake. His unbelievable generosity toward my parents. Caring for them because he considers them his family.

I grin in the darkened theater. Liam wants this marriage, he's in it for the long haul—he wants me.

The Justice is quiet as the cab pulls up to the back door entrance. It always seems too quiet, almost eerily so, when the mansion is silent like this. I enter the elevator with my new passkey, grateful I don't have to hunt someone in security down to let me into my own home. I smile at that thought. My home. With Liam.

The doors open and it's as if my thoughts have conjured him up and he stands waiting for me. Neither of us says a word as he steps up close. He reaches to cup the side of my face, his eyes holding mine. As he leans down toward me, his other hand comes up to cup the other side of my face. He holds me firmly as his lips cover mine.

The kiss starts slow as Liam tastes and nibbles at my lips. It's soon not enough for me as my desire is unleashed and I strain against him. My hands frantically pull at his shirt with every intention of touching bare skin.

His kiss intensifies, sucking the very breath from me as his tongue strokes mine. I rake my nails across his chest, down his stomach going for the button on his jeans as he grips my bottom pulling me closer, grinding his erection against me.

When he lifts me, I wrap my legs around his waist while his tongue continues to plunder my mouth. I moan and Liam steps off the elevator and the next thing I know, I'm slammed up against the wall.

His shirt buttons are a barrier to what I want and I grip the fabric, pulling until buttons pop, hitting the tiled floor.

"How do you feel, darlin'?" His words murmur against my lips.

"Really good." My voice sounds husky as I lean in to nip at the skin stretched tautly over his collarbone.

"Do you feel well enough for me to fuck you?"

I raise my head, dazed eyes meeting his smoky blue. I know he's referring to me being sick last night. "Liam, I'm not sick."

I watch as the heat I see in his eyes intensifies.

"That's all I need to hear, sugar."

My stomach does a free fall as his hand comes between us, releasing his erection from his pants. He holds me against the wall with his body as his hands rip my thong from me, tossing it aside as his hot gaze holds mine.

Holy hell. I'm panting as my arms come up around his shoulders, my mouth finding his neck. I moan and lick, pulling at the chain to his medallion with my teeth. My fingers reach up to thread through his hair as I writhe against his body, desperate for him to be inside me.

He doesn't make me wait long as he positions the head of his erection and thrusts up into me. I groan loudly from the glorious feeling of his large shaft stretching, filling me to capacity. The feeling is exquisite.

He yanks the strap of my dress off my shoulder, pulling my dress and strapless bra down to bare my breast, latching onto the nipple as he continues to thrust in and out of me.

It's fast, hard and the most satisfying quickie we've ever had. He thrusts at an unrelenting pace, and I hold on for dear life as my body explodes with what seems to be the never-ending orgasm, my inner muscles pulsating around his rigid length.

A growl starts low in his chest as the depth and force of his thrusts intensify. He squeezes my bottom pushing me harder into the wall. With one last unbelievably deep thrust, he finds his release.

He continues holding me against the wall as we both struggle for breath.

"Fuck," he groans, leaning in to bite my shoulder, I gasp then shiver against him as he runs his nose up the side of my neck, taking the lobe of my ear between his teeth.

"Mmm..." I hum as my hands move over the muscles on his back. At some point, he's lost his shirt and his skin has a light sheen of sweat.

He lifts his head meeting my gaze.

"Hi," I say softly.

One corner of his mouth lifts. "Hi, darlin'."

"Miss me?"

"What gave me away?" He lets me slide down his body until my feet hit the floor.

I unlock my hands from around his neck, smoothing my dress back in place.

"Are you hungry?" he asks as he steps back. He doesn't bother with zipping his jeans and I can't take my eyes from him as he picks up his shirt. He holds it up inspecting the damage.

"Darlin', this was my favorite shirt."

"I'm sorry!"

He looks up, a twinkle in his eye. "I may have to take retribution out on you."

My stomach clenches at his words and I close my eyes. I am truly a mess when it comes to him. I open my eyes to find him holding my torn thong up in front of my face, quickly drawing it back as I reach to take it from him. When I reach for it again, he holds it at arm's length above his head. I huff a breath and cross my arms.

He brings the scrap of material up to his nose, inhaling deeply, his eyes smiling down at me.

"Sugar, *that* is the sweetest scent."

My face suffices with heat as my hand shoots out to grab my thong from him.

"I didn't think guys had favorite shirts. Isn't that a girlie trait?" I ask with irritation.

"Girlie?" I look up to catch his grin. He certainly is in a good mood. "Are you questioning my masculinity, darlin'?"

I snort softly and then I can't hold back my giggle. The thought of Liam as anything other than all man is amusing. "I wouldn't dare."

Liam laughs, pulling me into his arms, giving me a swift kiss. My breath catches at how much I love this man. He releases me to step back and slip into his shirt.

"I asked you a question, Caitlyn."

I meet his gaze and raised eyebrow.

Holy hell. What was the question?

"Are you hungry?"

Oh. "No. I'm full of popcorn."

"Good." He studies me for a moment, his eyes moving over me before he meets my gaze. There's a gleam in his. "Come with me."

"Okay," I say, breathless again at the thought of what that gleam means.

He holds out his hand and it seems so symbolic of him leading me astray. I lay my hand in his. He leads me back into the elevator.

"Where are we going?"

His answering smile makes me a little nervous, and I watch as he touches the number one on the control panel.

"Why are we going — ?"

He grips my arm and pulls me to his side. "I have a surprise."

When I smile weakly up at him, he laughs as the doors open.

It's pitch black beyond the lit security of the elevator.

"Stay right here."

"Okay." I absolutely will. However, once he disappears into the darkness, I wish I'd gone with him.

I don't like this.

"Liam?"

I definitely don't like this.

When I see a glow of lights, somewhere deep in the bowels of the room, suddenly come on, I take a deep, relieved breath. As I watch, the lights get brighter as more turn on. The light sconces right outside the elevator light up with their flickering imitation of real flames. I now see that directly across from the elevator doors is a large desk and chair.

Liam is back, holding out his hand. "Did you think I'd left you?"

I look around nervously. "Or something dragged your body away."

He laughs out loud as he pulls me close. His skin is warm against my hands. It's chilly down here.

"Don't worry, I won't let anything drag me away from you, darlin'."

I look up, my heart giving a hard lurch against my ribcage.

"Let's go." He grasps my hand and stops when I draw back. He looks down, his eyebrow inching up. "Is there a problem, darlin'?"

Why are we down here?

"It depends" — my voice is soft and breathy — "what your surprise is."

He just looks at me with one of his unreadable expressions.

"No," I say softly, in answer to his question.

He leads me out of the elevator into a corridor. The ceiling, floor, and walls are stone. I hurry to keep up with his long strides as he leads me down the short passageway, and when we reach the end there is an iron gate. It's probably seven feet high and wide enough to securely block entry any farther. It's open now though and Liam leads me into a large cavern type room.

"Stay right here," he says, releasing my arm. I barely hear him.

I saw this place on one of the monitors weeks before when I was in the security office. My eyes immediately find the large cross that holds precedence in the room. I vividly remember the young woman tied to that cross as a man used a whip on her.

My eyes release that nightmare as I take in the other items that occupy the chamber.

Holy Shit.

Situated around the room are tables, positioned against the stonewalls, with straps attached. From my web search, when I first started working here, I recognize more than one spanking bench. There is even another smaller wooden cross on the opposite side of the room. Near it is a contraption that resembles a stockade. This one appears to accommodate more than one person at a time.

Lighting provided by dim, flickering wall sconces placed at intervals along the walls, adds to the medieval ambiance of the basement of Justice House.

When Liam takes hold of my arm again, it startles me.

"Relax, Caitlyn."

"Why are we down here?" My free arm wraps around my waist.

He looks slightly amused. "You don't wish to see your entire home?"

What? I search his eyes, wondering if he's teasing.

"I told you, darlin', I have a surprise for you." I look away. "Let's go."

As he leads me across the cavernous room I notice the back wall has a section where there are racks attached to the stonewall. The racks hold floggers, whips, paddles, belts, and canes.

A rolling, fluttery feeling in the pit of my stomach has nothing to do with the baby and everything to do with my sudden urge to run.

As Liam leads me down another passageway, we pass

what looks to be doorways set into the stonewalls. There is nothing but eerie blackness beyond.

He suddenly pulls me to a stop.

"Close your eyes."

"What?" I glance around and then up to catch Liam looking at me and even in the dim lighting, I see his dark eyes take on a hard glint.

"Perhaps you'd prefer a blindfold, darlin'?" His eyes narrow in warning.

"No!" I immediately close my eyes.

This is freaking scary!

I feel Liam's warm breath against my ear before I hear his softly spoken words. "Why so nervous darlin'?"

I lick my lips. "It's — scary down here."

After what seems like too long and he still hasn't said anything else, I shift uncomfortably from on foot to the other.

"Open your eyes, Cait."

I frown before slowly doing as bid. He's watching me closely, his expression pensive.

"I'm not trying to scare you, darlin'. I have something I want to show you."

With that said, he leads me up to the darkened door-way at the end of the long passageway. Reaching up, he opens a panel and suddenly a blue glow seeps up to us. Within the next second, another set of lights come on illuminating stone steps leading down. The blue glow is at the end.

Liam grins down at me. "I had this added on about five years ago."

What *this* is, I have no idea, but I'm not scared anymore. I'm not exactly sure why, maybe it's the excitement I feel radiating off him.

He takes my arm again. "Hold onto the railing."

When we reach the bottom of the steps there is a rock wall in front of us and we can go either side of it. The temp has changed, it seems warmer and the blue glow beckons as Liam leads me to our left.

Do I smell — my breath catches. Stretched out in front of us is water. A pool. Blue lights illuminate the water from beneath the surface and the water vapor coming off the pool gives the area a mystical ambiance. It's a round room with rock walls and a wide rock pathway circling all the way around the pool area.

The ceiling has stars! Small LED lighting but in the dark height of the ceiling, they look like tiny twinkling stars.

"Oh, Liam — it's beautiful," I whisper.

He pulls me close. "I thought you might enjoy a swim, darlin'." I look up at him. "I've wanted to bring you down here for some time now."

"Thank you."

He smiles as he reaches for the hem of my dress. "Arms up."

When I hesitate, looking around, Liam huffs a laugh, the sound echoing off the rock walls.

"There is no one but us down here."

I raise my arms and after my dress goes, he turns me to unhook my bra.

"I should have had you put your hair up," he murmurs.

I shrug as I slip out of my sandals. I turn to see him slipping out of his jeans, his medallion reflecting the faux starlight, his erection springing free.

I take a deep breath and look up to see his knowing smirk.

He holds my arm again as we step down the two wide steps into the shallow end of the pool. The water is deliciously warm and I sigh appreciatively. Liam releases my arm and I glide through the water toward the opposite side of the pool. The water feels wonderful, like silk against my skin.

I turn to watch as Liam skims the surface of the water with powerful strokes. When he reaches me, he grabs my hips. I squeal just before we both go under.

When I hit the surface, I splash water in his grinning face, then I'm cutting through the water but I'm no match for him as he quickly catches up, pulling me under again. I come up laughing and head for the shallow end. A strong, warm hand grabs my ankle, pulling me back under. I let him pull me close before pushing off against his stomach, breaking away.

We both surface, treading water. I laugh, splashing him again before ducking under the water. He treads water as I go deep and then come up behind him to grab his shoulders and I have time to wrap a leg around his waist before he takes me under. This time he doesn't let me go, holding onto my leg as we surface again.

His deep laugh echoes off the walls as I giggle, trying to clear my face of hair and water. He pulls me around and up close as he treads water, holding us both afloat. He feels so good, skin on skin, his erection pressing hard against my belly. I wrap my legs around his waist once again as he cradles my bottom.

His smiling eyes meet mine as he rubs his chest against my nipples causing them to harden even more as I bite my lip.

"I've never been skinny dipping before," I announce.

His mouth lifts at one corner. "Why does that not surprise me?"

"What?"

"There's a lot of things you've never done." He brings his mouth close to my ear. "I was right all those weeks ago —" he nips my earlobe " — about you being innocent." His warm breath sends shivers over my skin.

"I'm not innocent," I insist.

He leans back, looking down at me. "No, you are not. Not anymore," he says his eyebrow lifting as he grins wickedly.

He's moved us into shallow water so he is now standing. My arms are still wrapped around his neck, my legs around his waist with the water up around our shoulders. His hand comes up to cup the back of my head.

"And there are many more wicked things I want to acquaint you with, my dear."

Oh. His mouth takes mine, his kiss hot and his tongue insistent as it delves between my lips. The hand, supporting my bottom, slides between my legs. I lift up in surprise, moaning in his mouth as his fingers stroke me. Deepening the kiss, both hands come around to grip my bottom as he presses his shaft against me, maneuvering me up and down against his rock hard erection.

I pull my mouth from his with a loud gasp and then a tortured moan as my clit is massaged in a most delicious way. When my head falls back in wild abandon, Liam's hot mouth comes down on my shoulder.

"Liam!" I cry as the nerve endings in my clit sizzle with the beginnings of an orgasm. He lifts and angles my body for better stimulation as I continue to slide up and down his thick, hard length. I grip his shoulders and my body begins to undulate, keeping pace with his rhythm, absorbing every sensation.

"That's it, darlin', feel how hard I am. This is what you fucking do to me." I moan again as the pressure begins to build deep inside of me. "Imagine my cock, deep inside of you, sugar, fucking you deep" —his voice is hoarse and raspy— "hard, making you scream my name." His fingers slide between my spread cheeks, his thumb pushing deep into my anal passage.

My legs stiffen and my back bows as my orgasm peaks, sending me over the edge into the precipice. Liam leans his head down to take a turgid nipple between his teeth as I grip his arms, grinding against the base of his throbbing shaft, half out of my mind with the exquisite pleasure that washes over me.

"Fuck!" Liam pulls me close against his chest, his thumb flexing inside of me.

I cry out, his action seeming to prolong my orgasm.

"Fuck, Cait! I'll never tire of watching you come, darlin'." He pulls his thumb from me, his arm encircling my waist, holding me tight. My head rests against this shoulder with my eyes closed. I'm exhausted, a combination of exerting swim play and a mind blowing orgasm.

"I can't move," I murmur as I snuggle against him. His erection still hard as steel against my hip.

Liam walks through the water and I shiver as the air brushes against my sensitized skin. He carries me out of the pool and I soon discover the walkway around the pool only looks like rock. It's some type of cushiony material as Liam lets me down to stand. My legs shake slightly and he keeps his hold on me as he looks around.

"Can you stand while I find some towels?"

"Yes." I watch the play of muscles as he walks away. He has a gorgeous body. I smile. And he's my husband.

He's soon back, a towel wrapped around his waist, with a stack of towels and a spa robe.

"Here you go, darlin'." He wraps me in the large robe, rolling up the sleeves as I snuggle into the warmth of the terry cloth. "Are you okay?" His eyes move over me and then he's using a towel to squeeze the water out of my hair.

"I'm fine. We don't have to go yet, do we?"

His mouth lifts at one corner. "Not if you want to stay, baby."

He spreads out the towels and I lie down, using a wad of towels for a pillow. I stare up at the twinkling lights as Liam stands looking down at me before coming down to lie beside me, facing me.

"It's so beautiful." I turn to look at him. "Thank you for bringing me down here. I had fun." I smile.

He reaches for a damp lock of hair. "Why do you assume the fun is over, darlin'?" He twists my hair around his finger.

"I always have fun with you, Liam," I whisper.

His eyes lift to meet mine. They glow with an intense, blue heat. His gaze moves over my face.

"Cait—" he reaches for my hand and brings it to his mouth, his lips brushing over my knuckles.

I roll to my side, reaching to touch the soft scruff on his chin. My fingertips brush up his jawline, and I flatten my hand against the side of his face.

"There's something I need to tell you, darlin'."

He sounds too serious. I lick my suddenly dry lips. "Okay."

His brow furrows and I want to smooth the frown away.

"I need to tell you about Miranda."

I shake my head. "Liam —"

He puts a finger against my lips "Please, hear me out."

I don't want to hear about Miranda. I've been praying I'd never have to hear her name again.

"I fired Miranda."

I nod slightly. "I know. Holly told me."

"Did she now?" He tucks the strand of hair he's been twisting behind my ear.

"She said you were really upset."

"It was time for her to go. She'd caused enough damage."

"So —" I know I should feel bad about her losing her job but I just feel immense relief that she's gone. "No more Miranda." I try but the smile slips out.

Liam shakes his head, smiling wryly and then leans over to kiss me on the forehead, his lips lingering. "Let's go back upstairs, you're starting to shiver."

We stand and I reach down for the towels.

"Leave them."

"Can we come back again?"

"Absolutely. I still want to fuck you in that pool, sugar." He looks down, grins wolfishly, and then laughs when I blush.

Liam drops his towel, picking up his jeans as I gather up my things.

"Wear the robe, darlin', you'll stay warmer."

I ogle him as he steps into his pants, pulling them up over his hips, his eyes on me the whole time. When he finishes he crooks his finger. I take the few steps to stand in front of him. We just stand there looking at each other, Liam's eyes intense. He reaches out, his hand cupping the side of my neck.

"Are you okay?"

I grin. "Yes." I'm better than okay knowing I'll never have to deal with Miranda again.

He gives me a quick kiss. "Let's go."

As we walk back to the elevator, he surprises me again. This day has been full of revelations.

"There's something I've been meaning to talk to you about."

I look up at him.

"I've been thinking about turning Justice House into a health club only."

"You have?" My voice is heavy with shock.

"A sex club is no place to raise children, and I have no intention of leaving my home."

Children?

Liam throws together one of his famous pasta dishes as I sit on the kitchen counter where he placed me when we first came into the room. I watch him as he moves around the kitchen, occasionally brushing up against me to deliver a quick kiss or a tickle. I love the kisses but squeal with the tickles.

We're quiet as we eat. We're both hungry.

"Can I ask you something?"

He takes a sip of wine, his eyes looking at me speculatively, before answering. "Yes."

His cellphone rings and he holds up a finger, frowning as he looks at the screen and then shakes his head in irritation.

"What?" he says curtly when he answers.

I smile as I take another bite of pasta, certain it's Bryce.

"Not tonight, Cait's tired. I took her downstairs." He looks at me and winks.

Those two are definitely little boys.

"None of your business, fucker."

I stand for a re-fill of juice and feel Liam's eyes follow me as I cross the kitchen. We had a very quick, but pleasurable shower when we first came back upstairs and I'm dressed in a faded pair of very short cut-off jean shorts with a tank top and no underwear as directed by my bossy husband.

I take my time on the way to the fridge and then go for maximum effect, bending and stretching as I reach into the refrigerator, all the while feeling Liam's eyes on me.

"Now's a hell of a time for him to decide on that," he says irritably. As I sit back down, he lifts his eyebrow. "I'll get it ready." He lays his phone on the table.

"What's wrong?"

"I have to work for a while tonight. Bryce and I have a meeting tomorrow that I need to do some additional prep work for."

I bring my napkin up and dab at my mouth. "Emily came by to visit with me last week."

"Did she?" He forks a bite of pasta.

Why do I think he already knows this? "She told me about the baby she and Bryce lost." Liam looks up. "I feel so bad for them."

"It was hard on them both." He reaches for his glass of wine. "It still is," he murmurs.

"I wish you had told me."

He gives me a steady look, his eyebrow lifting. "I didn't want you to worry, darlin'."

"That's what Emily said," I say softly.

He smiles before forking in another bite of salad.

I stand to carry my plate over to the sink.

"That's all you're going to eat?" I look back to see his frown.

"I'm full."

While I rinse my plate, I feel the back of my neck tingle as Liam comes to stand behind me. When I turn around he steps close, and I tip my head back, looking up the long length of Liam Justice.

I bite my lip as he stares down at me. His lips lift in a slow, sensuous smile before he braces his hands against the counter on either side of me. My pulse rate accelerates, and I feel the energy that sparks between us like static against my skin.

"I'm going to work for a couple of hours in my study, darlin' and when I finish, I'm going to come find you—" He leans down, bringing his mouth close.

"Yes?" I say breathlessly, his eyes making me forget to breathe.

"—and tie you to the bed before I fuck you into next week." I make a small choked sound just before his mouth claims mine. When I raise my arms up to place around his neck, he grips my wrists and pulls them to the small of my back, leaning in to press me against the counter, effectively immobilizing me. When he lifts his head, my eyes are slow to open, my senses drugged. I breathe in deeply, absorbing his scent.

He laughs softly, making sure I'm steady before releasing me.

Liam's hired a company to come in to handle the re-decorating of the nursery and while he's working, I decide to look over paint and material samples they provided for us. I need to make some decisions on what colors we want. I spread the fabric swatches and paint chips before me on the bed. Liam told me to come up with my three favorite and then we'd pick from those.

After about an hour, I start craving something sweet. I decide to go downstairs and check out the cooler in the restaurant's kitchen, hoping to find chocolate covered strawberries. I decide not to disturb Liam since I won't be gone long.

I take the elevator that lets me out at the back of the mansion, close to the kitchen. They leave the main hall lights on at night, dimmed but on, which is good because it always seems so eerie when the great house is silent, void of members and staff. There is one ceiling light left on in the kitchen and I make my way across the room to the cooler, flipping the light switch before stepping inside. I say a silent thank you to Chef George when I find a tray of the delectable strawberry treats on a shelf inside. I grab a saucer and put a few of the strawberries on it. And then a few more. In case Liam has a sweet tooth too. I smile recalling how he likes to play with his strawberries. On me.

I close up and head back to the elevator. As I reach the main hallway and turn the corner, I hear something back down the hall in the opposite direction. I stop to listen and just as I decide that I'm imagining things, I hear it again.

I stand still, indecisive of what to do. Maybe someone left a window open or— I turn to walk back down the hall. I'm not really afraid, the alarm system is on, Liam's not far away, and there is a security guard patrolling the grounds.

As I pass the dining room, I stand in the doorway letting my eyes adjust to the low light of the recessed nightlights set in the wall at intervals around the room. While I stand there almost ready to head back to the elevator, I hear the faint, repetitive clunk of what sounds like something rolling down stairs.

Maybe there really was a window left open and a cat has gotten in, or a bird has managed to find its way into the house through one of the fireplaces. Or — a bat!

Shit.

I head for the front entryway, cautiously crossing the foyer not noticing anything out of the norm. I look up the shadowed staircase and take the four steps to the wide landing where the stairs turn to continue up to the second floor.

The hairs on the back of my neck suddenly stand on end as my eyes strain to see what — or who — is up there in the dark. I'm being watched. I can feel it and I no longer believe it to be an animal.

I'm frozen in place with a mixture of indecision and fear. I'm down here alone. Liam has no idea that I'm even out of the apartment. No one knows I'm here except for the person I sense watching me. If they come out of the shadows, the really frightening thing is I'm not sure if I can run fast enough to make it to the elevator in time.

I slowly take a step back. My heart feels as if it will beat right up out of my chest. One more step, and I know I see movement. I'm certain of it.

"Who's there?" My voice sounds scared. Not good.

Someone grabs my arm and I scream.

"Cait!"

"Mike!" My free hand comes up to my chest, over my heart as my other hand clutches the plate of strawberries with half of them now on the steps. "There's someone upstairs!"

His gaze flashes to the top of the darkened staircase as he fishes his phone out. "Lockdown," he says into the receiver.

Without taking his eyes from above, he says, "We'll wait right here, understand?"

"Yes." It doesn't escape my notice that he sounds just like Liam.

He puts the phone back to his ear and without him saying, I know he's calling Liam. "Get down here. I'm with Cait at the main staircase. We have an intruder on the second floor." He pauses. "I am. Hurry."

He pockets his phone, his eyes never wavering from his view of the landing above.

"What did you see?" he asks softly.

"Nothing at first. I just knew someone was watching me and then I saw movement—I'm certain—in the shadows."

I hear noises coming from the back of the house, but it's not until Liam calls out to me that Mike starts on up the stairs.

I'm grateful that he stayed with me, but I hate that it may have allowed someone to get away.

"Be careful," I call up to him as Liam and one of the security guards rush into the entryway.

Liam paces back and forth from the entryway to the living room of the apartment as he talks to the security company on the phone. I know he's angry. Mike and the security guard, who came in with Liam, conducted a search of the upstairs but found no one or any sign of a break-in.

Bryce and a couple more of the security team are searching the grounds but so far have found nothing.

"Mike just called. He and Bryce are on their way up," Liam says. He stands in the doorway and regards me steadily before crossing the room. He stops in front of where I sit on the couch. Reaching down, he pulls me to my feet, his arms encircling me in his warmth.

"Are you okay?"

I smile, snuggling against him. He keeps asking me that.

"I am."

He leans back so he can make eye contact, his eyes moving over my face. It's gratifying, his concern. When he came around that corner downstairs earlier, the relief when he saw me was apparent.

"What I'd like to know, darlin'" —he releases me and steps over to his corner bar— "is why the fuck you went down there without letting me know?" He walks back to hand me a glass of water, his eyebrow raises as he waits for my answer.

I take a long drink of the cool water. He's mad.

"I didn't want to disturb you. I was only going down to the kitchen."

His eyes narrow. "Then why were you in that part of the house?"

Oh, shit.

I know I'm about to be in serious trouble.

I lick my lips. "I heard a noise," I say softly.

And sure enough, Liam's eyes suddenly shoot daggers at me.

"So" —his voice has that quiet, lethal tone to it—

"instead of coming back up here, so I could handle the situation or simply going to security, you decided to investigate a strange noise by yourself."

I already know it was stupid of me. I realized the dangerous situation I put myself in when I was standing on the stairway, but it's our freakin' home!

Liam's eyes have taken on a blazing intensity.

"What did you see?" he grits out from between clenched teeth.

I know he's only angry because I put myself in danger and he's feeling at a loss to control what's happening within Justice House.

"Nothing but movement in the shadows."

He frowns. "You didn't actually see anyone?" He glares at me.

"I heard a noise—"

"What did it sound like?" he asks curtly.

I take a deep breath. "I—maybe something hard. I heard what sounded like something rolling, falling down each step."

He stares at me, not saying anything for several moments and I shift in nervousness.

"So you saw nothing but shadows. Maybe you just spooked yourself."

The tone of his words makes me feel—a fool. And pissed. I feel my face warm with an angry flush.

"I don't think so," Mike says from the doorway where he and Bryce stand.

How long have they been standing there? My face grows even warmer as I realize they witnessed Liam's anger and his sarcastic attitude with me.

I raise my chin, summoning up my own attitude,

catching Liam's frown before he turns his attention to Mike.

"Why do you think that?" he demands.

"Because…" Mike holds out his closed hand and when he opens it, one of those large shooter marbles and a regular sized marble sit in his palm. "I found these in the foyer."

"Someone lost their marbles," Bryce quips.

I snort softly.

I've been listening as Mike and Bryce inform Liam of what their search of the house and grounds have found — or not found. How can a person find their way in and out of the mansion undetected? If it weren't for the fact that Mike found the marbles, I would be thinking that I had "spooked myself" as Liam so eloquently put it. The thought someone rolled not one but two marbles down the stairs, to lure me to the main staircase —

I shudder.

When I look back to where the others sit across the room, I find Liam watching me.

"I think it best" —he says as he stands, his gaze holding mine— "that we continue this conversation in my study. It's getting late and we have several things we need to discuss."

I stand and look toward Mike and Bryce. "Good night."

"Good night, Cait," Bryce says and Mike gives me a quick nod.

At the doorway, I stop and turn back. "Mike, thank you for being there tonight." It truly does scare me what might have happened if he hadn't been.

Again, he gives me a slight nod. I start to turn but hesitate. "And thank you for not making me feel foolish." I cast Liam a quick glare.

"You're very welcome, Cait." I think I see amusement in Mike's expression when I look back at him. I turn then and walk out. As I turn the corner, I hear Bryce.

"Oh, man, I think you're in trouble."

I quickly change and brush my teeth. I'm exhausted after the long day's emotional rollercoaster. I step into the bedroom to find Liam sitting on the end of the bed waiting for me. My anger has left me, having made my point with what I said to Mike, but I'm just too tired to discuss any of it with him.

"I'm tired, Liam. Goodnight."

I walk past to turn the bed down and he stands, reaching out to catch my hand, pulling me to a stop.

"I was an ass."

"Yes, you were." I look up at him.

He pulls me close, enveloping me in his heady scent and warmth. "The thought of someone breaking into our home, and I can't seem to stop them — is fucking pissing me off."

My arms slide around to his back. "I know that's why you were mad and said what you did."

"Yeah, well..." He leans back gripping my arms, pushing me away from his body, glaring down at me. "If you ever put yourself in that kind of danger again, I will blister your ass and you won't be able to sit down for a week. Do I make myself clear on this?"

I look up into fierce blue eyes and swallow convulsively.

"Answer me!" he snaps.

"Yes."

He pulls me back close, one hand cradling the back of my head as the other squeezes me so tight I can barely breathe. "The thought of something happening to you —"

"I'm sorry, Liam. It scared me too. I realized how stupid I was in what I did."

He leans back enough to kiss my forehead as his hand slides under my hair, his fingers curling around the side of my neck. He uses his thumb under my chin to tilt my face up. For an instant, before he hides it, I see an unfamiliar expression on his face but it's quickly forgotten as he leans down, his mouth taking possession of mine.

CHAPTER THIRTEEN

LIAM DIDN'T COME TO BED until long after I did and already this morning he's downstairs, busy with the security people who have come in to do another assessment of yesterday's late night activities.

I've just finished drying off from the shower, and I'm slipping into my underwear when Liam is suddenly standing in the bathroom doorway. His eyes rake over me and I slowly turn to look at my reflection in the mirror, my hand going to the very slight swell of my belly.

Our eyes meet in the mirror and then he's stepping up against my back, his arm sliding around my waist. He flattens his hand over my belly, holding my eyes in the mirror with his enigmatic gaze. His mouth slowly lifts at one corner.

"I do believe, darlin' that you're developing a bit of a baby bump." The tone of his voice makes his words sensual.

I lean back against him. "Do you like baby bumps?"

His warm breath tickles my ear. "I like your baby bump." He runs his nose down the length of my neck as he inhales deeply. "I think I've related to you often enough that the thought of you, your belly swollen with my child is immensely — pleasing to me."

I whimper when he bites down on the spot where shoulder and neck meet. My head lolls against his chest and I close my eyes, breathing in deeply. Hands, that are exceedingly warm, slide down into the cups of my bra, pinching my hard nipples, elongating them farther.

He pushes me against the vanity and my eyes meet his again in the mirror. I moan softly at the erotic site of his hands in my bra.

"I really want to fuck you right now," he growls. "But I have someone waiting on me downstairs." One hand comes out of my bra to slide down my stomach and with practiced ease, slides right inside my panties. I jump at the shock of electricity that his fingers produce when they meet my clit. "I just came up to tell you I won't be home for supper." He takes my earlobe, biting down, as his wicked fingers slide between my folds.

"Liam!" I gasp.

"Yes?" he whispers as he presses two fingers into me. I unconsciously take a step to widen my stance, enabling him to thrust his fingers deep into my core. He moves them widely apart inside of me and my grip tightens on the edge of the counter top.

His fingers still. "I need to go, darlin'."

My eyes open wide and I see his smile as he pulls his fingers from me. I want to stomp my foot. He loves doing this to me.

"Go then." I try to make my voice sound normal, unaffected.

He grins and steps back, popping his fingers into his mouth. I don't think I'll ever get used to him doing that.

He laughs as he steps to the door where he stops. "We're going baby and mommy shopping next week."

I look agape at him. "Mommy shopping?"

"Maternity clothes, darlin'." He continues to the bedroom. "I need to change and get back downstairs."

Liam's going shopping with me? For maternity clothes? I smile at my reflection.

While I brush my teeth, my cell rings. "Do you mind answering that?" I call out. "It's probably Julie. I called her before my shower and left her a message to call me." The phone continues ringing and I hurry to rinse when Liam appears in the doorway.

"Liam, why —"

My voice tapers off when I see his face, dark with anger. He steps up to tower over me in a menacing way.

"What —"

"Why the fuck is Walter Justice calling you!" His tone drips with acid.

Oh, no!

I look at the phone he still holds, shaking my head in disbelief. Walter said he'd be calling, but I never dreamed he'd call this early in the morning.

"Don't pretend you don't know," he seethes with anger.

"I —"

"I am not going to ask you again, Caitlyn!"

"Give me a chance and I'll tell you," I snap. I also want to tell him to stop trying to intimidate me the way he is, hanging over me, threateningly.

His eyes narrow. "Get dressed. Now." He turns on his heel and walks out of the bathroom.

I follow him out but he's already left the room. I dress quickly, pulling on a pair of jeans that feel a little too snug around the waist and a T-shirt. I find him in the living room, pacing.

When he sees me, he comes to a stop.

"He called me the day Emily came over."

He frowns. "You shouldn't have answered the phone," he says sharply.

"I answered without looking to see who it was."

"How did he get your number?"

I shake my head. "I have no idea."

"If he calls again — do not — answer. I don't want you talking to him. Am I making myself clear?" He glares at me again.

I huff a soft breath. "Perfectly."

He walks over to where he's laid his suit jacket.

"Don't you want to know why he called me?"

His eyes slash back to mine. "No — I do not." He shrugs into his jacket as he holds my gaze. "I mean it, Cait. Do not answer. Do not talk to him if he calls."

What the hell?

My arms cross over my chest. There's so much more going on here.

Liam steps close, his eyes demanding my acquiescence.

"Liam, why won't you talk to me about your father? There has to be a way for you two to mend your relationship."

"I don't talk to anyone about my father, and I don't *want* to mend our relationship. Now drop it," he snaps.

He leans down to give me a quick kiss. "I won't be home until late."

He stops in the doorway and looks back. "Don't forget the decorators are coming to take measurements of the nursery this afternoon."

I spend the rest of the morning at Paul and Julie's. Julie and I go out for an early lunch and then I head back to Justice House. I can't stop thinking about Liam's anger toward his father. I wonder if there will ever be a reconciliation between the two.

"Cait."

Mike catches me just as I summon the elevator.

"The decorator and her assistant arrived early. I took them up and Annie was available to answer any questions they had."

"They came early?" I sigh, a little irritated that I missed them. Why did they even bother to make an appointment?

"They've come and gone," he informs me.

"Okay. Thanks."

He nods and then heads back toward the security office.

Since I now have a free afternoon, I decide to pay Holly a visit.

"Hey, Cait. I thought you had an appointment with the decorator."

"Me too. They came while I was gone. I have my afternoon free and I thought I'd stop by to see how things are going."

"Have a seat," she says and then gets up to close her office door. "What the hell is going on?" she asks as she sits back down.

"I don't know but Liam is extra testy."

"Yeah, he was a royal pain in the ass this morning. It scared me for you when I heard what happened last night."

"Me too, Holly. Did the guys say anything to you about where they think the intruder is getting in or who it might be?"

She shakes her head. "They're usually pretty upfront with me, and as far as I can tell, they don't have a clue.

I do know that Liam's having security inspect the floors every couple of hours at night now."

"Bryce and Mike were talking to him last night after the search and they think someone is hacking into the security system and cameras, regardless of what the security company says."

She stands again. "Well I hope they figure it out soon or Liam is going to explode. Want to come with me? I need to talk to Leon."

The dining room is nearly empty but the bar has several members enjoying an after lunch drink. Leon greets us and then he and Holly head to the back to go over a couple of reports. I'm sitting at the end of the bar, enjoying a glass of juice when I look up to see Leon's cousin, Tony.

"Tony. How are you?" I ask when he gets closer to where I'm sitting. The look he gives me is not overly friendly and he just nods.

I frown, watching as he virtually ignores me. I try to recall if I've done something to offend him.

"Have I offended you in some way?"

He looks up from putting away clean glasses. "I'm surprise you want to talk to me."

I frown again. "Why would you say that?"

He turns toward me. "You much too busy playing wife to owner," he says in his halting English. "No time for people who were friends." He gives me a deadpan stare.

My mouth drops open, but before I can say anything to his ridiculous comment, he's headed to the other side of the bar to wait on a couple of female members. He says something that causes the two young women to look my way and they both laugh. Tony glances over his shoulder and smirks, then turns his attention back to the women. The three of them laugh out loud and I know whatever they find so amusing, it's about me.

I immediately want to confront Tony, but I can't do that here. I don't know what his problem is since we were never close friends, but even so, I certainly never snubbed him as he insinuated because I was too busy being the boss's wife.

Holly soon joins me and we grab Tansy as her shift ends, and spend the rest of the afternoon in Holly's office catching up.

The evening is filled with things to keep me busy, my mind occupied as Annie, and I make lists of items we need to prepare the apartment for a baby.

I miss Liam. I'm so used to him being with me in the evenings. I had hoped he might call and I think about texting him when I hear nothing, but I decide he must be busy.

I know I've been asleep for a while when he comes in. He swears when he stumbles into the dresser.

"Are you okay?" I look over at the bedside clock. It's three in the morning!

"Go back to sleep, darlin'."

I sit up and hug my raised knees. "Are you just getting home?" Somethings not right here.

He turns off the bathroom light and when he reaches the bed, I hear him unzip and then the rustle of clothing as he undresses. When he's finished, he plops down on the side of the bed.

"Sorry I woke you, darlin'."

I frown. "It's okay."

I lie back down and he flips back the covers before sliding in. He pulls me close and I snuggle against his warmth. He smells so good. Like Liam and... I raise my head.

"Have you been drinking?"

He laughs. "Yeah." His large hand comes up and he pushes my head back down onto his chest. "Go back to sleep, Cait."

Yeah, right!

Who's he been drinking with? He was mad when he left earlier.

"I know how that mind of yours works, sweetheart." His voice rumbles in my ear. And *I* know now why he sounds different. His drawl is more pronounced. "I was out drinking with Bryce and Mike. No women," he mumbles.

"Well—I can rest easy now."

He doesn't respond as he's already asleep, breathing slow and deep. I pull the covers up over him and settle back against his side, my head on his shoulder. My fingers find his medallion and I lie awake, my fingertips rubbing over it.

Liam is still asleep when I slip out of bed the next morning, heading for the shower. It looks as if he's skipping his morning exercise routine. And the morning meeting. If Bryce and Mike are in the same condition, who's minding the store? Maybe they cancel when they get shit faced the night before.

In the time I've known Liam, I've never seen him drink too much. Did his father calling play a part in his overindulgence?

I'm just rinsing the conditioner from my hair when the shower door opens and Liam steps in. My eyes slide over his broad chest, down his hard muscled stomach to his erection just begging for attention.

I bite my lip as he moves to stand under the spray of water, leaning his head back, letting the water cascade over his body.

"Good morning," I say cheerily and probably a little too loud for someone with a hangover. "How are you feeling this morning?" I ask equally as loud, enunciating each word.

He lifts his head from the spray of water. One eye opens to look down at me.

Oh, shit.

Maybe I shouldn't be poking the bear. I sidle toward the door.

"I'm finished," I say in a normal tone. "I'll just let you—"

I squeak when his hand flashes out, latching onto my arm, pulling me back against his hard frame. His erection settles against my belly as if it belongs there.

My eyes are wide as I watch him. "How do you feel?" I whisper, licking my lips nervously.

He leans his head close to mine. "Like fucking you into next week, sugar," he growls.

I give a little, "Eeeep" as he turns until I'm under the spray of water.

"Grab the safety bar," he orders with a growl. "Hold on and don't let go, Caitlyn." As soon as I do, he delivers a stinging slap to my derriere.

I jump and yelp at the same time. One hand unconsciously letting go of the safety bar to move around as protection for my backside.

"I said—don't let go." He pushes against me and I grip the bar, my body already quivering with need.

He places his hands over mine and presses even closer into my body, sliding my hands up on the vertical bar while at the same time, his foot pushes between mine and I take a step, widening my stance.

"Spread your legs," he growls.

He certainly is growly this morning, but I do as bid, my stomach muscles clenching in an almost painful way. He positions his erection between my legs at my entrance, nudging against me. I bite my lip to still my panting.

When his hands cup my breasts, pinching my nipples between his fingers, my back arches.

"Liam," I moan as I wiggle my body in a way that I hope will get him inside me quicker.

With one powerful thrust, he surges up into me, lifting me onto the tips of my toes. The breath is knocked right out of my lungs, and I moan when my muscles tighten around his thickness as he fills me.

"Fuck!" he growls.

"Ahhh!" I cry softly when he eases back slowly and then thrusts upward again.

"You want to be loud, darlin?" His voice is raspy against my ear. "Let me hear you scream."

It takes me a moment to decipher what he's saying and then I shake my head. I know Annie is up, moving around the apartment at this time of the morning.

"It wasn't a request."

"Liam—"

He withdraws again and then thrusts me right off the tips of my toes. I cry out with the intensity of the sensation as his shaft hits that spot deep inside of me.

"Please," I cry.

He withdraws and thrusts deep again, my cry muffled

as I press my mouth against my arm. He sets up a punishing pace that pulls a long moan from between my lips when I feel the tell-tell tightening of every muscle in my body, signaling my impending orgasm.

When his hand strokes down the column of my spine, my body shudders. The sudden quivering that vibrates in my core makes me mewl in reaction to the unbelievable pleasure that courses through me. And then his finger pushes into my backside as he thrusts deep, impaling me on his shaft and finger at the same time.

I scream his name.

I am mortified as I come to my senses.

Liam's arm is around my waist, holding me upright as his other arm braces against the shower wall. We're both breathing hard with labored breaths.

"You scream so beautifully when you come, darlin'." He grunts when I elbow his stomach.

"You—"

He snorts softly and releases me, reaching for the body wash.

I don't say another word as I open the shower door and step out on shaky legs. I'm pissed, knowing Annie heard me screaming. He wasn't content with me screaming his name. He used his knowledge of my body and his fingers until I couldn't stop screaming.

I wrap my hair in a towel as I hear the water turn off. I slip on my robe and exit the en suite as he steps out of the shower.

I have plans to meet Paul for lunch and decide that I'll leave a little early so I can go by a children's shop that is located close to Query Magazine. I've walked by it any number of times and always notice the cute baby items that are on display in the window.

I step into the closet and pick out a yellow sundress. When I walk back into the bedroom, Liam is coming out of the en suite.

"What are you doing, darlin'?" He steps in front of me.

"I'm going to dry my hair."

"Not yet you're not. I'm not finished with you."

Before his words register, he scoops me up into his arms, striding for the bed.

"Liam!" I push against his chest. "I'm mad at you, put me down!"

He tosses me somewhat gently onto the bed. The towel flies off my head, my hair comes loose to tangle around me, and Liam's on top of me in one swift move, pinning my arms above my head in one hand. I struggle beneath him, to little effect as his legs press against mine to push them wide.

I pull against his hold on my wrists, and work at dislodging his legs. I try to arch my back but it's all futile. He's too heavy and infuriating as he calmly smiles down at me.

He smooths the hair back from my face. "Why are you struggling, sugar? You know you want me to fuck you again."

"I don't. Let me go!"

He leans in to kiss me and I turn my head. The fingers of his free hand grip my chin, turning my face back to him. I glare into his eyes and I'm further incensed when he laughs.

"You'd better behave or I'll open the bedroom door before I make you scream when you come this time."

"I fucking won't!"

His eyes widen in surprise. "I reckon I'm just going to have to fill that dirty mouth of yours, sugar."

My eyes narrow and I shake my head wildly. Damn, him. I'm pissed and he's just trying to piss me off further.

"Shall I tie you spread open and fuck you senseless? You know I'll have you screaming the house down in no time."

I glare at him.

He chuckles and changes his position to lie beside me, still holding my wrists above my head as he flings one of his well-muscled legs over mine. He smooths the hair off my face again.

"You are so fucking beautiful." My breath catches as his eyes hold mine. "And you belong to me." I swallow at the carnal need I see in those eyes.

His hand moves down to loosen the belt of my robe.

"No!" I glance toward the door and then back. "Don't please!" I beg, knowing it's a lost cause. He will do what he wants.

"Why are you doing this?" I ask softly.

His eyebrow lifts. "You started it, darlin'."

"What?" I frown.

"You thought it amusing that I might be hung over."

"No, I didn't. I promise, Liam." I bite my lip to stop my smile.

He shakes his head as he looks down at me. His hand parts my robe exposing my breasts, then pushes it apart the rest of the way down my body. His head dips, and my breath catches as his hot mouth sucks on an extended nipple.

"Ahhh!" My back arches sharply. My nipples are

extremely sensitive, unbelievably so when he sucks on them.

His eyes gleam up at me before he moves to the opposite nipple, sucking forcefully. I grit my teeth as an electrical current travels straight to my clit. I can't stop my hoarse cry.

He continues to suck as his fingers pull and pinch the opposite nipple. He has me writhing and ready in a matter of seconds.

"Please — let go of my hands." He does and my fingers immediately slide into his hair.

My breasts swell, my core tightens, and my back arches again as he gives one last hard suck to each nipple before his mouth travels down over my stomach. His tongue licks around my belly button and I can't stop the giggle that erupts from between my lips. It's the oddest place to be ticklish.

Liam glances up, his eyes smiling and then he rains kisses around my belly, almost reverently. When he lifts his head the look of intent I see on his face — in his eyes, causes my breath to catch. His head dips and he buries his nose at the apex of my thighs, inhaling deeply.

I moan and my back arches from the influx of sensation as my hands grip the sheets beneath me.

"That's it, darlin', I want to hear you."

My head moves back and forth on the bed. Why is he doing this? I don't want Annie to hear us.

Liam rises up over me, his hands braced on the bed on either side of my shoulders.

"Look at me, sugar." My eyes immediately meet his.

He leans down, taking my mouth in a soft kiss as his legs push mine wide. He enters me slowly and I groan as his large shaft fills and stretches my sensitized tissues.

"Fuck, you feel good," he growls as he arches his hips.

I cry out. He feels incredibly deep. He slowly pulls out and then pushes back in, agonizingly slow. My legs come up to wrap around his hips as my hands grip his arms.

He fucks me with slow, deep thrusts that soon have me begging and pleading for more.

"Liam—" My head thrashes back and forth. I can't take it any longer. My insides tighten and I feel the quivering begin to radiate out.

He stops, holding himself perfectly still as he looks down, his eyes gazing deeply into mine. The intensity of emotion I see there stills my breath.

"You are mine. You belong to me. Don't ever make the mistake of forgetting that, darlin'." His voice holds a warning note.

I frown and then reach up, my fingers touching the side of his face. "Why would I do that, Liam?" My eyes search his looking for the reason behind his words. Here is a man who is afraid to lose what he loves. He keeps his love reserved for the people who have been in his life for years. The ones he feels secure in loving.

It hits me with a jolt that Liam is afraid of his feelings for me.

"I love you, Liam." I raise my head as my hand moves to the back of his head. My kiss is soft as my tongue slips between his lips to stroke his. He suddenly groans, returning my kiss with increased vigor.

He begins to thrust again, still excruciatingly slow, hitting that sweet spot that elicits the most delectable sensations—

I tear my mouth from his. "Please, Liam!" I need

more. My arms and legs wrap around him as I try to pull him closer, encouraging him to go faster. Harder. Deeper.

He's leaning on his forearms, his hands on either side of my head, holding my gaze.

Oh, please! My head tips back as everything tightens and the surge of energy that passes between us ignites our passion. Liam's thrusts become faster and when he abruptly pulls out of me, I almost scream with my anguish. But he quickly flips me over raising my hips, and before I have a chance to right myself, he plunges into my wet channel.

My choked gasp and subsequent moan is guttural sounding.

"So fucking tight."

His words, his hard, deep thrusts are all I need as my orgasm builds and then wrings cry after cry from me as it twists my insides and ravages my senses. His continued thrusts lift me completely off my knees as he maintains a firm grip on my hips. He soon cries out my name as he empties himself into me.

After our second shower, I hurry to dress. I really feel the need to nap after our strenuous morning sexcapades, but I cancelled the last lunch date Paul and I had planned. Liam steps into the en suite as I finish applying the little bit of makeup I use. Our eyes meet in the mirror and his mouth lifts in a wickedly, satisfied way.

"I wouldn't be so smug if I were you."

His brows go up in feigned surprise.

I snort softly. The man has no embarrassment gene. "Annie likely heard you too."

He steps up close behind me. "The difference being, darlin' — I don't care if she heard me." He runs his finger down the side of my neck before meeting my eyes again in the mirror and giving me a cocky wink. He's chuckling as he walks out.

I stick my tongue out at his back.

I enter the kitchen where Liam sits on one of the stools at the island counter, talking on his phone. A cup of coffee sits on the counter in front of him; the aroma causes me to look longingly at the pot on the cabinet.

Oh, how I miss coffee. I rub my stomach and smile. *You're already putting the squeeze on your mama, little one.*

I look back at Liam to find him intently watching me.

I glance around, suddenly realizing there's no Annie. She's usually in the kitchen, offering to cook us breakfast. Come to think of it, I didn't hear her as I usually do while she moves about the apartment doing her morning routine. I frown.

Where's Annie? I mouth at Liam.

"Excuse me one moment," he says before tilting the receiver away from his mouth. "She called me late last night before she left. Her sister's ill."

I nod and then inhale sharply.

He knew she wasn't here this morning to hear us, but he led me to believe —

I glare at him, but he's already back on his phone conversation, a hint of a smile on his lips.

I pick up the potholder lying on the counter and throw it at him. His hand shoots up and he catches it in mid-air, not even looking my way.

I lock my packages in the Range Rover and then head down the sidewalk to the coffee shop across from Query

Magazine where Paul and I are meeting for lunch. As I reach for the door, I hear a man say my name, recognizing his voice before I turn around.

I know he's probably in his early fifties, but he looks much older. He's tall like his son, but he's very thin. His hair is mostly gray and his complexion is sallow. He doesn't look well.

"Mr. Justice, I'm sorry but I can't talk to you." I don't want to be rude to him but—

"Liam found out I called."

I look away and take a deep breath before looking back. "Yes."

"Please, can you sit for a moment?" He gestures to one of the outside patio tables.

"Liam—doesn't want me to talk to you," I say softly, hoping my words don't unnecessarily hurt him.

His shoulders visibly droop and his head hangs for a moment before he looks back up.

"I understand."

Damn it.

"I tried to talk to him but—" My voice trails off.

"I know he can never forgive me."

I'm not sure what to say to him.

He looks up with a haunted expression. "I haven't forgiven myself either. I was mean to his mother and him."

I look around again as people pass close by us on the sidewalk. I glance back.

"I'd like to help you reconcile with Liam, I really would but—I can't right now."

He gives me a weak smile. "I understand but you see it's urgent that I talk to him." I frown. "I need to explain some things and I need to warn him."

"Warn him?" I'm alarmed at his words. Why does he need to warn Liam?

"Yes, he needs to know what happened. If you could convince him—"

"I can't. Not at this point." Maybe never at the rate I'm going. Hard to talk it through with Liam when he has such volatile emotions concerning his father. "I'm sorry, Mr. Justice, maybe at a later date—"

"No! It will be too late by then. I have to tell him now."

He's beginning to scare me and I'm relieved to see Paul crossing the street.

"My friend is here for lunch and I need to go. I'm sorry."

His disappointment is palpable and I can't help but feel sorry for him. Maybe after the baby is born and Liam experiences the bond of fatherhood he will be able to forgive his father.

He looks so forlorn. "Are you going to be okay?"

"Yes," he says absently and steps away. "Thank you."

I watch him walk down the sidewalk as Paul reaches me.

"Who's that?" he asks as we watch the man with the stooped, defeated posture walk farther away from us.

"Liam's father."

On the drive home, my cell rings. I smile seeing that it's Liam on the cars display.

"Hi."

"Where are you?"

"Headed home and I'm still mad at you," I say with a smile.

He laughs. "Fun times."

"Ha! For you."

"You didn't enjoy it, darlin'?" The low, sexy timbre of his voice causes a delicious shiver to run down my back. I bite my lip and hear him laugh softly. "I'm headed for the airport, something's come up."

"Is everything okay?"

"Yes, don't worry. I'll be home tomorrow around noon and I'll tell you about it then."

I frown. "Okay."

"Annie called and she'll be home this evening."

"Okay."

I hear him inhale deeply. "You're certainly acquiescent, darlin'. If I were there, I'd see what else you might be agreeable to."

When I laugh, I sound breathless. "Maybe."

"So you're not mad at me any longer?"

I smile "Don't push your luck."

He laughs and I know it's going to be a long and lonely night without him.

"I probably won't be able to sleep without you snoring beside me."

"I don't snore!" I answer his teasing, my voice indignant. "Do I?"

He's laughing as he says, "Okay, I have to go. You take care of you and our son."

Son?

"After your snoring remark, I'm having a girl on purpose."

There's silence on the line and my hands tighten on the steering wheel. *Oh.* Wouldn't he like a little girl?

"Darlin'—I think I'd like that," he says softly.

I'm not sure why, but my eyes suddenly tear up.

"I have to go, baby."

"Okay. I love you, Liam."

"Now that's a nice send off," he says right before he ends the call.

I was right. I don't like Liam being gone. I can't sleep without him, tossing and turning half the night. Part of the reason, I feel anxious about not telling him that I saw his father.

And — talked to his father.

I just didn't want to upset him right before he left on a business trip that must have been important for him to leave so suddenly.

Finally, I fall into an exhausted sleep only to have the alarm go off at what seems to be moments later. Holly and I have plans to eat breakfast together in her office. We're going to brainstorm a plan to convince Liam to let me work, in some capacity here at the Justice, at least part time.

I don't feel the pressure or worry I felt before Liam arranged to help my parents financially. And I do feel better about the fact that we have a future together. But I need to work. There's not enough to keep me busy full time yet. I do realize how fortunate I am that I'll be able to stay at home with our child but, right now, I need to feel productive.

We're making a list of pros and cons of the benefits of me working. So far the pro's are winning.

"This is so good," I say around a bite of the breakfast casserole Holly made at home.

"I know, right? How can you go wrong with potatoes, sausage, and cheese?"

"We should start doing this once a week. I'll bring breakfast next time."

"Sounds like a plan to me."

About the time I feel a sizzle along my nerve endings, I see Holly look over my shoulder.

"Liam! What are you doing here?" she asks.

I smile and turn in my chair.

He's standing in the doorway and I don't think I've ever seen such unmitigated anger on his face. His eyes burn as he stares at me.

"What's wrong?" My voice comes out in a whisper.

"What's wrong?" His voice is that controlled angry that is so scary. "I think you know what's wrong."

I shake my head as he enters the room and steps up to my chair. I have a terrible moment realizing he knows I've spoken with his father.

"Get up."

"Liam—"

"Stay the fuck out of this, Holly!"

His anger is barely controlled and I'm frozen in my chair.

"I said—get up."

As angry as he is, I think I'll stay right where I'm at.

He continues to glare at me, his eyes like cold, blue shards of glass.

"I told you, you were not to speak to Walter Justice."

I hear Holly's gasp, but Liam holds my eyes captive. I'm conscious though of Holly rising to shut her office door.

I swallow against the sense of doom I feel settling around my heart. "I... he approached me—"

"And I told you not to talk to him." His quiet anger scares me.

"I—mostly listened," I whisper, which is the wrong thing to say as he takes a step closer, looming over me.

"Liam!" Holly says sharply. "You need to calm down."

"I don't understand why you're so angry with me for just talking to him."

"Well let me enlighten you!" His eyes burn with a blue fire that causes me to shrink back in the chair.

"Liam, please," Holly pleads, but he ignores her.

He leans down, placing his hands on both arms of the chair.

"Walter Justice murdered my mother."

"What?" I breathe. I shake my head in denial, suddenly feeling lightheaded, faint.

"I've spent months working to keep that bastard in jail. Not once, in twelve years have I spoken to the sonofabitch. And now — you've let that fucking viper back into my life!"

"I didn't know," I whisper. "You should have told me."

He stands and steps back.

"Liam, you can't blame Cait. She had no idea —"

His burning gaze holds mine. "If you had done as I asked —"

"But you didn't ask."

His jawline tightens as he grits his teeth.

"I didn't do anything but talk to him," I say softly, looking down at my hands.

"I don't want him in my life!" he snarls.

"Liam, so he's talked to Cait, but that's all. It doesn't mean —"

Liam turns to level his burning glare on her. "No. That is not all," he sneers before looking back at me. "A reporter from The Tribune contacted Ryan to see if I'd like to make a statement — about my *wife's* relationship with my estranged father."

My breath rushes out with an audible gasp.

My relationship with his father? The father who killed his mother?

"It makes me wonder what else you're not telling me."

There it is. The distrust he'll always hang on to.

"How about what you keep from me?" I know I shouldn't do this right now, but my mouth won't listen. "*You* should have told me. Especially after you knew he contacted me." I stand. "It gave you the perfect opportunity to let me know what was going on in your life, Liam." I'm unable to keep the hurt from my voice.

He runs his hands through his hair. His anger seems to have scaled down a notch, but he doesn't look at me again as he turns and heads for the door.

Holly calls after him but he continues out, closing the door behind him. Her troubled gaze meets mine.

"Cait, if you don't mind, let me talk to him."

I just look at her. What is there to say to him? After she leaves, I sit back down.

Liam's father murdered his mother. My eyes tear up. The horror of what he went through, losing his beloved mother and for it to be by the hand of his own father is unimaginable.

So many things are clear now. When I first came to Justice House, I knew there was something very upsetting going on in Liam's life. He later told me his mother's killer was up for parole and he was doing everything in his power to keep the man behind bars.

I swallow against the tears.

Not telling me about his father says so much about Liam's opinion of me.

CHAPTER FOURTEEN

T HE DOOR TO HOLLY'S OFFICE opens and I look up quickly, disappointed when Mike walks in.

He frowns when he sees me. "What's wrong?"

I'm still a little surprised when he talks to me. He's been a lot friendlier ever since the night we had an intruder. That will probably end now. I know how much he mistrusted me, believing I had something to do with the break-ins.

I shake my head in answer, afraid if I try to speak, I'll burst into tears.

He crosses the room to perch on the front edge of Holly's desk, crossing his arms over his chest. He doesn't say anything and after several minutes, I look up at him.

"I wasn't supposed to talk to Walter Justice but he showed up yesterday while I was waiting for Paul." I look back down, frowning.

His brow lifts in surprise. "You spoke to Walter Justice?"

"Yes. He called me the first time. Liam found out and—" I look back down under his piercing stare.

Someone is spying on me. Or Walter.

I look back up. "Someone is following me or maybe Walter."

"Why do you say that?"

"A reporter contacted Ryan to get a comment from Liam." Mike purses his lips in a silent whistle. "I didn't know Liam's father killed his mother. When Walter wanted to talk to me I had no idea."

"What did Walter want to talk to you about?"

"He wanted me to convince Liam to talk to him. He said he needed to tell him the truth."

Mike's brow lifts again.

"He said he needed to warn Liam."

"Warn him about what?"

"I don't know. He—doesn't seem well. He wasn't making sense, but he insisted he needed to talk to Liam before it's too late. That's twice now that he's insisted it's important that he speak with Liam."

"This is why Liam came back early?"

"Yes." I draw a deep breath. "He's really angry," I say softly.

Mike stands abruptly. "Liam is usually pretty level headed—except where his father is concerned, and with good reason. Give him some space and he'll realize you did nothing intentionally wrong." He walks around Holly's desk and reaches down to open one of her desk drawers. He holds up a candy bar when he straightens.

"Don't tell Holly."

"Okay."

After he leaves I clean up the breakfast we abandoned, and then decide to head upstairs. I take the back elevator. Liam and Holly might be in his office and I don't want to interrupt them. It's not even noon and I feel like crawling back into bed.

When I walk into the bedroom, Liam is busy packing

a bag. I stop mid step, my heart in my throat. He looks up and then returns his attention to his task.

Is he leaving me?

No. Surely if that were the case, he'd just throw me out. Maybe not though — because of the baby.

"What — are you doing?"

He glances up again. "Unpacking." The relief I feel is immeasurable.

He picks up a couple of items and the overnight bag, walking past me to the closet.

At least he's talking to me. Kind of. I wait, not sure what to say or do. When he re-emerges from the closet, I take a deep breath.

"Liam — I know you're really angry with me and I—"

He steps right up to me and my words cut off as I look up into his blazing eyes. They burn into mine and I wince at the anger I see in their depths. Without a word, he steps around me and leaves me standing in the middle of the room as he walks out.

For the rest of the day, Liam stays holed up in his study and when he does come out, he doesn't say much.

Annie keeps giving us concerned looks.

I go to bed alone that night, and when I wake the next morning, the only way I know Liam slept with me is the indentation on his pillow.

I shower and eat breakfast alone with Annie, who informs me, Liam left early without eating breakfast. I'm at a loss, but I want to follow Mike's advice and give Liam space to get over his anger. I know moping around the apartment isn't good for me, so no moping — at all.

I choose a pretty, white eyelet sundress to wear and

put my hair in a single side braid. Next I give Paul a call to let him know I'm coming by the magazine to see him. I take the elevator that goes down to Liam's office. If he's there, I want to let him know where I'm going.

He's not.

As I walk out, I notice Holly's door is shut and there's no answer when I knock. I've not spoken with her since the incident in her office yesterday. I thought about calling her last night but I hate putting her in a "taking sides" situation. We've become good friends, but I know she has to be loyal to Liam, and I don't hold it against her, that she didn't tell me about Liam's father. Liam should have.

When I walk past the dining room, it looks quiet and the new hostess is talking to one of the servers. I'm busy looking and not paying attention so I give a little squeak of surprise when strong hands grab my arms.

"Cait."

"Bryce! You startled me."

His eyes positively sparkle. "You need to pay attention to where you're going." He grins broadly.

"Sorry."

He falls in beside me, walking with me down the hall. "How's Emily?"

"I left her exhausted, so I'd say she's good."

I huff a little laugh, shaking my head at him. "I'm certain putting up with you is exhausting."

"Hey!"

I give him a quick smile, and he chuckles.

"Does Liam know you're going out looking like that?"

I frown. "What's wrong with the way I look?" I stop at the back door looking down as my hands smooth the skirt of my dress.

He laughs out right and tugs my braid. "You tease so easy. You look beautiful."

"Thanks. I think." Emily definitely has her hands full with him.

Reaching out he pushes against the back door, holding it open for me. "Don't forget, we're all partying at InJustice tomorrow night."

I'd forgotten. Will Liam still want to go? With me?

"I'll be there."

I see the slight frown on his face and before he has a chance to ask, I'm out the door.

"I'll see you later, Bryce."

As I enter the garage, the spot where the Porsche usually sits is empty.

"Is it okay if I do some research on your laptop?" I ask Paul as I flip through the latest edition of Query Magazine. He's just hanging up from a phone call.

"What's wrong with your computer?"

I lay the magazine down. "I don't want what I need to look up on my search engine."

He raises his brows. "Porn?"

"No!" I laugh sharply.

He chuckles. "So you just came over here to use my computer."

He swivels in his chair and lifts his computer bag onto his desk, taking out his laptop.

"Pretty much." I take the laptop as he hands it over the desk.

We're both quiet as we work. Paul busy on his office computer writing up an article, me searching for what I can find on the murder of Liam's mother.

Maren Justice was only thirty-six when she was strangled in a small town in Georgia. Her son came home from school and found her. The description and pictures of the crime scene are horrific; knowing that was what Liam saw when he entered the house. His mother fought hard for her life.

"Hey, what's wrong?" Paul asks as he stands. I look up and wipe at the tears. He walks over and stands behind me reading.

"Do you have a tissue?" I lay my bag back down after my unsuccessful search.

"Yeah, hold on." He has to go out of the office, but he's soon back with a box of tissues.

He squats down beside me to finish reading the article I've pulled up. It's all there in vivid detail, the last day of Maren Justice's life and the subsequent arrest of Walter Justice for the brutal murder of his wife.

He looks up at me when he finishes.

"This wasn't in the file Valerie had on Justice either?"

"No." Both Paul and Julie know Liam's mom was murdered, I told them after Liam and I broke up. They knew what I knew. The file Valerie had on Liam contained nothing about the murder. At the time, there was no reason to do further research. Or so I thought.

"When did you find this out?"

"Yesterday."

"Damn, Cait." I nod in agreement. "You never asked about her murder?"

"I didn't. I thought about searching for details but a part of me didn't want to know, and I wanted to respect his privacy. He never wanted to talk about her and you know me, I wouldn't have been able to hide what I knew."

"So why is Walter Justice contacting you?" Paul stands and leans against his desk.

"Like I told you—he wanted me to help him re-connect with his son."

"The son-of-a-bitch! When you didn't refuse, he had to know you weren't aware of the circumstances."

"Liam found out."

Paul frowns. "That Walter called you?"

"Yes. He was adamant about me not talking to his father. But, as you know, I did." I snap the laptop closed. "Liam—came back early from his meeting and—" I shake my head. "Mad doesn't describe his temperament."

"You didn't know his father killed his mother, Cait."

"No, but if I'd done as Liam—requested and had nothing to do with Walter—"

Paul's brow furrows further. "You talking to the man couldn't have done any harm."

"A reporter from the Tribune contacted his attorney, Holly's husband, wanting a comment from Liam about his wife's relationship with his estranged father."

"Damn."

"Yeah."

"Do you know who the reporter was?"

"No. Liam didn't say. But if we could find out who contacted the reporter— Paul, someone's following either Walter or me."

Paul picks up his phone and at the same time, his door is pushed open as Valerie steps into the room.

"I couldn't help overhearing." Paul arches a brow. "Your door was ajar, Paul."

I look from Valerie to Paul.

"Caitlyn, we need to talk, or to be more accurate—I need to talk to your husband."

I look back to stare at her, my mouth agape. When I don't respond, she says, "Today."

I give a short laugh. "Valerie, you are the last person my husband would talk to."

Other than his father.

"I'm sorry, that sounded—I don't mean to be rude."

She waves away my apology. "None of that matters, but it is vital that I speak with him."

I stand. "I'm sorry. Since you overheard our conversation, I'm sure it won't surprise you to know that Liam is barely speaking to me." I feel my face warm admitting this to her.

"Valerie, why did you keep the information about Maren Justice's murder out of Liam's file?"

She smiles wanly. "Because I know you, Caitlyn and your emotions would have let it slip."

Paul hangs up the phone and Valerie and I both look expectantly at him.

"The reporter is Natalie Byers. She said she received an anonymous email, sent from a local coffee house."

"So she has no idea?"

"She said she'd get back to me." He gives me a blank look.

Whatever—but I know it usually means that this Natalie knows more than she's willing to say at this point.

"And what's more, she's been ordered by her editor to drop the story and not look into it any further."

"What?" I quickly look at Valerie.

"I told you he has friends in high places," she says.

Holy shit.

"Maybe if I call the editor, we can find out if they know anything more," Valerie suggests.

"Let's wait and see if she gets back with me first," Paul says. "Cait, she said there was a picture attached to the email. It was of you and Walter, in front of the coffee shop."

I pull into the garage of Justice House, and the Porsche is still gone. I wonder what Liam has been doing today. An overwhelming loneliness settles over me, which is silly, because he's not gone, but I miss him. And on top of that, I'm still a little emotional about his mother's death. I have a lump in my throat over the thought of him, as a teenager, coming home to find his beloved mother strangled.

I have to talk to him. I have to make him understand why I spoke to his father. That I unwittingly wanted to mend the rift between them.

I rub my stomach. "What are we going to do about your father?" I say softly.

I enter Justice House and almost collide with Holly as she comes around a corner.

"Cait! I've been looking for you."

"What's up?"

"We need to talk."

"Okay. You want to come upstairs? It'll be more private."

"Perfect."

The apartment is quiet and as we enter the kitchen, I find a note from Annie laying on the island. Nothing from Lim.

"We have the apartment to ourselves, Annie's shopping and Liam—" I reach for glasses out of the cupboard. "Who knows where Liam is," I mumble.

"I'm so sorry, Cait. Liam should have told you about Walter."

"It would have helped."

"I hope you understand why I couldn't say anything." Her eyes implore me to understand.

"Oh, Holly, I do." I hand her a glass of iced tea. "Please don't think I'm upset at you. I know it puts you in an awkward position."

"I want you to know that I encouraged Liam to tell you. He just can't bear to talk about his mom or what happened. But if I'd known that Walter had contacted you, I would have told you myself. You needed to know."

"I didn't tell you because, again, I didn't want to put you in a position that made you feel pulled between your loyalty to Liam and our friendship."

"Have you and Liam talked about Walter?"

I huff a soft breath. "No, he's pretty much not talking to me."

She takes a sip of her tea. "Well there's more that you should know," she says as she sets her glass down. Her tone of voice causes alarm bells to go off.

"What?"

She takes a deep breath. "The trial was a nightmare. If it weren't for his mother's parents, I don't think he would have made it through the ordeal."

"He told me they helped him buy Justice House."

She looks around. "Yeah, but that was later, after—" She looks back at me. "Walter's lawyers used the defense that Liam was the one who murdered his mother."

The air sucks right out of my lungs and I feel lightheaded as I grip the table edge.

"They said he murdered his mother for the insurance money."

"No!" I shake my head in disbelief.

"Yes. It was horrible."

How could his father do that? I'm sickened at the thought that through me, Walter Justice tried to insinuate himself back into his son's life.

"Needless to say, the trial took a terrible toll on Liam. We were all worried about him. He spent years growing up with the shame of his father being the town drunk and then suddenly people started whispering behind their hands whenever he went out in public.

"The only good deed Walter Justice ever did in his miserable life, was put an end to what his lawyers were trying to do."

"What do you mean?"

"There was one particular grueling day in court, while Liam was on the stand. You should have seen him. He was so calm and so strong but when they put pictures of the crime scene up, it almost broke him. Walter stood up and told his lawyer to stop. He said that his son had nothing to do with his mother's death. And then he started apologizing to Liam. He said he never wanted them to accuse Liam. The whole time Liam wouldn't even look at his dad."

I hear the elevator, coming up from Liam's office, in the hallway.

"Liam's home."

We both stand.

"I need to take off. Ryan and I have dinner plans." She gives me a quick hug as Liam walks in.

"Hi," I say softly.

"Hey, bro." Holly gives Liam a hug and his eyes meet mine over her shoulder.

"Don't let me chase you off." He moves to the fridge to get a beer.

"Ha! Funny," she says as she sets her tea glass in the sink. "Have a good night; I'll see you both tomorrow."

"I'll walk you to the elevator." I glance at Liam to find him watching me.

"Oh!" Holly turns back at the doorway. "Don't forget we're all getting together tomorrow night."

"You're probably going to have to count us out, Holly."

So he doesn't want to spend time with me. For some reason, that pisses me off more than him not speaking to me.

"I'll have Bryce talk to him," Holly says as we walk toward the back elevator.

"I don't think it'll matter, Holly."

She takes my hand and squeezes it as we reach the door. "It will work out." She gives me a reassuring smile.

I step out into the rotunda with her. "I'll see you tomorrow. Have fun tonight and tell Ryan hello for me."

"I will." The elevator doors close on her little wave.

I head back into the apartment with newfound resolve. I find Liam still in the kitchen talking to Annie.

"Do you need help with the groceries?" I ask.

"Oh, no dear. You sit down and talk to your husband. It won't take me but a moment to finish up here."

I have no intention of having a one sided conversation with my husband, but I do have something to say to him. I stand there staring at him until he looks up. He lifts that damnable, sexy brow.

"I'm going tomorrow night." I turn on my heel and head for the bedroom. I'm smiling as I walk down the hall, knowing he won't be far behind.

As he enters the bedroom, I'm on my way to the closet. I take my time getting a fresh change of clothes. When I walk back into the bedroom, he's standing in front of the French doors looking out.

I falter for a second. He looks good. Distractingly good. His white shirtsleeves are rolled to his elbows and paired with his vest, dress slacks, and a loosened tie with the top two buttons undone on his shirt, he's the picture of sexy male perfection. I swallow hard and continue to the en suite bathroom.

He hasn't touched me in two days, and my body has always had a mind of its own where Liam Justice is concerned. But, hopefully, I'm about to "stir him up" as Holly says. I want an end to this rift between us and the only way I know to do that is to defy him. There's a part of me that cringes at the thought of his anger but the other part feels a sense of excitement.

I step back into the bedroom on the pretense of retrieving an overlooked item from the closet. As I walk back out, he turns, watching me again.

"Was there something you needed?" I lift my brow in copycat of his trademark expression.

He cocks his head and I bite my lip as my heart rate increases from its steady beat to an irregular thump. I reach and pull the hair tie from my hair, using my fingers to unbraid the length, shaking my head as my loosened hair spills over my shoulders.

His sultry gaze holds mine and I know at once that there is no way I can ever best him in the art of seduction. I'm no match for him, no matter what he's taught me. I will my breathing under control as he watches me with his enigmatic expression.

"You are not going tomorrow night," he states firmly

and from his expression, I know he thinks that is the end of it.

I smile letting my lips lift slowly. When his eyes focus on my mouth, I know I've caught his attention. It's an almost heady feeling. I lick my lips, watching him closely as I lift my hand to the top button on my sundress. The second and third buttons come undone as easily as the first.

I see no outward reaction as I slide the straps of my dress off. First one shoulder and then the other. My other hand clutches the bodice to keep it from falling down my body to the floor.

"Why?" I ask the single word, loud in the thick quiet of the room. Can he hear my heart trying to beat its way out of my chest?

He cocks his brow and his eyes lift to meet mine. "Because it will create gossip if you go alone."

"I thought you didn't care what people think."

"I don't. But you do."

"I'm going tomorrow night — with or without you." I let the dress drop and I'm left standing before him in my panties.

His eyes lazily rake over me, taking their fill as my stomach muscles squeeze tight in reaction.

At his casual perusal, I feel the heat of a blush move over my skin and I suddenly lose my confidence. I reach down, grabbing up my dress to hold in front of me and move toward the bathroom.

In the next instant, I'm pushed up against the wall; my wrists seized and lifted high above my head, held in one strong hand. He steps just close enough that the material of his vest abrades my sensitive nipples. I moan softly as I feel the flush of desire, hot and molten in my belly.

My eyes close against the blatant need he elicits. His foot pushes against mine until I take the step, widening my stance. When he grips me between my legs with his free hand, my head drops back and I moan in response.

"Look at me," he orders, his voice raspy. His eyes blaze as I meet his gaze. "You best do as I say, darlin'. I have ways of making you regret defying me." My mouth dries at the subtle threat. "And just so you know" — he takes that step that brings his hard body up against mine— "you seducing me, to get your way, will get you fucked, sweetheart—but you still won't be going tomorrow night."

He releases my wrists and steps back.

I rub my wrists under his penetrating stare and then he's striding from the room.

Well, that went well. Maybe I should have groveled at his feet, begging him to forgive me.

I suck at seduction.

I dry off from the shower and slip into my robe. As I wrap my hair up in another towel, I hear the house phone ring. After five rings, I decide no one else is going to answer and I cross the room to the bedside table. When I look at the caller ID, my breath catches in my chest.

Melanie Langford.

I do my best to take a deep breath. "Hello."

"May I speak to Liam please?" Her voice is soft and young sounding.

Why is she calling Liam? Unbidden, all of Miranda's snide insinuations and the conversation between her and Liam at our wedding party come to mind. A white-hot jealousy grips my heart.

"Hello?"

"Sorry." I take another labored breath, my hands shaking. "I don't think he's in the apartment." I'm not sure why, but this is the defining moment that I know there *is* something serious between her and Liam. "If you'll hold on — I'll check." I can't believe I sound so calm or that I'm offering to find my husband so she can talk to him.

"I'm calling long distance from Paris, so if you would just give him the message to call me back?"

Paris!

My legs almost buckle as I grip the phone.

"Hello, are you there?"

"Yes," I whisper. I drop down onto the edge of the bed.

"Okay, thank you." The line goes dead as she hangs up.

The Niels live in Paris. I recall the veiled comments of Charles Niel at our wedding party. And I remember Liam's anger at the man.

What is Melanie to Liam? Is she the one who gave him his pendant, promising her love will always be with him?

I jump up, pulling the towel from around my head, my fingers combing my damp hair as I storm out of the bedroom, marching straight to Liam's study. He's on his cell phone, his brow arching in surprise when I enter without knocking.

Is he talking to her?

"Boyd, I need to cut this call short — I'll get back to you." He calmly places his phone on the desk.

My hand tightens around the phone I'm still holding,

moving it behind my back to help control the urge to throw it at him.

"What can I do for you, darlin'?"

I grit my teeth at his mocking tone. "I think it's time you tell me about Melanie Langford."

Other than him leaning back in his chair, there is no outward show of emotion, not even a blink as he gazes at me.

"I want to know what is going on with her. What she is to you."

His eyes become glacial and then he sighs, running his hands through his hair. "I'm not going to talk to you about Melanie. It's none of your business."

My mouth drops open. "I'm your wife."

He sits forward, his eyes taking on a threatening glare. "Then act like my wife. Trust me and when I tell you to do something—fucking do it!" He practically shouts.

Oh! My temper rises even more. He's seriously mistaken if he thinks I'm going to let him continue to make me feel bad about his father when he's carrying on with another woman. I cross the room with angry strides and slam the phone down on his desk in front of him.

"Well, *husband*—you need to call your mistress back. The one in Paris." Some emotion burns in his eyes. "And you can go to hell!" My eyes blaze right back at him.

I turn but don't manage to take two steps when I hear him move. My first thought is to run, but he reaches me before the next thought has a chance to form. He spins me around and walks me backward until I'm up against his desk. When I push against his chest, he grips my wrists and pulls them to the small of my back. I'm all too aware of the fact that I have nothing on but a thin robe.

"Stop it!" I struggle against his hold as he presses

against me until I'm leaning back over his desk. He brings his mouth to mine and I jerk my head to the side. Taking my wrists in one large hand, the other comes around to grip my chin, turning my face back to his as he forces his kiss on me. His tongue pushes its way between my pressed lips, delving deep inside.

I continue to struggle, the whole time fighting against my body's desire to submit to him.

When he releases my hands, his arm encircles my waist, tightening in a firmer hold. He releases his hold on my chin, his hand going to the belt of my robe. He pushes the material apart, baring my body. My nipples harden even further from the cool air.

I bring my hands around to half-heartedly push against his chest and try to wiggle out of his hold as I feel my body succumb. He continues to devour my mouth, his large hand squeezing and kneading my breast.

I whimper against his merciless onslaught, and my arms go around his neck, my hands tangling in his hair. When he releases my mouth, I suck in great gulps of air. His hands close around my waist and he lifts me, laying me down on the top of his desk. Resistance is futile—I want him.

His face is set in strong determination, his eyes holding mine as he releases his erection. My breasts heave with each breath I take and my whole body tightens in anticipation.

He grips my legs and pulls me to the edge of his desk, entering me with one hard, deep thrust. My back bows, my moan long and plaintive. He feels so good.

"Fuck! You feel good, darlin'," he growls, his voice harsh with need. Pulling my legs up, he drapes them over his shoulders as his hands support my bottom. "So fucking tight."

He pounds ruthlessly into me as he holds my gaze. It's fast and quick, my orgasm slamming into me with a ferocity that steals my breath. He continues thrusting, fucking me deep and hard. It's a sweet/sharp sensation, that line between pain and sweet agony.

When I feel the next orgasm build, I mewl softly. I'm not sure I can survive another one. My body arches and wave after wave of intense sensation scalds my insides.

Liam reaches his release at the same time, shouting my name.

He's heavy as he partially rests his torso on mine. His hand buried in my hair, his mouth pressed against my neck, his breath hot and moist as we spiral down from our fast and frantic coupling. His medallion is hot, pressed into the spot over my heart, and I feel the sudden need to cry.

He pulls out of me, causing me to writhe beneath him. Lifting up off me, he pulls his pants back up his hips. When I won't meet his gaze, he sighs and pulls me up into his arms. My arms come up in front of me in an unconscious protective manner.

"Are you okay?" he asks softly.

I nod, not trusting my voice.

He presses the side of my face against his chest, his hand cradling my head as he presses his lips against my hair. "Please, don't cry, darlin'."

Tears choke my voice. "You made me trust you."

He stills. "You can trust me." His voice rumbles against my ear.

I pull back and his arms fall away as I move from between him and the desk. I look down, shaking my head as I pull my robe up around me. Maybe, because I love him so much, I've fooled myself into believing that he wanted our marriage to be real. Tears are threatening and I need to be by myself.

"Cait—"

I shake my head, my face still turned down. I head for the door on shaky legs.

When his arms go around me, it breaks what little control I have left.

"No. Please, let me go," I sob.

His arms tighten. "I am *never* going to fucking let you go, darlin'," he says, his voice deep and adamant.

"I can't do this, Liam."

"What?" he says sharply.

I look up. "I can't live with you angry like this. I'm sorry I talked to Walter. I only wanted to help you. I thought you could heal if you made peace with him." I hiccup. "I didn't know—you should have told me."

"Shhh... " His hand slides under my hair to the side of my neck. "I can't handle you crying, darlin'."

I bring my arm up and wipe my nose on the sleeve of my robe.

"I know you don't trust me."

"What?" He pulls back to look down at me.

"You didn't trust me enough to share one of the most important things about your life."

"I'm sorry," he says gruffly. "I should have told you. I just—" When he doesn't continue I look up, meeting his gaze. "Fuck, Cait! I don't like talking about—I don't even like thinking about any of that shit."

I sniff and rub my sleeve across my eyes. He brings

his hand up to brush his thumb across my tear dampened lips.

"I should have told you and I'm sorry for taking my anger out on you."

I sniff again. "I'm sure you wish I was the obedient little wife."

He snorts softly and his lips lift at one corner, his eyes sparkling with humor. "I reckon it will take some time to get you trained, darlin'."

It's my turn to snort and he laughs. His expression suddenly becomes serious, his eyes intense as he looks deep into mine. I think he's on the verge of saying something when he pulls me back close, his arms wrapping tightly around me.

"You were so mad at me — still are," I mumble against him.

He pulls back and I look up. "Yes, I am mad. But not in the way you think." His arms drop, releasing me. "Please sit." He nods toward the chair before he moves behind his desk. His face is set in grim lines and I swallow against my sudden nervousness.

His intense gaze finally meets mine.

"I've been mad as hell — and worried. One of the reasons I was so mad that you didn't do as I asked —"

I give a choked laugh. "There was never any asking." His eyebrow lifts in censure and I press my lips together.

"I'm not sure what that bastard is up to, but he's not in this alone." My eyes widen. "Someone took pictures of the two of you when he confronted you the other day."

"I know," I admit. Liam frowns. "Paul called the newspaper and found the reporter who contacted you. She told him that someone sent her an email with the picture attached."

"And that disturbs me. That and how the hell he found your personal cell phone number." He turns and paces to the window. His shoulders are rigid and when he turns, my breath catches at his expression. It's a myriad of emotions. Anger, ruthless determination and a power that seethes just beneath the surface.

"I'm—concerned that he was able to get that close to you."

It has me concerned too. "As long as I don't talk to him again—"

Liam's face darkens. "Do. Not. Talk to him!"

I raise my hands in a placating manner. "I won't," I say firmly.

His eyes narrow. "I've spent the last two days doing my damnedest to make sure he doesn't come near you again." He turns and moves to the window, his hands on his hips.

What has he done? "Made sure, how?" I ask cautiously.

He looks back over his shoulder. "Let's just say I've made sure that if he comes anywhere near you"—he turns to face me—"He *will* go back to jail."

Oh.

"And you won't be going out on your own without Mike or me being with you."

What?

"This is not open for discussion, Caitlyn," he says, his voice stern.

I stand, moving around the desk. I lay my hand on his arm and feel the tightening of his muscles.

"I'm not arguing. I know you're just trying to keep me safe."

He pulls me into his arms as mine slide around to his

back. I bury my face against his chest, breathing deeply of his scent.

We stand like this for several minutes, each taking comfort. I love this man more than I could ever have imagined. He's never said the words to me, but he shows me in so many ways. But that doesn't get him a free pass.

"Liam—"

He kisses the top of my head. "Yes, darlin'."

I take a deep breath. "Tell me about Melanie."

Liam's body tenses and I look up to meet his gaze, mine not faltering when he gives me his best scowl.

"Fuck, Cait!" His arms drop and he takes a step back, his hand slashing through his hair.

I pull out his desk chair, sit, and look up expectantly at him.

I have to know.

He closes his eyes and shakes his head. "Mel—is pregnant."

CHAPTER FIFTEEN

THE BREATH IS KNOCKED RIGHT out of me. If I weren't sitting, I'd fall straight to the floor.

When did he sleep with her?

I feel as if the rug's been pulled out from beneath me. All of his out of town trips, have they been to see her? And why is she not here? Why is he keeping her in Paris. Because of me?

Angrily, I start to rise and Liam leans down, his hands landing on the chair arms, trapping me.

"Darlin', the baby is not mine. I have never had sex with Melanie," he says firmly.

I frown, searching his fervent gaze. "Then why —"

"I helped her leave the country to get her away from her abusive boyfriend. The last time he beat her, she nearly lost the baby. I had to send her someplace he couldn't find her."

"Paris," I say softly.

"Yes."

I frown again, remembering some of the things Charles Niel said at our wedding party. "Why the secrecy with the Niels, am I wrong in assuming that they know?"

"She was still working here when she called me from the hospital. She was desperate to get away from the boyfriend. I sent her out of state, but the bastard tracked her down. Thankfully, one of her neighbors became suspicious when he noticed the boyfriend lurking around her apartment, and called the police. I decided then that she needed to leave the country." Liam closes his eyes briefly. "I'm sorry Charles was being a fucking jerk at the party." He grips my chin, tilting my face up. "This has to remain a secret—for Mel's continued safety. No one else knows. The Niels help her, for me. They assume" — the skin around his eyes tightens — "that she's my mistress."

"Oh."

Liam releases my chin and runs his hand over his mouth and jaw. With a heavy sigh, his eyes come back to mine. "You are not leaving me." His voice is low, filled with an undercurrent of emotion.

Even with the relief I feel that he's not kept something from me as important as fathering a child with another woman, I feel heartsick for Mel. She's alone in another country. I can't imagine how I'd feel if I were in her place.

"Say something," he demands.

"You have to help her."

His brow lifts. "I am."

"I mean, she's all alone in a strange country, Liam."

"She's good. She's made a life for herself there. She's even talking about staying after the baby's born."

"How far along is she?"

"Seven months."

Wow.

"Cait, you cannot say anything to Paul or Holly—no one."

"I won't, I promise." He's told no one, not even his best friends. *But he told me.* "You probably should call her back."

"I will. She would have said if it were important. I'll call her later."

How often do they talk? I'm ashamed to admit that the vice of jealousy squeezes my heart. "Does — does she know you're married?"

"Of course she does." He laughs and then sobers. "Don't be jealous, darlin', there is no reason." His eyes suddenly become guarded. "But you need to know, Cait, I am going to continue helping her."

"Of course! You have to. I want you to, Liam."

He studies my face for a moment and then gives me a quick kiss.

"Damn, darlin', you're going to be the death of me."

"What?" I frown. What's he mean by that?

"Every time I fucking turn around I think you're about to leave me, or you're defying me, or you put yourself in harms way —"

My eyes widen.

He shakes his head and laughs. "Let's go see if Annie's fixed supper. I'm hungry."

I'm busy the next afternoon in the nursery with a few wallpaper swatches the designer dropped off when Mike calls to tell me I have a delivery and he'll escort them up. Curious as to who or what is here, I hurry down the hall to the rotunda.

When the elevator doors open, two young women, one carrying a garment bag and the other a large case step out. Mike remains inside and I look at him curiously, catching his smile as the doors slide closed.

I look back at my visitors.

"Mrs. Justice," the woman holding the garment bag

steps forward, "my name is Candee Blair and this is my assistant Emma. We are here at your husband's request." She holds out a folded note card.

I tentatively reach for the note.

Darlin', meet me in the entryway at six sharp.
Ms. Blair has a dress for you,
and she will help with your preparations.
Six sharp, don't be late!
P.S. I have at last purchased you lingerie.

I laugh at his postscript as I re-fold the note.

"Are you ready to begin?" Ms. Blair asks.

I take one more look at myself in the mirror. Candee and Emma are Goddesses! I'm not sure how they managed to curl, twist, and pin my hair up into the elaborate style they achieved, but it is a testament of their amazing talent. They then turned their magic to applying my make-up with the flair of artists. It's more than I usually wear but it looks good. Especially with my dress.

My dress is beautiful. Candee informed me that Liam came into the boutique she worked for and picked out the dress himself. It's a beautiful, luxurious, deep red velvet with capped sleeves, a scooped neckline with the bodice tucked and the skirt falling to drape beautifully around me, ending above my knees. And the lingerie he chose makes me blush at Candee and Emma's subtle teasing. There's barely anything to it at all, but it feels incredibly sexy.

Liam also provided strappy black, killer heels that make my legs look long and toned.

I turn slowly in front of the mirror. I feel very

glamorous and pampered. I smile. I don't know what Liam has planned but I feel the excitement building.

At two minutes to six, I head for the entryway of the apartment and just as I reach the elevators, the doors open.

Holy shit.

Liam's wearing a tux and surely no man has ever looked so unbelievably handsome and sexy. No man that I've ever seen.

I know I'm looking at him as if I'm an idiot, but I can't take my eyes off him. He looks even taller than usual. His hair is in the casual, combed with his fingers, style he favors that is so damn alluring to me. All that paired with the bit of designer scruff on his handsome face, and he looks as if he just stepped off the pages of GQ. I simply want to jump him.

His eyes sweep over me, and then his burning gaze meets mine. He smiles and my equilibrium leaves me for the night. His sensual mouth forms the word beautiful, and my breath escapes in a little puff as I bite my lip.

He smiles in that sexy way of his that leaves me witless, before stepping forward to take my hand, pulling me into the elevator. His arm slides around my back as he presses the control panel.

"Don't look at me like that, darlin'."

"Okay," I breathe.

He looks down then, his sexy mouth curving into a slow smile. He lowers his head, bringing his lips to mine in a soft kiss.

"You look beautiful, sugar."

"Thank you," I say softly. "Thank you for this lovely dress. I love it, Liam."

He cocks his head, his eyes slowly moving over me.

"I saw it and knew immediately it needed you to make it beautiful."

I feel my cheeks warm with his compliment. He takes my arm when the elevator doors slide open and leads me across his office.

"Are you hungry?" he asks.

"I'm very hungry." *Just not for food.*

He laughs softly as he opens his office door. When we step out into the hall, he pulls me close. "I bet I can guess what you're hungry for, sugar."

When I glance up, he gives me a lascivious grin and I know my face probably turns as red as my dress. Liam laughs out loud and farther down the hall I see a couple of members turn to look our way and smile. We continue down the hall as he leads me toward the mansion's main entryway.

"Where are we going?"

He gives me a sideways glance. "I'm taking my wife out to dinner."

Seven simple words but they elicit an immediate response in me. A glow settles around the vicinity of my heart and I suddenly feel exceedingly happy and lighthearted.

Liam greets a couple as they descend the grand staircase. They both greet us and I smile as I slip my hand into Liam's. He promptly squeezes and then lifts it to his lips, kissing my knuckles.

When he opens the front door of Justice House, I see the black limousine parked at the curb waiting for us.

"A limo?"

He smiles down at me.

The driver opens the door for us and as soon as we settle in, we're on our way.

Liam reaches to the side of where we sit and a panel opens, revealing an ice bucket containing a bottle.

"Sparkling cider, darlin'?"

I grin when he looks at me, holding up a fluted glass, his eyes gleaming.

"Yes, please." I practically bounce in the seat. *This is so fun.*

As music begins playing softly in the background, Liam hands me my glass. I beam at him, taking a sip as he leans back with his own glass.

"You're drinking cider too?" I ask with a little laugh.

He raises his brow. "Well now, I reckon there's a lot to be said for cider." He leans close to bring his lips to mine, his tongue swiping the last remnant of cider off my lip before his mouth takes mine. I turn more fully into him and his free hand slides behind my back, moving up to encircle the nape of my neck. His hand is so warm goosebumps erupt across my skin. When his lips slide across my jaw nipping lightly with his teeth, I moan softly, arching my neck.

"We'd better stop or I'm going to mess up that pretty hair-do, darlin'," he murmurs near my ear.

"I don't care," I breathe.

I feel him smile against my neck. He kisses the spot behind my ear and leans back. "I look forward to ravishing you later, but the night is young and when I fuck you, sugar, I want your undivided attention to be on me, not food."

"I'll always take you over food," I murmur softly, my cheeks heating as I take a sip of the cool cider. The smoldering look he levels on me dries my mouth and I take another sip.

That sexy eyebrow of his lifts. "We may need to take another ride later, after we leave the club."

I frown. "Why?"

His salacious grin causes my stomach muscles to tighten in a most delightful way. He leans close. "I have a sudden desire to see you on your knees between my legs, sugar." My breath hitches at the seductive timbre of his voice. "My hands buried in your hair."

When I realize what he means, I gasp. "You're very naughty."

He laughs out loud. His arm slides behind my shoulders and his fingers caress my ear. "Yes," he says, his voice a soft growl. "With you, I can think of all manner of naughtiness." His eyes are mesmerizing as his gaze holds mine.

I desire this man more than my next breath. The love I feel for him is an all-consuming passion and since the moment I first saw him, I've belonged to him.

His finger strokes the side of my face. "Don't look at me like that, darlin'."

I look away and take a long sip of my drink. Liam pulls his arm from behind my back, taking hold of my hand to bring it to his bulging erection. I quickly look up, sucking in a sharp breath.

"Now look what you've done," he says in his slow drawl. "And we're here."

Liam exits the limo first, reaching to help me out, pulling me close. "Now who's the naughty one?" he whispers against my ear. I giggle.

We're dining at an exclusive club where I know you have to be a member and I also know only the rich can afford the price tag. As we're led to our table, I can't ignore the ardent looks of the women. Liam looks like a wet dream in a tux. Well — in anything.

"The fuckers need to stop looking at you," he growls, his arm sliding possessively around my waist as we cross the dining room. I glance up to notice his clenched jaw and can't help but laugh.

We're seated at a table and Liam takes the chair beside me as our server greets us.

"Would you like me to order for you, darlin'?"

I glance up at the server and he smiles. "Please."

"Would you like a glass of sparkling cider?" he asks, his eyes flashing with humor.

"No, thank you. I've had enough and the night's still young."

Liam's mouth lifts at the corners. "The lady will have an ice water with lime and I'll have a Macallan single malt scotch. We'll also have the grilled beef tenderloin, well done for the lady. A wedge salad and the twice-baked sweet potatoes. That'll be all," he tells the waiter.

I glance around in awe of the dining room with its arched ceiling, Neo-Gothic stained glass windows, and old world charm. It's décor is opulent and beautiful.

When my gaze meets Liam's again I find him watching me. I bite my lip nervously. "This is—" I hesitate as our waiter delivers our drinks "—lovely."

Liam lifts his glass to his lips, his eyes watching me intently. "Yes, it is." The low, sexiness of his voice causes me to shift in my chair. His arm comes up to rest along the back, and his heady scent inundates my senses. I look up, my eyes settling on his lips.

He leans close. "We're going to shock the poor waiter

when I ask for our meal to go, darlin'." He smiles into my eyes.

"Why would you do that?" I ask softly, running my finger around the rim of my glass.

He sits back. "Why? So I can take you home. That look you keep giving me just begs me to fuck you proper, sugar. I'd fuck you right here but I don't want anyone else to enjoy what is mine."

"Liam!" I quickly look to see if anyone has overheard him.

He laughs and that does garner a few looks our way. Mostly women, their appreciative glances lingering on him.

I look down when I can't stop the smile that pulls at my lips. He is irresistible when he teases like this. Hell, he's irresistible when he breathes, and I know he's not teasing.

I lean toward him. "Will it shock him too badly?" I murmur for his ears only.

He gives a choked laugh, setting his drink down. "Well now, darlin' — are you trying to seduce me?" he asks softly. His leg presses against mine as he leans closer. "I have a notion that I'm living under the false assumption that I'm calling the shots in this relationship."

Is he kidding? I search his eyes, catching the unmistakable gleam of humor. I nudge him with my elbow.

"I'm glad you're having fun with your teasing," I say playfully, raising my chin in feigned disapproval.

"Who's teasing," he murmurs as he sits back. "Here's our food, darlin'."

By the time we leave, I'm completely full from the

delicious meal, but my arousal gnaws at me with a vicious hunger. I'm ready to ditch the party at the club back at Justice House.

As we settle into the supple leather seat of the limo, Liam pulls me close, his hand cupping the side of my face as his kiss steals my breath. His fingers slide beneath the scooped neckline of my dress to caress the swell of my breasts as my erect nipples throb.

I turn more fully into him, lifting my hand, stroking the light scruff on his jaw with my fingertips. I'm on the verge of unbuckling my seat belt so I can crawl into his lap when his cell phone rings.

He lifts his mouth slowly from mine. I moan softly and he gives me a quick kiss as he pulls his phone from his pocket, scowling when he looks at the screen.

"Fucker," he murmurs and I know it's Bryce. "This better be good," Liam growls when he answers.

I settle back in the seat, my hand lifting to pat my hair back in place. It's a testament to Candee and Emma's expertise that it's still up.

"Actually, I'm not sure we're going to make it, buddy." Liam reaches for my hand and brings it to his bulging erection. "Somethings come up."

I giggle and quickly slap my free hand over my mouth. Liam's mouth lifts at the corners.

"Sorry, Bryce. I think we'll skip this one. My wife's a demanding little thing."

I grin when he winks at me, his smile contagious. He grunts as I squeeze him through his slacks.

Damn. He's hard as steel and I feel him throb against my fingers. His legs spread wide and when I glance up, his eyes are narrowed as he looks down at me.

I suspect we might not wait until we get back to Justice House.

"What?" he demands into the phone and then sighs, his head tilting back against the seat. "Okay." He looks at me. "Yeah, we're here now."

I look out the window, surprised that we have indeed arrived home. Liam ends the call and then buzzes through to the chauffer, instructing him to deliver us under the Porte cochere.

"We're going?" I ask, disappointment evident in my voice. I truly am insatiable when it comes to him. It's his fault though with his sensuous touches and heady kisses. And I pray that never changes.

"Yes. Bryce says it's imperative we join them." Liam's voice holds a note of skepticism.

We're greeted by several club members as we enter InJustice. I honestly see several women's jaws drop at the site of Liam in a tux.

It's still early enough and not overly crowded that it doesn't take us long to cross the room. Liam grips my arm protectively as we climb the stairs to the private balcony above. It's a good thing, as these heels aren't made for climbing stairs. They're for looking good.

Liam leans his head close. "This is the last time you're wearing heels like this until after the baby comes."

Sometimes his bossiness is a little —

"But I plan to enjoy them later when they're wrapped around my neck." He smiles down at me when I gasp.

He loves embarrassing me with his sex talk. I bite my lip, hiding my smile and yearning to be alone with him.

Maybe I should feign not feeling well and get us out of here early.

Some of our extended family are already gathered around one of the tables. I sit down beside Julie. She greets me smiling and then looks up at Liam, her mouth dropping open. I pat her hand.

Everyone's in good spirits as we greet each other.

"You look beautiful, Cait," Ryan says from across the table. Holly beams at me, nodding in agreement. "What are you doing with someone who looks like Liam?"

The table erupts in laughter and I glance up at my husband. He smirks, his arm encircling my shoulder to pull me close. Leaning his head down, his mouth comes close to my ear.

"Go on, tell him it's the fucking, darlin'." He promptly laughs and moves out of my elbows reach.

"Cait, you do look beautiful," Julie says, leaning over to give me a quick hug. "I love this dress."

"Thank you. You look beautiful too." And she does. Julie is one of the most beautiful women I know. Her personality enhancing that beauty.

Paul leans back to look past her. "You two are certainly gussied up. What's the occasion?" he asks.

I glance at Liam but he's talking to the waitress who's brought us drinks. She looks dazed as she stares at him. I look back at Paul and shrug.

"They don't need a special occasion to dress up Paul. Some people just dress up when they go out," Julie teases.

"Where the hell is Bryce and Emily?" Liam asks Holly. He hands me a glass of ice water with lime slices. I smile inwardly; I like how he knows I like lime over lemon with my water.

"They went to find Mike," she says.

Liam rests his arm along the back of my chair, his fingers stroking the back of my neck. I glance up at him, breathing in his erotic scent. He shakes his head in irritation and leans close again.

"We'll give them another fifteen minutes." I smile and nod agreeably.

Our waitress is back and she sets one of those iced champagne buckets on a stand, beside our table.

"Hey!" Bryce calls out as he and Emily arrive.

There's another round of greetings.

"Hi, Cait." Emily leans down to give me a hug. "I love your dress. And your hair! How did you do that? It's so cute. You have to show me how."

I laugh. "I don't have a clue. I have to give all the credit to Candee Blair and her assistant."

Emily's eyebrows rise. "Wow. I know Candee, she's amazing. Must have been a special night out." She looks at Liam. "You look okay too," she says with a laugh.

"Yeah." Bryce slaps him on the back. "What's with the monkey suit?"

Liam knocks back what remains of his drink and before he can set the glass down, a new one is placed before him. "Where's Mike?" he asks.

"Michael is on his way," Emily says.

Bryce's arm encircles her waist, pulling her close. He whispers something in her ear and she blushes beautifully.

"Here he is," Bryce says as he looks toward the stairs.

Mike is quite friendly when he greets me. I'm glad we're on better terms with each other. I watch as he greets everyone else. He's quieter than his friends. Quiet and somewhat mysterious. When I asked Liam about him, all he would say was that Mike was a very private person. I watch as Emily stands on tiptoe to give Mike a hug. She's the only one to call him Michael. If I want to know more about Mike, I'm going to have to ask her and Holly.

I turn to Julie. "Do you and Paul want to go out to dinner next week?"

"Yes. I've been meaning to call you."

"Paul said you were working on a big campaign."

"Oh, yes. Thank goodness, we've wrapped it up. All the hours I was putting in were killing me."

"Can I have your attention, please?" Bryce calls out.

"I'll call you the first of the week," I tell her and then turn my attention to where Bryce and Emily stand.

Emily is looking up at Bryce, adoration vivid on her face. I know I look at Liam the same way.

Bryce leans his head down and gives Emily a quick kiss.

"Come on, let's have it," Holly teases.

Bryce grins. "We're getting married."

No one says anything.

I thought they *were* already engaged—just taking a break.

"Next month," he adds.

"What?" Holly squeals as she jumps up, hurrying around the table to give Emily a hug.

Everyone is at once, standing and talking, laughing at the same time. A waitress appears with a tray of fluted champagne glasses as another waitress opens the chilled champagne. The party turns quite festive with celebration after that as the champagne flows freely.

I enjoy myself immensely, but I am more than ready to leave when Liam suggests we do so a couple of hours later.

"We have plans," he tells Bryce.

"Yeah, I know what kind of plans." Bryce grins and then winks at me.

I turn quickly so he doesn't see my flushed face. "I'm so happy for you," I tell Emily as I give her a hug.

"Let's all go out to lunch this week so I can fill you in on the plans," she suggests.

"Sounds good." I give the others a little wave as Liam's arm encircles my waist.

Instead of taking the steps down to the main floor, Liam leads me to the small bar area in the far corner of the balcony. There's another elevator that he leads me into and then pulls me into his arms, kissing me so soundly, I'm dazed when the doors open and he lets me go, leading me out into a hallway.

"I didn't know there was another elevator or that this was here," I say as Liam leads me to a door that opens into the restaurants kitchen.

"Secret passage." He grins.

There are still a few people cleaning up in the kitchen at the end of a busy Friday night. They smile and greet us as we pass through. Just before we exit the room, one of the kitchen help calls out to Liam.

"Wait right here, darlin'."

He's soon back holding a small white box, which I eye curiously. He takes my arm again, leading me out of the kitchen, toward the back of the mansion. I assume we're headed for the elevator but when he leads me past, I look up questioningly.

"Where are we going?"

"We have a date, remember?" he says. "On your knees, between my legs, darlin'."

I giggle, looking up and he looks down giving me a wolfish grin.

"Here, take this." He hands me the white box. It feels as if it's been in the cooler. "Chocolate covered strawberries," he says at my quizzical look.

What? My heart swells a little more in love with him.

He pushes the back door open, and as I step through, I see that our limo awaits.

I feel guilty the next afternoon when Mike has to come in on his Saturday off to drive me to the baby specialty shop where Liam and I ordered the baby's crib. Liam had a meeting with a member from out of town, so Mike was volunteered when someone from the store called and wanted me to come in to look at the crib before they delivered. I also plan to place an order for the dressing table Liam and I have decided on.

I'm quiet on the way to the shop, dreaming about the night before. I had the most wonderful time. Liam made it such a perfect night, first with the lovely dress and then the special dinner, not to mention the fun time we had on our trip around the city after we left the club. We didn't get back to Justice House until two in the morning.

"I'll wait here for you," Mike says as he pulls up to the curb.

"Okay. I'll hurry," I say as I unbuckle and open the door.

"Take your time; I have a couple of calls to make." He's already pulling out his phone as I look back.

The sales clerk I met the first time I came to the shop, greets me.

"Good afternoon, Mrs. Justice."

"Hello, Janet. Please call me Cait."

She smiles. "Come on back with me. I have to say, you chose the most beautiful crib I've ever seen."

I agree, it is beautiful. I'm having so much fun getting the nursery ready.

After I place the order for the dressing table, I wander through the open doorway to the connected shop next door. They are having a sale on their baby clothes, and I just want to take a quick look since Mike is waiting.

As I'm looking through the most exquisite selection of baby girl dresses, I hear my name. My hand stills. I recognize his voice, and before turning around, I scan the store. How did he know I was here?

Before he can speak, I hold my hand up. "I can't talk to you. To be more precise, I don't want to talk to you." I look around again, hoping to catch a clerk's attention, trying to ignore the fact he looks unwell.

"Please. If I could just have a moment of your time—"

"No. I'm sorry Mr. Justice but you have nothing to say that I want to hear."

"Please, I need to speak to my son." Up to this point, I still felt a little sorry for him. "I need to warn—"

"Your *son!* You murdered his mother!" I hiss.

"Is everything all right?" A young sales clerk with a worried expression comes up to us.

"Do you mind getting my driver, please? He's just outside, in the Range Rover parked at the curb."

I turn back to Walter as she hurries off to do as bid. "You need to leave." I watch as his posture straightens.

"I may have been a mean, drunken son-of-a-bitch, and I admit I was guilty of many things—but I did not kill Maren. She was my wife and I loved her."

I glance across the store when I hear the jingle of the outside door opening. When I look back, Walter is gone.

"Cait!" Mike calls as he hurries to my side. "What's wrong?"

"Walter Justice was here," I whisper, conscious of the fact most of the people in the shop are staring at us.

Mike scans the area as he takes hold of my elbow. "Let's go."

On the way home, he questions and has me repeat my conversation with Walter. I know I'll have to re-tell it all to Liam too.

As Mike pulls up near the back door to let me out, I look over at him. "Thank you."

He nods and I give him a smile, exiting the vehicle.

I get to Liam's office to find he's not there. Checking in with Holly I discover he's been called away, leaving a message for me to call him when I return. I really don't want to tell him about Walter on the phone, and I know he'll be able to tell something is wrong in my voice.

"Do you know where Liam went?"

"Something about a problem at The Heartbeat."

It's not the first time I wonder about Liam's part in that business. And I know I shouldn't, but I ask Holly about his involvement.

"He's a partner with Jimbo."

"I thought it was something like that."

"Liam owns interest in several businesses here in Chicago and in Lansing."

Of course he does. I don't want to think about how rich he might be. It makes me very uncomfortable. Like a woman who has married way above her station. Like a gold digger.

"Cait!" Holly laughs. "You look as if you've just heard the worst news possible."

I smile weakly at her.

"Are you okay?"

"I'm fine. I'm just in need of a nap."

She looks unconvinced as she searches my face.

"I'll talk to you later, Holly."

I head back to Liam's office. I wasn't kidding when I told Holly I needed a nap. Liam keeping me up half the night and then the stress of running into Walter has taken its toll. I smile, recalling the fun of the night before with our sexcapades in the limo.

The office is dark as I cross the room, the corners shrouded in shadow. I've been in this room any number of times when the lights are all off, save for the dim, recessed lights set in the wall. This is the first time I've ever felt uneasy though, as if there were something lurking in those shadows.

I chide myself for being silly. Evidently, a vivid imagination comes with pregnancy.

My phone rings, startling me and I know, without looking, that it's Liam.

"Hi."

"You should have called me immediately."

"I'm sure Mike told you that we came right home. I thought I'd tell you here." I look back at the darkened room once I reach the elevator, my eyes peering toward the shadows.

"Are you okay?"

"Yes." I swipe my card and step inside as soon as the elevator doors slide open.

"I'll be there in a few minutes."

"It's okay. I'm going to lie down."

"Tired, darlin'?" I hear him chuckle, a deep sound that causes a gut-tightening response. "Answer me, Caitlyn."

I bite me lip at my body's further reaction to the forceful tone of his voice.

"Yes. My husband is not easily satisfied."

"Are you sure you're okay?" His voice has softened.

"Yes, the baby's just demanding that I rest."

I hear a woman suddenly laugh on his end of the call. Close.

"I shouldn't have kept you up so late, darlin'. I need to go, I'll be there shortly." The line goes dead.

I press the control panel, peering into the darkness as the doors slide closed.

The house phone is ringing as I enter the apartment. Annie is usually gone on the weekends, so I hurry to the kitchen.

"Mrs. Justice, this is Aaron, at the gate, there is a Valerie Sharp here to see you."

What?

"Tell her" — Liam will have a fit — "I'll be right there."

What the hell is she doing here?

I told her Liam wouldn't speak to her. I dump my bag and head through the apartment to take the elevator down to the back entrance.

"Caitlyn, it is imperative that I speak with your husband."

"Valerie—" I glance toward the street, conscious of the fact that Liam could be arriving at any moment to find me standing inside the gates talking to Valerie. "He won't talk to you. In fact, I'll warn you, he's probably going to be very angry to find you here."

"That may be," — she says in her concise manner of speaking— "but, I'll take that chance."

"Well, I won't. I—"

"Caitlyn, I insist on speaking with your husband," she says firmly. "He *will* want to hear what I have to say."

I doubt it.

For the life of me I can't imagine what Valerie has to say that Liam would want to hear. But I also know that she doesn't play games.

"If it's about what happened before, when I came to work here... we've moved past that."

"It's not."

I take a deep breath. Liam will probably stop speaking to me — or deny me orgasm for a month.

"Okay."

When Liam walks into his office, I know the last person in the world he expects to see is Valerie Sharp, sitting on his fine leather couch, drinking his expensive bourbon.

He comes to an abrupt stop, his gaze slashing to my worried one. The anger I see there is not surprising, but the utter shock of betrayal is.

"Liam—"

He turns his back, cutting off my words. Without a word, he steps to his desk, picking up the phone.

"Liam wait." I set down my glass of water. "Valerie needs to speak with you."

He looks over his shoulder his forehead creased in a

scowl. I sigh and in my peripheral vision, I see Valerie stand.

"Mr. Justice, I have information you will be interested in hearing."

"I doubt that." He turns and the look he gives her intimidates me, but Valerie seems impervious. "As I told your lawyer *and* you before—you have nothing to say that I am interested in hearing."

Her lawyer? I glance at Valerie.

"Security is on their way, so I suggest you get the fuck out of my office before I forget my manners and throw you out!" His voice ends practically on a shout.

"I have information about the death of your mother."

I look at Valerie in surprise and then at Liam. If I thought he was angry before— by the look on his face, I know he is about to follow through with his threat to throw her out.

"Liam," I say sharply. "You need to listen to her." His anger filled gaze turns toward me, but I ignore it as I make my way across the room to him. "I know her, Liam. And I know if she says she has information about your mother, she does."

"There is no news about my mother that I don't already know, Caitlyn." His anger is palpable. "She's looking for a story. It's what she does, and you should know that."

"Please hear me out Mr. Justice. Give me five minutes."

My eyes plead with him as his burning gaze holds mine. "Please." My lips form the word. I want him to hear what Valerie has found out about his mother.

"My sister was murdered twelve years ago. Three months before your mother," Valerie says, sensing an opening.

I gasp and quickly look at her. *Murdered!*

I look back at Liam to find him watching her with an enigmatic expression.

"The M.O. was the same for both victims — your mother and my sister Elise. Both strangled. Elise in Oregon and then your mother in Georgia." Valerie pauses as she picks up the drink she set on the small table at the end of the couch. "At the time of my sister's death, your father was in the hospital with an emergency appendectomy."

The door opens suddenly and Mike enters the room, coming to an abrupt stop, his eyebrows rising when he sees Valerie.

"Escort Ms. Sharp out, please. Make sure she is never again allowed on the premises — even if she is with my *wife*." He levels another glare on me before turning to stride toward the elevator.

"Was a piece of jewelry that your mother wore missing?" Valerie calls out. "Something that the authorities never disclosed to the public?"

I look at Valerie and then back at Liam as his hand stills on its way to press the call button. I turn to look at Mike, a frown on his face as he watches Valerie.

"My sister always wore a bracelet our mother gave her. She never took it off." Valerie takes a step forward. "What item of jewelry was missing from your mother?"

Liam slowly turns. "A St. Christopher's medallion," he says softly.

My breath is indrawn sharply, loud in the stilled quiet of the room.

Liam is suddenly striding back toward us.

"Tell me everything you know."

CHAPTER SIXTEEN

"I WAS EXTREMELY CLOSE WITH ELISE. I raised her after our parents died in a plane crash. I was happy she was accepted to the college of her choice, even though it meant she would move to Oregon, but she was ready to spread her wings. I stayed in California, visiting often, and we talked every day on the phone.

"Elise came into contact with Vincent Hale quite by accident, and from that moment on, he stalked her. I of course was upset, but Elise insisted she wasn't worried. That was before the night she came home to discover him, waiting for her in her apartment.

"At my advice, she filed a restraining order the next day and I made plans to leave for Oregon later—" Her voice trails off. She's quiet a moment and then knocks back the rest of her drink.

Liam gives Mike a glance and he brings a bottle from the bar to re-fill Valerie's glass.

"They found her body the next day, dumped in a secluded area. She had been raped and strangled."

"Oh, Valerie!" I reach out to place my hand on hers. She glances down and then back up at me.

"I know you've often wondered why I hired you Caitlyn. As I told you before, you remind me so much of Elise. I couldn't help but want you around." She gives me one of her rare smiles.

"Please go on Ms. Sharp," Liam says from where he sits across from the couch where Valerie and I sit.

"Vincent Hale was the main suspect in Elise's murder — to the point that the police never looked at anyone else. One of the detectives on the case admitted that they knew he murdered Elise but they couldn't prove it. It seems he had an airtight alibi. And he is very good at what he does."

"Why were they so sure?" Liam asks, flicking a quick glance at me and then back at Valerie.

"He'd been a person of interest to them and the authorities in Idaho for quite some time. He's a nasty piece of work and has a rap sheet to prove it." She reaches into the bag sitting at her feet. "The only picture I have of Vincent Hale." She hands it to Liam. "Not a very good one, mug shots seldom are, and that picture is fifteen years old."

Liam studies the picture for a moment before handing it to Mike. I watch as he stares at the picture, his brow furrowed.

"That is the man who killed my sister and I've hunted him for twelve years."

I'm still watching Mike. Does he recognize the man in the picture?

"As I said, I was living in California, but from that moment, I travelled around the country following the trail of Vincent Hale. At times, it led me out of the country."

"That's who you were speaking of that day at the magazine, when you first returned from your — trip." I sit forward. "You told me at that time you'd been trying to find someone and the trail led you to Justice House — a year ago!" I quickly look at Liam.

"Yes, but years before, one of my private investigators discovered the connection between Walter Justice and Hale."

Liam has shown little emotion while Valerie has talked but now he sits forward. "What connection?"

"My investigators learned that Walter Justice's mother, your paternal grandmother, re-married after the death of your grandfather. The man had a young son, close to the age of your father. His name was Vincent Hale."

Liam is frowning as he digests this information and then glances over at Mike.

"Your grandmother and Dennis Hale divorced eight years later. Hale and his son moved shortly thereafter to Arizona. The investigators discovered that Vincent Hale turned up in Georgia — twelve years ago. Three months after murdering Elise."

I'm watching Liam and I see a host of emotions cross his face.

"I don't remember anyone coming to see Walter — "

"All I know is that Hale was in Georgia and there was an individual that one of my investigators spoke with. A Hadley Morris?"

Liam nods. "He was a good friend of Walter's."

"Well, this Hadley said that your parents were out with Hale at a local bar, shortly before your mother's death. Hale was all over your mother, she had to practically fight him off. He was extremely persistent and your father was... inebriated. Morris finally stepped in and there was an altercation between the two men. Morris said that Hale threatened to gut him."

I glance at Liam.

"Hale disappeared the day after your mother —"

I feel tears threaten as I watch the pain on Liam's face.

Valerie clears her throat. "After I heard of the similarities in your mother and Elise's murders, I was satisfied that Hale killed them both. When your father was convicted and incarcerated, I decided I needed to stay close to you. You moved here to Chicago, and I followed."

"Why didn't you contact me then, so we could have worked together?"

"At first, I didn't have enough information to convince you that Hale murdered your mother. Once I did, I tried. You declined any contact with me."

I glance quickly at Liam but his expression is inscrutable.

"I've kept my private investigators trailing Hale all this time, knowing he'd slip up somewhere, and he did, but he always managed to elude the authorities. And me. Imagine my surprise when, after eleven years, he shows up here in Chicago, right on your doorstep."

Liam frowns. "What do you mean?"

"He was here — at a couple of your special events."

"That's impossible," Liam says, glancing over at Mike, who shakes his head.

"I assure you, he was here at Justice House."

Liam stands and paces across the room to look out the window, his hands thrust in his pockets. I want to go to him, but will myself to remain seated.

"That's when I made the decision to put one of my people in here." Her gaze shifts to mine and then back to Liam. "Hale stayed in the area a couple of weeks and then he disappeared again. On a hunch, my investigator discovered Hale made a trip to visit your father in prison. I have since learned Hale visited your father several times over the past ten years."

Liam turns. "All this time — all your investigating and you couldn't find anything to pin on him?" Liam's voice holds a measure of anger.

Valerie stands. "Mr. Justice, please believe me when I say, if I ever have the slightest chance, I will see Vincent Hale dead. I won't call the police and wait while Hale manages to slip through their fingers again. I will see the deed done."

Liam's eyes narrow slightly as if gauging the validity of her words. At last he nods. "What do we need to do?" Liam glances over at Mike.

"Whatever we do will have to be carefully orchestrated. Hale is slick." Valerie gives me a quick look and then sits back down before looking at Liam. "There is a reason for Hale coming to Chicago and it coincides with the release of your father from prison."

The first inklings of fear crawl up my back and I shudder slightly.

"I believe Hale is here because of you, Mr. Justice."

"Maybe it was just — a coincidence," I whisper, glancing across the room to meet Liam's eyes.

"When Walter Justice was released from prison, he didn't go home; he came straight here to Chicago and immediately hooked up with Hale. We are carefully keeping tabs on them both."

Holy hell.

"How can Walter come here like this? Isn't he on probation or something?" I ask. And why would he associate with Hale? It doesn't make sense.

"He served his full time," Liam says. "I made certain of that." His eyes meet mine again and I see the guilt there before he quickly hides it.

Oh, no. I can't imagine how he must be feeling to find out, there is a very good possibility, his father did not murder his mother. Liam has held onto the anger toward his father and now faces the likelihood — it was unfounded. At least for killing his mother. But — what is the connection between Walter and Hale?

Liam sits in his office chair and runs his fingers through his hair before looking over at Mike.

I glance at Mike too, curious what he has to say since he was with Liam through the whole ordeal of his mother's murder. But in typical Mike fashion, he says nothing, he only shakes his head.

Valerie stands again and Liam immediately rises. "Mr. Justice, I have a meeting planned for Monday morning. I'm meeting with the private investigators on the case and my lawyer. You and Mr. Bowen" — she glances at Mike — "are welcome to join us. I imagine you would probably like to go over the surveillance material I have garnered through the years."

"Yes, we would like to be there for that meeting." Liam glances at Mike. "Thank you, I'd be most interested to see what you have on Vincent Hale." He crosses to shake her hand.

"Very well." She turns toward me. "Caitlyn, I'll talk to you later."

I stand and before I can think twice about it, I give her a hug. "Thank you, Valerie. And thank you for being so persistent."

She hugs me back and then bends down to pick up

her bag. "I'm desperate to catch this monster and I will do everything in my power to accomplish that goal."

As we move toward the door, Liam takes my arm. "I'm going to walk Ms. Sharp out, you need to go upstairs and lie down for a while, you missed your nap."

What? I can't lie down now, I have too much going through my head.

He must see the argument taking shape. "Now, Caitlyn," he says in his firm, not to be argued with voice.

I huff an exasperated breath. "Fine!" I grab hold of the front of his shirt. "But you have to tell me everything you talk about."

The corners of his mouth quirk up slightly and he makes a sound of repressed laughter, before leaning down to give me a quick kiss.

There is no way I can sleep, not with everything I learned today. I almost want to see Walter Justice again so I can rip him apart. How does a parent do that to their child? How could Walter have anything to do with Vincent Hale? And what are they up to, are they planning to try to extort money from Liam? Unease settles over me at what exactly the two men could be planning. I'm terrified at the thought that some harm could come to Liam.

At least we now know that something is in the works. I re-play my conversations with Walter over and over. He seemed so sincere about wanting to talk with his son.

I roll over and punch my pillow, angry for Liam. Angry that he now has to contend with the likelihood that he made sure his father served his full prison time for a crime he didn't commit. But at this moment, I feel like

Walter Justice deserved exactly what he got, especially if he is in cahoots with Vincent Hale. And if that is the case, I know that they are out to hurt Liam.

I toss and turn for about an hour before I hear Liam enter the apartment. I bound out of bed and I'm running down the hall to meet him, practically leaping into his arms as he scoops me up. I wrap my arms around his shoulders as I bury my face against his neck, breathing in his spicy male scent.

He holds me tight, one arm around my waist, the other fisting a handful of hair at the back of my head. When I lift my legs to wrap around his waist, he moves the arm around my waist to my bottom, supporting me.

"You shouldn't run, darlin', you might fall." I snuggle closer. "Did you sleep?"

"No," I answer, my voice muffled against his neck. "I've been lying down this whole time, though."

"Good."

His arm slips back up to my waist, he holds me firmly against his body, and we stand there as such, each taking comfort in the other. When he begins walking, I look up into the face of the man who means so much to me that I can barely breathe with the onslaught of emotions I'm feeling.

"Are you mad at me?" I whisper.

His beautiful eyes meet mine. "No, darlin', I'm not mad at you."

I lean in and kiss his neck, his arms tightening around me.

"Where are we going?"

"Kitchen."

"Why?"

"I'm going to ravish you on the kitchen counter."

I giggle.

He does set me down, right on the counter, his warm hand stroking my leg from the thigh down to the calf, causing goosebumps to erupt over my skin. I reach up to stroke the side of his face, my hand moving up into his hair.

"Are you okay?" I ask softly.

He turns his face down, but I can see his furrowed brow. He nods and then looks up to meet my eyes. "I'm fine, darlin'. I won't have you worrying about all of this."

"The only thing I'm worried about is you."

His mouth lifts at one corner as he reaches to tuck a lock of hair behind my ear.

"I'm so sorry," I whisper.

"Me too," he says softly. He leans his forehead against mine.

"What can I do to help?"

He lifts his head to kiss my forehead and then takes a step back. "Honestly, I just want to lose myself in you for the evening. Forget about this for the night."

"We can do that." My voice sounds breathless. The thought of how he needs me, is empowering. "I love you, Liam."

He grips my chin and lifts my face, searching my eyes and then lowers his head, his mouth capturing mine. His tongue seeks entry to stroke mine and he tastes of bourbon and Liam. A heady combination. I grip his shirtfront, pulling him closer.

Releasing my chin his hands land on my thighs before slipping between them to push them apart as they move up under my skirt. His mouth slides across my jawline to my ear, taking the lobe between his teeth. I whimper when he bites down.

"We need to eat first and then I'm going to have you for desert, darlin'." His breath is warm and delicious against my neck.

"Mmmm," I hum as he nibbles his way down my neck, his hands continuing to slide up my legs to the junction of my thighs as my hands move up under his shirt, my fingers grazing lightly across his back.

He lifts his head. "Your panties are soaked, sugar." He leans back and grins wickedly. "We may have to skip right to desert." I bite my lip to keep myself from begging him to do just that.

When his fingers slip into my panties, pressing against my clit, my back arches uncontrollably.

"Liam," I moan. I close my eyes absorbing the sensation, but when he pulls his hand from between my legs and steps back all in one move, my eyes fly open. "What—"

"Food first, darlin'." He grins.

I make a disgruntled sound and give him my best pout. He steps back close, his arm going around my back, tugging me forward against his chest.

"Oh." My breath whooshes out softly.

"It will be worth your wait, darlin'."

He is the most exasperating man.

I glare at him and almost laugh when he grins cockily as he takes a step back, moving away from me.

"So you say." I lift my chin and look at my nails as if I'm extremely bored. From my side vision, I see him stop on his way to the pantry, turning back to look at me. I give him raised brows.

"Are you questioning my ability to satisfy you, darlin'?" His mouth lifts at one corner.

He is so damn cocky! I love it.

I nonchalantly lift my shoulder. "I'm—not satisfied."

When he doesn't say anything, I sneak a peek from under my lashes. He's standing with his hands in the front pockets of his jeans, his enticing eyes glowing with amusement.

Without a word, he steps to the cabinets and starts opening drawers. I hear things rattling around as he digs.

What is he doing?

When he turns, his arm drops to his side, effectively hiding what he's holding. He walks toward where I still sit on the island counter.

"What are you doing?" I'm suddenly worried about what he's hiding from my view. I nervously glance up, meeting his amused gaze.

"Well, now, darlin', you're the one implying you need more than I can provide."

"No," —I shake my head— "no I'm not." I shift uneasily.

When he holds up a long pair of kitchen tongs and squeezes them so that they clack together in a menacing manner, I squeal and pull my legs up, scooting back on the countertop.

"Liam!" I squeal again when he points the tongs at me and makes them clack once more as he steps close.

Laying the tongs on the counter, he reaches for an ankle and pulls me back across the countertop to him. I wrap my legs around his waist and as my arms reach for his shoulders, I knock the tongs onto the floor out of his wicked reach.

His mouth comes down, taking possession of mine, moving his tongue against the inside of my mouth in a way that soon has me needy with passion. I clutch his shirt tightly and return his kiss in equal fervor.

When he raises his head, he presses his forehead to mine.

I sigh. "Can we just go to bed and eat later?"

He laughs as he lifts me into his arms. "Yes. Dessert first little girl."

I grin and squeal, grasping at his shoulders as he suddenly leans down, scooping up the tongs.

"No!" I laugh, kicking my legs.

"What? Darlin', I'm going to need these for what I have in mind."

I laugh and turn more fully into him squeezing his neck. When we enter the room with the sex swing, I look up, meeting his dark gaze.

"Ready to try something new?"

"Yes," I say without hesitation, excitement at once running rampant through my body.

The ringing of his cell phone halts what he's about to say. He shifts me in his arms as he digs for his phone, making a disgruntled sound when he sees who it is.

"I need to take this darlin'," he says as he lets my legs down, releasing me once I'm standing. "Here, hold these." He hands me the tongs, his eyes gleaming with amusement.

"What's going on?" he asks as his hand comes out to cup the side of my face. He frowns at whatever the caller says, his hand dropping as he steps aside. "Did you call Bryce?"

I glance around the room. There are still dust covers strung over everything. I came in here one day when both Liam and Annie were gone, peeking under the covers, thankful I didn't see anything that looked too scary.

Where the sex swing previously hung, there is now two chains hanging down with what looks to be wrist straps on the end of each chain. My stomach muscles tighten.

"Okay, I'll be right down."

My eyes flash back to his.

"Sorry, darlin', I'm needed downstairs."

"I understand. It's Saturday night."

Liam's already headed for the door when he stops, looking back. He holds out his hand. "Come with me and we'll have the kitchen fix us something to eat."

"Can I change first?"

"If you hurry. I need to get a file from my study."

I choose a short red dress with pockets, raising it up above my head, I slip my arms into the armholes and let the silky material glide sleekly over my body as it falls into place.

Going downstairs with Liam will be better than staying here alone in the apartment. Sometimes when he's needed downstairs, it's hours before he returns. And after all that's happened today—I feel the need to stay near him.

"Where did you put my tongs?" he asks as we head for the back elevator. I snort softly. "Don't be hiding my tongs now." He grins.

I love it when he's playful like this. "I returned them to the kitchen where they belong and need to stay."

"Well now, what I have in mind for you won't work in the kitchen, sugar." His honey smooth voice, stirs all manner of butterflies in my belly.

I take a deep breath. "Can I ask you something?"

"About earlier today?"

"Yes."

He looks at me. "You can ask me anything, Cait."

"What else did Valerie say when you walked her down?"

He hesitates before answering. "We talked about the meeting that's scheduled for Monday, and I told her from now on, she has a partner in her search for Vincent Hale."

"You did?"

"I did."

"I had no idea Valerie had a secret like she did. She never said a word about what happened to her sister." He holds the door to the rotunda open for me. "Liam, I kept going over my conversations with Walter. He told me he needed to talk to you to make things right.

"He played on your emotions, hoping you'd convince me to see him."

"The thing is" —I look up meeting his gaze—"I believe he was sincere."

Liam frowns slightly and as soon as he presses the call button, the doors to the elevator slide open.

"Walter said he needed to warn you."

"Caitlyn—" He shakes his head and then motions for me to precede him into the elevator. "I don't want you talking to Walter. I don't want you anywhere near him. I mean it. We have no idea what's going on, and if he calls you, *do not* answer your phone." He gives me his stern look.

Geez. I've never known a person who can move from playful to just shy of mad as quickly as he can.

"I don't want to talk to him."

He sighs deeply. "It may be that they were both involved in my mother's death."

I quickly look up at him, fear slicing through me. "Please be careful, Liam," I whisper.

He looks down and must see the fear in my eyes because he pulls me close, kissing the top of my head. "Don't worry, darlin', I won't let anything take me away from you and our child."

I turn more fully into him, pressing my face against his chest.

"You just remember that you don't leave Justice House without Mike or me. Understood?"

"I won't. I promise." I agree with him that we have no idea what's going on, and I have no desire to meet this Vincent Hale.

I look up. "Do you think you should call the police?"

He meets my eyes, a smirk on his handsome face. "Already taken care of, darlin'."

The doors slide open and we're on the second floor.

"Go on down to the bar. I'll try to hurry, and we'll eat once I'm finished. Have Leon order you an appetizer," he says before dipping his head, his mouth near my ear. "I'll show you what I can do with kitchen tongs later, sugar."

"That's what all the boys say."

His eyebrow rises in his cocky fashion. "You better not let anyone else bring their tongs near you."

I can't help but giggle. He's teasing but there's also a warning note in his voice.

"I'll meet you downstairs," he says, giving me a kiss that makes my toes curl against the soles of my shoes.

"Mrs. Justice, how are you this evening?" Leon looks over my shoulder, his gaze scanning the room. I know he's looking for Liam.

"I'm fine Leon. I'm going to wait down here for my

husband. Leon — please call me Cait." I nod my head and give him an encouraging smile. "I'm still Cait."

He smiles as he takes down a couple of glasses and sets them on the bar top.

"How have you been?" I ask, glancing around the bar. All of the tables are occupied and there are several club members sitting around the bar counter. I know that most of them are probably waiting on a table in the dining room. "It's busy tonight."

"Saturday night and I am very well, thank you. What can I get for you, Ms. Cait?"

I grin. "Water with lime?"

I look toward the dining room as Leon steps away. I know Tansy is working but as I came through to the bar area, I didn't see her. Just the new hostess. When The Justice House is this busy, two hostesses are usually on duty.

"Have you seen Tansy?" I ask when Leon delivers my ice water.

"She's in the night club. Mr. Bryce left his phone here in the bar earlier, and she's taking it to him."

"Was he with Emily?"

"Yes. Good to see those two together."

One of the members calls to Leon from across the bar and he leaves me again. I pull my phone out of my dress pocket to text Liam.

I'm going to find Bryce & Emily in club

"Good evening, Mrs. Justice." The security guy at the door greets pleasantly. "Would you like to have someone escort you? It's really busy tonight."

"That won't be necessary."

He seems about to argue, but quickly opens the door when I reach for the handle.

The club is packed and as usual, the music is at a decibel that renders normal conversation non-existent. But most people are here to dance, not talk. I work my way through the throng of people, wondering if an escort might have been a good idea. I head around the dance floor for the table area, hoping Bryce and Emily are there and not upstairs in the private balcony.

Several people greet me as we bump into each other. When someone grips my upper arm, I spin around to face Bryce. His gaze immediately moves over my head, looking for Liam, I suppose.

"What the hell?"

I read his lips and stand on tiptoe as he leans down.

"I'm waiting on Liam."

He gives me that mischievous grin of his and nods. Holding my elbow, he leads me to the table where Emily sits talking to an older man. When she sees us, she jumps up to hug me.

She gestures to the older man and he scoots his chair back to stand. Leaning in close, she says, "This is my dad, Robert Bronson." She leans close to her dad to speak and then he's holding out his hand to me.

He's a very handsome man. I guess to be in his early fifties. Very distinguished looking. I know from what Holly's told me that Emily is an only child and her parents dote on her. He's also a member of The Justice House.

We all sit down and a waitress is immediately at my elbow, leaning close to get my order of grapefruit juice.

"Where's Liam?" Bryce asks as he leans close. I point

up and he nods, looking at his watch. "Does he know you're in here?"

"I sent him a text."

Bryce throws back his head and laughs. I glance at Emily and she smiles before turning back to her dad.

"Did Tansy find you?" I ask and he nods.

The waitress is back with my juice and Emily leans close.

"Sorry. My dad just returned from a trip and I haven't seen him in two weeks."

I smile and gesture for her to go back talking to him.

Another couple joins us, both members, and it looks to me as if the woman scoots her chair closer to Emily's dad. I glance at Emily to catch her frown.

The woman's partner stands and comes around the table, leaning down, asking me to dance. Before I can shake my head no, Bryce stands and says something to the guy who mouths a "sorry" to me before he goes back to his side of the table.

What? I give Bryce a narrowed glare as he grins.

Emily leans close. "Bathroom?"

When Bryce starts to stand, she waves him back down.

"I think we can safely make it by ourselves," she says loudly as we head that way, making our way around the loop. Just before we reach the far wall where the bathrooms are located, someone Emily knows stops us. I motion to her that I'm going on.

The door closing behind me, shutting out the blare of music and people is a welcome relief. Thank goodness there's no waiting line. I exit the stall and as I walk around the corner to the sink area, I'm startled to see Miranda.

What is she doing here?

"I thought you were banned from Justice House." I walk past her to the sinks.

"So you managed to get yourself knocked up."

I look up and glance around, thank goodness the bathroom is empty, save for Miranda and me.

"Go away, Miranda."

"I don't know why I didn't think of it to begin with, when I was trying to reason out why he would marry *you*. You quickly figured out what a child would mean to Liam."

I pull out a towel and turn toward her. I know it would be best just to ignore her.

"Yes, Liam and I are expecting our *first* child."

I'd always thought Miranda beautiful, but in that moment, her face displays true ugliness. Her soul is shining through.

"You gold digging bitch!"

I toss the towel in the trash and move to walk past her.

"Thank goodness Liam had the foresight to draw up a prenup." Her smile is gloating when she notices my hesitation.

"You know nothing about Liam and me."

"I know that he was aware of your true nature. He knew you got pregnant on purpose."

"You're pathetic," I murmur as I walk past her.

"Me? You're the one who sold her child for money!"

I spin around, truly pissed now. "What the hell are you talking about?"

"Oh, please, save your innocent act." She steps up to the mirror. "Now that I think about it, it was probably your idea to put the clause in the prenup that stipulated if you leave, you give up all rights to your child and receive five million dollars to simply go away."

I think my heart actually stops beating. I know I feel an instant light-headedness that causes me to reach out, steadying myself against the wall. I'm barely conscious of Miranda walking past me.

That day in Liam's study comes back to me. Ryan's insistence that I read the prenup.

I hear the bathroom door open and then Emily's saying, "What are you doing here?"

Ryan wanted me to read the prenup. He offered to go over everything with me.

"Cait!" Emily puts her hand on my shoulder. "Are you okay? What did Miranda say to you?"

I shake my head. "Nothing. I need to go."

I have to read that document.

"Cait, wait! What happened?"

I turn back, hearing the distress in her voice.

"I'm okay. It's just so noisy—and I'm tired. I'm going to go upstairs."

"Let me text Bryce and we'll walk you out."

"No, it's okay." I edge toward the door. I need to go now. "Go back to Bryce and your dad. I'll talk to you later."

I head back toward the bar area near the back of the nightclub, skirting the table so Bryce doesn't see me. I leave, using the back door Liam showed me the night before.

I discover that Liam doesn't lock the files in his study. I start looking through, hoping he'll at least have a copy of the prenup and I'll find it before he finds me. I have no doubt that Bryce called Liam immediately after I left. I wish I'd come up with a different excuse for why I was leaving the club, so I'd have a little more time.

There are three tall, oak file cabinets and I almost need a step stool to look in the top drawer of each one. My fingers glide across the file folders, and I hope I don't miss it in my hurry.

I find it.

I pull it from the folder and flip through the pages until I find what I'm looking for. As I read, I move to Liam's desk, slowly sitting down in his chair. It's worded in such a way that I might have read it differently if I weren't aware of what he'd done.

When I finish I just sit there, numb.

I put most of the blame on myself. I should have read it, taken the hint from Ryan that I needed to read the prenup. But how could Liam do this to me? He'd told me more than once that he could be ruthless if need be.

But there was no need.

I leave the prenup lying on his desk and hurry to the bedroom to retrieve my purse. I have to leave before he finds me. I can't see him, not until I have time to process all of this. I call a taxi as I head for the elevator that goes down to Liam's office. I hope my hunch about him taking the back elevator is correct.

I exit his office, peeking out to see if the hallway is clear first and then hurry to the main entryway, letting myself out the front door.

My first thought as I settle into the cab is to go home to my parents, but I know my showing up there, unexpected will only upset and worry them. Plus, I'm holding a tight reign over my emotions and I don't know how much longer I can hold the anger and tears at bay.

I pull out my phone and there's a text from Liam.

No! Stay in the bar

I frown and then realize it was from earlier after I sent him a text about going into the nightclub.

How could he so coldly trick me in to signing away my child?

For money?

Grant it, it's my fault for not reading the prenup but it hurts like hell that he would do that to me.

My phone rings and without looking, I turn it off.

There's only one place I can go until I figure out what to do. I know Paul and Julie's will be the first place Liam looks, but I also know it won't do him any good. I will be safe from having to see him.

When Paul answers his door, I immediately burst into tears.

"You rest. Paul and I will be right here for you," Julie says as she turns the bedside light down until it gives off a dim glow.

"I'm sorry to come here like this. I just need time to think about what I'm going to do."

"Cait, we're family. Of course you should be here with us."

I pull the sheet up under my chin.

"Try to get some sleep and we'll talk more tomorrow, get the next step figured out."

I close my eyes. I'm exhausted. When I hear the door to their spare bedroom close, I roll to my side, my hand going to my stomach.

"Your daddy can be an ass," I whisper brokenly.

As upset as I am, I know why he did it. But it was such a callous way of guarding against the threat of losing his child. Part of the pain of his betrayal is my own fault. I let myself believe that he wanted me.

When I open my eyes, the first thing I see is Liam. He's sitting in a chair pulled up next to the bed, watching me. Neither of us say anything as his dark, penetrating gaze holds mine. We remain silent just looking at each other.

I'm going to kick Paul's ass, because I know the only way Liam made it into this apartment was if Paul allowed him in.

He looks tired. Rumpled clothes, mused hair, and sexy scruff take nothing from Liam Justice's blatant good looks. Just looking at him makes the tears well up. He must see them because he leans forward, resting his elbows on his knees his hands clasped.

"Please don't cry."

I don't say anything. I'll cry if I want to. I feel like crying. I love him so much and for a time, I believed that was enough. But then, I also believed he wanted me, he wanted — us.

Liam closes his eyes and inhales deeply before his gaze settles on me again.

"As I told you, when you first left Justice House, I wasn't sure how I was going to get over you." His voice is low and husky. "I lived in fear of seeing you out somewhere. Seeing you with someone else. And then — there you were." His eyes are intense as they continue to hold mine. "That first morning, when you woke and needed me to help you to the bathroom, when I picked you up, I felt as if I were kicked in the gut. I never thought I'd hold you like that in my arms again. When I realized I was not only holding you, but also our child for the first time, I knew in that moment that I would never let either of you go again. I spent most of that day trying to figure out how to make that happen. My first decision was for you to move in with me. But when you told me you were thinking of going home to your parents, I knew I couldn't let that happen. I couldn't bear the thought of letting you out of my sight again. So I decided to move up my second decision, asking you to marry me."

"There was never any asking," I whisper. His eyebrow lifts. "You told me I was marrying you." There's anger in my voice as I remember he didn't hesitate to threaten me with his plans to file for sole custody if I didn't agree.

He leans back in the chair. "That's because I knew if I asked—you would say no." His eyes move over me. "And I couldn't have that, darlin'."

I swallow hard against the lump in my throat.

"And you did say no." His eyes are suddenly guarded. "Cait, I won't apologize for forcing you to marry me. I will always do what I have to, to keep you in my life. And, I do remember asking you later and you agreed." He smiles slightly. "I just didn't plan for it to be so sudden. I wanted you to have a fairy tale wedding."

My throat squeezes tight with the threat of tears again. Our wedding was beautifully romantic and Liam made that happen. He made that happen—for me.

"So my plan for us to marry was put in place and I came up with the despicable idea of the prenup. I bullied Ryan into hiding that little clause in there that stipulated you gave up all rights to our baby if you left me." He leans forward in the chair and reaches out to take my hand, lying beside me on the bed. "The only reason I had that clause put in there was because I knew — if you feared losing our child —" he swallows deeply, the skin tightening around his eyes "—you would never leave me."

"Caitlyn —"His eyes are an intense blue as they search mine. "*You* are my all-consuming passion. I need you, darlin', like I need my next breath."

I can't breathe. I stare into his eyes as he repeats my words from so many weeks ago, of the type of love I'd always desired.

I throw back the covers and crawl across the bed into his lap, his arms closing tightly around me, crushing me to him. I bury my face against this neck, breathing in my favorite scent.

"Darlin', I've told you this before, but you need to believe me when I say I did not marry you because you're pregnant. I married you because I. Want. You." His voice is soft and raspy. "When you left, it scared the hell out of me. For the first time in my life, I couldn't envision my future. Without you — there was nothing." His thumb brushes away the tear on my cheek. "You are my life, Caitlyn."

"Liam," I cry softly as his hands weave into my hair, his mouth coming down to capture mine.

CHAPTER SEVENTEEN

"WHAT I'D LIKE TO KNOW, is how the hell Miranda made it into the nightclub," Holly asks as she sets her wine glass down.

We're all together sharing the amazing meal Annie prepared of lasagna, salad, and lots of crusty bread. The wine is flowing freely and we're enjoying each other's company. Liam felt we should all get together and talk over what's happening with the situation involving Walter and decided doing it over a meal was a good idea. He even invited Paul and Julie but they were unable to make it.

Our conversation has now turned to the matter of security at Justice House.

"I grilled my men and I'm certain no one knowingly admitted her," Mike says. He's been quiet most of the meal.

"Do you think she wore a disguise?" I ask.

He looks across the table and smiles. "Yes. That's what we think."

"So how do we keep her out?" Holly asks.

"That won't be a problem," Liam says quietly.

The day before, he and Ryan went to see Miranda after his meeting with Valerie. I didn't want him to. I don't want him anywhere near Miranda, but he said he needed answers. But she wouldn't tell him how she managed to see the prenup.

"Ryan suggested I file a restraining order against her," Liam adds. "And we let her know that if she was connected to anything to do with the break-ins or Walter — I would see to it she went to jail."

Ryan smiles wryly. "I believe Liam got his message across to her."

I glance at Liam. We still don't know how she managed to see the prenup, and it's disturbing to think that she might have been here in the apartment.

Liam turns to look at me.

"Don't," he mouths, sensing my dark thoughts and lifts my hand, kissing my knuckles. I smile weakly. He turns my hand over, kissing my palm, his eyes holding mine. His kiss on my palm is a direct line to my libido and that familiar spark jumps between us. I bite my lip as my breath hitches.

"Let's talk about happier things," Holly suggests. "Cait's birthday bash!"

I groan inwardly. Holly has planned a huge party for the coming weekend. The nightclub will be closed to the public, only members allowed. My problem with it is I don't like being the center of attention.

"Maybe we should cancel." As soon as I see Holly and Emily's shocked expressions, I hurriedly add, "At least postpone, with everything going on — "

"Cait, you're not cheating us out of an excuse for a party," Bryce teases.

"Why don't you have a pre-wedding celebration?" I ask him, smiling sweetly.

"We already did that when we were first engaged.

We thought it better to wait and have a reception when we get married," Emily says.

"I'm sorry." I feel bad that I forgot that they had already postponed their marriage.

"It's okay, Cait," she says.

"That was then and this is now," Bryce says. "We have no regrets because we're ready to move on and we're stronger for what we've gone through." He pulls Emily close and when she looks up adoringly at him, he leans over, cupping the side of her face as he kisses her.

Amazingly, Bryce can be serious when he wants to be.

"Get a room!" Ryan says.

We all laugh. It's Bryce's favorite line.

It's been a fun evening and as everyone is saying good night, Holly, Emily and I make plans to go out to lunch. I glance across the room, my eyes meeting vivid blue.

Holy shit.

My heart rate kicks up a notch. The expression in his eyes renders me speechless. They are full of sensual promise.

"Cait?"

When I look back, both Holly and Emily are looking at me, waiting for my answer.

"I'm sorry—"

Holly grins. "We just wanted to know if Thursday is okay?"

"Thursday is fine," I say distractedly as I glance back at Liam.

I'm putting the living room back in order, carrying glasses to the kitchen while Liam escorts everyone downstairs. He said he needed to talk to Leon and he'd be back soon. I'm plumping the pillows on the couch when I feel the back of my neck tingle. I turn to find Liam standing in the doorway, watching me.

His eyes glow with a heat that causes an instant response in my body.

"I think we have a date, darlin'."

"We do?" I whisper.

He nods as he walks slowly toward me. The look on his face, his eyes burning with hunger suddenly makes me nervous and excited at the same time. When he reaches me, he scoops me up into his arms and I grasp his shoulders, giving a little squeak of surprise.

"We were interrupted the other night, darlin', but nothing will save you from me tonight."

What?

"What are you going to do to me?"

His eyes meet mine as he strides down the hall. "Well now, darlin', I thought it was understood what I plan to do to you." He reaches to open the door to the sex swing room. "I'm going to fuck you."

"How?" I ask breathlessly, glancing around the room. The sex swing is still missing but there are plenty of other, unknown items in the room. I look back, meeting his heated gaze. Sudden uncertainty of what he has in mind assails me.

He smirks, his lips twitching suspiciously. "How?" He sets me down to stand on shaky legs in front of him. "Well, since you suggested I might be *lacking* in that skill" — he grins — "I had better do it very well."

I giggle at the absurdity of that statement. I sober quickly though when I look up into his intense eyes. The heat they emit is almost palpable.

"I want you to go into the bathroom and take off your clothes."

I don't move immediately and his arm shoots out, his hand wrapping around the back of my neck, pulling me up against his hard body. His hand fists in my hair, pulling my head back.

"I might should warn you, darlin', when we're in here, you do what I tell you without hesitation." He tugs on my hair, pulling my head back farther. "Do you understand?"

"Yes," I breathe, my heart in my throat.

His arms fall away. "Go," he orders.

It's a mix of excitement and apprehension that besets me as I slip out of my clothes.

"Caitlyn" —he knocks lightly on the door— "Put your hair up."

What? Why does he want my hair up? I pull the top vanity drawer open and find hair ties and a brush but no hairpins. I brush my hair up into a ponytail and pull the length back through part of the way.

I swallow down my nervous tension. Not knowing what is in store for me is immensely exciting, arousing, and scary all at the same time. There's a part of me, something deep inside that sparks and comes to life with this man. I crave his touch and his control over me. I have from the very start. At times, it's a little overwhelming, like right now. I take a couple of deep breathes, trying to calm my racing pulse. I do know that whatever he has in mind, he won't hurt me.

As I step back into the room, Liam gives me a cursory glance as he pulls and adjusts the chains hanging from the ceiling. Almost immediately, his gaze flashes right back to mine, and my body heats as his eyes move slowly over me.

He walks purposefully toward me, his eyes never

leaving mine. Desire pools dark and potent deep in my belly and my breath hitches.

As he draws closer, I watch as his eyes darken. Stopping in front of me, he reaches out a fingertip to touch my nipple. An immediate spark of energy shoots straight to my clit and everything south of my navel tightens deliciously.

I sway slightly as he moves around to my back, pressing up close against me, his hands cupping my breasts. I moan softly, leaning back against his front when he pinches and pulls at my nipples.

"You are very beautiful, darlin'."

"Thank you," I gasp and then mewl as the pressure of his fingers increases.

He releases the engorged peaks, one large hand sliding down to the soft swell of my belly. I bite my lip as my desire intensifies. "Especially beautiful with your body beginning to show you carry my child." He leans down to whisper against my ear. "Are you nervous?"

"Yes." My voice is breathy and I turn my head, pressing the side of my face against his chest.

"No reason to be nervous, darlin'." His hand caresses my stomach before moving back up to my breast. I bite my lip as it swells in his hand. He shifts as he leans down, his face pressing against my hair, and I feel his chest expand as he inhales deeply.

"You know I would never hurt you or our child."

"Yes," I say softly, barely able to speak. The low timbre of his voice is erotic, weaving his spell over me. He's still fully clothed, but I feel the warmth of his body seep into mine. The thick length of his erection presses hard against my lower back.

"There is nothing in this world more precious to me than you and our child."

I moan softly, his words sending a pleasurable thrill straight to my heart. *Oh, this man knows how to seduce.*

His hands slide up over my skin, his fingers curling around my throat as my breasts rapidly rise and fall at this subtle reminder that he's the one in charge.

"You belong to me. You are mine."

"Yes," I breathe.

"You are mine to do with as I please." His breath tickles my ear as his low, impassioned voice causes my skin to tingle.

Holy hell.

He drops his hands to my shoulders, turning me in his arms, his mouth coming down on mine, rough and possessive.

I know that whatever he wants, I will give to him. He owns me heart, body, and soul. My hands grip his shoulders as his mouth devours mine, our tongues tangling in an erotic dance.

I'm unaware he's walked me backward until he releases me and I discover I'm standing beneath the chains that are hanging from the ceiling where the sex swing once hung.

He takes a step back. "Don't move."

I swallow convulsively as he moves behind me, my belly tightening as my breathing escalates. I almost laugh in nervousness, my nerves stretched thin, not knowing what he has planned for me. He first reassures me that he won't hurt me, only to reinforce he will do as he pleases with my body.

I hear him moving about, and when he steps close up against my back, the heat from his bare chest is like a furnace and I inhale sharply. He takes hold of one wrist, wrapping it securely with a padded cuff, my gaze following as he raises my arm above my head to attach the cuff to one of the chains. I feel a little anxious as he repeats the process with the other wrist.

He steps around in front of me. "You look fucking beautiful, darlin'."

I look up again, pulling at the chains, testing their strength. I am truly at his mercy. I feel a flutter in my throat as my eyes meet his, all dark and glowing.

He steps close and I inhale sharply as my sensitive nipples brush against his chest. He reaches up to pry my clenched hands open before linking our fingers together. I tremble at the intensity I see in his eyes as they stare into mine.

"There are so many things I want to do to you, sugar, when you are under my control like this. At my mercy." I shiver with anticipation at his words. "But since we have never stepped to that level of intensity and in regard of your delicate condition" —his words are spoken softly, his scent deluging my senses as he stands close— "I will curtail my natural tendency to take advantage of your vulnerable state."

I think he's teasing since he's had me tied to the bed more than once. But admittedly, this feels very different.

He moves around to my back, pressing his body close. His arms come up to wrap around me, one across my chest as his hand covers a breast, the other arm curls around my stomach, holding me close to his body. His mouth comes down on my shoulder and he works his way up my arched neck, his voice low and raspy at my ear. "I love how you submit to me, darlin'." A delicious quiver runs down my spine at his erotic words.

Oh! I need him to take advantage of me. "Well" —my voice

has a husky undertone— "you need to do something. I'm dying with anticipation here."

His arms drop and he steps around in front of me. That sexy eyebrow lifts, and I'm relieved when I see his eyes glimmer with amusement.

His hands slide down my arms until he reaches my shoulders. When he suddenly tickles me under my arms, I yank at the chains, trying to escape his merciless fingers.

"Liam!" I give a choked cry as I jerk and struggle to evade his torture. "Stop!"

His fingers move down, tickling along my ribs.

"No! Please!" I cry as I dance on tiptoe.

I'm gasping for breath as he gathers me close, his body shaking with laughter.

Bastard!

I hate to be tickled. "I'm so glad you're amused," I grumble.

He leans back and laughs full and deep while I scowl at him. His large hand reaches up to grip my hair, pulling my head back as his mouth comes down to take mine in a soul-searing kiss.

I moan as his arm releases my waist and moves between us to undo his jeans. His erection feels like a brand against my belly. Without breaking our kiss, he grips the back of my thighs, lifting me.

"Grab the chains," he growls against my lips as he positions himself, his hands gripping my hips as he thrusts up, burying himself deeply.

My head drops back, my body bowing. I groan loudly as Liam grunts.

"So fucking tight."

He gives me a moment to acclimate to the sensation of being stretched and filled beyond comfort.

"You don't come until I say," he growls, his eyes intense.

I moan softly.

He pulls out and thrusts hard enough to make me gasp. Setting up a relentless pace, he continues with deep thrusts. His hands slide down to my thighs, angling my body so that each thrust hits a different spot.

He holds me firmly so there is no pressure or pull on my arms, but my hands are already numb from my grip on the chains. They are my lifeline. The only hold I have on my slipping control. My stomach muscles tighten and my body stiffens as my orgasm looms over me. With each deep stroke, my control quickly falters.

"Liam!" I cry, not sure how much longer I can hold on as the need to come becomes intense. "Please!" I beg.

He continues pounding into me, deep thrust after deep thrust until I can no longer hold on. I scream as my body explodes around him. Without thought, my legs wrap around his waist as my body stiffens. I'm consumed with an influx of sensation as wave after wave of intense pleasure washes over me.

I gradually come to my senses as he holds me close, my body shuddering with the tremors of my orgasm. He strokes my back, his face pressed against my neck. When he leans back, I look up, my gaze languid. Slowly, he lowers my legs to the floor.

"You came." He shakes his head, his expression somewhat reproving.

"It's not like I had any choice," I gasp.

My legs are still quivering has he runs his hands over my body, tweaking my nipples sharply.

"Ahhh!"

He moves to my side, his hand sliding over my belly,

moving down to the apex of my thighs. I moan softly as his fingers part my labia. Two fingers sink deep inside me as his other hand rests against my bottom, pushing me against his fingers.

My head drops back, my eyes closing as he moves his fingers widely apart, stretching and pulling at my sensitive nerve endings. I can't believe how quickly my body responds to him as I feel my insides tighten.

His hand leaves my bottom and in the next instant, it comes back with a resounding, stinging smack.

"Ahh!"

Shit!

The blow forces me forward and I don't know if my yelp is from the swat on my ass or the pressure of being more firmly seated on his fingers.

The second whack comes quick and even harder. I cry out again as I surge forward and before I have time to brace myself, he delivers two more sharp blows.

This time I cry his name.

"Shhh." His hand rubs my stinging bottom as he moves his fingers in and out of me. My body's reaction to the mixture of pain and pleasure is startling.

He pulls his fingers and steps around to face me, his hands sliding around to grasp my already sore bottom, hauling me up against his front.

"Don't come again unless I tell you to," he warns as he kneads my bottom.

Holy shit!

His hands come around to pinch and pull once more at my nipples. My head tips back and my back arches as he rolls and tugs with his fingers until my nipples ache.

I moan and open my eyes to find him watching me, his scorching gaze studying every reaction on my face.

His mouth comes down to suckle my nipple, drawing firmly on the sensitized flesh.

I mewl softly and squirm.

"Hold still, darlin'. You won't like it if I chain your legs too."

I shake my head at the thought of being totally tethered, at the mercy of his every whim. I usually like his whims but — my ass is on fire and I'm a little leery of what else he might have in store for me.

He moves to the other nipple, sucking firmly. I feel the sensation all the way to my clit. I bite my bottom lip as he sucks, his hand moving down between my legs. The sensation of his hard fingers sliding over and around my already sensitized clit sizzles along my nerve endings and my whole body stiffens. Muscles clench deep in my belly as he continues to suck my nipple firmly while his fingers drive me to the edge. I pull the chains tight as his fingers massage and press against the bundle of nerves centered between my legs.

"Please," I beg, gritting my teeth as I feel my insides quiver.

He releases my nipple only to take it between his teeth, biting down. I cry out, bucking against him.

Shit!

"I like this, darlin'."

I huff a breath. Easy for him to say, his nipple isn't throbbing and his ass isn't on fire.

When he goes to his knees in front of me, my body quivers in reaction, knowing what he's about to do.

"Oh, God…"

His hands slide between my legs and push until I widen my stance.

"Liam," I plead.

"Quiet, Caitlyn," he growls as his thumbs open me for his assault.

I feel my insides coil tightly as his ruthless tongue strokes my clit. It hardens and swells as he continues to lick and suck gently. When he closes his mouth over me and draws strongly on my now engorged clitoris, I grit my teeth, my body arching sharply as the chains rattle.

His mouth releases me and he brings his fingers between my legs to stroke the swollen nub.

"Fuck, you taste good, sugar. Do you like this?"

I'm panting, the intensity of the sensations I'm experiencing from his touch is almost painful.

"Answer me, Caitlyn," he says sharply.

"Yes!" I gasp. I open my eyes and the sight of him on his knees as his fingers pump in and out of me, is immensely erotic. When he leans forward to lick my clit, I can't control the shudder that racks my body with the deluge of sensation.

I go up on tiptoe, tilting my hips and bucking against him when his hot tongue touches me.

"Hold still," he growls.

Oh!

His hands slide under my bottom, lifting me higher, his tongue swirling once more around my clit before licking my length, only to delve deep into my channel, and I cry out again.

"I said quiet." He looks up with a warning expression in his eyes.

It's impossible to stay quiet. It's impossible to remain still as he mercilessly tortures me with his tongue. As he licks and tastes, I discover that I am very sensitive to the rough texture of that tongue. It's almost unbearable the sensations in my body that he's creating. Mind blowing. I grip the restraints and pull hard against them, trying anything that will help me focus and not come. My back arches as he concentrates on the tender spots. When his fingers sink deep inside me, my head falls back and a low moan escapes my throat.

He sucks hard on my clit and it's too much, he's too skilled at this. He's very thorough in his technique, torturing me into a mindless state where all I'm aware of is his fingers as they pump in and out of me, rubbing against that sensitive spot deep within. And his tongue. Oh, sweet mercy—his tongue...

Just as the pleasure becomes too much, just to the point of exquisite pain as my body tightens... he stops.

My pants and soft cries echo around the room and he's suddenly standing, pulling me into his arms.

"Easy darlin'," he soothes as he brushes away tears, I didn't know I was crying, from my cheeks.

He holds me close as he reaches up to release first one and then the other wrist. I moan as he slowly lowers each arm, rubbing the stiffness from them and my shoulders. I'm exhausted as I lean against him. He scoops me up and I lay my head on his shoulder, my eyes already closing.

"Don't go to sleep on me, Caitlyn. We're not finished."
What?

Even as tired as I am, my body quickens at his words. He carries me across the room where a large sheet covers an item sitting against the wall. Not only is it covered from sight but also an area of wall above it. Liam sets me to my feet, making sure I'm steady before whipping the sheet off a padded bench. The muscles in his back flex as he reaches up to tug the sheet from the wall, revealing a large mirror that is as long as the bench.

Our eyes meet in the mirror.

"Lean over the table, darlin'."

When I hesitate, he raises his eyebrow. "Now, Caitlyn," he says firmly.

He is so freakin' hot. His jeans are still undone, sitting low on his hips and his erection juts up along his belly. *Holy shit.*

I step to the bench, my gaze meeting his again. I hesitate and he steps up close behind me, pressing against my backside.

"Lean forward, on your elbows. I want to see your breasts as I fuck you."

I flush at his words but I also feel a slow sizzle begin in my belly.

My eyes are wide and I'm in desperate need of a hairbrush as I watch us in the mirror. An unbelievably handsome man standing behind me, his erection pressed against my bottom.

Liam pushes on my back. "Down, darlin'."

I rest my forearms on the table as his gaze holds mine. His hand runs over my bottom and I shift slightly. I'm sore where he hit me.

"Spread your legs," he orders softly, his eyes cast down watching as his hands grip my bottom. I bite my lip, watching him as I do as bid.

He pulls my cheeks apart and I shift nervously, moving my legs back together. He glances up, his eyes meeting mine. I quell under the look he gives me and then his hand grips my hair, pulling my head back.

"Do I need to remind you about doing what I say in here?"

My mouth dries at his subtle threat. "No," I whisper.

I continue to stare at him and his eyebrow lifts. I lean over the bench.

He runs his hands down my legs and back up over

my bottom, quickly igniting my need all over again. When his fingers probe between my cheeks I bite down on my bottom lip and close my eyes, concentrating hard to stand still.

"Open your eyes, darlin'."

His are filled with an unknown light meeting mine in the mirror. He gives me a roguish smile and then sinks two fingers into my wet channel as his thumb probes my backside.

I suck in a sharp breath, closing my eyes, moaning.

"Open."

He moves his fingers, setting every nerve sizzling. My hands are fisted and I'm panting as his eyes hold mine.

He strokes against that sweet spot deep inside that quickly has my body trembling in response.

"You're so tight" — his voice is hoarse with his own need— "I can't wait to be inside you."

I mewl softly when he pulls his fingers, positions himself, and thrusts hard, burying himself balls deep.

I cry out.

"Fuck! You feel good," he growls as he plunges in and out of me. "I love how you grip my cock."

I feel my skin heat at his words but they're quickly forgotten as I moan with pleasure. *Oh – he feels good too.* My whole body is shaking as unimaginable pleasure courses through me. The sensation of his thick, hard shaft rubbing my sensitive vaginal walls is exquisite.

He grips my hips hard as he pounds into me, watching my breasts sway and bounce with each thrust. I watch him as every muscle on his torso, his arms, bunch and flex. Watching him as he fucks me is one of the sexiest things I've ever seen, and I know it's what pushes me over the edge so quickly.

I try hard not to come but I also know he is ruthless in his determination to make me fail. It's an exquisite agony when he reaches around, his fingers coming to rest on my clitoris, circling round and round, rubbing across the sensitized nub.

My orgasm rips through me with a vengeance. My arms stretch forward, my body flattens against the bench as my fingers dig into the leather. I cry Liam's name needing him to save me from a climax that threatens to consume me.

He continues with punishing thrusts that raise me to my toes, finally calling out my name when he finds his release.

When I wake, I'm lying with my head on his chest, his arm curved around my back as his fingers sift through the length of my hair. My leg, bent, lies over one of his. I shift to place a kiss on his chest.

"Awake, darlin'?"

"Hmmm."

"Want to go another round?"

"Hmmm."

He chuckles, a deep sound against my ear.

"Hungry?"

"No."

"Don't you be starving our child," he scolds softly.

"I like that you think of her as our child," I murmur.

I feel him shift as he raises his head and I look up, meeting the most gorgeous pair of blue eyes, I have ever seen. Eyes that have held me in their power since the moment our gazes met in the dining room of Justice House.

"Well now, my son *is* ours, darlin'," he teases as he touches the tip of my nose with one long finger.

I smile and lay my head back down, snuggling close as his arms close around me.

"Are you okay?"

I lift my head to look up at him. "I am. Why wouldn't I be?"

"It wasn't too rough?" His finger strokes the side of my face.

"No." I lay my head back on his chest. "I had a good time," I say softly. Why do I still feel embarrassed with him after all this time, after everything we've done together? When he doesn't say anything, I tilt my face up. His mouth lifts in a cocky grin. "Are you going to spank me again?"

He leans his head closer to mine. "Let me tell you a secret, sugar," he whispers. It still unnerves me that the tone of his voice alone wields such control over my body. "Just the thought of spanking you — turns me on." My eyes, wide and bemused, flash to his.

He laughs softly as he lays back, his hand tightening on my hip. "But everything about you turns me on." He raises his head again, looking back down at me. When he wiggles his brows, I can't help but laugh.

I press closer against him, pleasure at his words making me feel giddy. "Everything about you turns me on too," I whisper.

He rolls me to my back, his body covering mine. "I know, darlin'." His mouth comes down on mine in a soft, tender kiss.

It's a busy week as workmen come in and out of the apartment each day, converting one of the spare bedrooms into the nursery Liam and I have envisioned for our child.

I'm overseeing the work on the nursery while Liam puts in extra hours in meetings with Valerie and her investigators. He's also been busy hiring a PI team of his own.

He's opening up to me, talking about his mother. He doesn't say, but I know he's holding onto the hope that his father didn't murder his mom. He still doesn't say a lot about Walter. Years of hurt hold him in its grip.

I'm amazed, all over again as he reveals more of his childhood. How he managed to become the successful man he is today is testament to his strength of character. I am so proud of him.

Saturday comes too soon. I would be happy to celebrate my birthday with just our close friends but those same close friends are geared up and excited about the birthday party planned for me in Justice House's nightclub.

I sit at the mirrored vanity in the dressing room of the en suite, putting the finishing touches on my makeup.

I'm wearing the dress Liam took time out of his busy day to buy and have delivered to me. It's one of the loveliest dresses I've ever worn. It's an off the shoulder number in a soft gold color with silver trim and wide lace crisscrossing my body. It makes me feel glamourous and I still can't get over Liam's ability to choose exactly what I would.

I've curled my hair and left it hanging down my back

and I'm touching up my lipstick as he walks in. Our eyes meet in the mirror as he crosses the room to stand behind me.

He's dressed in jeans that hug his ass and thighs in such a delicious way and a white linen shirt with the first two buttons undone. His sleeves are rolled, exposing his strong forearms and with the dark scruff on his jaw and hair that he's just run his fingers through, he looks positively — dangerous. Sexy dangerous.

I smile shyly at him noticing his eyes hold a glint of something I can't decipher.

He leans down and kisses my bare shoulder and I close my eyes briefly, inhaling his devastating scent. I wish we didn't have a party to go to and we could just spend the evening alone.

"You look beautiful, darlin'."

"Thank you. You do too." He snorts softly. "I love my dress, thank you."

He reaches out to place his hand on the side of my neck, his fingers curling around to the front of my throat. "You can thank me proper later, sugar." His deep voice is low and seductive.

My cheeks warm at the thought of how I'd like to thank him.

"We could stay here," I whisper, aroused by his thumb stroking the side of my neck. "I could model the pretty lingerie you bought me."

His mouth lifts at one corner and he shakes his head. "No," he mouths. "The way you look in that dress, I want to show you off." His eyes continue to hold mine in the mirror. "I have something for you."

I frown. "What?"

"For your birthday."

"Liam, you already gave me this beautiful dress, I—"

"Cait." His hand slides down my neck to my shoulder, his fingers splaying across my chest to the soft swell of my breasts. My pulse instantly begins to race as he holds out a small jeweler's box.

I turn to take the box, puzzled by his expression. "What's this?"

"Open it, darlin'."

I gasp softly when I do. Nestled against velvet is a small white gold St. Christopher's cross. It's similar to the one Liam wears, only smaller, dainty looking. I carefully lift it from the box. It hangs on a slender, delicate chain. I can't resist, I turn it over, stunned at the engraving.

Remember,
my love is always with you,
always yours.

Embedded at the end of the word *yours* is a sparkling diamond. It's not large because the pendant is small, but it's perfect.

Tears come to my eyes; I look up to find Liam watching me closely.

"Liam—" My voice is thick with tears.

His hands settle on my shoulders. "Don't cry, I'll think you don't like it."

I give a choked laugh and sniff. "Okay."

"Let me help you with it." His fingers deftly open the clasp and I gather my hair to hang over one shoulder. "My mother always wore one like this," he says softly. "Her mother gave it to her." He places it around my neck and the pendant rests in the valley of my breasts. I reach up to straighten it as he fastens the clasp.

"My mom gave me the one I wear on my sixteenth birthday. It has the same engraving as hers."

I reach up quickly to stop the tear that threatens at the corner of my eye.

"I added to your engraving—it seemed appropriate."

"I love it." My heart is beating a fast tempo.

"I'm not sure it goes with your dress, perhaps I should have bought you diamonds—"

"No!" My fingers cover the pendant. "Liam, this is more precious to me than any jewel you could ever give me."

He reaches for my hand and pulls me to my feet, straight into his arms. His hand slides under my hair to encircle the nape of my neck as he leans down, his lips pressing against my forehead. My hands smooth across the rippled planes of his stomach, around to his back. Tipping my chin, his eyes meet mine.

"I love you, Caitlyn Justice."

I swallow against the sudden emotion of joy that threatens to spill out as tears while at the same time I can't stop the huge smile that covers my face. "I know," I whisper.

His eyes sparkle and the corner of his mouth twitches. "Do you now?"

"Yes," I say softly. "You show me every day."

The smile slowly leaves his face, replaced by a deeper emotion and as I watch, his eyes darken. He brings his mouth down to mine, and his tongue flicks out against my bottom lip before sucking it gently.

I moan, my hands sliding back around to his chest, up until my fingers can stroke the soft scruff on his jawline. I run my fingers through his hair and he deepens the kiss, his hand pushing against my bottom as he presses his erection into my soft belly.

When he lifts his head, I'm slightly dizzy and breathless.

"We best stop this or we won't make it to your birthday party, darlin'."

"Okay by me," I whisper.

He laughs. "Let's finish up and head that way."

I give him my best pout and he grips my chin, giving me another quick kiss.

"I have something else for you, darlin'."

"I don't need anything else, Liam."

One side of his mouth lifts in a sexy, lopsided smile. "Well this you do need." He holds out a large manila envelope.

Frowning, I take it from him. Opening the flap, I pull out a legal document.

"What's this," I ask, looking up at him.

"It's a copy of the paperwork I had Ryan file to nullify our prenup."

My breath draws in sharply. "Liam—" I look at the papers. "You didn't have to do this," I say softly.

"Yes, I did." He takes my arm, pulling me close, his arm encircling my waist. "My whole intention of the prenup to begin with, was to bind you to me." His free hand raises my chin and my misty gaze meets vibrant blue.

"I love you, Cait, and everything I have is yours."

"I don't need—" His mouth cuts off my words.

I cling to his upper arms, deeply affected with the depth of my love for this man. When he ends the kiss, he presses his forehead to mine.

"Just know, darlin'—you are never leaving me."

I laugh softly and nod. "I know."

He cups the side of my face. "Let's go."

Liam follows me out of the elevator on the first floor and glancing back, I catch his frown.

"What?"

"That dress is very short."

"I know. I love it." My hand smooths over the material. "You picked it out," I remind him.

His arm slides around my waist. "Well, you don't wear it anywhere but with me."

I giggle.

"I mean it." He squeezes my waist.

The nightclub is packed with people. Not too surprising since I learned soon after I started working here that everyone at Justice House loves a good party.

We make our way amidst birthday wishes. I still feel very grateful to be accepted and welcomed by the members, ex-coworkers, and Liam's friends.

Liam keeps his arm around me as we cross the large room, first heading to the alcove located near the bar area. There is a buffet set up with a huge tiered cake set in the middle and to my utter dismay, another long table loaded with gifts.

Why would they bring me a gift? I look up, narrowing my eyes at Liam.

He smiles. "Holly and I both stipulated no gifts."

I swallow against the sudden lump in my throat and Liam pulls me close, kissing my temple.

"Just go with it, darlin'. They don't expect you to open them tonight."

"Cait!" I turn toward Holly and she leans down to give me a hug. She's even taller than normal in killer stilettos. "Wow. Now that is some dress."

I beam at her. "One of my gifts from my handsome husband." I smile up at Liam. *He loves me!*

My gaze moves over him. He slipped on a dark blue suit jacket right before we left the apartment and the jacket heightens the blue of his eyes, making them positively lethal. He looks perfect. And sexy. Definitely sexy.

He leans his head close. "Stop looking at me like that, darlin'," he growls and then softens his words with a smile.

Holly laughs and then links her arm with mine, pulling me from Liam.

"Let's get this party started!"

It *is* a wonderful party. Being the center of attention isn't as bad as I worried it would be. But after four hours of dancing, eating birthday cake, and opening gifts, I'm exhausted.

I was especially pleased that almost all of the gifts were donations in my name to various charities. So very thoughtful.

Paul hands me over to Liam after our dance ends, and I melt gratefully into my husband's arms.

"Enjoying yourself, darlin'?"

"I am, truly, and I know it's early but do you think anyone would mind if I go upstairs for a bit?"

He leans back, frowning as he looks down at me. "Are you okay?"

"Yes." I smooth his shirt down on his chest. "I'm fine, don't worry. I just need a break. I'll sit in the quiet for about an hour and I'll be back down."

"I'll go with you."

"No, please stay."

"Darlin' I'm not staying if —"

I reach up and put my fingers against his lips. "Please, Liam... stay. I don't want the fun to end and I promise I'll be back in an hour. I'd like to give my parents a quick call before it gets too late."

He smiles beneath my fingers and takes hold of my hand, kissing the palm. "I'll walk you up."

I'm not sure how I convince him to just walk me to the door that leads back into the mansion, but I do and I'm surprised when he pulls me into his arms, kissing me passionately in front of everyone.

"I'll be up for you shortly," he warns.

Now, as I walk across the darkened dining room, I almost wish I had let him escort me to the elevator, at least. The restaurant and kitchen closed early so everyone could join in the party and the usual eeriness associated with the lack of noise and people, so characteristic of Justice House, is unnerving.

I have the uncanny feeling of being watched. The same feeling I experienced the night I came down alone to the kitchen and an intruder was here in the house after hours.

I breathe a sigh of relief when the elevator doors close. In my hurry to get on the elevator, I inadvertently dropped my passkey into my clutch, so I'm digging for it at the door to the apartment when I hear a noise coming from the stairwell. *Why would someone be in the stairwell?* My heart gives a lurch in my chest as my fingers latch onto the passkey, but in my hurry, I slide the card too quickly. It doesn't scan properly, the doorknob rattling, refusing to open. I glance back at the door and almost scream as the stairwell door slowly opens.

CHAPTER EIGHTEEN

FUMBLE AGAIN AS I SLIDE the card, but this time it works and just as I open the door, keeping my eye on the stairwell, Walter Justice steps forward.

"How did you—"

He quickly crosses and pushes his way into the apartment with me, slamming the door shut.

"What are you doing here?" I step away from him, alarmed by his actions and by the fact he has blood running from a gash above his temple down the side of his face.

"Don't be afraid!" He holds up his hands.

Too late for that. How the hell did he get into the stairwell? How did he get into the mansion?

"Walter—this is no way to get Liam to talk to you. He'll be really upset—"

"No! I'm here to help you, you're in danger!"

He runs his fingers through his hair as he looks toward the door. When he looks back at me, I can't help but notice he has a wild look in his eyes.

"He has it all planned." He steps closer and I shrink back against the wall. "No! Please, don't be afraid. I just went along with his plan to fool him."

I don't know if it's his demeanor or his rambling that

frightens me the most. He reaches behind his back and then he's holding a gun.

I think I'll faint. I give a soft cry of alarm and press my body even closer to the wall.

"No! I'm not going to hurt you! But we have to hide." He frantically looks around. "We have to go before he gets here. He's on his way!"

He grips my arm and proceeds to drag me farther down the hall.

"You have to stop this, Walter." I try to pull my arm free but this only makes his hold tighten. "If you stop now, I... I can help you leave. Liam need never know you were even here." My voice sounds breathless.

Gripping my arm, he pulls me into the kitchen when we reach it. I'm so thankful Annie is not here.

"We'll go up. Yes! The roof."

Oh, no!

"Walter, stop!" I use my free hand to try to pry his hand from my arm. It doesn't do any good, though. He may look frail but he's surprisingly strong. He drags me through to the utility room, over to the door that opens to the stairwell to the roof.

How does he know about the roof or the layout of the apartment?

He reaches up and swipes at the blood still oozing down the side of his face.

"You're—hurt. Let me help you clean up that cut." I need to do something to stall or distract him.

"No, we have to hurry, you don't understand."

To my utter dismay, the door that's always locked—is not. He reaches around the doorframe and I hear the flip of a switch and then another, turning on the lights that

400

illuminate the stairwell. Again, I wonder how the hell he knows where the light switches are located.

He grips my arm tighter as we ascend the stairs.

"Hurry, we have to hurry!"

We break through to the top of the roof and Walter slams the door shut. He turns, scanning the roof area. He must have turned on the floodlights that light up this part of the rooftop when he turned on the stair lights.

"We need to block the door," he says anxiously.

I find myself looking around too. There's not much left up here and what is, is broken or smashed. My heart constricts seeing the devastation of what once was a beautiful, romantic oasis. I was the reason Liam destroyed it.

Liam. He'll be coming for me soon. I'm not sure why Walter has a gun, but one thing is for certain, he's delusional and I don't want Liam anywhere near his father.

Walter jerks my arm and we move across the roof toward the front of the mansion. I try to act as if I'm having trouble walking in the shoes I'm wearing, hoping—I don't know what to hope for. I guess I'm hoping I can think of something to make him come to his senses.

"Walter—I need—" I lean against the chimney we stop beside. "Please, give me a moment." I try to wrench my arm free again.

"There's no time. I don't think he knows about it up here. I hid that information from him."

I frown.

"Let's go!"

"I don't think there's anywhere to hide up here, Walter."

We don't stop again until we're near the edge of the

roof and Walter releases my arm. I rub the circulation back.

There's a three-foot high edge around the perimeter of the roof in this area, but it wouldn't prevent someone from falling off. My legs begin to shake uncontrollably. I've kept my cool up to this point but now fear is getting a strong hold on my emotions. What are we doing up here?

"Please, Walter" — my voice sounds shaky — "let's go back down. Liam will help you."

He rapidly shakes his head. "No! You don't understand," he hisses. His eyes seem overly bright in the glow of the floodlights.

I take a deep breath, trying to calm my rapidly beating heart. "Walter, tell me what is going on—so I can understand what I need to do to help you."

He frowns. "We need to find a place to hide."

A sudden frightening thought comes to me. Up to this point, I've believed Walter was just rattled, confused. What if the "he" Walter's referring to is Vincent Hale? My gaze travels around the rooftop.

"If he finds you" — my eyes flash back to his — "he'll hurt you."

I inhale sharply. "Who, Walter? Who will hurt me?"

"I told him I wouldn't do it." He reaches up with his gun hand to touch the place on his temple.

"Dad."

Both Walter and I immediately turn toward Liam. He's standing a few yards away, his hands raised in a placating manner, his eyes focused on his father.

My eyes widen in alarm. *No!*

"Liam!" His gaze locks on mine. I shake my head and

quickly look at Walter and then back, hoping to convey the fact that Walter is out of it.

"Are you okay?" he asks softly.

"Yes."

His eyes flash back to his father. "Dad," he says softly. "Please, Dad, don't hurt her. Let Cait go. She has nothing to do with what's between us."

Walter turns to look at me as Liam moves closer.

"Give me the gun, Dad." Liam takes another step forward and Walter swings the gun toward his son as he turns.

I cry out and Liam looks at me briefly with a subtle shake of his head.

"Dad, please let Cait go. Don't hurt her." There's such pleading in Liam's voice that tears come to my eyes. "Please, Dad." Liam moves slowly toward his father.

I look at Walter, he seems confused as his forehead wrinkles and he shakes his head.

"I'm not going to hurt her, son. She's carrying my grandchild. I'm trying to keep her safe."

"I think he's worried about me."

We all three look in the direction of another voice. A slim, dark complected man steps out of the shadows. He's holding a gun. Pointed at Liam.

I inhale sharply, recognizing the stranger from months ago. He was the man who was upstairs and followed me as I made a room delivery for Leon. The same man who managed to get in and out of Justice House undetected. If not for my run-in with him, we might never have known he was even in the mansion.

"Yes, I see you remember me."

I glance at Liam but he has his attention trained on the stranger. I know he recognizes him too, from the security video. Movement from Walter catches my eye. He's standing with his head dropped, rambling incoherently.

"What do you want?" Liam demands.

"Well, my plans have changed — somewhat." When he grins, it reminds me of a snake. "I really wanted to kill you first and then enjoy the charms of your wife." His black eyes move over me and I almost gag when his tongue flicks out, greedily licking his lips. "But in order for Walter to inherit and not your in-laws, she'll have to go first. I'll keep you alive just long enough and then you'll join her."

No! I shake my head.

"You are not going to hurt them!" Walter steps forward, facing the man for the first time.

"You fool!" the stranger snarls. "If you had done as you were told, this would already be over."

"What do you mean?" Liam asks.

The man looks back at Liam. "Your father is in on the plan to kill you both so he can inherit your money."

"No! I had no part in this!" Walter turns toward Liam. "I let him think I was going along with his plans, son. I tried to talk to you, to tell you—"

"Shut up you fool!" The stranger points his gun at Walter, taking it off Liam for the first time. "It doesn't matter now. The end will be the same."

"Let Cait go," Liam says. "I will give you whatever you want."

"No! I'm not leaving you!"

Liam doesn't look at me as he keeps his eyes on the stranger. "Shut up, Cait," he snaps.

The man laughs. "You'd give me anything I want, until she calls for help. No, I don't think so."

"Why did you break into Justice House, what were you looking for?" Liam probes.

The man laughs again. "I didn't find anything with my first attempt but with the second, I discovered a copy of your will." He looks at me with an apologetic smile. "Marrying and leaving everything to you my dear sealed your fate."

I look at Liam. *He left everything to me?* We were in St. Louis with my parents right after the wedding when the second break-in happened. When did he change his will?

"So you kill us and my father inherits everything."

The man smiles, his eyes back on me, making my skin crawl.

"How does that benefit you?"

"Walter and I—have plans, which I won't bother sharing with you since you won't be around."

"Who helped you get into Justice House?" Liam asks.

"You have a very disgruntled employee. It seems your bartender is a little bitter about your wife marrying you."

What? I shake my head in disbelief and look at Liam again. He continues to focus on the man with the gun who has once again pointed it on my husband.

"Leon wouldn't do that," Liam says firmly.

"His cousin would."

My mouth drops open and I recall Tony's attitude toward me. I did notice. Maybe if I'd said something—

"You're lying," Liam states. "Tony has no way into the mansion after hours."

"Awww... but getting into the mansion was easy once the bartender found the passageway."

I see Liam frown.

"There are secret passages, son. Old blueprints of the mansion showed them all."

That's how they came into the house and remained undetected.

"Enough chit-chat. Here's what we're going to do—"

"You're Vincent Hale, the man who murdered my mother."

"What?" Walter's head turns toward the man.

"You murdered my mother and before her, that young girl in Oregon"

The pure evil that suddenly emanates from the man is perceivable in the utterly chilling smile on his face.

"Yes, she was a pleasant diversion."

I want to scream at him. In all my life, I have never wished for harm to come to another, but in that moment, I would gladly cause this—monster—physical injury.

"You hurt my Maren?" Walter takes a step toward Hale who swings the gun toward him again, halting Walter. My eyes look down to the gun that Walter still holds at his side.

Vincent Hale laughs. "*Your* Maren? You never paid any attention to her. You spent your time in a bottle. She was a beautiful woman, and she enjoyed my attention. She wanted me."

"You touched my wife!" Walter's face fills with rage.

Vincent Hale's expression chills my blood.

"I can still feel her lovely neck in my hands—"

I cry out as I see Liam's face darken, right before he makes his move toward Vincent Hale, murder on his face.

A shot rings out.

And then, a second one.

CHAPTER NINETEEN

T HE FUNERAL WAS THE HARDEST thing I have ever had to do.

But Liam is at peace now.

I roll over onto my side. I'm supposed to be napping, but sleep eludes me. I move my hand to my belly to soothe my child. The fluttering is stronger now.

The last few days have been hard. So much pain and anguish—for what? Vincent Hale was a horrible person and I'm not sorry that Mike's bullet took him out, but not before he destroyed one more life.

The bedroom door opens and Julie quietly slips in.

"Why aren't you sleeping?" she asks as she sits on the edge of the bed.

"I tried."

"You need to sleep honey."

"I know," I whisper.

She reaches for my hand. "A Detective Jerome is here to speak with you. I showed him to the study."

I frown. "Thank you." He's already spoken to me twice, what more does he want?

"And Valerie called; she's on her way over."

I smile slightly. She's certainly been supportive through everything. I know she feels a sense of peace for the first time in years. She shared that with me the day of the funeral.

"What's my mom doing?"

"She's on the phone with your dad."

My parents love for me knows no limits. My dad insisted my mom come here to be with me, arranging on his own, for a health care provider to come in and stay with him. I know how difficult it is for them both to be separated from each other, but having my mom here with me — I have no words for the comfort it brings me.

"I better go talk with Detective Jerome."

I pause at the study door. This is so painful, having to relive the night on the roof over and over. I've decided to tell the detective that this is the last time I intend to talk about that devastating night. He has two statements from me. It's enough.

I take a deep breath and open the door.

I don't even look at the detective who quickly stands. I barely register him in the room as my gaze connects with disarming blue. My husband holds out his hand and I cross the room to be engulfed in his heat, scent, and that sizzling connection that sparks between us.

"Did you rest?" Liam kisses my temple as his softly spoken words caress my ear.

"Yes." I look up and raise my hand to rest against the side of his face. "I would have rested better if you were with me."

He snorts softly, then smiles. "We both know better than that, darlin'," he whispers softly, a wicked gleam in his eye.

Oh, it's so good to see him smile. The death of his father has devastated him.

Once he learned everything Valerie knew about Vincent Hale, he felt the anger he'd had against his father begin to soften. He confessed that he longed to repair and forgive their previous relationship, but there will be no re-building of trust between a father and son. Liam has found a sense of peace though, knowing his mother's killer was finally caught—finally finding justice. It's bittersweet that he had to lose any chance of reconciliation with his father in the process.

We learned that Vincent Hale had an uncanny hold over Walter. The two men had obviously bonded as young boys and from what the investigators, that Liam hired, discovered, it seemed Vincent had always had the upper hand in the relationship.

The forgotten detective clears his throat and Liam and I both look at him. My husband continues to hold me in his arms, in no hurry to let me go.

"If you could spare me a moment please."

I look up to catch Liam's frown as he slowly releases me.

"Detective Jerome," Liam begins as we both move to sit on the couch facing the chair the detective takes. "I hope this will finish—what you need from my wife and me?" Liam's tone leaves no room for argument, and I almost smile, watching as his eyebrow lifts.

The detective nods, clearly not missing the message. "Yes. I appreciate you seeing me. Once again, my condolences on your loss."

Liam nods.

"I spoke with your head of security, Mr. Bowen and we now have everything we need, so this should be the last time we need to speak."

Liam starts to stand.

"But I'm actually here to let you know, we have connected more than eight murders to Vincent Hale."

I gasp softly and Liam's arm slides up over the couch back, his hand resting on my shoulder.

"Eight we can prove — the rest we're working on.

"When we searched his belongings at the motel, where he and your father were staying, we discovered information that led us to a storage facility located outside of Chicago. We found two suitcases, one of them containing —" he clears his throat " — items that belonged to his victims."

"Jewelry," Liam says.

"Yes. But we did not find the pendant you described belonging to your mother."

"Oh, no," I whisper.

Liam takes hold of my hand and raises it to his lips. His mesmerizing eyes gaze into mine before slowly closing. He breathes in deeply.

"But we have new information that is promising," the detective continues.

"No," Liam says firmly. "I don't want it back. Do what you need to do to bring closure to others, but I don't want my mother's pendant back."

"Why?" I ask softly, searching his face.

He turns to look at me. "Because, I don't need it. But more importantly, I don't want it. Not after he held it and gloried over it as if it were some type of trophy."

My eyes fill with tears.

"Don't, darlin'," he says softly, his hand squeezing my shoulder as he pulls me close.

"I understand," the detective says. I see a glimmer of something in his eyes. I think it's respect for my husband.

"We have more information from your previous

employee, Tony Kallis. Evidently, he saw several pictures of documents that Vincent Hale was interested in. He admitted to sharing some of this info with a" — the detective turns the page of his notepad— "Miranda Davis."

So that's how Miranda knew about the prenup. Did she know about the tunnel that led from the back property behind the greenhouse to the mansion, and the hidden passageways? I look up at Liam and notice his jaw clenched.

"Mr. Kallis insists that he knew nothing about the original blueprints showing the hidden passageways." The detective reads from his notes before looking up. "We will continue to question him and I've contacted Ms. Davis. She will be coming into the station tomorrow to answer questions. But it looks as if, from everything we've found, that neither of them were involved. Mr. Kallis was approached by Hale and paid to find the tunnel opening, but other than that—"

"But they knew about the break-ins. And isn't it a crime, Tony finding the tunnel for Hale? He had to know it was for unlawful entry." I look at Liam and then back at the detective.

"Cait," —Liam gives a quick look at the detective— "Ryan has contacted the prosecuting attorney, and the proper steps are being taken to insure Tony pays for his part in all of this. Miranda had knowledge of Tony's involvement and that will be dealt with also."

I give a slight nod. Good.

"I heard your security people now know how Hale eluded the security cameras?"

"Yes," Liam says. "Hale definitely knew how to hack into and manipulate security systems. Wired and wireless." He gives me a quick glance. We're both aware of Mike's anger over Hale's ability.

"I would also like to let you know" —the detective continues— "that we found a journal kept by your father. He recorded his conversations with Hale and it would seem your father was telling the truth about trying to thwart Hale's plans concerning the two of you."

I glance up at Liam and though I'm sure the detective can't see the subtle pain that crosses his face, I catch it right before Liam stands abruptly.

"According to the journals, Hale made arrangements for the both of them to exit the country for South America after your father inherited your estate. He had plans already in motion to sale the assets of your estate and move the money to an off-shore account."

I watch as Liam's brow furrows. I suspect he's thinking the same thing I am—how could Vincent Hale control his father as he did?

"Detective Jerome, thank you for stopping by to share what you know with us, you can contact my lawyer if you have anything further," Liam informs him.

The detective stands and Liam gives me his hand as I rise.

"I am very pleased neither you nor Mrs. Justice came to any harm. That was very good forethought on your part to have a panic button, alerting your security."

I clutch Liam's hand and lean into him. When he came to retrieve me the night of my party, he quickly found the door to the roof stairway ajar. As soon as he saw his father holding a gun, he pushed the panic button on his phone.

The detective holds out his hand to Liam. "Thank you for your time and... I probably shouldn't say this but, I'm not sorry that your man took out Vincent Hale."

I glance up at Liam but see no reaction to the detective's words.

"He will never harm another young woman. I'm just sorry he was able to shoot your father." The detective looks down and then up to meet Liam's eyes. "I know a little of your history and... your father saved your life that night, stepping in front of you to shield you from a bullet."

Liam remains stoic as the detective clears his throat again.

"Thank you, Detective Jerome. I'll show you out."

"Mrs. Justice." The detective nods toward me.

"Good bye and thank you, detective," I say softly.

I stop in the kitchen doorway. My mom's perched on one of the kitchen stools as she and Valerie talk. Valerie is smiling and nodding at something my mom is saying.

Emily and Julie are laughing as Bryce pours wine into glasses. Whatever he says next, has them both blushing bright pink.

Liam walks up behind me and places his arm across my chest, pulling me back against his body. My hands come up to his arm as I lay my head back against his solid chest.

"Are you okay?"

I turn in his arms, mine going up around his neck.

"Me? Are *you* okay?" I ask softly.

"I am now, darlin'." He smiles as his head lowers taking my mouth in a soft kiss.

The sudden thought of how close I came to losing him washes over me and I tighten my hold on his neck.

His arms tighten around me, and he deepens his kiss as if he has the same thought.

"Hey, you two! Get a room!" Bryce shouts.

Liam grins against my lips.

I turn a teasing glare on Bryce but he's looking sheepishly toward my mom and Valerie. "Sorry, ladies."

I move to step away and Liam's hand catches mine, pulling me back. "Ryan's on his way over. I need to have a short meeting with him."

"Oh. What about?"

"My idea for Justice House."

"You're sure?"

"Absolutely." He leans close so my mom or Valerie won't overhear him. "We need to turn this into a family home, darlin'. A place to raise children and grow old together."

"Anywhere you are is home to me and any children we have, Liam."

His mouth lifts slowly at one corner before he leans down, giving me a short, sweet kiss that lingers with a promise for later.

"Bryce?" Bryce turns to look at him. "Ready?"

"I am."

Liam grips my chin and gives me another quick kiss.

"Ladies, please excuse us, we have a meeting. Good to see you Valerie."

She returns Liam's smile.

As Liam and Bryce head down the hall, Liam looks back, catching my gaze with his incredible blue eyes. I feel my world tilt, just a little as the man I love, my whole world, gives me one of his panty dropping smiles.

Eighteen months later.

I sit cross-legged on the floor of the living room as my daughter sits in front of me. Her small hand reaching for another block as we stack them.

"What color is that?"

Bright blue eyes the exact shade as her father's meet mine.

"Bwu."

"That's right, blue," I enunciate.

At the same time, we both hear the elevator.

"Oh! Who's here?" I ask softly, exaggerating surprise.

My daughter's beautiful little mouth forms a perfect O as her eyes widen in excitement.

I hold out my hand in case she needs help as she clambers to her feet, but she's definitely an independent little girl.

I clap my hands. "Who is it?"

"Da-dee!"

"Daddy!" I say excitedly.

She toddles toward the door just as Liam walks in and scoops her up.

"Hello, princess."

She throws her arms around her daddy's neck as he cuddles her close, burying his nose in her dusky curls. His eyes immediately search for me.

His mouth lifts at one corner. "Hello, beautiful."

I stand and Liam reaches out to pull me into his embrace. We stand like this for several minutes, my eyes closed as I give a silent prayer of thanks for my husband and child. I look up, my breath catching when I see the heat in Liam's eyes. He leans down to bury his nose in my hair while his daughter digs through his shirt pocket.

I go up on tiptoe and Liam takes my mouth in a soft, sweet kiss.

"How are you, darlin'?" he breathes against my lips.

I'll never tire of him calling me that.

I raise my hand to caress the side of his handsome face. The bluest eyes smile down into mine.

"Perfect, now that you're here."

AUTHOR BIO

Rivi Jacks has a lifelong love of books, and she is a true believer in holding onto a good love story. One reason her attic and barn are full of the books she has collected over the years.

She lives in the Missouri Ozarks on a farm with her husband, and when not writing or reading, she likes to take long walks down country roads, cook, fish and spend time with family and friends.

CONTACT LINKS

https://www.facebook.com/Rivi-Jacks-234024470093905

https://www.pinterest.com/rivijacks

https://www.twitter.com/rivi_jacks

https://www.goodreads.com/book/show/27836107

http://www.instagram.com/rivi_jacks

PLAYLIST FOR FINDING JUSTICE

Dance Me to the End of Love — The Civil Wars
I Surrender (Piano Version) ~ Digital Daggers
Fallin ~ Alicia Keys
Say Something ~ A Great Big World
Slipping Away ~ Barcelona
I Won't Give Up ~ Jason Mraz
All Good Things (Come to an End) ~ Nelly Furtado
Apologize ~ One Republic
Blue Blood ~ Laurel
Thinking Out Loud ~ Ed Sheeran

51018767R00252

Made in the USA
Charleston, SC
13 January 2016